BLOOD OF THE LAMB

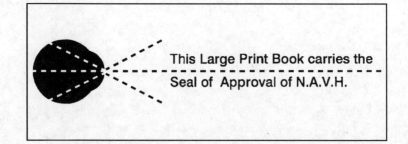

This Large Print Book carries the
Seal of Approval of N.A.V.H.

BLOOD OF THE LAMB

A NOVEL OF SECRETS

SAM CABOT

THORNDIKE PRESS
A part of Gale, Cengage Learning

Detroit • New York • San Francisco • New Haven, Conn • Waterville, Maine • London

GALE
CENGAGE Learning

LIBRARY OF CONGRESS CATALOGING-IN-PUBLICATION DATA

Cabot, Sam.
   Blood of the lamb : a novel of secrets / by Sam Cabot. — Large print edition.
      pages ; cm. — (Thorndike Press large print thriller)
      ISBN-13: 978-1-4104-6395-1 (hardcover)
      ISBN-10: 1-4104-6395-8 (hardcover)
      1. Large type books. I. Title.
PS3603.A364B56 2013b
813'.6—dc23   2013034054

Published in 2013 by arrangement with Blue Rider Press, a member of Penguin Group (USA) LLC, a Penguin Random House Company

Printed in the United States of America
1 2 3 4 5 6 7 17 16 15 14 13

Rome

Palace of Justice

Tiber

Santa Maria Maddalena

Pantheon

Trevi Fountain

Piazza del Colosseo

Colosseum

JANICULUM HILL

TRASTEVERE

VATICAN CITY

Exit

Thomas's Room

Library

Cardinal's Office

Saint Peter's Basilica

Saint Peter's Square

Gendarmerie Office

Tiber

Palazzo Farnese

Santa Maria dell'Orazione e Morte

Ponte Sisto Bridge

ORTO BOTANICO

Piazza Trilussa

Apothecary

Santa Maria della Scala

Spencer's House

Livia's House

Il Pasquino

Tempietto

Santa Maria in Trastevere

Ellen's Apartment

Piazza di San Cosimato

Ministero della Pubblica Istruzione

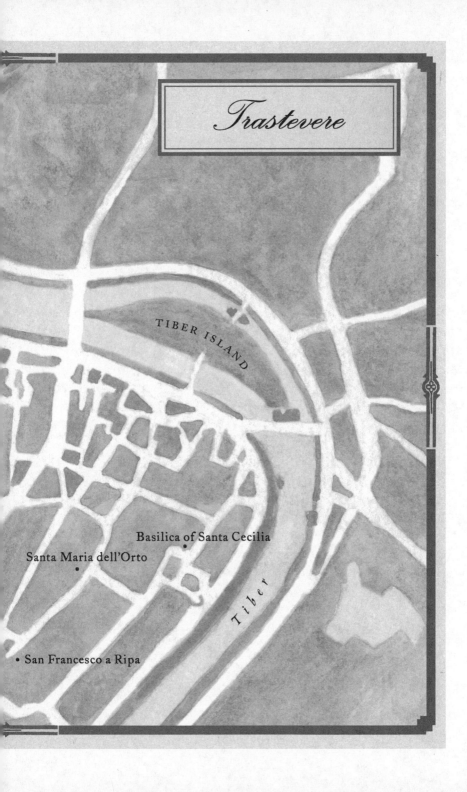

Trastevere

TIBER ISLAND

Tiber

Basilica of Santa Cecilia
Santa Maria dell'Orto

San Francesco a Ripa

Prologue

April 21, 1992

He wasn't prepared.

He never could have been. As the Fire rose in him he understood that.

They'd discussed it, so deeply and so long. The right thing, or wrong? She'd cautioned, counseled patience. But he knew what he wanted, knew with a certainty rock-solid and also rolling, cresting, an endless ocean wave. She wanted the same, he knew that, her restraint an attempt to protect him from irreparable error — if error it were. It wasn't, he was sure: the reverse, it was the choice that could join them together, give each to the other in ways beyond, even, the love and the bond they already shared.

They decided; and once *whether* was behind them, *when* and *where* became simple. Now: this soft spring dusk, the sky fading from violet to onyx as it had the night she'd first revealed to him that this was possible. Here: in the parlor of her ancient home, a tower that had stood centuries upon this spot and watched Rome grow around it, watched the world change.

In the dark and silent room she lit no lamps, put on no music. The streetlight's distant gleam, footsteps in the piazza below: "It's enough," she whispered. They'd had wine, velvety Barbaresco, but now the wineglasses stood forgotten. On a cloth of cobalt silk spread across an intricate carpet, she leaned over him, the pale streaks in her long black hair glittering in the dim light. Silver to his gold, as her green eyes were ocean to his sky. She paused for a moment, but she didn't ask if he was sure; the time for that had passed. She brushed his lips once with hers. He was seized, suddenly, with a yearning to wrap his arms tight around her, to press her body against his, but he didn't move. He couldn't move.

She took his hand. She kissed his palm and a moan escaped him. She moved her lips slowly to his wrist. Another kiss, another moan. Then a fierce sharp pain, a searing that flashed to shoulder and fingertips. It faded as fast as it had come, to nothing, to numbness. Time passed, he didn't know how much.

And now this. Everywhere, every cell —

he swore he could feel them each, individually — in every one, a warmth, a generous, suffusing heat began, intensified, rose. The sense of it made him joyous, wild. As it heightened he was sure he was ablaze, would be consumed by fire from within, and he couldn't stop himself: he laughed.

Slowly, the burning faded, too. He turned amazed eyes to her. She was smiling. Her breath, her blood, her gardenia scent: he knew them all, his blood knew them all as it knew, as he knew, the cat out on the cobblestones licking its paw, the soft murmur of lovers crossing the piazza, hand in hand. Intoxicating perfume drifted in the open window: the blossoms on the magnolias, too faint for him before. Somewhere, not close, someone played a piano. He heard the instrument. And he heard the distance.

He had Changed.

1

May 27, 1849

Dear Margaret,

I write to you tonight on a matter of utmost consequence. Please, my friend, give your gravest consideration to what I am about to ask of you. I am guilty, I know, of a fondness for the grand gesture, and I imagine you are rolling your eyes at yet more melodrama from your little poet; but I am in earnest when I say that what is contained herein, as fantastic as you may find it, is simply — and momentously — the truth.

With this letter I send you a small sealed box. It holds a copy I made of a document obtained from the Library of the Vatican itself. Obtained! Margaret, I stole it! As you no doubt know by now, Pius the Ninth has fled, taking refuge from our righteous cause in the Kingdom of the Two Sicilies. Here in Rome his craven disappearance had been rumored for months — thus the Pope defends his faith? Hah! — but we were not assured of it until this Easter last. As the news spread our soldiers were hard put to choose between festivity and fury. The coward Pope has summoned the French — the French! — and crawled away.

In the end, being unable to dissuade my men from their consuming rage, I chose to channel it. I led them to the very gates of the Vatican, barely more than a howling mob. (Barely, but yet more: soldiers still, and under my command. Since receiving my commission from General Garibaldi, your fat and laughing poet has become a very good officer, indeed I have!) They would have eagerly stormed the walls at any spot, but I conducted them to the gate nearest the Library, though the purposeful nature of my orders was, perhaps, not apparent.

Wait, I hear your voice, and you are shocked: **Wild soldiers, marauding through that storehouse of wisdom? Papal possessions or not, the glories contained therein are world trea-**

sures! You, Mario, deliberately led soldiers thence? Margaret, your reverence for learning causes horror to ring loud, drowning out the **bravo!** you are no doubt otherwise heaping upon me for my martial prowess.

Withhold your judgment, I beg of you. I was in search of the very document, a copy of which I send you now, and under cover of my soldiers' rampages, I found it. Immediately, I ordered them out, and they obeyed. Yes, there was damage, and there was pilfering; these were unavoidable, my intent being to create a chaos in which my retrieval of these papers would go unnoticed.

This document, dear friend, will shatter the Church.

I retain the original, and believe me when I tell you I have taken steps to conceal it well, in a place that will resist flames, floods, and the predations of the French. I fully intend and expect to employ it myself, at a moment of my choosing, to maximum effect.

But Louis Napoleon's army, led by that jellyfish Charles Oudinot, remains camped outside the city. We were told they were impartial, come to mediate between Pius the Ninth and his subjects

— his subjects! my God! — but Oudinot has thrown his lot in with the Papacy. I cannot say this surprised me; his master is that Napoleon elected President by free vote of his people, who is rumored on the verge of declaring himself their Emperor. Emperor, Margaret! Does he intend to be Caligula, or perhaps to rule Cathay?

This is why I write to you now. It is likely but a matter of time before Oudinot takes action on behalf of Pius the Ninth and lays siege. If he does he will succeed. It is that simple. Our army will be defeated. But we will not. This document, Margaret, will be the salvation of the Republican cause. Of more than that! It will throw the Papal boot from the neck of the Italian people, of my people, and be the agent of its fall from the necks of those who love freedom in every corner of the world.

But know this: once the inner cabal of the Church understands that it is gone they will stop at nothing to get it back. Thus your friend, full of buoyant confidence though I am, might at some point be no more. Improbable, Margaret, so do not fear — I am a hard man to kill. More credible is the prospect that, despite all my planning, the document itself will be destroyed; or that I will be prevented from recovering it to make the use of it that I so ardently wish and so wholly intend.

Why not, then, just say where the document is, instead of this over-wrought business of copies, locked boxes, and other absurdly theatrical goings-on? you ask, and though I shall not tell you where it is, I will say how very much I am enjoying this imaginary conversation, hearing your voice once again! I shall not tell you, because, although I am consigning this package to a trusted (and well paid!) courier, the possibility exists that it will be inter-cepted and this letter read by eyes for whom it is not intended. (And if you who are reading this are not Margaret Fuller, I say: shame on you, sir!) No, the hiding place of the original document is my secret alone. But, dear Margaret, as you have been in our mutual explora-tions of scholarship, of literature, and of statecraft, I am asking you in this, also, to be my invaluable collaborator. I send you this copy of the document sealed and ask you to retain it thus. Margaret, do not read it. I promise you what is found therein will tell a tale you would scarcely credit. You will think your good friend mad, but I assure you, I am not. I beg you, follow these instructions faithfully. Keep this box unopened and always near you; and tell none you have received it.

In the months to come, once the impending battles have been fought and decided, I will send word. But if you have not heard from me in a year's time, take this box to safety. If he still lives, deliver it into the hands of General Garibaldi. He will read the document and, though at first he will recoil, if he is the man I know him to be he will acknowledge the truth and understand the use of it. If he lives not, Margaret, you must publish the document yourself. Remember, as you know me, and on our friendship, I pledge to you that this document is no fiction and the bargain it makes is irrefutable and real. The other signatory — my people — retain possession of their original manuscript, signed and sealed as is the Vatican's that I have hidden. Once your copy has seen the light of day, though the world may at first refuse to believe, my people will have no choice but to bring their copy forward. Then will the Papacy and the Church come crashing down, and a new era begin!

Ah, Margaret, how often and how fondly do I think of you, imagining you intensely at your work, quietly at your reading, joyously with your family! How I miss you! The brilliance of your arguments, the passion of your debate. Here in the Army of the Republic, I find much excitement, but little, alas, in the way of conversation.

Spencer, of course, predicted this, arguing against my decision to offer my services to General Garibaldi. He takes, as might be expected, a longer view of the unfolding of history than I myself. I would send you his greetings, but I cannot, because he has, at my insistence, left Rome. My thought was not so much of danger to him, but to the objects in his collection. Planned or unplanned, destruction in war is inevitable; what good, I argued, is a historian without relics of the past, the very objects that prove history? So (upon a laden oxcart, with another following, how you would have laughed!) Spencer has gone to the Piedmont. The result of my silver tongue is that I sit in a leaking tent eating badly boiled polenta, while he sips cognac in a warm villa in the North.

Oh, but how I digress! Your poet is a willing, even an eager, soldier, but a lonely one, and apparently no less garrulous than in civilian life.

Your dashing Giovanni cuts a grand figure in Riete, I am sure; you must send him my compliments. And little Nino is no doubt flourishing. I look forward eagerly to the day when, in a free and united Italy, we are all together once more!

Until that day, Margaret, please: upon our friendship, promise me, though I am not there to hear it, that you will faithfully accomplish what I have asked of you.

Until we meet again, dear friend, I remain

Devotedly yours,
Mario Damiani

2

July 5, 1850

They didn't roar. Flames. They didn't roar; and pumping his thick legs as hard as he could, slipping and stumbling on the rough stones of Via della Madonna dell'Orto, plowing through the bedlam of shouts, carts, and the ripe smell of fear, Mario Damiani laughed. The celebrated poet, renowned for his love of the concrete and real, of physical facts and sensory truths, was surprised to find a cliché untrue? Damiani's experience of fire was, naturally, limited, but not entirely lacking. Caged fires had warmed his homes and cooked his meals, had lit gas lamps and other men's cigars. Not one of them had roared. The flames he and all around him now raced to escape were of a wildly grander scale, but still distant — though a single errant cannonball from the French position on the Gianicolo and more were sure to bloom.

21

These flames snickered, sizzled, whispered, telling of the mindless destruction of places he had loved. They broke his heart, but they didn't roar, and he laughed to acknowledge the fool he was.

Not entirely a fool, though. A sharp turn, another minute's elbowing through frantic, fleeing crowds, and before him, suddenly, the gates leading to the dark, aloof façade of the Basilica of Santa Cecilia. Cecilia, patron saint of poets. **How apt,** Damiani thought, **and how marvelously arbitrary.** His choice of this place, like the others he'd hastily visited tonight, was dictated by happenstance: all were churches on the path from his home to the river, and his little notebook of praise poems already held a page celebrating each. Damiani creaked open the courtyard gate, closed it behind, and stood panting. Perspiration dripped from his brow. He wiped it with his sleeve, grinning to think how horrified Spencer would be by the gesture. Damiani, a year a rough soldier, would have to relearn gentlemanly ways when he reached the North. As his breathing slowed he crept across the courtyard, keeping to the shadows.

This was the last place he'd visit tonight. Six times already, Damiani had torn poems from the notebook and concealed them.

Across the bottom of five he'd block-printed five letters with an artist's lead — inelegant but serviceable, and it was wartime, after all — and he'd hidden each where it would be safe for as long as it would need to be. Here in Santa Cecilia, he'd do something different. The page from his notebook that he'd hide here held no poem. It bore only the last five block letters, the final pieces of the puzzle.

He pulled open the basilica's heavy door and slipped inside. Shouts and panicked footfalls fell away, replaced by the patient hush of old, worn stone. Traces of incense lingered in the cool air, hardly discernible to most, perhaps, but murmuring to Damiani of desert caravans and exotic Eastern cities. Lately, Spencer had been wanting to travel, to see distant lands and wonders. Damiani had always maintained that Rome was enough to satisfy the soul of any man; but now, for the first time, he felt something of Spencer's yearning. Yes, he decided: once reunited, he and Spencer would travel, to see miracles and marvels. Perhaps Spencer, though he'd always scoffed at the idea of going west to the young land, might be persuaded to journey to America, to see cities of vigor, of ferment.

Damiani shook his head and grinned.

Fine, Mario. An Atlantic crossing. Perhaps you'd care to find your way out of Rome first?

Three votive candles, evidence of someone's concern for the next world even as Louis Napoleon's soldiers tramped the streets of this one, provided the basilica's only light. No matter; Damiani saw well in the dark, and had spent countless hours in this place. He trotted up the center aisle, knelt, and crossed himself. It was an old habit, one he'd found he could not break. Spencer had accused him of not trying so very hard to break it, of actually enjoying the atavistic nature of the gesture. Well, perhaps.

Rising, he vaulted the altar rail.

There he knelt again. Before him lay Stefano Maderno's breathtaking, delicate statue of Santa Cecilia, head so oddly turned away from those who looked on her. The executioner's ax had fallen on Cecilia three times, but her neck had not been severed, and for three days she hadn't died. A beautiful, terrible thing for a sculptor to depict; made more terrible, and more wondrous, by the model Maderno had used: the remains of the saint herself, uncorrupted when disinterred twelve hundred years after death.

Terrible, wondrous, and to the Noantri, Damiani's people, a particular and secret astonishment.

For Damiani, it was a bittersweet thing that his chase should end here, at the small, tender work he loved most of all Rome's glories. From his notebook he tore the leaf, blank but for the five lead letters. He folded the paper and, after a brief pause, slid it deep into a gap at the statue's base. He reached out when he was done to trace his finger on the thin line across the saint's marble throat, where her life should have left her but had not. Then he rose, crossed himself again (hearing, in his mind, Spencer's sigh), and, after a glance about him (even in the dark, he knew the angels, he knew the saints), made his way back up the center aisle.

Opening the groaning church door, Damiani flinched at the way the din of the invaded streets splintered the stillness. Across the courtyard he took a deep breath and pushed through the gate. Here, as before, swarming people, burdened wagons, horses and donkeys being ridden or desperately pulled along. Damiani laughed again, as Spencer's sardonic voice rang inside his head. **Really, Mario. Such vast drama — is it necessary? Concealed clues, a hunt**

25

for treasure — it seems like a great deal of bother.

Oh, Spencer, Damiani thought, hurrying on the ancient stones (did he hear the snort of warhorses, the in-step tramp of troops?). **Oh, yes, a great deal of bother. But when you find the treasure, when you hold in your hands the document itself, you'll understand why.** Rash and reckless Damiani, who never planned anything beyond the next line of verse, had hidden the document a year ago. Had first made a copy and sent it out of Rome. Now, this evening, he'd left a note in Spencer's study at the deserted villa: *Look to your poem.* It was an instruction that would be cryptic to all but Spencer, and with it he was proposing to lead his historian lover in a merry dance. All this should in itself convince anyone of the gravity of his intention.

Except, of course, Spencer would laugh at him in any case, as they sat sipping cognac in the Piedmont. None of the steps Damiani had taken to secure the document would be of the least importance except in the case of his own death. He raced now to render them all useless, for he did not intend to die.

On Via di Santa Cecilia he charged left, toward Via dei Genovesi, the river, his hidden boat, and, if his purse of gold had been of any use, his hidden boatman. He'd reach the mooring well before the arranged time. If the boatman had been seized with fear and had fled? Mario would handle the boat himself. If the boat was gone? He'd jump into the Tiber and swim until he reached a French-free shore. He'd fight his way to the Piedmont, sweep triumphantly into the villa, drink the excellent wine Spencer could be trusted to lay in wherever he found himself, and make poems until his moment came. Then he'd return and retrieve his hidden treasure, and the world would change.

He plowed headlong through the tumult, his ears so full of shouts and his own labored breathing that he didn't hear the clip-clop of horses' hooves until the horses themselves pranced into Via di Santa Cecilia, practically on top of him.

Damiani pressed into the shadow of an overhanging window. The street's panic swelled, though most of these people had nothing to fear from the French. Nothing immediate, in any case. Damiani himself was a different matter. He still wore the trousers and rough cotton shirt of Garibaldi's troops, though he'd prudently thrown aside the officer's coat he'd so proudly donned the year before. The general himself,

27

seeing Rome was lost, had wisely negotiated a truce and taken his army north. Oudinot's plans to deliver Garibaldi with Louis Napoleon's compliments into the hands of the Pope being thus foiled, his troops were now hunting soldiers who had remained in Rome — men like Mario Damiani.

Were hunting, and had found. Shouting, the lead cavalryman reined his horse so hard it reared, and charged forward with his saber raised.

An instant to decide: left? right? Damiani had once assured a friend he was a hard man to kill, and so he was; but to capture would be easier, and especially compassed round, as now, with tons of stone and horse-flesh. To his right, down Via dei Genovesi, lay the river, so close he could smell its damp stone channels: but that street was wide enough for horses. Even if he were to successfully bolt, a straining fat poet is no match for a galloping horse. In the dark wall on his left, a slice of deeper darkness: an alley's opening. It would be more useful if this alley connected to another street, which Damiani, who had walked every public inch of Trastevere (and many of the private inches, too) knew it did not. Still, the horses couldn't follow. If the cavalrymen dismounted and chased him on foot, perhaps the shadows of the tiny inner piazza would shelter him until they gave up, decided he'd ducked into a doorway, and went away. Fighting foot soldiers, if it came to that, would still be preferable to fighting horses. He exploded out from the wall.

The soldiers, without pause, swung off their horses and swarmed after. Damiani crouched behind the piazza's absurdly tinkling fountain. The French captain gave an order: one man with him, circling left, two more going right. The rest remounted at the alley's mouth. One of each stalking pair tested doors while the other watched the shadows. These men might be French fops, but they were no fools and they were closing like pincers. Still, they were only four. Damiani was Blessed with tremendous strength, in the way of his people, and it was not unreasonable that he could defeat four Frenchmen. But then what? Into the street again, to where the rest of the troop waited? Diving under the horses' bellies to escape?

That, he thought as the first to see him shouted, was a question for later.

They rushed him; he leapt back from the fountain to a recessed doorway. Let them come at him from the front. Let them come.

They came. The captain first, a privilege

of rank. Ducking the saber-swinging arm, Damiani rammed his shoulder into the man, throwing him into the soldier behind. For a moment all movement stopped. Any plan they'd had to attack him singly, as gentlemen would, was abandoned now that they saw his strength; and he'd just made a fool of their captain. All four charged in a gale of shouts and swords. He felt the sting of a blade on his wrist, then a fiery slice down the length of his thigh. Meaningless in the end but distracting in the moment, as pain always was. Two soldiers tackled him, knocking out his breath, throwing him down. He shoved a hand up under one man's sweaty chin, pushed and pushed, straining until suddenly the man tumbled off; but the other was still pummeling him and two more dove down hard. Damiani's head rang. He drew a great breath and with a roar and a thrashing of arms, he erupted. Jumping to his feet, he hurled one man against the wall, punched another squarely on his thin French mustache. But still they came, fists and sabers sweeping the night air.

Mario, Damiani thought, **this may not turn out as well for you as you hoped.** He ducked a blade that chipped the door-post where his head had just been, then twisted his arm to throw off a hand clamping his wrist. That hand, though, did not yield. Its strength was as great as his, and it yanked him left, then backwards. Damiani braced to slam the wall. Instead he fell flat on his back in darkness. An urgent voice whispered, "Come!" and a door was slammed and barred against angry French pounding. Damiani jumped up and ran, following a shadow down a dark passage, followed himself by a tall shadow behind.

The thumps and angry cries faded as Damiani and his rescuers — his own people, he now knew — emerged into another alley. A horn sounded, the French patrol raising the alarm. "They will be everywhere now," the man behind Damiani said, a calm dark voice Damiani simultaneously recognized and was astounded to hear. "We cannot risk the streets. Filippo, that door. Ahead, on your left." The lock would not give, but Filippo — Filippo Croce, it must be; he was the other man's personal secretary — threw his shoulder against it twice. The wood shrieked as it tore. A nail plinked on the cobblestones. The door, complaining, opened, and the three stepped through.

The light in the room was low but the aroma was unmistakable. Before Filippo lit a torch, Damiani, hands on knees as he drew breath, knew they had entered a stable. Dancing shadows showed him to be correct. The smells of dung and hay thickened the air, but the place was silent: the horses were all in the North, under the backsides of Garibaldi's troops.

"Thank you," Damiani panted, still bent over. He rubbed the wound on his leg, painful but not as deep as he'd thought. "How did you find me? Or am I just lucky beyond belief?"

The tall man shook his head. In his deep, slow voice, he said, "We have been searching for you, Mario. Do I have to tell you why?"

A jolt caused Damiani's heart to skip. Heat suffusing his skin, he straightened slowly. After a moment he replied, "No, Lord."

"Then tell me where the document is hidden."

Another moment; another breath. In a voice at once trembling and sure, Damiani said again, "No, Lord."

"Mario." A shake of the dark head. "I understand your cause. I know you believe I do not, but I do. It is not time. The time will come, but it is not come yet."

"Lord." Damiani steadied his voice. "My Lord, the time will not 'come.' In all these years it has not yet come. We must make it come."

"We cannot. To everything there is a season."

Damiani blinked. "You'd quote Scripture to me? On this question?"

"And why not? Your argument, as I understand it, is with the papacy, not the Church."

"If only the papacy allowed for the distinction!"

All three froze as rushing footsteps and jangling swordbelts in the next street told them the French were near.

The tall man said, "We cannot debate now. You must give me the Church's copy of the Concordat that you have stolen. You will come to understand when you have lived as long as I have."

"It is precisely those years that blind you to the chance these times create! The world has changed. It will continue to change. Reason and scientific thought gain the upper hand. We no longer need the Church!"

"You are wrong, Mario." A slight nod signaled Filippo; Damiani saw it, but not in time. Together the two threw themselves on him, and though he was strong, they were stronger. He kicked and heaved, but heard a clanking, felt a constriction, found his arms and chest bound in iron. Filippo wound the chain tight and fastened it about a post. Trussed, Damiani lay on his back in the straw, staring up at the others.

"Filippo," said the tall man. "Leave us."

"My Lord —"

"Leave us!"

After a moment Filippo bowed and obeyed.

Damiani tugged at his chains, feeling them bruise his arms. Perhaps he could break them or tear down the post, but it would take time.

"Mario." The words came gently. "Tell me."

Damiani did not speak.

"This is useless, Mario. Garibaldi's army is defeated and the Pope still rules. The Noantri must keep peace with the papacy and the Church."

"Peace!" Damiani repeated bitterly. "This is not peace! This is serfdom! We wait, and wait, concealing ourselves, feigning and dissembling. You know what our lives are! But we need not! When the agreement comes to light, when the Church falls —"

"*It is not time!* If the Church falls, we also fall. The life you've had — the villa, your poetry, your fame — you are a wonderful poet, Mario. A great talent."

Damiani stared stonily, not acknowledging the compliment, and the other man sighed and went on. "This agreement you so despise is what allows it all. You did not know the times before." He paused. "You have been impatient, a hothead from the day you joined us. I should not have permitted it."

"No, I didn't know those times," Damiani retorted. "But these are different times. You are living in the past. I am looking to the future."

"The future." The tall man's voice held a new, sad note. "Do you not understand? Unless you give me the stolen document, I cannot let you live."

Damiani's blood ran cold.

"This is not something I want to do," the other went on. "It will haunt me forever, I fear. But my responsibility is to our people. If you live, though it will take years, you will retrieve the document and you will publish it. Am I wrong?"

Slowly, Damiani shook his head.

"Then, unless you return it to me, you cannot live."

"My Lord." Damiani's voice was ragged. He tried to strengthen it. "Do not do this, I beg of you." Meeting the steady, silent gaze, he said, "It will be futile in any case. I made a copy. I gave it to a friend."

The dark eyes held him. "No, you did not."

"I did. With instructions to publish it, in the event of my death."

"To whom?" A contemplative frown. "Not to Spencer George, I think. He's been ensconced in the North for some time. And would not, I think, approve of your actions, if he knew."

"No, he wouldn't. He is a historian. His view is long." Damiani said this calmly. He hoped he was wrong; but, for Spencer's sake, he hoped he was convincing.

"If it's true you've made a copy, you have put a friend in danger. It is not only we who will be searching. Did you think the Vatican would not discover your theft, not chase after what they've lost?"

"In truth, my Lord, I thought only they would. I did not think I had anything to fear from our own people."

A thought seemed to come to the tall man. In a voice equal parts wonder and disappointment, he asked, "Is this why you joined Garibaldi's army? With this sole intention: to put yourself into a position to raid the Vatican Archives?"

Bound and prone, Damiani had to laugh. "Sir. You think too highly of my cunning. I never understood what I might bring about until I found myself with my troops at the gates of the Vatican. No, my Lord, I joined the Army of the Republic to unite Italy and throw off the papal yoke, not just from the necks of our people, but of all people."

"Ah, Mario, you laugh. It was that laugh, that excitement, your boundless joy in life, that convinced me you could be one of us. Please, remain one of us. Tell me where the document has gone. Allow me to free you and all will be as before."

Damiani breathed deeply. He smelled the straw he lay in, saw shadows flicker on the walls. He drew another breath and said, "No."

"We will find it, Mario. We will find your friend. This is a grand gesture, but it will be in vain." After a long, silent time, the tall man nodded. "I see. I'm sorry, then. Very sorry."

He turned and strode to the rear of the stable. A great wave of fear broke over Damiani, banished, to his surprise, almost immediately by this thought: **All men die. In the end, you are a man, Mario, as you were at the beginning.** It calmed him, that realization; and another thought almost made him smile. Margaret would succeed. The death of Mario Damiani would mean something, mean more, even, than his life. Margaret Fuller, well known and wealthy, famously resolute in her endeavors, beyond the reach of both the Pope and the Noantri, would bring about the liberation of his people and the destruction of the Church. **It's in your hands now, my friend. I know you will not fail.** Damiani was thinking this when the other man returned, carrying a blacksmith's hammer.

"Mario?"

He waited, but Damiani did not speak.

Finally: "I understand. At least, I will not make you suffer." He swung the hammer high above his head and down again with rushing force. Pain seared Damiani's skull and blackness flooded in. Through it, he saw the other man take the torch from the wall and set it to the straw. As the world faded, Damiani had to laugh one last time. Flames, when they were racing to devour you, did, indeed, roar.

3

September 14, 2012
This document, dear friend, will shatter the Church.

Father Thomas Kelly read the words again, absently tapping a pencil on the table, an old seminary habit. A glare from his left and a "shush!" from his right; he grabbed the pencil up guiltily, offered an abashed smile. Serious researchers, brooking no distractions, were clearly to be found in London's Transcendentalist Archives. Thomas sympathized. He was one himself. How else to explain his joy in rooting through these (rather ill kept, if truth be told) shelves and boxes, searching for a path probably not there to find?

And while he was on sabbatical, too.

Unlike many of his fellow Jesuit scholars, Thomas Kelly enjoyed teaching under-graduates, feeding happily off their enthusiasm and energy; but they required direction to the same strong degree that they resented receiving it. His own student days were barely a decade behind him, and his occasionally headstrong approach to his studies were still a clear enough memory that he couldn't fault them. Teaching did sometimes feel like sailing into a headwind, though. Exhilarating, but exhausting. Time without classes was restorative, no question.

More so if you actually used it productively, of course. Or, on the other hand, found a way to relax. Maybe he should go down to the Thames and sail a real boat, not a metaphorical one. Instead of spending his days sifting through the disordered collection of papers left behind in 1850 when the American journalist Margaret Fuller sailed for New York. Although, he reminded himself, that journey ended in a shipwreck that took the lives of all the passengers, Fuller included, and most of the crew. So much for real boats.

Thomas glanced at his watch. What he *should* do was stop daydreaming and get back to campus. He had a meeting soon at his office at Heythrop College with a student whose thesis he'd agreed to advise even while theoretically student-free. Why not? His own academic career had received generous help from some of the Church's top scholars. Now that he was regarded as in those ranks — a standing Thomas viewed with skepticism, but there it was — it was his duty to offer help in the same spirit.

It was not an entirely altruistic gesture, though. What was? On days like this it was good to feel you'd gotten something done. Thomas's morning had been a waste. The letter with the dire phrase ("shatter the Church," indeed!) had been written by Mario Damiani, a fiery anti-Papist poet of the Risorgimento — the nineteenth-century uprising of the Italian people against the power of the Church. Thomas considered the idea that any document could be that dangerous flatly absurd. For one thing, Damiani's politics plus his tendency toward hyperbole suggested he might be putting forth more hope than fact. For another — and Thomas said this as a churchman who'd himself been through a momentous crisis of faith, who loved his Church yet saw it with clear eyes — if the scandals, disasters, and wrong turns of the past decades, or millennia, hadn't shattered the Church, he suspected there wasn't much that could.

He was curious about what Damiani thought had that power, though; but his real interest in Damiani grew from another part of this letter. Thomas's focus as a scholar encompassed the Risorgimento and the other Italian political movements of the time. He'd written a number of groundbreaking papers, and two books, in that area, and when he'd found Damiani's letter to Fuller the implications made his scholar's heart pound. The Vatican Archives had been looted in 1849. The letter made it clear Damiani had been involved; in fact it claimed he'd led the troops himself, though Thomas suspected the poet of being a bit of a blowhard. Church scholars had long given up hope of recovering treasures stolen in that raid, partly because Vatican record-keeping had been so imprecise it was hard to know exactly what was gone. But no one, to Thomas's knowledge, had taken the route he was following: through Garibaldi's partisans.

He'd struck a vein with this letter: Damiani had sent a copy of something to Margaret Fuller and hidden the original. Whatever it was, the copy no doubt went down with Fuller, and the location of the original must have died with Damiani. But maybe he'd done it more than once, or maybe others had done the same — hidden things or sent them away. A study of Damiani's papers and those of his circle might, just possibly, lead somewhere new.

It was the lot of historians to interpret events, to stand to the side and study, not participate. Thomas had chosen that role and for the most part was content. But as he gathered his coat, laptop, notepad, briefcase, and errant pencil, he thought — not for the first time — how satisfying it would be to be instrumental, just once. To be a part of history instead of a follower of it. One small discovery, one document found because Thomas Kelly had thought to look where others hadn't — well, well, if that wasn't the sin of pride rearing its ugly head. Thomas grinned and, probably to the gratification of the other researchers, left the Transcendentalist Archive.

Heythrop College stood at the other side of Holland Park. Since coming to London from Boston seven years earlier, Thomas had become rather the sedentary scholar. A fast walk, he decided, would do him good, and he trotted down the steps and into the park. The brilliant gold of linden leaves overhead and their crunch underfoot called forth from him a silent prayer of thanks. Thomas loved the change of seasons, both the fact of it and the idea. Yellow leaves, bare branches, pale buds, bursting blooms, then yellow leaves again: it all happened whether you wanted it to or not. If at the height of summer you couldn't quite believe in winter, if in the depths of winter you thought summer would never be back — it didn't matter. Flowers, autumn colors, snowfall, they were all on the way; faith not required. For Thomas, that very fact was enough to bolster faith.

He'd traversed the park, reached the campus, and was climbing the stone steps to the doors of Charles Hall when his cell phone rang. Juggling briefcase and office keys, he stuck the phone to his ear. "Thomas Kelly."

"*Buongiorno,* Thomas. It's Lorenzo."

"Father!" Thomas stopped, smiling in delight and surprise. He hadn't spoken to Lorenzo Cardinal Cossa in three or four months. His own fault, he knew. His former thesis adviser — and spiritual adviser and friend, more to the point — had much to occupy him since his move to the Vatican four years ago. It was Thomas who should have made the effort to keep in better touch. "An unexpected pleasure! How are you?"

"Very, very well, Thomas. And you?"

"I'm fine, thanks."

"You sound out of breath."

"Rushing as usual, is all."

"With your coat unbuttoned and your arms laden."

"I'm afraid so."

"You're busy."

"Always. But don't —"

"You're about to be busier. Thomas, I need you."

"Of course." Thomas shifted his load and started up the stairs again. "Tell me what I can do."

"Here."

"I'm sorry?"

"Here, Thomas. I need you in Rome. And now. As soon as you can get here. Much is happening. The day has finally come."

"I — I'm sorry, I'm lost. What day? What's happened? Is everything all right?"

"Much better than all right. I've wanted to call you for the last few months, since Father Bruguès took ill, but of course that wasn't possible. But now it's official. Two weeks ago he took a well-earned retirement. Thomas, I've been honored with both of his positions. I've been made Archivist and Librarian of the Vatican."

"Oh!" Thomas stopped again, causing a rushing student to plow into him. The student, seeing he was on the phone, mouthed, *Sorry, Father.* Thomas smiled and waved him off. "Oh, that's wonderful! Congratulations! Both positions — what an honor."

"And a responsibility. Thank you, Thomas. Now come help me."

"I — My classes, my students . . ."

"You're on sabbatical, aren't you?"

"I'm advising three theses."

"Our Lord has given us glorious new technologies to allow you to do that from here."

"I —"

"Thomas. You and I spoke about this back in Boston, when it was barely a dream. This priceless, irreplaceable, and deeply chaotic collection needs a comprehensive steward-ship, an approach of methodical care it hasn't seen yet. The opportunity to partici-pate in that work was why I came to Rome. The chance to take the lead in it has been what I've wanted most, for a very long time, and I don't deny it. Assisting Monsignor Bruguès was the beginning. Now the entire Library has been given into my care. It's always been my intention that you should have a role."

"Yes, of course." Thomas entered the building and turned down the hallway. Outside his office the waiting student jumped to his feet. Thomas held up a delay-ing finger, unlocked the door, and shut it behind him. "And I hope —"

"A specific role," Lorenzo went on. "The

overall work is important, but there's a particular task I need you for. Your skills and your knowledge. It's something we haven't discussed yet. I was waiting for the right time, and now the time has come."

"I'm supposed to start teaching again in the spring semester," Thomas said weakly.

Lorenzo Cossa sighed. "Your obsessiveness as a scholar is the positive side, I suppose, of your . . . lack of flexibility. Thomas, I'm a Cardinal. I'm the Vatican Librarian and Archivist. I can get you reassigned and Heythrop College will be proud, not dismayed. I promise you. Please, come help me here."

Thomas shrugged out of his coat, looking around. His plants, his pictures, his books and papers. Seven years of settling in. He tossed the coat on the chair. "Yes," he told the Cardinal. "Of course."

The call to the priesthood had been the most compelling force in Thomas Kelly's life. A rangy Irish redhead, he'd found baseball, girls, and garage bands also part of his South Boston youth, and he had a nodding acquaintance with illicitly acquired six-packs and smokable non-tobacco products. But behind it all, beyond the breathless rush of childhood and above the clang

47

and crash of adolescence, hovered something still and silent. Something as calm and deep, endless and inviting, as the sea. Later he would come to understand this as faith; early on, he only knew the peace, the sense of being home, that he felt at Mass. It took him years to recognize most people didn't feel what he did, even longer to see the path open to him. When he understood, he took to his vocation with joy and gratitude.

He'd been an exemplary seminarian, drawn to the cerebral, scholarly life. After ordination he'd headed along an academic route, happily exploring obscure byways of Church history. His powerful intuitive gift for research had drawn the attention of other scholars, of journals and publishers. Doctoral, postdoctoral, and teaching positions had sought him out, for which he was thankful. Whatever intellectual talents he possessed were matched — no, actually, overshadowed — by a pronounced clumsiness as a pastoral counselor. His efforts to comfort the occasional undergraduate or old friend who came to him at times of crisis only left Thomas feeling intrusive, cliché-ridden. He greatly admired priests who ministered directly to people's spiritual needs, but he accepted that his own contribution to his Church would be less immediate, more ethereal. That his work was unlikely to rock anybody's world, however, did not lessen his joy or confidence in his vocation and the direction he'd chosen within it.

It had therefore been a shock to him when, the fourth winter after ordination, he'd found himself plunged into a terrifying abyss by a single word.

In the midst of consoling the young widow of a high school classmate who'd died unexpectedly (one of those times when Thomas felt it his duty to attempt the solace a priest should be able to offer), a previously unheard voice came whispering inside his own mind. "The Lord has a plan for each of us," he'd said to the distraught woman. "It's not ours to know, but you must never doubt it exists. To everything, there is a season, and a time —" He'd stopped, dumbfounded, hearing a silent question: **Really?**

The widow, mistaking his stillness for pastoral manner, smiled sadly and completed the phrase. "— to every purpose under heaven. Yes, Father, of course." She had, he recalled, taken strength from whatever he'd gone on to say and left with renewed hope. He, on the other hand, sat motionless in his study for the rest of the day. The afternoon faded and the street-lights spread an anemic glow across the slushy sidewalks. The voice that had asked the question didn't stop, asking others, all different but with only one meaning. **Are you sure? How can you be? Isn't it convenient that God has for each of us what we most desperately want — a purpose, a reason to exist — but keeps it secret? Thomas,** the voice whispered, **you're a smart man. Isn't it just as likely we invented all this, a huge absurd theological security blanket, because we're scared? That nothing has purpose, nothing has meaning, and God is just a lullaby we sing ourselves? Thomas — really?**

"Thomas, the only men of God who've never felt what you're feeling now are sheep. Hah! Lambs of God. Followers. Not think-ers." In his austere, book-crammed study Lorenzo Cossa flicked the Red Sox lighter Thomas had brought as a gift and grunted in satisfaction at the steadiness of the flame. He pulled in air until his cigar glowed, and settled his long, gaunt frame in an armchair. "It's a crisis of faith. Everyone goes through it."

"Yes, Father."

"Doesn't help at all, does it? Knowing that?"

Thomas shook his head. Three weeks after his counseling session with the widow, he was still spiritually dazed and unable to find footing. He'd requested a leave and flown off to Chicago, hoping his mentor could help him make sense of this onslaught of uncertainty.

When Thomas was in graduate school at Boston College, Monsignor Lorenzo Cossa's history seminars were legendary for their rigorous intellectual demands and equally for the priest's galvanizing oratory. Monsignor Cossa maintained the Church had long ago strayed from the spiritual high road and, far from being a path to salvation in the debased world, was itself in danger of being devoured by it. This wasn't a belief Thomas shared — where was the Church, and where was it needed, if not in the world? — but such was the flair of Lorenzo Cossa's rhetoric that Thomas would have studied algebra with him for the pleasure of hearing him talk. That his courses fit Thomas's interests was a bonus. That Lorenzo Cossa seized on Thomas Kelly as the most promising student he'd had in years was a mixed blessing. He leaned harder on Thomas than on other students; but even

51

alone in the library at three a.m. Thomas understood he was being forced to his cerebral best, and, though exhausted, was grateful. The year after Thomas got his doctorate, Monsignor Cossa had been elevated and given charge of Church educational programs in the Midwest. They'd remained in touch, but such was the power of this earthquake that Thomas knew the telephone and computer screen would be powerless against it.

"No," Thomas said, in Lorenzo — now Bishop — Cossa's study. "It doesn't help."

The Bishop wasn't fazed. "Of course not. It's like going to the dentist. Knowing everyone who ever sat in that chair suffered the same agonies doesn't reduce your pain. But remember this: they all survived."

"I'm not sure about that. Some men leave the priesthood. Some leave the Church."

Around the cigar, Lorenzo grinned. "I was talking about the dentist. Thomas, in all seriousness. Yours is one of the strongest vocations I've ever come across. But what made you think you'd never have doubts? Jesus himself had doubts. Doubt is the coin which buys our faith. That this never happened to you before might be lucky or unlucky. You're farther down the road than most when the first crisis comes. But eventually everyone arrives at this chasm and has to find a way to jump it."

"First crisis? I can expect this to happen again?"

"Forget I said that."

"No, it's actually hopeful. It almost gives a context."

Lorenzo regarded Thomas in silence. Knocking ash from his cigar, he said, "I saw this coming."

"You did? Why didn't — why didn't I?"

"Why didn't I warn you, you mean. Could I have said anything you'd have believed? What's happened to you is one of the hazards of scholarship. Knowledge is power, isn't that what we say? But power corrupts. An institution based on knowledge and learning can't help but be a corrupt institution."

"You're calling the Church corrupt?"

"There's the flaw!" With a joy Thomas remembered from the classroom, Lorenzo pounced. "The Church isn't based on knowledge! It's built on faith! What drew you to the priesthood, Thomas? The spiritual magnet of faith. Indefinable. Mystical, even. If you'd chosen the contemplative life and locked yourself in a monastery you'd have been fine. But you made the mistake of engaging your faith with the world. In your case, through the study of history."

"With you as my guide."

"Yes, all right, I made the same mistake. And had a similar crisis, if that's what you're fishing for. Until I realized that all the knowledge in the world can't stand against faith. No matter what you learn, Thomas, your faith is still there behind it all. The magnet's still pulling." The Bishop's cigar had gone out; he lit it, puffed on it, and resumed.

"It's the learning that's troubling you, isn't it? The evidence is too heavy to ignore: that no one associated with this enterprise, by which I mean the Church, is divine, with the exception of our Lord. It's a shining exception. But the discovery makes you wonder. Thomas, I want you to remember this: Knowledge is about facts. Faith is concerned with truth. They're not necessarily the same. That's what you've flown halfway across the country to discuss, isn't it? Come, it's time for dinner. I don't think there was ever a discussion of faith not improved by a bottle of wine."

That evening didn't set Thomas back on firm ground, but it gave him a life preserver to cling to in the frightening waters of misgiving. They talked for three days; it was,

54

finally, a practical suggestion by the Bishop that realigned the world, showed Thomas a direction to follow while he waited to see if his faith would return.

"One of your strengths as a historian," Lorenzo said as morning sun poured through the window, "has always been your broad range of interests. Periods, places. Now I'm going to suggest another approach. Something different has happened to you, Thomas, and perhaps it calls for a response in kind." The Bishop stretched out and crossed his legs. "The intellectual life of the nineteenth century, in America and Europe, revolved around faith. What it was, who had it, where and when it was needed. It was a powerful set of questions, sometimes created by, and sometimes creating, political and military movements. Questions of faith moving secular societies. I'm suggesting you focus your attention in that arena."

Thomas considered. "Randomly? Or do you have something specific in mind?"

"Of course I do. You sure I can't give you one of these?" He gestured to the humidor. As always, Thomas shook his head. He couldn't think of half a dozen times outside of meals and the celebration of Mass that he'd seen Lorenzo without a cigar. Early on he used to take one to be polite, but he'd never enjoyed them, and their friendship hadn't required that sort of courtesy for years.

"I want you to head straight for the lion's den," Lorenzo said, drawing on his cigar to get it going. "In the nineteenth century, before there was an Italy, rebellions up and down the peninsula raised questions about the secular power of the papacy. The Church in the world, Thomas."

"Your favorite subject."

Lorenzo rolled his eyes in mock despair. "*In* the world, *of* the world — completely different states! Have you learned nothing, Father Kelly?"

If he'd learned nothing else, Thomas had learned that particular distinction well and truly in his years with Lorenzo Cossa. He couldn't help grinning.

Lorenzo grunted. "You're having me on, aren't you? I suppose that's a good sign, that your sense of humor, such as it is, is returning. May I get back to the nineteenth century?"

"Please."

"The questions about the Church's secular power became questions about spiritual power. Do you see what I'm saying? These men followed their doubts to their logical end. Don't run from that: study it. If your faith is strong — as I know it is — you'll survive this encounter and be the better for it."

"And if not?"

Lorenzo held Thomas's eyes. "I'm offering no promises. But at the least, you'll have added to the store of human knowledge. Is that, in itself, such a poor goal?"

It had not been, and Thomas had worked toward it, at first mechanically, then with growing animation. Lorenzo's prescription had proven to be precisely the cure for Thomas's spiritual ailment. Close study of the words and actions of men whose sworn enemy was the Church gave Thomas the tools, the time, and in some way the courage, to sort out the roots of his own faith and the roots of his doubts. The doubts, he'd begun to understand, flowed from received wisdom, unexamined assumptions. **Thomas — really?** The faith sprang from someplace simpler, deeper: the peace he'd always felt in the presence of God. The questions the new voice was asking were only that: questions. Not sly statements of fact, just uncertainties. Legitimate; but standing against them was that undeniable, palpable sense of being home.

Thomas was rock-certain that without

Lorenzo's help then, and in the late-night calls in the weeks and months that followed, he'd have made the huge and heavy mistake of valuing the new voice over the old peace. He'd have left his vocation, he'd have left the Church. Now, eight years later, with Thomas secure in his decision and the direction of his life, Lorenzo was asking Thomas for help.

How could he say no?

4

Lorenzo Cardinal Cossa replaced the ornate receiver and stared sourly at the telephone on his desk. How much had been spent to rewire these ridiculous porcelain antiques to modern standards? He relit his cigar, sighing. That they'd go to that trouble proved, yet again, the soundness of his argument: the Church, Lorenzo Cossa's home, his chosen and very nearly his sole family, had lost its bearings. Was wandering in the wilderness. The useful elements of the modern world — functioning electronics, for example, and comfortable clothing — it eschewed in favor of gilt and ermine. But suggest a Latin Mass, or offer the once-obvious idea that the contemplation of a saint's relics could be of spiritual use, and you were derided as pathetically old-fashioned.

All right, then, he was. And from now on, he'd use his cell phone.

As he puffed the cigar, the Cardinal's mood improved. Thomas was coming, would be here in two days. Unlike Lorenzo, Thomas didn't grow short-tempered at the Church's frivolities; he either shrugged them off, or actually didn't notice them, so focused was he on the high-altitude joys of recondite research. Not only a born churchman, a born Jesuit. Born and, once Lorenzo had found him, led, directed, and guided. Thomas Kelly had been that once-in-a-lifetime gifted student, and Lorenzo Cossa had uttered daily prayers of thanks for him. The Good Lord knew what he was doing when he sent Thomas to Lorenzo. In fact Lorenzo saw it as a sign: his time was coming.

And now, had come.

Many of those around Lorenzo assumed that, having achieved his current exalted positions (both at once!), he'd fulfilled his ambitions and would now happily putter among the manuscripts and books for the rest of his days. A valued and important cardinal, a senior official, and a trusted adviser, yes of course — but sidelined, as the Librarians always were.

Not true. Oh, no, not true. Lorenzo's work had just begun.

5

The wind made a grab for Livia Pietro's hat as she raced out the door. The magnolia's thick green leaves gleamed in the sunlight but she dashed by without a glance, charging across the uneven stones of Piazza Trilussa, heading for the bridge. A strong breeze carried the loamy scent of the Tiber; the more she sped up the harder it pushed against her. As an external manifestation of her internal state, that was perfect; she'd have laughed if she hadn't felt queasy. She didn't remove the wide straw hat, only clamped her hand on it as she ran. She felt foolish, hand square on head like that, though her neighbors' indulgent smiles would have told her — if she hadn't already known — that eccentricity from her was nothing new. The hats, the sunglasses, her ancient tower house, the gray streaks she refused to banish from her long, dark hair, and, worst, her unmarried state at the age of gray streaks, all conspired, though her academic status provided partial explanation. (*"Professoressa,"* they'd confide to one another knowingly.) Gossip, Livia was resigned, was inevitable. Through friendliness and liberal spending in the local shops she managed at least to keep the gossip benign.

A horn bleated. She let a *motorino* pass, then darted across the road in a nimble dance with oncoming traffic. She hurried over the bridge as fast as she dared, though not as fast as she could. Among Livia's Blessings were agility and speed. A horsewoman in her youth, she retained a high level of athletic skill. But a middle-aged *professoressa* speeding like Mercury along the Ponte Sisto would invite exactly the kind of attention Livia was at pains to avoid.

Odd, she thought as she ran, to be rushing someplace she so very much didn't want to go; but a Summons was neither a happy event nor an occasion for choice. Although the Conclave met regularly to debate issues of importance to the Community, it was possible to live a long and happy life without ever being Summoned before it. In fact that was the experience of most Noantri; but this was Livia's second time.

Worse, she feared this Summons was not

unrelated to the first.

Across the river she cut left, onto Via Giulia, where the cobbles led past the Palazzo Farnese's ivy-draped wall. The Fontana del Mascherone — the Big Mask Fountain — looked particularly apprehensive and unhappy today. Before her Michelangelo's bridge curved over the road. Livia loved that bridge, its perfect arch and trailing leaves, but right now her heart lurched at the sight. Immediately past it stood, to the right, an apartment building where people lived comfortable, normal lives; and to the left, her destination: Santa Maria dell'Orazione e Morte.

The art historian in her wanted to stop and stand, to drink in the church's bone-bedecked façade, her eyes tracing the path the sculptor took as, inch by inch, he'd coaxed cherubs and skulls from the stone. At times, before a statue or a painting, Livia felt tiny contractions in her arms and hands. Her body, more insightful by far than her mind or even her heart, was re-creating the artist's movements, teaching her how the piece had come to life. Those moments of perception, which after so many years still thrilled her, had been part of the Change for Livia; the works where she felt them were the ones she knew and loved best.

This church's façade was one of those, but she didn't linger. She slipped a five-Euro note from her pocket and slid it into the collection slot. In that same movement she found and threw the hidden switch to unlatch the church door. Each Noantri Summoned before the Conclave was told about the switch and how to operate it. Livia had been told the first time; now, she regretted to say, she knew.

Inside the church she took off her dark glasses and moved through the sanctuary to a point behind the altar. The crypt door stood ajar. She removed her hat, smoothed her hair, listened for a moment to the thumping of her heart, and headed down the uneven stone steps into the dank air of the crypt.

At least she was on time.

The stairway curved down to a brick-arched, stone-floored room whose niches held meticulously stacked bones and pyramids of skulls. Rosettes made from hands and arcs made from ribs adorned the walls. Four centuries of the poor and the un-claimed had found sanctified ground here, their bones painstakingly cleaned and positioned for the devout to reflect upon as they prayed. Not for the first time, Livia considered the oddness of her people's penchant for the trappings of death. It was akin, she had decided, to the woven streams that flowed through the carpets of the Bedouins.

This church, though, odd as it was, was an excellent choice for meetings of the Conclave. Like so many of Rome's small churches, Santa Maria dell'Orazione was now rarely used, and the crypt visited even less often. A discreet and sizable annual contribution from the Noantri to the church's burial society procured private access to the crypt at any time; thus the latch in the collection box. For uninterrupted meditation, officially, and no priest or bone cleaner had yet sought to investigate more deeply. The Conclave would be undisturbed, and the weight of centuries in the scents of earth and rock would, as always, serve to remind those who met here of the consequence of their deliberations.

The crypt housed an eternal flame, also appropriate. Its flicker was often the only illumination, but now, as was usual when the Conclave met, great iron candelabra on either side of the room cast pools of wavering light. Puffs of air from cracks in the ancient walls danced shadows against the blacker darkness. As she stepped through the doorway, Livia heard no sound but her own footsteps and their timid echoes, fading as she walked forward and stood before the Conclave.

All were assembled, silent, waiting: the twelve Counsellors sitting in rows right and left, and between them the Pontifex, whose dark gaze made Livia uneasy even when she encountered him in the most casual of circumstances. Here, in the hush of stones and skeletons, it was all she could do not to squirm. She stood silent; it was protocol that the Pontifex should speak first, though in truth Livia could not, at that moment, have spoken at all. A shuddering conflict had enveloped her, familiar from her first Summoning. Like all Noantri, Livia felt an immediate comfort, a sense of grateful belonging, in a group of her own people. It was physical and instantaneous, a calling of blood to blood. The relief of it had flooded around her when she walked into the crypt. But here, it was illusion. These black-robed Counsellors were not her friends. Standing before them the first time, she'd sensed individual flashes of sympathy behind the unanimous disapproval. This time, though she didn't yet know why she was here, nothing but anger filled the dank air.

"Livia Pietro," the Pontifex said, his deep, slow voice echoing in the stone chamber.

"I'm dismayed to see you before us once again."

Not as much as I am, Livia thought, but she only nodded in acknowledgment.

"Years ago, when you were called here," the Pontifex went on, "you spoke eloquently. You admitted your error in judgment, but you pleaded movingly the case of Jonah Richter. Your plea was heard. He was initiated and allowed to remain. Many of us, through the years, have made similar mistakes in the name of love." Though the Pontifex's eyes did not stray from Livia, the black-robed man at the end of the row to his left — the position of the Conclave's newest member — lowered his gaze. Livia struggled not to do the same. "In the event," the deep voice continued, "your breaking of the Law seems to have been in vain. Jonah Richter left you not long after he became one of us. You look surprised that I know this."

"We were — we were in Berlin at the time, my Lord."

"Because we allowed him to remain, did you think we would not be watching him? The New always bear watching, Livia."

Now Livia did look away, her face hot. Her separation from Jonah was no secret, but she hadn't understood it to have happened in a public spotlight, either.

"Livia," the Pontifex said in tones that were, to her surprise, gentle, "we haven't called you before us to settle that account. This Conclave deliberated and, once you'd made Jonah Richter Noantri, permitted him to continue. That was our decision. Nor could any reproach from us be as painful as his forsaking you has already been, I'm sure. That's the way it is with affairs of the heart." Livia looked back up, meeting his dark eyes as he said, "No, we're here because of a different betrayal. Larger and much more dangerous."

He turned to the woman on his immediate right. Senior in the Conclave and one of the Eldest — like the Pontifex, a bridge to the times Before — she was known to Livia as Rosa Cartelli, although of course that would not have been her name at birth.

"We have received a letter." Cartelli's words were clipped and businesslike. "From Jonah Richter. In German," she added. Livia heard clearly the contempt in Cartelli's voice. To the Counsellors, from various lands and all highly learned, Jonah's native tongue wouldn't have presented a problem; but by tradition, communication with the Conclave was initiated in Latin. From courtesy, the Counsellors usually replied in the language of the petitioner; with Livia called before them, all were speaking Italian. But the choice was always theirs. That Jonah had defied tradition this way did not bode well.

"The letter is a threat," Cartelli said flatly. "He is telling us to choose: either we can make public the contents of the Concordat, or he will."

"But . . ." Livia was at a loss.

"Do you doubt he would carry this through?" the Pontifex asked.

After a moment Livia shook her head. "No, Lord. Jonah is . . . impatient. He feels the Concordat constricts us all. There are many who think the same way," she added. "Who feel it is past time we stepped into the light. And that the world is ready to accept us."

Why had she said that? To defend Jonah? After all this time and in these circumstances? Absurd.

"Yes," the Pontifex said patiently. "I know that. They are wrong."

Livia glanced at the faces of the Counsellors. Most appeared in calm agreement with the Pontifex — as, on this point, despite having just articulated the opposing view, Livia was herself. Three Counsellors, however, glared with an accusatory fierceness that could only mask doubt. Well, why would that not be? Unveiling was a topic of endless interest to, and discussion within, the Community; why wouldn't it be debated in the Conclave as well? Still, whatever their individual beliefs, none of the Counsellors spoke, save one: a woman two seats from Cartelli, whose features were Asian and whose name Livia didn't know. "They are wrong," she echoed the Pontifex in a soft, clear voice, "and there are others in our Community more radical than Jonah Richter who would seize on the chaos this revelation would cause to advance plans yet more perilous."

Livia waited for more explanation; none was forthcoming, but she didn't doubt that what the Counsellor had said was true. She looked again to the Pontifex. "But, Lord, this threat. Why would any of the Unchanged believe him? He can try to reveal whatever he wants — he'll sound like a ranting fool. Surely this isn't any real danger."

"It could be." The man at the end, the one who'd looked away when the Pontifex talked of mistakes made for love, spoke now. "If he can prove it."

"But how could he?"

"The Vatican's copy of the Concordat disappeared in 1849," the Counsellor said.

Taken aback, Livia asked, "It did?"

"Yes. And Jonah Richter claims to have it."

"Is that possible?"

The Counsellor looked to the Pontifex. "The man who stole and hid it," the Pontifex said, "a poet by the name of Mario Damiani, was one of us — a Noantri who believed as Jonah does. Damiani died without revealing its location." The Pontifex spoke steadily, but a shadow passed over his face that Livia thought was not from the flickering candles. "We made a search. I can assure you the Church did also, starting even before the Pope returned from Naples to reestablish his rule in Rome. The Vatican eventually concluded their copy had been misplaced, or possibly destroyed, in the looting and the subsequent attempt to restore order. For the past century and a half they've believed it most likely lost somewhere in the vast disorganization of their collection."

Livia nodded slowly. "It would be plausible. Artworks and documents surface in the Vatican all the time. Sometimes centuries after they disappear."

"The cumbersome bureaucracy at the Vatican — in the Church in general, in fact — has always worked in our favor. The very fact that the Concordat never came to light convinced the Church it hadn't fallen into the wrong hands. For our part, the Conclave was satisfied it had either been destroyed or was hidden so well it would never be found. But Jonah Richter claims he's discovered its hiding place and will reveal its location unless we reveal its contents. That, of course, would be tantamount to Unveiling."

Livia tried to think clearly. "Is it possible Damiani never took it at all? That Jonah knows that story and is bluffing?"

"Jonah Richter might be bluffing, but Mario Damiani did steal the Concordat. He made a copy."

The Pontifex turned to a round man, an American, Livia recalled, named Horace Sumner. "He sent it to a friend, a journalist named Margaret Fuller," Sumner said. "Sealed in a silver box. He instructed Fuller not to read it, and we don't believe she did. In any case she didn't speak about it and she died within a year, in a shipwreck. Her papers and possessions were all lost — except for the silver box, which we were able to retrieve. We've read the copy. It's the Concordat, word for word."

Livia understood. Though the general terms of the Concordat were known to all in the Community, none but the Conclave had seen it. Mario Damiani couldn't have quoted it unless he had it before him.

"Jonah Richter has given us a deadline. Impudent man!" Cartelli's anger was barely contained. "Three days hence, on the feast day of San Gennaro. How symbolic." Her curled lip told Livia that if they'd been alone, woman to woman, Cartelli's next words would have been, *Really, what did you ever see in him?*

"Richter has since gone into hiding," the Pontifex said. "Because of the way he phrased his threat, we don't believe he has the document with him. We think he's discovered its location but left it where it was."

"Why would he do that?"

"Perhaps it's in a place too public, or too private, for easy access. Now, we could find him and eliminate the immediate danger." The casualness with which the words were uttered, in this crypt of the dead, chilled Livia's blood. "But that won't lead us to the Concordat. Unless we find *it,* we're at risk of this happening again. Livia, *you* must find them both. Jonah Richter and the Concordat. He is your responsibility. You know him well, know how he thinks. Do whatever he did, follow whatever trails he followed. Find them before the deadline."

"And then?" She asked this with a tremor in her voice, because she knew the answer.

"You will bring us the Concordat. And you will kill Jonah Richter."

6

Forty-eight hours ago Thomas Kelly had been in cool, fall-fresh London, facing a comfortably predictable day of students, books, and his plant-filled office. Now he sat in a silk armchair watching dust motes dance on a shaft of sunlight at the Vatican. He was still trying to comprehend this shift in the pattern of his life when his thoughts were interrupted by a cheerful young priest, an African with a lilting voice, who led him across the anteroom and ushered him through a grand pair of doors. Lorenzo Cossa looked up from behind a gilt-trimmed desk.

"Your Eminence!" Thomas couldn't help grinning. "You look well." The Cardinal was thin as ever, but a glow of purpose suffused his sharp features. Thomas knew that look: Lorenzo Cossa was at the start of a major new work. Neither the Cardinal nor anyone else involved would be sleeping much for a while.

"You're clearly flourishing yourself, Thomas." Lorenzo stood and came out from behind the desk, looking his protégé over as the African priest left, discreetly shutting the door. "Come, sit. There? Here? Shall we try them all?" With theatrical despair he waved a hand, taking in the throng of furniture, the inlays and rare woods; and the silk-covered wall panels, the marble statuary, the paintings. "What do you think? Too early to redecorate?"

"You haven't changed." The suite, like every inch of the Vatican, was luxurious and ornate, these rooms even more than some because they were the office of a cardinal. Most Princes of the Church took seriously their status as Princes. But Lorenzo had always found luxury distasteful. "All that gilt," he'd say, shaking his head. "Distracting. We have work to do." If Lorenzo had his way, Thomas knew, this room would be emptied and painted white. Filing cabinets would replace cherubs, bookcases would line the walls where Renaissance Madonnas now hung. Everything would go but the desk — and the humidor.

"And you, Thomas? Have you changed your ways? One of the advantages of Rome over home — I can smoke wherever I want.

Father Ateba's arranging for coffee. Can I offer you a cigar?"

"No, thanks." Thomas sat in a velvet armchair, smoothing his cassock under him. He rarely wore it, preferring to teach in jacket and collar; but presenting himself at the Vatican for the first time seemed to call for more formal attire.

"You can wear whatever you want, by the way," Lorenzo grunted, appearing, as so often, to read Thomas's mind. He himself was in a black jacket and shirt. A heavy gold chain draped into his jacket pocket, where his cardinal's cross was tucked to keep it out of the way of his work. That and the gold ring on the hand that had swept the air were the only changes Thomas could see in the cantankerous scholar he'd met years ago. "I want you focused on your work, not the trim on your ferriaolo. They take the trappings seriously here but don't let that fool you. A lot of what goes on is less pious than you'd think. Than you'd hope. More of a business, sometimes, than God's holy work." Briefly, Lorenzo glared; then he relaxed. He thumbed an onyx lighter, puffed his cigar. "That's why you're here." He settled against the gilt and velvet of an armchair and looked at Thomas steadily. "The Church was founded by our Lord, but it's run by men. Good men, most of them, and some not, and all of them — all of us — make mistakes. Sometimes those mistakes, large or small, come back to haunt us. You've seen that happen."

Thomas nodded, unsure where Lorenzo was headed.

"A serious mistake was made six hundred years ago. I'd like to undo it, but I can't. The best I can do is make sure it never comes to light." Lorenzo tapped ash from his cigar. "In 1431, shortly after he became Pope, Martin the Fifth signed an agreement known as the Concordat. The Church has been living with its provisions ever since. It was wrong to sign it, wrong to abide by it, but at this point the Church would be seriously damaged if its existence became known. Much more than the damage that's already been done by continuing to follow it."

Thomas frowned in thought. "The Concordat? I haven't heard of it."

"No, you wouldn't have. It's hidden even from you deeply learned scholars. It's a secret even most cardinals aren't privy to."

"I see. But now that you're Archivist and Librarian —"

"That's what they think. But I was familiar with it already. I've known for some time."

"This Concordat — it's an agreement with whom?"

"I can't tell you that. When you read it you'll know, but until then — Thomas, I'm afraid of what it will do to you, to your faith, to hear me tell it without proof."

Thomas stared, and then laughed. "My faith? I've been through that fire and out the other side. Thanks to you. Whatever this is about, it can't be worse than that was."

"You're wrong." Flatly, Lorenzo returned Thomas's gaze. A silence stretched, and Thomas became aware of an unseen clock ticking in some distant corner.

Lorenzo shifted, puffed on the cigar again. "The Concordat is missing."

"Missing?"

"The Vatican copy. The other party has evidently been able to keep track of theirs through the centuries — at least, I haven't heard otherwise. Ours, however, seems to have vanished sometime after 1802. That's the last time a comprehensive inventory was attempted. Though even then, I can't be sure the records are accurate." Lorenzo shook his head. "I told you: this collection is chaotic. Disastrously so."

"But the renovation — the entire Library was closed for three years."

"Renovated chaos is still chaos. That was

all about electronic security chips, computer workstations, and bombproof bunkers. What's here, and where it is — still anybody's guess."

The door opened and the young priest returned, bearing a silver coffee service and china cups. "Thank you, Father," Lorenzo said. "You didn't have to bring it in yourself. They tell me that's what the valet is for."

The priest smiled. "I had a sense you wanted a certain level of discretion, Eminence. And coffee is not so heavy."

"A fine young man, that," Lorenzo told Thomas once Father Ateba was gone. "He has a future here in Rome. Or he could go back to Cameroon, and he'll become a bishop, without question. The future of the Church lies in Africa. In Latin America. In Asia! Do you know why?"

Thomas took the coffee Lorenzo handed him and added cream and sugar, marveling at the delicate porcelain. "You're about to tell me, aren't you?"

"To enlighten you, yes!" Lorenzo's tone was self-mocking but he continued seriously. "Because they believe. It's about faith with them — with us it's logic, it's reason, it's rationalism. Other words for compromise. So-called fairness — accommodation! — they'll be the death of this Church. Oh,

80

wipe off that smile."

"It's a pleasure to hear you fume again, is all. Your Eminence."

"Yes, fine. You think I'm Cardinal Chicken Little. Still, indulge me. This is serious business. I may be wrong, and you're certainly entitled to keep that thought in your head as you do your work, as long as you do it. I need you to find the Church's copy of the Concordat. That's why I called you here. I had a search made when I took this office. No trace of it's turned up. But we need to find it. Before someone stumbles over it by accident and everything comes out."

Thomas sat back against the chair and let his gaze wander the high-ceilinged room. The weight of history was palpable in the paintings and the statues, in the thick, figured carpets. The worries and triumphs, the work and the scheming — the prayers and uncertainties — of centuries of church-men could be breathed in with the air. Two days ago, he'd sat in a dusty archive in London, reading a letter from an implacable enemy of this place, and now, he was breathing this air. He set down his coffee cup.

"It's not here."

Whatever Lorenzo had been expecting Thomas to say, it clearly wasn't that. "Excuse me? You've suddenly developed unshakable faith, and it's not in vital theological doctrine but in the efficiency of the Archivist's staff? Just because we can't find it, you conclude it's not here?"

"That's not what I mean. I've never heard of this Concordat until today, but . . . Does the name Mario Damiani mean anything to you?"

"No. Should it?"

"Possibly." Thomas resettled himself, hearing his cassock rustle. "Damiani was a poet of the Risorgimento. A captain in Garibaldi's army. It's likely he was involved in the looting of the Archives in 1849."

Lorenzo's gaze was steady. "You think that was when the Concordat disappeared?"

"I think he stole it. Deliberately."

"Do you now? Based on what?"

"There's a letter he wrote to Margaret Fuller. The American journalist?" No light went on in the Cardinal's eyes, but it didn't matter. "It's what I've been doing in London. Going through Fuller's papers. She was enormously important in Italy. Her reporting shaped the American view of the uprising and helped make Garibaldi a hero. She was married to a partisan, knew them all, and didn't pretend to be objective. Damiani and she were particularly close. In his letter he tells her he stole something from the Vatican. He's coy about what it is, but calls it, quote, 'a document that will shatter the Church.' "

Briefly, Lorenzo was silent. Then: "No, I don't think so. If he had it and knew what it was, why didn't he use it?"

"I'm not sure he got the chance. He claims to have hidden it somewhere safe. He made a copy and sent that to Fuller with instructions not to read it, but to take it to Garibaldi if anything happened to him. Something did, though it's not clear what. That letter, from 1849 just before the French entered Rome, is the last time he's heard from."

Lorenzo sat very still. "There's a copy?"

Thomas shook his head. "Fuller headed for New York a year later, on a sailing ship. No one's ever been sure why."

"Why she went? Or why a sailing ship?"

"Either. But both make sense in light of Damiani's letter. He tells Fuller to take care, because the Vatican will be after the document, and to give it to Garibaldi if she hasn't heard from Damiani in a year. By then Garibaldi was already in New York. Steamships had just begun to cross the Atlantic, faster than sailing ships but also bigger. More danger of being followed. On Fuller's ship, besides her family, there was only one other passenger, an American named Horace Sumner, who boarded at the last minute. The ship turned out to be a legendary mistake, though: they sank in a storm within sight of the New York coast. Most of the bodies were never found, and all Fuller's papers were lost. Besides her published books and articles, she only left behind a few scattered items."

"Which you, my eminent scholar, have discovered?"

With a grin, Thomas said, "This is my period, you know."

"Well, don't you look pleased with yourself? I seem to recall it wasn't your period until some wise man recommended it to you. Nevertheless, a little back-patting might be in order, if you're correct." The Cardinal smoked in silence for a time. Finally he said, "If that document was the Concordat, it would answer two questions: why we haven't located it here, and why it hasn't come to light."

"Exactly."

"Well." Lorenzo laid his cigar in a crystal ashtray. "Do you think you can find it?"

"I have no idea. But why not leave it hidden?"

"You mean, since it hasn't been found in all these years, assume it won't be? For two reasons. First, we're not sure Damiani — is that his name? — was talking about the Concordat. I'd hate to think he'd unearthed yet another document equally dangerous, and I'd like to know. For another, assuming it *is* the Concordat, it's too big a risk. Maybe it's been destroyed by now, but if it hasn't, it could still be found. Someone will be digging a foundation or knocking down a wall, leafing through an old book or re-framing a picture . . . No, what I need is either the thing itself or some believable proof it's gone for good. Can you bring me that?"

"I really don't know. Do you want me looking for the Concordat, whatever it is, or the document Damiani stole and hid, whatever *it* is?"

"Both. Pursue whatever trails make sense. But I have a feeling you might be right. Follow your poet. Find what he stole. If it's the Concordat, you will have done your Church a great service."

In the opulent room with the unseen clock faintly ticking, Thomas nodded. "I'll start this afternoon."

7

Standing in the dank silence of the bone-decked crypt, Livia Pietro struggled to find her voice. She'd been given the instructions of the Conclave, delivered by the Pontifex himself; no argument was possible, but still, she spoke. "My Lord. I can't."

"On the contrary," the Pontifex replied calmly. "You will kill Jonah Richter, or we will. He is your Disciple. He is your responsibility."

Livia felt faint. Of course he was right. She knew the Law. Her first transgression — bringing Jonah into the Community without prior permission — had been a major one, and it was by grace of the Conclave that she hadn't been exiled for it. They wouldn't be so lenient again.

"The search for the Concordat, right now, takes precedence over the search for Jonah Richter," said the American, Horace Sumner. At that, Livia felt a spark of hope.

Perhaps if she found the document and returned it, Jonah would be spared. He was impatient, yes, but he was still New, and he was young. He could be made to understand — to see that many others had thought through the position he'd taken and that the results of Unveiling would not be what he hoped.

Sumner went on. "As far as that, we've fallen into a bit of luck. A priest has recently arrived in Rome, sent for by the new Librarian of the Vatican. Father Thomas Kelly, from Boston by way of London. Father Kelly's field is the history of the Church. His specialization is Italy in the nineteenth century."

"The Cardinal is searching for the Vatican's copy of the Concordat," Cartelli said. "He had people comb through the collection when he arrived, and of course they didn't find it. He knows when it was last seen, thus more or less when it disappeared. Our sources say he's brought Father Kelly here because of that expertise, but we think the priest doesn't know the nature of the document."

Livia looked from Cartelli to Sumner. "An odd coincidence. The timing, I mean."

"No." Sumner shook his head. "It's more likely that Jonah Richter, seeing the Car-

87

dinal make such a serious effort to locate the Concordat, feels his hand's been forced and so is forcing ours."

The scholar in Livia, trying to stay calm, focused on an unanswered question. "Why, in fact, is the Cardinal making this effort? From what you say, the Archivists before him have been content to let this secret lie."

The Pontifex spoke. "Just as we have always been divided between those who are grateful for the Concordat and willing to abide by its provisions and those who believe it constricts us and that the time is past for Unveiling, the Church has had for centuries its own internal debate. Among those in the Church who know about the Concordat, all — *all,* Livia — find it repugnant. But an extremist faction feel that in agreeing to it, Martin the Fifth poisoned the Church's very soul. They believe any relationship with us beyond the murderous enmity of old is a tragic and irresponsible mistake and argue Martin's act delegitimizes him and all Popes since. That it is proof he was never fit to lead the Church. They maintain it was we who engineered Martin's rise, in exchange for this contract. A charge," he added with a small smile, "not entirely without merit. We didn't engineer it, but once assured of the transformation in our lives Martin was prepared to bring about, we . . . took part in events already under way."

"A fine distinction," Cartelli sniffed, "which is lost on the extremists. A sour and unsubtle crowd. Their dearest wish is to go back to the apostolic line of the man who would have been John the Twenty-third, now called Antipope. It was he who was defeated by Martin."

Livia considered this. "They want to install whoever's in that line today, as Pope? The Church would never allow it."

"Whether they would or wouldn't does not signify!" Cartelli snapped. "For myself, I believe they might indeed. But can you not see the danger of the argument erupting, irrespective of who wins it? If the Church were to split publicly on this issue, our existence would be revealed. In order to gain sympathy for their cause, the militant faction would paint us in the darkest of colors. Vicious and bloody rhetoric would be used to terrify the faithful, as in years past. The power struggle within the Church would be couched in terms of us: *Are you a true and pious child of the Holy Mother Church? Or a friend of the Godless Noantri?* Those currently in power would try to make people understand the Concordat as a lesser-of-two-evils way to keep the wicked Noantri under control. The others would claim no compromise is possible with such demons. And no one, Livia Pietro, would claim us as their friends."

Ice sat in Livia's stomach; she wanted to argue, but long experience of the world silenced her. Cartelli, in fact, was probably correct.

"The new Librarian," the Pontifex said, and Livia was grateful for his calm, measured tones, "Lorenzo Cardinal Cossa, is of the extremist camp. He would happily use the Concordat as a scourge against us. But he is bound in obedience to his Church. We believe his search for the lost copy, therefore, is his attempt to do the next best thing: to ensure this compromise never comes to light."

"I see," Livia said slowly. "But if it does —"

"If Jonah Richter were to reveal the contents of the Concordat and prove its existence, the Cardinal, we think, would be bitterly grateful. The ensuing hysteria within the Church — and around the world — would set him free to argue to the current Pope and the Church powers that nothing could restore the Church's legitimacy but an abrogation of the Concordat and the destruction of the Noantri."

The Pontifex paused, then spoke like iron. "That will not happen." His echoing voice seemed to agitate the shadows, to make the bones dance on the candlelit walls. Livia did not doubt him. One of the Eldest, the Pontifex was a man of great learning, wise judgment, and respected counsel. And something more, also: a depth and delicacy of understanding of the Community, their lives and their situation, that set him apart and above. There were those, like Jonah, who believed that they needed no Conclave and no leader and after Unveiling, would have none. But while they had a leader, no Noantri had ever argued that another was more suited than this man.

In a quiet voice, the Pontifex spoke again. "That Cardinal Cossa has not already begun this argument within the Church indicates, we believe, that he does not know about Jonah Richter's threat. Nor will he. As I said, if you make no progress in your search for the Concordat, the Conclave will attend to Jonah Richter. But there will be other Jonahs, other cardinals. Until the world becomes more enlightened, this danger will be with us. The document must be recovered."

In the silence, all eyes rested upon Livia.

It seemed to her she was seeing the Pontifex, the entire Conclave, from a great distance; but with exquisite clarity just the same.

"The priest," she heard herself say. "Father Kelly."

"You will need him," the Pontifex replied. "We're fairly certain Mario Damiani left instructions of some sort to the place where he hid the Concordat, where Jonah Richter stumbled upon it."

" 'Stumbled upon'!" Cartelli scoffed. "More likely, has been obsessively searching for under our very noses."

"Perhaps," the Pontifex said evenly. "In any case, Mario Damiani was a man with enormous contempt for the Church. A very intelligent man, also. He would have understood the Concordat might have to pass decades, perhaps centuries, in its hiding place. Concealing it on Church property would be a sensible decision: Church-owned buildings are the last to be demolished, are rarely even renovated beyond minimal structural repair. Such a course would have appealed to Damiani's sense of irony, also. He'd have chosen carefully, appropriately. If Jonah Richter has already located the document's hiding place, an expert in Church history might be able to right the balance."

"Also," said Cartelli drily, "we do not like the idea of a priest running around loose, digging into our past. We'd like an eye kept on him."

"So you want me to enlist Father Kelly in my search?"

"Or offer to aid his," said the Pontifex. "An art historian who's lived a long time in Rome — you could be valuable to him. Our information is that Father Kelly is an obsessive researcher. He's been charged with an important task. He might welcome the help. But bear in mind, the priest has no deadline and feels no sense of urgency. We do."

"If he refuses?"

"Persuade him."

"If that involves telling him — the truth? About the Noantri?"

The Counsellors glanced at one another. The Pontifex didn't take his eyes off Livia. "Then you will tell him. We have debated this. Father Kelly is a scholar of great achievement and deep intellectual curiosity. It strains credulity to think that Cardinal Cossa expected once he found the Concordat, he would not read it."

"Does he believe as Cardinal Cossa does, about us?"

"They all do," Cartelli said with disgust.

The Pontifex, for the first time, turned on Cartelli a look of mild impatience; but he didn't correct her.

"If Father Kelly doesn't yet know the contents of the Concordat, he most likely doesn't know the truth of our existence, either," he said. "But Cardinal Cossa has been grooming this young man for some time. He probably intended to make him privy to that secret as he advanced in the Church. Father Kelly will almost certainly know one day."

"And so you are giving me permission to tell him now?"

"My," Cartelli said, "why suddenly so obedient? I don't recall you asking for permission the last time."

Livia's cheeks burned. The last time: when she had told Jonah. Revealed what she was, who the Noantri were. She had wanted to share with him the deepest part of herself, and to make him comprehend her certainty and her fears: what could be theirs in a life together, and what could not. The risk had been that he'd react as so many always had, with fear, with revulsion. She'd wanted him to know she understood that and was willing to take that chance, for him. From the start of time lovers had promised to climb the highest mountain, swim the deepest ocean, to prove their love, but Livia had offered Jonah a greater gift: their love itself, to claim or destroy.

And he'd been neither afraid nor repulsed. Nor merely accepting. Amused, at first, believing she was joking with him. Then, once persuaded, he was thrilled, and soon was asking, pleading, to join her. To be Noantri, too. She had thought, at the time, that it was from love. That he wanted to be everything she was.

"Livia." The dark voice came to her as though from far away. "Livia. You must begin." She looked up to see the Pontifex leaning forward in the flickering light. "Time is short." He smiled a tiny smile, acknowledging the irony in that statement.

"My Lord," she said. "I may not succeed."

He shook his head. "You will. You will search until you find the Concordat. If the deadline is near and you haven't found it yet, you will continue the search and we will see to Jonah Richter." He sat back again. "Jonah cannot escape this sentence, Livia. It will be far better for him if you are the one to carry it out."

The Counsellors, the Pontifex, all sat motionless, eyes on Livia in the candlelit gloom. She had been given her instructions and dismissed; she understood that. Still, in

95

a shocking breach of protocol, as though she were not part of the proceedings, but only watching, she heard her own voice whisper, "Is there no other way?"

The Pontifex may have been about to speak, but Cartelli slapped the arm of her chair. The sound rattled like a gunshot. "*What* other way? Are you a fool, too? Or" — her eyes narrowed in her wrinkled face — "are you in sympathy with Jonah Richter? Do you, also, believe the time for Unveiling has come?"

Livia shook her head. "No, no. I wish I could say I think so. But I don't believe it has."

"Then go. Do as you've been told. Or six centuries of peace will be destroyed. The fires will come again. In fear and raging fury we will be hunted, driven out, and we will die. You did not know those times. I did. We did." She nodded to the Pontifex, to a few of the others. "All this will be repeated, magnified a thousand times, if the world learns once again whom to label 'vampire.' "

8

The blue eyes that had watched Livia Pietro enter the church now saw her emerge, pale and shaken. She shut the door gently, as though it were fragile, and stood unmoving on the cobblestones until a gust tangled her long black hair. That seemed to wake her: she smoothed her hand over her head and put on her hat. The watcher's heart leapt. He remembered the feel of her hair, thick and untamed, under his own hand. Her skin, also, supple velvet despite her age. He smiled, understanding now what he hadn't the first time he touched her: the full and double meaning there. And the scent of her. He stood behind a closed window in a flat across Via Giulia, so what stirred him now must be not real, but remembrance. Still, he caught his breath. Few of the Noantri wore perfume. To senses awakened by the Change, the world offered sights, sounds, and aromas in infinite and startling intricacy. Not the least of these was the scent of one another; few cared to mask or even augment this signature. With this, as with so many of the Community's customs, his Livia was out of step. She delighted in a range of essences, rare and delicate, each applied with a fine hand — and each acting on him differently but irresistibly. He had tried, so many times and in so many ways, to persuade her of what was clear to him: that her unconcern with Noantri convention proved that what she claimed to want — a comfortable, invisible, assimilated life — was not her real desire.

His Livia. He shook his head. He still thought of her that way. They hadn't spoken in more than two years, and if he was correct, she'd just been instructed to kill him.

Jonah Richter had known his letter to the Conclave would call them into full battle mode — meaning, first, mind-numbing assemblies and debates. Ultimately, though, they'd have to act. He suspected he knew what form their response would take, and apparently he'd been right. Livia had been Summoned, had gone in looking apprehensive, and come out looking like hell. Maybe he was flattering himself; but if the Conclave had been as alarmed by his threat as he expected, his destruction was an obvious solution. Livia — the Noantri who had Made him and thus the only Noantri inherently dangerous to him — was its obvious agent.

Many of his friends, Noantri who believed as he did about Unveiling, claimed the Noantri were superior to the Unchanged. Some had taken, in fact, to ostentatiously dropping "Unchanged" in favor of "Mortal," a label so fraught that its use had been abandoned by the Community long ago. The extremist opinion held that, far from being forced into hidden, constricted lives, the Noantri ought to rule. That their fine sensibilities, acquired wisdom, and distant view of unrolling time made them better suited to governing than were the limited Unchanged.

Jonah did not share this viewpoint, and he sniffed the stench of egotism in those who did. He suspected that each saw himself — or herself — as the Emperor of All when the transition came. And he remained skeptical at the idea that it was possible to benignly rule those who were, not to put too fine a point on it, your food source.

The vision shared by Jonah and his group was a different one. After Unveiling, the Unchanged would understand two things: that the Noantri were not a threat; and that to be Noantri was to live so completely, to have senses so finely tuned and a mind so fully awake, that everyone would want to Change.

And where would nourishment come from, when all blood was Noantri blood? The would-be Emperors sneered this question in the Noantri coffeehouses and bars, the baths and gathering places. The answer — offered patiently by partisans like Jonah, edgily by those less tolerant — was: science. Human blood, after all, was only a chemical compound. It could be cloned, synthesized, grown. Why not? Promising work was already coming out of Japan. More would follow. Until then, the Unchanged already donated blood by the barrelful, some of which found its covert way to the Noantri as it had for centuries. More to the point, many sold their blood to pay their rent or buy their beer. Why wouldn't they keep that practice up, especially at the prices the Noantri could offer?

The arguments went on and on. Talk of Unveiling was everywhere; according to those Elder than Jonah, it always had been, since the day the Concordat was signed. The Conclave had no objection to the discussion, in fact was willing at any time to hear a new line of reasoning pro or con. The position of the Conclave, however, had never yet been affected by argument. Unveiling would happen in time; this was not the time.

But it was. Jonah was tired of hearing the arguments. He was tired of pretending, of evading questions with a smile. He had become afraid, suddenly, of losing the friends of his youth, as he saw them change, saw their faces line and their eyes soften. Livia had tried to comfort him, telling him these losses were part of the dark side of Noantri life, unavoidable and balanced by so much else. She repeated to him an aphorism, a saying of the Noantri: The Unchanged change; only the Changed remain unchanging. But her voice held sorrow as she thought of people she'd loved, long gone; and far from being persuaded to accept his friends' bad fortune, Jonah had begun to see an entirely different course of action.

Livia, he thought now, as he watched her turn and start slowly down the street. **You'll come to understand. This is, without question, the right thing. Even the members of the Conclave will be glad this happened, once it's over. Then maybe — maybe — you and I can be**

together again. In any case, don't worry; you won't be killing me.

9

In the vast, marble-floored hush of the Vatican Library's *Manoscritti* Reading Room, Father Thomas Kelly jotted on a notepad, then pocketed his pencil to keep his bad habit at bay. No pencil-tapping here. Along with no photography, no food or drink, no ink pens, and no humming to yourself. And no touching the books without white cotton gloves. Ah, intellectual freedom.

Not that he minded the restrictions, really. He was amazed just to be here. He wanted nothing more than to wander through the bright rooms, along shadowed corridors, past towering windows, and across the thresholds of low, hidden doors. He yearned to unlatch cabinets, slide drawers, climb ladders. But you couldn't. You sat and looked through the electronic catalog, a legacy of a previous Librarian's reorganization of the treasures in his charge.

You requested the items you wanted to study, and they were delivered to you.

Thomas's clerical collar brought him considerable deference from the staff, but he had no freer access than any other scholar. Lorenzo, of course, could have arranged for Thomas to enter any room he wanted, handle any document he cared to, without interference. That arrangement would have been highly unusual, though, and would not pass unnoticed. Because of the sensitive nature of Thomas's research, Lorenzo had asked him to work within the system. "Unless it becomes absolutely necessary," he'd added. "If it is, let me know and I'll say the word."

Thomas had been tempted, just so he could wander those corridors; but that would be overweening and wrong. For the task Lorenzo had charged him with, the system was working fine. Right now, better than fine.

A day of intense research here, added to the work he'd been doing in London for the past few years, had Thomas convinced he was one of the world's leading experts on the looting of the Vatican Library in 1849. That, in itself, was no great accomplishment; but he was also more sure than ever that it was then that *Sottotenente* Mario

Damiani — who, braggart though he may have been, did actually seem to have led the raid — had stolen the Concordat. What the Concordat was and why this mattered so much, Thomas still had no idea. All in good time, though: Lorenzo had brought him here to discover its hiding place, not its meaning.

Methodical scholar that Thomas was, he'd spent his first afternoon following the few faint trails the first search team had found, just to make sure they'd missed nothing. When those trails faded out, he'd gone back to his original thought, and began tracking down Mario Damiani.

All day yesterday he'd uncovered nothing but the facts of Damiani's life and work and his service in Garibaldi's Republican Army. Some of what he found was straight information, and some of it had to be read between the lines; some he'd already known and some he hadn't; much was of interest to the scholar in him but little to the newly minted detective. But with the fresh new morning came a new thought and a hopeful find.

Damiani had written in Romanesco, the traditional dialect of Rome, a choice of some Republican patriots of his era that Thomas, if he were being honest, would have to call a self-limiting affectation. In Thomas's opinion, Romanesco wasn't different enough from Italian to make using it the statement of fierce independence the partisans intended; it was, though, just different enough to be irritating to the Italian speaker trying to read it. For scholarly purposes Thomas had long since become fluent in Romanesco, as well as a number of other Italian dialects, dead and living. Hoping to get an idea of who Mario Damiani had really been, of how he'd thought and therefore where he might have taken something as precious as the Concordat, Thomas had requested the Library's volumes of Damiani's works. When they arrived they told him little, but by then he was off on a different trail.

Waiting for the volumes to be excavated from whatever deep vault they were buried in, he'd stayed at the catalog computer and clicked idly through the list of other Romanesco poets, thinking perhaps the works of Damiani's fellow fiery patriots might help his project of getting inside the man's mind. The catalog included thumbnail images, usually the front covers of the works in question. Some seemed promising, and Thomas slipped his pencil from his pocket once or twice to make notes, books to request later if he needed them. At the end of the list he found a grouping of uncategorizable odds and ends: letters, records, fragments. An item listed as "Poems, handwritten, anonymous, damaged" caught his eye. He clicked on the thumbnail image to enlarge it. The item was a pasteboard-covered notebook, bent and beat. How extensive the damage to the pages might be, Thomas couldn't tell, but the front cover was in good enough shape that he could read the handwritten inscription on it: *Poesie d'Amore, per Trastevere, Gennaio 1847.* **Love Poems, for Trastevere, January 1847.** He hadn't been able to make out the words when the image was small, but the handwriting had seemed familiar. Now he could see he was right: it was Damiani's.

Thomas put in an immediate request for the notebook, and it was delivered soon after Damiani's other works on a silent-wheeled cart by a thin, solemn clerk who whispered, *"Prego, Padre,"* and slipped away. Thomas's white-gloved fingers put down the volume he'd been holding and took up the notebook. He leafed through it with a delicacy that belied the pounding of his heart. Could it be this easy? The stolen document, slipped into a notebook, then lost all these years because of a lack of attribution? Thomas imagined the Concordat rustling out of the pages, saw himself racing through the echoing hallways, bearing it triumphantly to Lorenzo; and he laughed out loud — provoking frowns from other researchers, which seemed to be his lot — when he turned the final pages. Of course it wasn't there. Nothing fell out, though the book was in sorry shape: back cover gone, some pages torn and some missing, looking as though it had been stepped on more than once. **Oh, Thomas. Still a hopeless romantic.**

He glanced at some of the poems. Just as the cover promised, they were love poems, or at least, poems of praise, to the buildings and streets, the statues and fountains of Trastevere. None of the poems was titled; it was left to the reader to work out the subject of each. A few seemed obvious to Thomas:

Du' angioloni de quell'angiolo stanno de
   guardia
ar martiro, buttato ggiù in ner pozzo

two angels of that angel keep their watch
over the martyr, thrown into the well

That had to be San Callisto, where two of Bernini's angels gazed perpetually across the church to the pit where the martyred

Pope had died. Or

*Cosmologgje de colore, rosso-sangue,
   bianche,
e le curve llustre de li pini in ombre de
   verde*

cosmologies of color, blood-red, white,
and shining curves of pines in shades of
   green

What came to mind was the floor — Cos-matesque, the style was called — at San Crisogono. Many churches had similar floors, but these colors were associated, in Thomas's mind at least, with that one. And *Cosmologgje/Cosmatesco,* was it wordplay? Maybe. But maybe not . . .

Well, it had been his plan to spend the morning studying Damiani's work. He might as well start here. He settled over the notebook, forearms on the table. He read a poem, turned a page, read another. So absorbed was he in the words he was reading that he actually jumped when a soft voice spoke beside him.

"Mario Damiani! I thought no one read him anymore but me!"

Thomas blinked, taking in the sight: a woman in a flowing, flowered skirt, a blouse, and a complicated jacket (how did women know how to wear things like that?) was removing large sunglasses and smiling in surprise. She took off a straw hat and smoothed her dark hair. She'd spoken in English, and, extending her hand, in English went on. "Livia Pietro. I'm an art historian."

Thomas took her hand automatically. Her grip was strong and cool, and her eyes were an extraordinary green: silver-flecked, deep and dark. Moonlight on the ocean. Thomas realized he was staring. "Thomas Kelly," he said. He started to stand, but she slid out the chair next to him and sat. He dropped back into his own chair and added, "A historian, too, but of the Church. From Boston."

"I know." Livia Pietro dropped her voice to a whisper as two scholars by the window frowned over at them. She laid her hat on the table and gave Thomas a mischievous smile.

"That I'm an American?" Thomas matched her whisper. "Is it that obvious?"

"Well, you Americans do sit, walk, and hold yourselves in your own way. You're not hard to spot. But no: I meant, that you're a historian. The collar might suggest theologian, but you're reading Damiani, a fellow not known for his religious subtlety."

"Brava." Thomas smiled. "Some fine deduction."

"Why, thank you, Father. I've studied Damiani myself, here and there. He was an excellent poet. Complicated, elliptical, but well worth the effort. May I?"

Livia Pietro unzipped her shoulder bag and removed white cotton gloves, pulled them on, and lifted a volume off the pile. **Prepared and making herself at home,** Thomas thought. Academic protocol demanded that he object, stake his claim now, or risk losing his proprietary rights to Damiani's volumes. But Pietro's good humor was appealing, and it occurred to Thomas that if she knew Damiani's work well, perhaps she could help him get inside the poet's head.

She looked up and asked, "Do you read Romanesco? Few non-Italians do. Few Italians these days, actually."

"My main subject is the Church in the nineteenth century, on the Italian peninsula and elsewhere around Europe, as affected by the political movements of the time. Many primary sources have never been translated. I found it easier —" At Livia Pietro's smile, Thomas stopped short, hearing with something like horror his own pedantic tones. "I'm sorry. I think I spend too much time with undergraduates. Yes, I read Romanesco."

"So do I. What's this?" With a quick, conspiratorial movement, Livia Pietro slid the battered notebook along the tabletop. One finger keeping Thomas's place, she leafed through the pages. Her green eyes seemed to sparkle. "Is this Damiani's? I don't know these."

Thomas, who until that moment had not known eyes sparkled except in novels, said, "Yes, I think so. It was cataloged with the miscellanea. I doubt if anyone's looked at it since it was accessioned. If they had, the handwriting would've —"

"Yes," she said. "I agree. How exciting! You've made a discovery. Added to the store of human knowledge." Her brows knit. "But look — missing pages. I wonder why?"

"I assume, poems that didn't go well."

"Perhaps," she said doubtfully. "But look at some of these. Cross-outs, rewrites, arrows, more cross-outs, lines up the margins. He didn't seem to mind poems that needed work."

"Maybe he thought these couldn't be saved."

"Ummm." Livia Pietro came dangerously close to humming to herself, Thomas thought, as she turned the pages of the small notebook. "Interesting." She nodded, said, "Ummm," again, and settled over the volume. After a moment, Thomas pulled his own chair closer and read along with her.

10

Under the glorious blue Rome sky the buildings of La Sapienza positively glowed with learning. Anna Jagiellon flopped down against the trunk of a golden-leafed *platano*. The morning was fresh and clear and she had an hour before her next class: twentieth-century Russian poetry, a miraculous trifecta of a fascinating subject, presented in a creatively organized curriculum, taught by, for once, a professor who, though Mortal, wasn't an idiot. Not only not an idiot, the man was hot: a grinning swarthy Serb. She'd caught the way he looked at her as she studiously took her notes, seen the corners of his mouth tug up when she swept her long blond hair back from her forehead. She'd have taken a run at him already, but her current life was a comfortable one that she wasn't prepared to complicate for a few rolls in the hay. Especially now, with her goal suddenly, after so long, within sight. If she was able to accomplish her objective, she and the Serb could take it up then. At that point they'd be fair game for each other.

Not that there was anything fair going on when a Noantri made a play for one of the Unchanged. The Noantri body was so intensely and elusively irresistible to Mortal senses that Noantri custom declared seducing the Unchanged unacceptable. Amazing, Anna thought, how her people had the same wide streak of pious hypocrisy as Mortals, who outlawed double-dealing, drunkenness, and debauchery and then feverishly committed every sin they had time for. In her Community, it was the same. If every Noantri who took a Mortal lover were punished, the Conclave would have time for little else. And, Anna suspected, would be missing a few of its own members.

Now that she was settled in the shade she pulled off her hat, a red straw Jason Wu, fizzy with random bits of crimson netting that would have done her no good if she'd actually needed to veil her features, if she'd had to go about with that air of elegant mystery women had affected a hundred years ago. Aha, progress! A century and now she could uncover her face.

Honestly, how could these Mortals stand it?

Of all the identities, professions, and trades Anna Jagiellon had had through a long, long life, being a university student was the one she returned to most often. True, her considerable intellect was rarely challenged except by Noantri professors, who, recognizing their own, quietly tailored assignments to take into account, and take advantage of, not only her intelligence but also the years of learning already behind her. Still, even without that, she'd found enough new knowledge at universities to keep her interested, and her own impatience and restlessness found an echo in the yeasty fervor of young Mortals. Mortals, damn it. She used the politically correct "Unchanged," or "Gli Altri" — "the others," as opposed to her own peoples' "Noantri," which meant "we others" — when she had to, but she hated those terms. It wasn't, as she pointed out to nods and mumbled agreement in the Circolo degli Artisti café, in that back room where you'd always find a compatible few, that they were *other* or *not changed* that made the vast majority of humans different from, and yes, lesser than, Noantri. It was that they were *mortal.* It was that they would die.

That kind of talk, naturally, was dangerous. It had gotten her exiled nearly a century and a half ago, sent to Buenos Aires. Far from Europe, but not any kind of hardship, not for her. The beautiful, wealthy, and wild port city had adored the beautiful, wealthy, and wild young Hungarian. She'd loved it back, its burning sun and broad, sparkling river, its *confiterías* where she sipped *café con leche* all day, and its sultry clubs where she danced all night. She'd considered turning her back on the Old World and making the New her home. But though the Noantri Community in Argentina was large, Rome was the center of the oppressor's power and also of her people's. Her people, her hidden, optimistic, absurdly contented people, who had every right to the entire pie and were grateful for the crumbs. The Conclave had eventually lifted her sentence, not called her back but allowed her to return if she chose. She did.

She was braiding her long pale hair over her shoulder, looking forward to an hour of reading Akhmatova, when her cell phone rang. "I Will Follow You into the Dark," which meant that fool, Jorge. Maybe she shouldn't have given him his own ring tone. Then whenever he called she'd have a few more exasperation-free seconds between the time the phone rang and the time she knew who it was.

"*Pronto,* Jorge." He'd speak in Spanish, she knew; his Italian, though earnest, was clumsy, and his laughable attempts to master even a few words of her native Hungarian were pathetic. If she'd wanted to make him comfortable she'd have picked up with, *"Bueno."* But Jorge was more useful if he wasn't comfortable. He tried harder to please.

"Anna." She could tell from that one word that he was excited. "I'm in the Vatican Library," he said. Yes, in Spanish and just a notch above a whisper.

She blew out a sigh, answered in Spanish to move this conversation along. "That's where you're supposed to be, Jorge. Did you call to tell me that?"

"No! No, of course not. I've been watching that priest the way you said to —"

"Good boy," Anna said, knowing he'd beam and completely miss her acid sarcasm.

"Thank you." God, it sounded like he was blushing! "For the last two days he's been asking for books by nineteenth-century Republican poets."

"And . . . ?" He might miss sarcasm but he'd hear impatience, at this high level anyway.

"And someone came to join him today," Jorge hurried on. "One of us."

Anna sat straighter. All right, the boy might be on to something. "Who? What do you mean, 'to join him'?"

"She introduced herself but I didn't hear. A woman, with long black hair. Some gray streaks," he added, with clear pride in his powers of observation.

"When you get a chance" — she suggested the obvious — "you might check the registry. Wouldn't she have had to sign in?"

"Yes, she would've." Again, sarcasm flew over his head. She wondered if that was a hearing defect, or a mental one. "I'll go look. But here's why I called."

"Oh, you mean there's a point?"

"Anna!" Finally, he was wounded. "The priest asked for a book, and when she saw it she got excited. They're leaning over it and reading it together."

He stopped again. Sometimes Anna doubted herself: Were the Noantri really the right choice to rule the world, if the Community included morons like Jorge? And like herself, whose fault Jorge was in the first place?

"Jorge," she said carefully, "what is the book?"

"Poetry," he answered promptly. "Nineteenth century, but unattributed until now. The priest thinks it's Mario Damiani's.

Anna, wasn't he one of —"

"Yes. Does she agree? The black-haired woman?"

"Yes, and she —"

"Get it."

"What?"

"The book, Jorge! I want that book! Do you understand me?"

"I — yes, but —"

"Call me when you have it." Anna added, *"Ciao,"* then thumbed the phone off with perhaps more force than necessary. She settled back against the tree trunk and took out a cigarette. Few of the No-antri smoked. A real pity, she'd always thought; it was a great pleasure, and the health dangers of this habit meant nothing to them. Of course, the problem was the fire. You needed a flame to get your cigarette going and it burned at its tip the whole time. Well, what of it? These miniature embers, so easily smashed out on the bottom of your shoe? Her people had been afraid of fire, and so much else, for far too long.

She drew in smoke and streamed it out contentedly. The Conclave had sources in the Vatican; well, good for them. So did Anna and her friends. She'd been told about Father Thomas Kelly, called to the Vatican to root through the Archives in clear — and clearly desperate — search of something. Now he'd been joined by a Noantri with Vatican Library credentials, thus obviously a scholar. And there they were, getting excited together over a book of Noantri poetry.

Of course, it could mean nothing. Just some academics getting their bookish thrills.

Though if it meant nothing, why was Anna's skin tingling like this?

11

"Interesting," Livia Pietro said again, still studying the pages of the poetry notebook.

Thomas, who'd been contentedly reading the poems alongside her, looked up. "What's interesting?"

Now she turned to him, considering. "Do you know Trastevere well?"

"I'm afraid I don't. It's across the Tiber from Rome proper and therefore through the centuries a neighborhood of noncitizens when only citizens were allowed to live within the city walls. It housed the Jewish ghetto until the ghetto was dissolved and has always been a magnet for people of many nationalities because of its proximity to the docks. It has a Bohemian reputation but has gentrified lately, with writers, galleries, cafés — you're smiling again. I've gone beyond pedantic into pompous, haven't I?"

"Just a little, around the edges. But you're spot-on. Damiani lived there, and as it happens, so do I. It's an extraordinary place. Though I suppose," she added, "most people feel that way about their hometowns. You probably find Boston extraordinary."

"Yes, I do." Thomas thought it sweetly polite of her to be at pains not to rank her hometown above his own. Though he had yet to meet a Roman who didn't consider everywhere else inferior to Rome. "It does seem a fascinating place. Trastevere," he said. "Damiani obviously thought so, writing love poems to it. Is that what you meant by 'interesting' — that he wrote love poems to buildings?"

"No." She shook her head thoughtfully. "We actually have a tradition of that here. But look. You wouldn't know this, but . . . These pages, there are forty or so poems here. Some are clearly in praise of what could be called major sites — important churches, statues, piazzas."

"You can tell which they are?"

"A few. They're unmistakable. Here — the martyr in the well has to be San Callisto."

"Yes, I thought so, too."

She glanced sideways with a smile. "Did you?" Then back to the book. "And here's Fontana dell'Acqua Paola, and I think I see Porta Settimiana. But there are so many poems. Some seem to be about places that are relatively insignificant. And I think some major places are missing."

"Well," Thomas said, "a lover writing love poems — he might find praiseworthy what others consider insignificant."

"Undeniably true." She inclined her head. "Still, there are one or two churches, for example, that no lover of Trastevere would ignore. What I'm wondering is whether the missing pages were about those places."

"They might have been. There's no way to know, though."

"I'm not so sure. I —" Livia Pietro snapped her head around. The solemn clerk who'd brought Thomas's materials wheeled his cart past their table. Livia Pietro's green eyes seemed for a moment to flash, another thing Thomas had thought eyes didn't actually do. The clerk, paying no attention to them, crossed the room to collect books left by a researcher finished for the day. Livia Pietro watched him wordlessly, then turned back to Thomas. "If you look at how the —"

Stopping, she leapt to her feet. Before Thomas had quite registered that she was standing in front of him, he felt himself gripped from behind and flung onto the cold stone floor. The echoes of clattering chairs pinged around the room, mixing with shouts from affronted scholars and from Livia Pietro, who, in a flurry of complicated jacket and skirt, seemed to be struggling with the silent clerk over Damiani's notebook. Thomas was briefly immobile in confusion — What was going on? Why had the clerk thrown him out of his chair? How had he come back across the room so fast? — but when a falling book thunked onto his forehead he unfroze and grabbed for the clerk's ankle. All he got was trouser leg, so he yanked on that. Thrown off balance, the clerk tottered and fell but rolled to his feet again. He ignored Thomas, who was clumsily trying to free himself from books and furniture. The clerk and Livia Pietro faced each other. For a half second both stood as still as the marble statues that stared disapprovingly from niches along the walls.

Then movement: the clerk's eyes, fixing on the notebook in Livia Pietro's hand. He lunged. Thomas, halfway to his feet, body-blocked him with a South Boston street corner move. As the clerk crashed to the floor and a chair toppled onto him, something brushed by Thomas: the complicated jacket of Livia Pietro, who, shoulder bag and hat in one hand and notebook in the other, was racing across the marble floor.

Appalled, Thomas yelled, "Wait!" He was

125

aghast at the sudden thought he'd gotten it wrong: Livia Pietro was stealing the notebook and the clerk had been trying to stop her. Thomas glanced down, saw the man trying to untangle himself from a heavy chair. No time to help: Pietro had turned a corner. In a hail of *"Silenzio!"* from the other researchers, Thomas sprinted after her.

12

Livia cracked the hidden door just enough to see Thomas Kelly race around the corner and skid to a bewildered stop a few yards past her in the bright, empty hall. A crash from the reading room announced the clerk was free of the chair; pounding footsteps said he was coming after them. If the Gendarmes weren't also, they would be any moment. Livia cursed herself for a fool. Why hadn't she been on her guard from the moment she became aware of the clerk? Of course a number of Noantri were in service at the Vatican — it only seemed prudent — but this was someone she didn't know. That should have rung an alarm, but it hadn't.

Or perhaps it had, but she'd been so intent on her mission and on Thomas Kelly's discovery that she'd ignored it. The priest's find, this notebook, could be crucial. She thought she'd seen a pattern to the places not written about, something Thomas Kelly wouldn't have noticed because he didn't know Trastevere. She might be wrong, or the pattern might be there but mean nothing. Until she was sure, however, she wasn't giving the notebook up. Not to the priest, and especially not to a sticky-fingered fellow Noantri.

Briefly she considered leaving the priest behind. He'd only slow her, and what did he really have to offer? Well, she reflected, he did read Romanesco, possibly better than she. If she was right about the pattern of what was missing in the notebook, and if the poems that remained turned out to be important, another viewpoint on Damiani's elliptical verse might come in handy. So, given the nature of the buildings, might an expert in Church history. Most importantly, the Conclave had told her to make use of, and keep an eye on, this priest. Obeying the Conclave in letter as well as spirit struck her as wise, right now.

Livia pushed the door open and showed herself.

"Father Kelly. Quickly! In here." The priest spun in surprise. She held out the notebook. Kelly dashed toward her; she seized his arm and yanked him through the door, then slammed it shut.

"I — What —"

"Shh," she commanded. "Come." She grasped the priest's arm and started towing him down the corridor. She knew he couldn't see a thing. Her own eyes, much sharper than his, could barely tell floor from walls in the faint light seeping through the high openings. In the rooms on either side, those slits would be invisible, shadows in moldings near the ceiling. The door she'd just slammed, too, was imperceptible once shut. The Vatican was riddled with hidden passages and the Library was no exception. Most were built to allow servants to travel invisibly. Some had been created to facilitate other exchanges or escapes. Over many years, in the course of many legitimate research projects in various libraries, museums, and study centers around the world — her scholar's credentials were impeccable — Livia had occasionally passed time wandering where she wasn't supposed to be. Those explorations had yielded a number of doors and passages and occasionally led her to some interesting scholarship. Some secret doors, like the one to this passage, were never meant to be locked and gave easily once you'd found the hidden latch. Others required more finesse. To aid in her private research projects, Livia had acquired locksmith's tools and the skills to use them, but she was glad not to be slowed down by the need for them now.

Of course, the clerk wouldn't be slowed down, either. Even if he didn't know about this passageway he'd find it. His heightened Noantri senses would lead him to her, by scent if all else failed. But she and the priest had a good head start. Livia's hope was that by the time the clerk discovered the hidden latch, they'd be out the passage's other end.

If, that was, Father Kelly could be persuaded to keep going. Shocked into silence by her sudden appearance and by her manhandling, apparently he'd now recovered. He tugged and twisted, trying to free himself or at least stop their progress. In the face of her strength he couldn't do either, which added to his confusion and panic. He dug in his heels and shouted, "No! Wait! What's going on?"

She stopped and turned, catching him gently so his momentum wouldn't plow him into her. "I'll explain," she said. "But not here. Stay quiet. We need to get out." She added, "I have Damiani's notebook."

"I know you do! You stole it! We've got to go back."

"There's no time. Come." She started forward again, hauling him with her.

"Don't pull! Let me go!"

Father Kelly sounded so surprised, so offended at her unexpected might, that Livia
almost laughed. Normally, like most
Noantri, Livia hid her Blessings — her
strength, her agility — from the Unchanged,
to avoid provoking exactly this unease. She
released his arm. "You don't have to come.
You can stay here. Work your way back
along that corridor. Or shout and they'll
find you. But I'm taking the notebook and
if you don't come, you won't know why."

"You can't! It's —" He stopped. When he
spoke again his voice was calm. "You came
here for that notebook. You're not studying
Damiani any more than I am. Who are you?"

"I'm an art historian, as I told you, and
on the contrary, I'm studying Damiani
exactly as much as you are. I didn't know
about the notebook, though I'm very glad
you found it. But I didn't come for it. I
came for you."

A pause. "What?"

"I need your help. And I can help you.
We're both after the same thing."

He said nothing. His eyes were wide in
the dark and she held them with her own
though he probably couldn't see it. "I'm
searching for the same thing you are," she
said. "We have to find it, and more urgently
than I think you know."

"*We?* Are you —"

"Wait!" She touched a finger to his lips. He startled. She listened, spoke again. "He's found the door. He could find the catch at any moment. Come, or stay." The priest didn't move. "Father Kelly. To find the Concordat, you must come with me." She heard his sharp intake of breath.

"What do you know about the Concordat?"

"More than you. You've been told to find it and you've been told it's dangerous, but you don't know its contents, do you? I do."

"All I know is that it's a secret the Church guards closely."

"You doubt me. You have that right. But I'm telling the truth."

"Why are you looking for it?"

"Not now. Come." Instead of seizing his arm again, she gently took his hand. He startled once more, but while he didn't fold his fingers onto hers, he didn't pull away, either. She waited, then gave a soft tug. After a moment he took a step toward her.

They made their way down the servants' passage, Livia listening for the clerk's progress. A tiny click — he'd found the latch. She sped up, as sure-footed as the priest was stumbling. Twice she had to keep him from falling, losing precious seconds each time. Without him she'd have eluded the clerk for sure, but now it was touch and go. The rhythm and minutely rising volume of the clerk's steps behind them told her he'd shortened the distance, was quite close by the time she and Father Kelly emerged through another hidden door into a tiny anteroom. Kelly blinked in the sudden wash of light. Livia slipped on her sunglasses and fixed her hat. "Be casual," she instructed, and stepped through a low archway into the Vatican Museum's Galleria Clementina.

Thomas Kelly alternately beside and behind her, Livia wove through crowds of shuffling tourists, keeping up a hurried but informed commentary on the paintings, statuary, and artifacts they passed. She was a private tour guide steering a visiting priest through the treasures of the Galleria Clementina and then into the Museum of Pagan Antiquities, behind in their schedule but still focusing on the art as they rushed. No one seemed to notice them, not even the security guards strolling casually, protecting the art while not alarming the tourists. One of those officers was Noantri, a man Livia recognized. They exchanged the tiniest of nods. Could she count on him to stop the clerk if it came to that? She wasn't sure; best not to chance it.

The clerk, of course, had found his way through the passage and was on their trail. He was two rooms behind them; Livia easily picked his footsteps out. Unlikely that he'd risk a confrontation in this crowd. He'd follow them, waiting for his chance. She heard him speed up as she and Thomas Kelly maneuvered through the crush of people and started circling down the bronze spiral staircase. As they reached the bottom, he took the first steps down. The same thick crowd that slowed them would hinder him, but still he'd be no more than a few seconds behind when they burst out into the bright, crowded piazza.

Burst they did, and as Livia feared, alarms began to shrill and clang when the notebook in her bag crossed the Vatican's threshold. Cardinal Fariña's parting gift, the new security system; she'd known it was a risk. Quick-walking beside her, Thomas Kelly blanched.

"Fifty people came out when we did." She spoke low, keeping a merry smile, not looking at him or changing pace. "Forty-five of them look more suspicious than a middle-aged lady tour guide and a priest. Just stay with me." Ignoring the alarms and the security guards now running through the crowd, she clasped Father Kelly's arm again and took off striding past the gelato and torta carts.

Camera-draped tourists flowed through the piazza, swarming after colorful umbrellas and pennants on poles. They circled water- and trinket-sellers like feeding fish. At the curb, buses disgorged them and, more importantly, waited in patient lines to scoop them up again.

"What are you —"

"Shhh." Livia scanned the crowd. The visored Taiwanese would do them no good, and the Americans were just arriving, but beyond, a group of mixed Europeans — Italians, Poles, and a gaggle speaking Greek — were loading onto a bright blue bus. "Come." When they were close to the bus she slowed, waiting until the guide turned away to answer the inevitable question from the inevitable guidebook-thumbing tourist. "Now!" she said, and hopped onto the stairs and into the bus. The engine was already running. She moved through to the back, smiling at her fellow passengers as though they'd been together for days on this whirlwind tour of Italy. She'd found a seat and was looking through the window when Thomas Kelly dropped beside her.

"Are you crazy?" he demanded in a whisper.

She turned to him with a smile. He was red-faced and sweating. "You're a tourist," she said quietly. "Act like one."

He dropped his voice. "Give me the notebook."

"I will. I will, and you can replace it in the Library. But we need it first."

"Need it for what? You can*not* just *do* that." He was spluttering sotto voce. "Who *are* you?"

"A historian, as you are. We can't talk now. Wait until we get where we're going."

"No. Give me the notebook or I'll call the police."

"No, you won't."

"I will!"

The harried guide climbed the stairs. The driver left the door open for the last of the straggling tourists.

"You could have called for help at any time in the museum," Livia said, "but here you are. You're curious." On his face, guilt fleetingly eclipsed confusion and anger. "Father Kelly, trust me, please. We're after the same thing: the lost copy of the Concordat. Damiani's notebook may be vital, and as soon as we get somewhere safe I'll tell you why."

"Safe? We were perfectly safe until you stole it!"

"No. The clerk was trying to steal it. I stopped him."

"The clerk? Who is he?"

"I don't know."

Kelly frowned. "It's ridiculous anyway. Why would he bring it to me and then try to steal it? He could've stolen it anytime, if that's what he wanted."

"I think it was my interest in it that called his attention. My interest coupled with yours, I mean. I think he was in the Library to watch you."

"Me? To watch me? And you say you came for me? I see. Thomas Kelly from Boston is the clueless center of a vast Vatican conspiracy. That's what you mean?"

"When you put it that way —"

"Well, maybe it's okay." The priest threw up his hands. "Maybe that clerk is after the same thing we are, too. Just another member of our happy clan."

The desperate edge of Father Kelly's sarcasm was impossible to miss but she answered him seriously. "No. If the people who sent me already had an agent in the Vatican Library, they'd have told me. I'm afraid he might be working for the other side."

"*What* other side?"

She touched his arm and nodded to the

aisle, where the guide was working his way along, greeting the group, answering questions. "Don't say anything. You don't speak Italian."

"Of course I —"

She stopped him with a look.

When the guide reached them he gave them a quizzical raise of the eyebrows. Before he could speak, Livia grinned and said in Italian, "Hi! Are you the new guide? Where's Aldo?"

"Aldo? Who is he?"

"Our guide from this morning. And yesterday, too. He's so funny! He made us laugh so hard when we were at the Trevi Fountain, didn't he, Thomas? Even though Thomas doesn't really speak Italian, but he understood Aldo! Everyone did, even those sour Scots! Does Aldo have the afternoon off or something?"

"Signora," the guide said carefully, "I have been with this group since Saturday. There is no one named Aldo."

"Oh, but —" Livia suddenly stopped. She looked blankly at the guide and glanced around. "Oh!" She clapped her hands together, then buried her face in them. "Thomas!" she said in English, muffled and laughing. "We're on the wrong bus!"

"Signora —"

She dropped her hands, switched to Italian again. "Our bus was blue, too! And we were so late that I was afraid everyone would be mad — oh, this is mortifying!" She craned her neck to look out the window, then giggled like a schoolgirl caught in a prank. "It's gone! We're so late they already left!" She rooted around in her bag and dug out her cell phone. "Don't worry." She peered at the guide's name tag. "Sergio? Don't worry, Sergio. I'll text Aldo. It's lucky he gave us his phone number! I thought, why would we ever need that, but you see? He was right! Where are you going next?" Her thumbs hovered above her phone's buttons. "This group — where are you going?"

Sergio blinked. "To the Colosseum, *Signora.*"

"So were we! Oh, good! Oh, marvelous! I'll text Aldo and tell him not to worry about us and we'll just get off and meet the group there and thank you so much, Sergio! I'm sorry to cause you trouble! Oh, how ridiculous!" She laughed again and bent over her phone, thumbing rapidly. "Thomas, what a pair of idiots we are! Why didn't you say something? You know I have no sense of direction! This is so funny!" She was still giggling and thumbing when Sergio nodded, said something about having been put

139

to no trouble at all, and walked quickly back
up the aisle.

13

The doors finally closed and the tour bus inched along the curb in front of the Vatican, the driver eagle-eyed for a gap in the traffic.

"Look." Pietro nodded back toward the piazza. Thomas leaned across her. The clerk, in the center of the tourist scrum, snapped his head left, right, left again, clearly at a loss and clearly livid. In the patternless milling another disruption caught Thomas's eye: two men in blue uniforms and a third in a dark suit charging the wrong way through the entry and shouldering through the crowd. Gendarmerie: the Vatican Police. Thomas saw the clerk catch sight of them, too, and fade back into the shadows. **Why?** Thomas wondered. The Gendarmes would have been alerted by the alarm, but they wouldn't know what they were chasing. The clerk not only knew what, but whom. Why not race over to the police and tell them? Help them?

Unless what Pietro had said was true: the clerk had been trying to steal the book for himself.

Thomas flopped back against his seat as the bus found an opening and dove into the stream of cars. What was he doing? **This is pride, Thomas. The sin of pride. You should have stood your ground in the passageway and shouted for help. You should have summoned a guard on the piazza as soon as the alarm bells rang. You should have wrestled Damiani's notebook right out of this mad historian's hands.** Though he wasn't quite sure how he'd have done that, given her baffling physical strength. Admittedly he had little experience of the female body, but he'd seen her outwrestle the clerk and he'd felt her iron grip — he touched his arm; it was tender and, under his sleeve, no doubt turning colors — and he didn't think he was wrong in suspecting Livia Pietro was, comparatively, a powerhouse. Still, that he'd likely lose a cage match against her didn't mean he shouldn't have tried. But she was right. He was, as ever, curious. Pride: his right to have his questions answered trumping ethical imperatives, like Thou Shalt Not Steal.

He turned his head to look at Livia Pietro.

142

She was still watching out the window.

"Well," Thomas said softly. "Gendarmes. You'd think someone had committed a crime. Theft, perhaps. I wonder if they're worried, the criminals."

At that she sat back also, and shrugged. "There's nothing I can do."

"I can."

She raised an eyebrow to him. She hadn't removed her sunglasses, dark against her pale skin. Thomas found himself, irrelevantly and annoyingly, wanting to see those ocean-in-moonlight eyes again. Those eyes that had found their way so easily through the black passages in the Vatican, where he'd been blind as a bat. He pushed away the thought of Pietro's eyes as she asked, "You can what?"

"Back them off," he answered. "But you'll have to give me the notebook." If she did, he'd call Lorenzo. The Cardinal would tell the Gendarmerie it was just a misunderstanding. The police wouldn't argue with the Librarian. They'd smell a fix but they'd drop it. Then Livia Pietro would owe Thomas, and he'd insist she tell him what the Concordat was and how she knew about it. And why she wanted it. And who —

"No." Livia Pietro looked straight at him, planting her handbag more solidly on her

143

lap as though issuing a dare.

Thomas, after a moment, settled again in his seat and stared at nothing. He should probably call Lorenzo anyway. He was cheered by the thought that Lorenzo would by now have gotten a report and that the events in the reading room would make Thomas look like a hero: madwoman steals book, clerk fails to stop her, Thomas runs after her. The body-block he'd thrown on the clerk might put things in a different light but even if Lorenzo heard about that — even from the clerk himself — the Cardinal would believe the Thomas-the-Hero version until he was forced to think otherwise. Which would be never, if Thomas called right now.

But he didn't. He meditated on the relationship between curiosity and pride, a relationship he hadn't noted before, as the tour bus honked its way down the Lungotevere, headed for the bridge.

The bus was pulling up at Piazza del Colosseo when Pietro, once again peering out the window, stiffened. "Gendarmes," she said quietly. Thomas looked past her, saw the same two uniformed men he'd seen at the Vatican now emerge from a tiny black-and-white Alfa Romeo. The man in the dark suit was already in the piazza, scanning the crowd from beside an unmarked Peugeot. The comfortable vehicle, a privilege of rank. "I didn't think they saw us get on this bus," she said.

Light dawned for Thomas. "I'm sure they didn't," he replied, with a smug smile he couldn't help.

"Then how?"

"That book." He thumbed at her bag. "Cardinal Fariña, before he retired. He spent years renovating the Library and Archives. Most of it was about security. The chip that set off the alarms, I'll bet it's also got a GPS. They tracked us. *Professoressa* Pietro? You're busted."

To his surprise she grinned as their bus squealed to a stop. "Think so? Watch." She pulled the notebook from her bag and turned it over, to the marbleized paper that had once been the last leaf inside the missing back cover. The security chip, wafer-thin and about an inch square, was attached to the blank page before that. Which, after Pietro gave it a quick rip, was no longer attached to the book.

"*What?* No! You can't!" Thomas, appalled, grabbed for the notebook but as always, she was faster. She stuck the book deep in her shoulder bag and the chip in the pocket of her flowing skirt. A part of Thomas, nonplussed, thought, **A lot of good that'll do: it's still on you. Why not toss it?** The rest of him was appalled to see himself abetting this thievery, even if only in his head. Pietro jumped to her feet as the rear door opened. Thomas couldn't believe he'd just sat and watched her vandalize a book from the Vatican Library. He was nearly ready to stay behind. Let her hop off the bus and get scooped up by the Gendarmes. On the other hand, that might not happen. If it didn't this would be a ridiculous time to stand on principle and lose the notebook. **In for a penny, in for the crown jewels.** He stood.

The doors opened and Pietro jumped out onto a bright sidewalk boiling with tourists. The crumbling hulk of the Colosseum towered a half-block in front of them, but Pietro dashed the other way, across the street. She wove between taxis, sedans, and Smart cars. Thomas, close in her slipstream and fully expecting to get flattened, muttered an automatic Hail Mary. Though he wondered whether prayer was effective when you were stealing from the Vatican. At least he was wearing his clerical collar. Maybe people would try harder not to hit a priest. In the end both he and Pietro made it across unsquashed, and Thomas caught up with her at the entrance to the Colosseo Metro station — caught up only because she'd screeched to a halt.

Standing between them and the turnstiles was the clerk.

Clerk before, Gendarmes behind, end of the road, *Professoressa;* but before Thomas quite finished that thought Pietro said, "Do you have a ticket?"

It took him a moment to understand she was speaking to him, not the clerk, and what the question meant. "A monthly," he stammered.

"Use it now. Wait for me."

He could see the Gendarmes, one of the uniformed men with a handheld device, the other frantically and uselessly trying to stop the traffic. They dodged and wove as Thomas and Livia had done, working their way across the frenzied lanes. A screech of brakes, a scream of metal on metal, a tinkle of breaking glass, and then a symphony of curses and car horns. Thomas stared into the street and saw the Gendarmes still coming, crumpled fenders, stopped cars, and furious motorists in their wake. One way or another, Thomas decided, the far side of the turnstile might be the place to be during whatever mayhem was about to erupt. He swiped his card; the clerk paid no attention to him, but stepped up to Pietro, to block her way.

Thomas expected her to sidestep. She didn't. Instead, she charged right at him. The clerk was as surprised as Thomas, probably even more when Pietro tackled him. They tussled, twisted, and rolled, scattering shrieking tourists and Romans. The Gendarmes reached the curb outside and pushed past the souvenir carts. In a swirl of flowered skirt and complicated jacket Livia Pietro leapt to her feet. She snatched her hat and sunglasses up from the tile floor and shouted, "Go!"

Thomas was rooted in place until he saw Pietro neatly vault the turnstile and race down the escalator steps. **Turnstile jumping, well, why not?** Thomas took off after her, though he wondered exactly why: the Gendarmes would do the same, would be along any moment, would either grab her in the station or have Carabinieri waiting at the next stop if she managed to get on a train. Whatever happened now, Thomas would be well out of it. He decided to watch the denouement from a distance, then go report to Lorenzo.

The first thing he saw when he reached the platform was the countdown clock, claiming a train would be along in under three minutes. The second was Pietro, sunglasses and hat replaced, calmly waiting for it. He turned back to the escalator to follow the progress of the Gendarmes. Only they weren't there. All he saw was the escalator's steady stream of well-dressed locals and backpacked tourists, undisturbed by a ripple of charging policemen.

Pietro, as though she felt Thomas watching her, turned to him and smiled. After an uncertain moment he walked down the platform to her. "The Gendarmes are coming, you know."

She didn't answer, just kept smiling. The Gendarmes didn't come. The train did. Pietro got on. Thomas, wondering what had become of the Thomas Kelly he'd been for thirty-four years, followed her through the closing doors.

14

No law enforcement officers — not Gendarmes, not Carabinieri — burst onto the Metro train at the next stop. None were waiting on the platform ready to pounce when they left the subway car at Piramide, nor were any lurking by the station when they emerged to switch to the bus.

Livia would have been surprised if they had been.

On the Metro ride, when the rumbling of wheels could have covered the sounds of their conversation, there was no conversation: the priest had been stonily silent. During the short bus ride to Trastevere he'd hissed a question or two but the bus was packed and Livia refused to speak. When they alit in front of the giant palazzo of the Ministero della Pubblica Istruzione, she and Kelly were finally alone. Livia, as always on these streets, felt a calm, a comfort. She'd been born in Trastevere, and though she'd lived for years at a time in other places — a necessity of Noantri life — her home was here.

As soon as she started forward she could feel Thomas Kelly about to start grilling her. The streets were still too crowded, though, so she walked just a little too fast for him, staying ahead until they reached the cobblestones of Piazza di San Cosimato. Two Carabinieri moving purposefully through the piazza made the priest draw a sharp breath. Livia smiled at them and they smiled back, one touching his cap in greeting. *"Buonasera, Professoressa."* They strode on past.

"They're going for coffee," Livia told Thomas Kelly. "That's why they look so determined. Nothing to do with us." She continued to quick-walk through the cobbled streets, the priest truculent but sticking with her. Once past the fountain outside Santa Maria in Trastevere, the crowds thinned and Livia slowed her pace.

"Why have we come here? What's going on?" When she didn't answer, Thomas Kelly grumped, "They'll find us, you know," amending it after a moment to, "They'll find you. Or maybe that clerk will, first. He seems to be persistent."

"The Gendarmes never saw us," she reminded him. They turned the corner by the ancient hospital. "And they have their chip."

He stopped. "They do?"

She grinned. "If you'd asked while we were on the train, instead of shooting daggers out of your eyes, I'd have told you." She tucked her arm in his to get him moving again. "I shoved it into the clerk's pocket when we had that little scuffle. So I don't think he'll be an immediate problem, either."

"I — Is that why you tackled him?"

"Well, it wasn't because I enjoy your American football." Her shoulder still hurt where she'd banged up against a turnstile. So did her shin where the clerk had kicked her. Neither injury was as painful now as when they'd happened, but what drew people to contact sports — especially the Unchanged, who healed much more slowly than Noantri — she would never know.

They'd just come into the small piazza in front of Santa Maria della Scala when the priest broke another dark silence to ask, "Where are we going?" His tone implied he was nearing the end of his patience. She couldn't blame him; luckily, they'd arrived.

"To see a friend." Across the square from the church stood an old house, less impressive from without, she knew, than from within. Livia stepped to the door and clanked the ring in the brass lion's mouth.

A few moments' wait, and the door was opened to them by Spencer George himself. He wore a chocolate cashmere sweater and tan trousers, his feet encased in butter-colored leather slippers. Livia always enjoyed the sight of Spencer, who seemed to delight in his own excellent taste. Though in little else: his thinning brown hair topped a long face perpetually on the verge of a glower. They were old friends, but she hadn't expected a warm welcome today, and she wasn't mistaken.

"Livia. What a pleasure." Spencer spoke in dry, guarded tones, and in English, his native tongue.

From courtesy — he was Elder — she replied in English, too. "You know, then?"

"Oh, I think everyone knows."

She wasn't surprised. Meetings of the full Conclave were infrequent enough to be noteworthy in themselves. No one appeared before the Conclave except by Summons. If Livia Pietro had been spotted going into Santa Maria dell'Orazione e Morte — for a second time — the Noantri grapevine would have sizzled with the news.

"I must admit I was halfway expecting you," Spencer said.

"And hoping I wouldn't come."

"On the contrary. I don't know what your instructions are but I'll be glad to help if I'm able. Though I rather think I won't be."

"Why not?"

"Because whatever it's about, if the Conclave had any hope of me, they'd have called me in, too. Who's your friend?"

The tone in which Spencer said "friend" implied it wasn't the first word that had come to mind. Livia smiled and said, "Father Thomas Kelly."

Spencer waited, but she didn't go on. Thomas Kelly turned to her, about to speak, but she shook her head. After a long stare of clear distaste at the priest, Spencer shrugged and stepped aside. "All right, then. Come in."

He led them through the entrance hall and upstairs to his study. At various periods, both since Livia had known him and before, Spencer had kept a full staff. At others he'd had a butler or valet; moving with the times, he now had a cleaning woman who came twice a week, and a cook. Some of the Noantri were indifferent to food and drink. Others, though they appreciated the pleasures of the palate, didn't go to the trouble of keeping stocked pantries or fully equipped kitchens. Livia herself was in that camp. She enjoyed a leisurely meal in the presence of friends, both Noantri and Unchanged; but at home, except for the *gelato al pompelmo rosso* that she bought by the liter, her larder was generally bare. Spencer, though, had been a gourmand before he became Noantri. The rest of the staff came and went with current fashion, the better for Spencer to blend in. A cook was nonnegotiable.

He rang for the current one as Livia and Thomas Kelly seated themselves in heavy leather chairs. "You'll have coffee?" Spencer said to Father Kelly. Livia smiled to herself. Spencer had little use for priests, but less for discourtesy. The priest was in his house; civility would prevail.

Despite Father Kelly's confusion and his angry impatience, Livia caught him peering around the room at the maps and prints on Spencer's walls, the odd arcana on the shelves and polished tables. **We historians,** she thought, **we're all alike.** Spencer's house had always been too overstuffed for her liking, but it suited its owner well enough. Livia took pleasure in surrounding herself with objects of beauty. Spencer, however, collected first for interest and meaning; beauty, if any, was a secondary concern. He was also a historian, but his study was their people.

The cook appeared; coffee was requested. When she'd gone, Spencer settled himself, tugging at his trouser legs. "So you've come for my help. What can I do?" He looked at Livia and then, pointedly, at Thomas Kelly.

"It's more complicated than that," Livia said. "I wouldn't feel right if I didn't tell you this from the start: the Gendarmerie are after us."

"The Gendarmerie?" Spencer's eyebrows rose. "Not the Carabinieri? My, what have you done?"

"We stole a book from the Vatican Library. I stole it," she amended, in response to a strangled sound from Thomas Kelly.

"Well, good for you. Presumably because it will help you do whatever you've been instructed to do? Can I expect those strapping young gentlemen to arrive at any moment, then? I can ring for more coffee."

"No, we've taken care of them for a while, I think."

"How grand. But really, Livia, before we continue, you'll have to explain the priest to me."

"I speak English, you know," snapped Thomas Kelly.

"No, I didn't know," Spencer drawled. "Then perhaps you'll be good enough to explain yourself?"

"If I had any idea at all I'd be glad to. As it is, I'm at a loss. I don't know why I'm here, and I should probably leave." He turned to Livia. "With the notebook."

"Notebook?" Spencer inquired mildly.

"The one I stole." Livia felt a surge of sympathy for the priest. "I asked Father Kelly to come with me. He doesn't know why yet."

Thomas Kelly started to splutter at "asked" but before he could speak the cook re-entered with a tray.

"Excellent," said Spencer, and it was unclear whether he was referring to the situation or the refreshments. He thanked the cook, dismissed her, and poured out from a silver service into fine china cups. With silver tongs he placed two small biscotti on each saucer. Father Kelly accepted the offered cup a little desperately, Livia thought. Spencer said, "You can explain to us both, then, Livia, why you've brought me a priest."

Livia took a sip of Spencer's always superb coffee, then put the cup on the inlaid side table. "I was called before the Conclave yesterday."

"I think I mentioned: everyone knows that."

"Does everyone know why?"

"Of course not."

"The Vatican's copy of the Concordat, it seems, disappeared a century or so ago," Livia said. "Now it appears to have been found. Not by the Vatican."

Before Spencer could speak Thomas Kelly blurted, "It's been found? Found where?"

With a wave of his cup toward Father Kelly, Spencer asked, "How much does he know?"

"His name is Thomas Kelly!" The priest sat forward, red-faced. "He's from Boston, he was brought here two days ago by Lorenzo Cardinal Cossa to find this mysterious Concordat, and he's about to call the Cardinal and tell him you people know where it is and he can come get it himself."

Spencer gazed at him, unruffled. "If you think invoking a cardinal in this house is going to occasion fear and trembling, you're misinformed. Father. What I'm asking is, are you aware of the contents of 'this mysterious Concordat'?"

Thomas Kelly met Spencer's stare. The bellicose set of his shoulders made it clear to Livia how very much he wanted to tell Spencer he knew everything he needed to know about anything and Spencer could go climb a tree, or whatever insult they'd use in Boston. Instead, after a frustrated breath, he said, "I'm told it's an agreement between the Church and another group. I don't know who the others are or what it binds each to do but Cardinal Cossa has impressed upon me that it's secret and highly dangerous. That public knowledge of so much as its existence, never mind its details, could seriously damage the Church. Which, with all due respect to the Cardinal, strikes me as alarmist poppycock."

Spencer's only response was a small, amused smile.

Livia said, "No, Father. It's true."

Thomas Kelly gave her a hard look, and then shrugged. "If you say so. I have no way to judge and I'm close to not caring. My job was to find it, and I seem to have done that." He stood. "Give me the notebook."

"Sit down," said Spencer. In all these years Livia had never heard Spencer raise his voice; but she also didn't know anyone who didn't obey without a second's pause the granite tone he'd used just now.

Father Kelly, to her surprise, remained on his feet, gave Spencer a calm, wordless stare, then turned back to her. "Give me the notebook."

"Father," she said, "please, hear me out. The Concordat's been found but I — we —

don't have it. None of us know where it is, except the man who discovered it."

"Ah," said Spencer, overriding whatever the priest might have been about to say. "And who is that? I assume there's some reason the Conclave didn't just ask the finder to gift wrap it and send it over. And some reason, Livia, why you were chosen."

Spencer's gaze was at once stern and sympathetic. Livia's cheeks burned. She nodded to confirm his guess. "It's Jonah." From the corner of her eye she saw Thomas Kelly give her an odd look. He didn't sit down, but he stayed silent.

"Oh," said Spencer. "Oh, my. I'm beginning to understand. Your young man isn't at all interested in placing it in the hands of the Conclave, is he? Nor of the Vatican. Let me guess. He's threatening to make it public."

"Yes."

"But he hasn't yet. So he's making demands, in return for silence. What could he possibly be asking for?"

"What could he possibly want? It's not about that. He's just giving the Conclave a chance to do it formally. He says either they publish the contents or he will."

"Really? Is he that militant? I had no idea."

"It was one of the . . . reasons for our split.

I tried to tell him the New often feel that way, but that over time he'd come to understand."

"Apparently he hasn't. And what does the Conclave expect of you? Surely they're capable of searching out and dealing with a renegade on their own?"

Livia's heart skipped at "dealing with." "Of course. But they don't just want Jonah. They want the Concordat. So this can't happen again. They think I can find both him and it because I know him so well."

"And because he's your responsibility," Spencer said, sounding severe. Spencer had his own opinions on some of the Laws, but the accountability of a Lord for a Disciple was one he believed in strongly. It was, she suspected, one reason he had never become anyone's Lord.

"Yes," she acknowledged. Her face flushed but she met Spencer's gaze. "That's right."

"Are they correct? Can you call him up and have a nice chat, during which he'll gladly disclose the location of his hidey-hole? Or skip over that step and go fetch the Concordat directly because you already know where that place might be?"

She shook her head. "For one thing, they think he's not the one who hid it. He only says he knows where it is — it's likely what's happened is, he's somehow found its hiding place. For another . . . It's been a long time, Spencer. I don't think I know him anymore."

Spencer nodded. "Well. I must admit to feeling a certain amount of sympathy."

Livia was about to thank him when she realized he didn't mean, for her. "Spencer, you can't agree? That the Concordat should be made public?"

"No," Spencer sighed. "No, of course not. Though in a perfect world making it public would yield benefits all around. But in a perfect world we wouldn't have needed it in the first place."

"One of the benefits of making it public," Thomas Kelly snapped, "is that some of the rest of us might have an idea what you're talking about."

Spencer turned to stare at the priest. "Livia," he said, "why is he here?"

"The Conclave instructed me to . . . involve Father Kelly in the search. Because his search is the same."

"Wait — they did?" Kelly said. "But we just met. Because you saw I had all those poetry books . . ."

She watched understanding dawn in his eyes. I'm sorry."

"Let me understand something," Spencer

said. "You" — to Thomas Kelly — "were brought here just recently, by the new Librarian, to find the Vatican's Concordat? Does the Cardinal know what the Conclave knows — that Jonah Richter has found it?"

"I'm sure he doesn't," the priest replied tightly, "because he wouldn't have had me looking through the Archives then, would he?"

"Your tone aside, I think you're correct. In which case, I have two questions. One, it's an odd coincidence, don't you think, that your search should come just when the Concordat has reappeared? But two, and more to the point, what possible help can you be to Livia? Livia, why not let me show him out? Without, of course, this stolen notebook. If you feel you need that to complete your task."

"For one thing," Livia replied, "he found the notebook."

"And for another, he's not leaving without it," Thomas Kelly said. "I'll call the Gendarmes if I have to."

Spencer rolled his eyes.

Livia said, gently, "Spencer? There's something else. The notebook is Mario Damiani's."

Color drained from Spencer's face.

"I'm sorry," Livia said. "I was told at the

Conclave that it was he who stole the Concordat. When the Vatican Library was looted."

After a long moment, her old friend slowly shook his head. "Well, well. Mario. There were always rumors that he'd done something big and bad, and had had to go to ground. I put them down to the fact that he was gone and therefore ripe to become the stuff of legend. I knew he wasn't in hiding. He wouldn't have vanished for all time without a word to me. Mario. I waited, you know. In the North. I really thought he'd come." Spencer trailed off. Livia shot the priest a look to keep him quiet. At last Spencer roused himself. "The Conclave," he said. "Have they known for long?"

"That Damiani stole it? Apparently since it happened. Back then, when it never turned up and a search didn't find it, the Conclave was satisfied it had been destroyed. Or at least hidden too well to be found."

"Did they tell you how he . . . What happened to him?"

"No."

Spencer nodded and finished his coffee, gazing at nothing. A tiny smile tugged the corners of his mouth. "That explains, then, why you were called in, but I was not."

Thomas Kelly now spoke, his scholar's curiosity clearly overpowering, for the moment, his anger and confusion. "I was right, then. It was the Concordat that Damiani's letter referred to."

Livia looked up at him. "What letter?"

Abruptly, Thomas Kelly sat again. "You have your secrets, I have mine. What are we talking about?"

As if from far away, Spencer asked, "Livia? May I see the notebook?"

Livia slipped it from her bag. She was prepared to fend off the priest, but although he didn't take his eyes from it once she produced it, he didn't grab for it, either. Handing it to Spencer, she said, "I think it might tell us where the Concordat is."

"How?" Spencer asked absently. He began slowly to turn the ragged pages.

"It's a book of praise poems. To churches, piazzas, fountains — various places in Trastevere."

"He was working on that, yes. This is it?" Spencer smiled. "Ah, yes. They're all *cinquini* — he invented the form, you know. A-B-A-B-A. He had to be different."

"Seven pages are missing. One of them might be a poem to the hiding place." She watched Spencer as he read a page of faded handwriting. "Are you all right?"

"Something about this book . . . I don't know what, but it's oddly familiar."

"You must have seen any number of Damiani's notebooks."

"No, it's more than that." Spencer fingered the paper. "But to what you were saying: if one of the missing poems identifies the Concordat's location, what about the others? Why are seven missing?"

"They're red herrings?"

"To mislead whom?" Spencer looked up skeptically. "And what's your plan, then? To discover what landmarks are missing and go to each?"

"I can't come up with anything better," Livia admitted.

"I'm not sure how you would even make that determination," Spencer said. "And the priest?"

"Is a Church historian. If any — or all — of these missing places are churches, he might —"

"All right!" Thomas Kelly exploded. "The priest is tired of being talked about in the third person and tired of feeling like he's — like I'm in a play without a script! Who's the Conclave? What's the Concordat? What's Mario Damiani to you? Who are you people?"

Livia and Spencer looked at each other.

"All right," Kelly said again. "Tell me or I'm leaving. I'll call the Gendarmerie and the Cardinal the minute I'm out the door. The Gendarmes will come for the book and the Cardinal will tell me what's going on."

He stood once more. Livia did, also, though she wasn't sure what she was about to do. Stop him, certainly. The Conclave wanted him involved; the Conclave would have him. But how? She could keep him here, but she couldn't force him to help her. He already knew this search was of great importance to his Church, yet he was ready to leave, so that argument wouldn't persuade him. And though the damage to his Church was certain and irreparable if the Concordat was revealed, she didn't have its interests at heart and he wouldn't believe her if she said she did.

It was her Community who concerned her.

It was Jonah.

She still had hopes of saving Jonah from his sentence; but if she didn't find the document, his death was certain.

And if he found a way to carry out his threat before the Conclave destroyed him, then the inevitable, unthinkable consequence would be the devastation of her people. The obliteration of six centuries of release from the terror and peril that had filled all the countless years before.

The priest still stood at the doorway, frustrated, furious, and ready to bolt. **He'll never understand what's at stake,** she finally admitted to herself, **without the truth.** She looked to Spencer for help, but he sat with the notebook, lost in its pages, as though she and Thomas Kelly weren't there.

"Father," Livia said, laying a hand on the priest's arm. "Please. Sit down."

15

Thomas Kelly charged down the stairs to the front door. He threw it open with such ferocity that the ring clanged against the lion's mouth. Turning blindly right, he swept around the corner and ran on, stopping only when, another block later, he found himself half-hidden by the tables and umbrellas of an outdoor café. His heart still pounded wildly. He drew a deep breath and peered back past the patrons sipping their espressos, reading their papers, and talking on their cell phones.

No one. He wasn't being followed.

In fact, he hadn't been followed down the stairs, he realized, playing the scene back for himself. His crashing steps were the only footfalls. Livia Pietro, after her insane words and the historian's calm, shocking display, hadn't even stood when he ran off. Nor had her mad friend. They weren't coming after him. He was safe.

Safe from what? What had just happened? What did any of this mean? Who were these people and why had they gone to all this trouble to terrify him? Which was obviously what it was about. These lunatics were playing with his mind. To distract him, that must be it. Yes, of course. To make him useless. To prevent him from finding the Concordat before they did. Why? Why did they want it? What was this document, that people would go to such elaborate lengths? Because it indisputably wasn't the document they'd described to him.

His heart had just about come back to normal now. He took out his cell phone. Before he could make his call he saw on its screen that he had seven messages from the Cardinal. He thumbed the button and stood staring back through the umbrellas toward the House of Crazy People.

Lorenzo picked up at once. "Thomas! Where are you? What's going on? Why didn't you answer my calls?"

"I didn't get them. I had my phone off. In the Library, so I wouldn't disturb people, and then I —"

"Well, apparently you disturbed a lot of people. What on earth happened? The reports say a fight, a stolen book? Which hasn't been recovered, though the thief's in

170

custody. Where are you? What happened? What book, and do you have it?"

"In Trastevere. No. It's a little hard to explain. He's not the thief. The clerk. She said he was trying to steal it but he was trying to stop her. She stole it. A notebook of Mario Damiani's. She still has it but I know where it is. I —" **You what, Thomas? Ran away? Because two mad people told you a crazy story?** Out here in the sunny morning on this quiet, cobbled street, he found himself unable to admit anything so ridiculous. "A historian who lives in Trastevere. Across from Santa Maria della Scala. We took it to him. They're up there now, the two of them. You can send the Gendarmes. The reason they think they have the thief — the Gendarmes think that, I mean — is because she stuffed the chip in his pocket. The clerk's pocket. But make sure they're armed, because they're crazy. Not the Gendarmes are crazy. These people. They're crazy."

"Thomas?"

"I should've taken the book from her, but she was saying such insane things. Who they were, what the Concordat is. Insane. And then — what he did — still, I shouldn't have left it. Maybe I should go back. Yes. I'll go back. I —"

"Thomas."

"There's no —"

"Thomas."

"I had —"

"Father Kelly!"

The last time Thomas had heard his name in those tones was during his second week in graduate school. A fellow student in his Augustinian Thought seminar had remarked that feeding the poor and fasting were two sides of the same coin, which set Thomas to wondering what the obligations of the poor really were on fast days. Apparently he'd been so deep in thought that he'd missed the next discussion question, and Lorenzo Cossa, not yet a cardinal but already a legend, had not been pleased.

"Father Kelly! Get hold of yourself!"

Thomas swallowed. "I'm sorry, Father. I've been babbling, haven't I? I'm sorry."

"Thomas. The people who have the book — have they left the house?"

"No, I don't think so. I'll go back and get it."

"You won't. I'm sending the police."

"For the book?"

"Stay until they get there to make sure those people don't leave. If they do, don't confront them. Just keep tabs on them and call me. If they don't, then soon as the

Carabinieri show up, come here."

"The Carabinieri? Not the Gendarmerie?"

"Do you know where the nearest taxi stand is?"

"I —"

"If you're near Santa Maria della Scala, there's one in Piazza Trilussa. When the police arrive, get in a cab and come here. I'll be waiting."

The Cardinal clicked off.

16

Lorenzo Cardinal Cossa sat motionless behind his ornate desk. He'd already instructed Father Ateba to bring Father Kelly in the moment he arrived, and he'd called the Gendarmes and told them to release the hapless clerk. Before any of that he'd called his nephew, Raffaele Orsini. He'd found the young Carabiniere on duty but available to do a favor for his uncle. That meant Raffaele's partner was probably not around, the anti-clerical detective whose name Lorenzo could never remember — Giulio Aventino, that was it. Julius Caesar of the Aventine Hill, Raffaele called him. How much clearer could it be that the man was from an old Rome family, one that predated possibly the founding, and at least the growth to power, of the Church? And, according to Raffaele, had a chip on his shoulder about it. Detective Julius Caesar; but Lorenzo, even as his lip curled with disgust, realized he was directing his bile at the absent detective in order to avoid focusing on his real and looming problem.

Even allowing for Rome traffic, Thomas would be here in fifteen minutes.

What then?

Lorenzo sighed. Was there really any question? Thomas had indeed been babbling, and Thomas Kelly didn't babble. Something had badly shaken him up, frightened him — something he didn't understand. The woman from the Library who'd stolen the book, and the historian who lived in Trastevere: they'd terrified Father Kelly. He'd said they were crazy, but Lorenzo had heard the tiny note of doubt in Thomas's voice.

There was only one possibility.

They'd told him the truth.

17

Gendarme *Vice Assistente* Luigi Esposito slammed his fist on his desk and clenched his jaw shut. Back home in Naples he'd be cursing a blue streak but in the years since he'd come up to Rome to join the Gendarmerie he'd learned to keep his language clean. Well, no. He'd learned to keep his mouth completely closed on infuriating occasions like this, so he wouldn't risk filling the security offices of the Holy See with the words the situation called for.

It was bad enough he'd had to go racing through the traffic-choked streets of Rome in the company of two provincial dolts whose entire ambition extended to putting in their years finding tourists' lost purses and then retiring on their piddling Gendarme pensions. Though at least the chase, as opposed to most of the work Luigi did here, had gotten his blood moving. They'd caught their quarry, too, a pale, sniveling clerk who'd stolen a book from the Vatican Library.

The uniformed idiots Luigi was saddled with laughed uproariously at how stupid he must be, this Argentinian punk, to work at the Library and not even think about the GPS-alarm chip in the book. And when it set off the alarm, to rip it out, stash the book somewhere — and forget he had the chip still on him! Oh, what a *scemo*!

Gritting his teeth, Luigi had thought, **No. You're the *scemi*. No one's that dumb, with the possible exceptions of yourselves.** Keeping the chip was clearly a well-thought-out red herring. The clerk had passed the stolen book to a confederate — probably the black-haired woman he'd pretended to be scuffling with — and kept the chip so they'd focus on him while she got away. This suggested to Luigi an organized burglary ring. Perhaps specializing in antique manuscripts, or perhaps just in stealing from the Vatican. Why not? There was wealth here beyond comprehension. Furthermore, as far as Luigi could tell, the possessions of the Vatican were like an iceberg. The ten percent that was visible was impressive enough, but the rest, besides being nine times greater, was hidden in murky waters. If you could get a precious item beyond the walls, there was a good chance no one would miss it. Which didn't mean it was easy to steal from the Vatican, but it was possible, and probably, if you were a certain kind of crook, irresistibly tempting.

Luigi was a cop, not a crook. Scratching out his childhood on the cobblestones of Naples, he'd dipped a toe in criminal waters. Which of his friends hadn't? He'd boosted the odd TV, raced off with the occasional dangling purse, run errands for a few local *malavitosi*. But it wasn't for him. He watched his pal Nino get sent away to reform school, which everyone knew was six kinds of hell; and then his cousin Angelo, at fifteen, was one night advised to leave Naples immediately and plan not to come back. Angelo kissed his tearful mother and didn't even pack a suitcase. Luigi could see early on that there was toughness and its attendant respect, but no real future, in crime.

There was a future, however, and other advantages, too, on the police. You could be tough and respected, and it was also useful to be smart. Luigi joined the local force, but ran up against a difficulty. His past as a booster and errand-runner wasn't enough to blackball him. This was Naples, after all;

if the police only accepted lily-white recruits there wouldn't be a dozen cops in the city. But Luigi had been smarter and more enterprising than most *ragazzi*, reliable, able to think on his feet. Every *malavitoso* in Naples coveted his services. If he'd elected to join one crime family over another the loser would have felt regret and congratulated the chosen. When he turned his back on them all and declared his loyalty to the other side, it stung. The investigation of crime depends on the cultivation of sources and mutual back-scratching; but no matter what Luigi Esposito offered, the word was out. No crook in Naples would talk to him. All doors were shut.

Luigi knew a cobblestone ceiling when he saw one. He began to despair at the vision of a future spent patrolling garbage-strewn alleyways and directing traffic on fume-filled streets.

One day, as he was responding to a purse-snatching on Via Santa Chiara, in the heart of his old neighborhood, inspiration struck. The American tourist's pocketbook was long gone — when would they learn not to dangle their bags so condescendingly from their fingertips? — but after he made short work of the report he took his hat off and entered the quiet church. Old Father Carmelo was delighted to see Luigi Esposito and to find he'd done so well. By which, given the nature of the parish, the priest meant that Luigi had graduated from high school and wasn't in jail. Luigi confided his problem to Father Carmelo, who had a word with a seminary mate whose cousin was a bishop, and so on, and Luigi had gone up to Rome.

It was quite an honor, so he was told, to serve on the Gendarmerie. That might be true, but Luigi soon discovered it to be an honor reserved for men like himself: people who knew people. Talent for the job, which Luigi happened to have, was secondary. In one way that was good. Surrounded by dull lumps of coal, a diamond shines all the brighter. Luigi, unsure he was a diamond but demonstrably not as dull as most of his colleagues, rose to the rank of *vice assistente* in an impressively short time. *Vice assistente* was a detective's title; the problem was that the Gendarmerie had nothing much to detect. The pickpockets of Saint Peter's Square needed chasing, and the occasional nut who insisted on speaking to the *Papa* — or insisted he *was* the *Papa* — needed to be quietly shooed from the premises. But anything juicy, any criminal activity an investigator could sink his teeth into,

180

ran headfirst into the fact that as far as the Holy See was concerned, silence was golden. *Make It Go Away* was the Gendarme's first directive. Find out who did whatever it was, and then explain in a soft and calm way that a dossier had been compiled and they'd best get themselves gone and keep quiet, did they understand? They always did, and the investigations of the few real crimes Luigi had come up against had ended as compiled dossiers in his desk. It was enough to turn a cop into a cynic.

Or to make him long for another move. Luigi began to dream of the Carabinieri. For a kid from Naples by way of the Gendarmerie, this was close to an impossible dream, based equally on the Carabinieri's heavy pro-Rome bias and the fact that Luigi had little to show for his six years on the Gendarmes.

Until today. This could have been it, this could have been big. Luigi could see that this Argentinian, this Jorge Ocampo, was no *scemo* and he hadn't acted alone. When they caught him he didn't have the stolen book. But Luigi had him. Luigi began his interrogation and it was only a matter of time before he'd have broken the punk down. That would have led to his confederates. As the detective on the case — as, in fact, the man who'd personally tackled the clerk after his bogus fight with the woman (though the skinny kid was unaccountably strong and it had taken all three Gendarmes to subdue him), Luigi would be in a fine position to make Carabinieri hay while this sun shone.

He was, he thought, not far — a few minutes, half an hour — from pulverizing the kid's innocent-victim act and getting him to spill it, when his *soprintendente* interrupted him. A call had come from the Cardinal Librarian: it was all a mistake. Nothing had been taken. Nothing was wrong. A faulty alarm system, a chip fallen from a book. A big uproar over zilch. Let the kid go.

Expressing his disappointment and his outrage to the *soprintendente* had gotten Luigi nowhere, not even winning him a sympathetic shrug. "We work for them, Esposito," had been his boss's cold reply. "Most of us are grateful for the opportunity to serve."

Thus it was that the Argentinian, pale and confused but not checking this gift horse's mouth, scuttled away, and Luigi Esposito smashed his fist on his desk and bottled up the curses that threatened to singe the office's air. A cardinal! Luigi's blue Carabinieri uniform torn from his grasp by a cardinal who was no doubt embarrassed by the traffic-disaster chase and the Metro-stop dustup. Not to mention the obvious involvement of Library staff. Like all of them, the Cardinal Librarian only *Wanted It To Go Away* and probably considered a missing book a small price to pay for maintaining dignity and decorum at the Holy See.

Luigi stepped outside. He'd been trying to cut down but this situation called for a smoke. He lit up, pulled deeply, and looked around at the groomed, disciplined, cross-eyed boring perfection of this place.

Maybe it was the change in perspective, or maybe the nicotine jolting his brain, but as he was grinding out the cigarette Luigi had a thought. The Librarian, Cardinal Cossa, wanted the problem to go away *from the Vatican.* If Luigi was right, though, this wasn't a Vatican crime, as such. It was a burglary ring, a criminal racket, an organized conspiracy, targeting the Vatican but possibly other places, too. Secular places. With at least one member inside the Vatican Library and others outside it. If Luigi could crack this racket, could at a minimum point the secular authorities in the right direction,

183

that could be the feather his cap needed to
get him in the Carabinieri's door.

18

Jorge Ocampo stood still, an island buffeted by the waves of tourists in Saint Peter's Square. The Gendarmes had escorted him out after that belligerent Neapolitan detective had suddenly decided to let him go. Jorge had been pleased that his protestations of innocence had finally gotten through to the man.

His satisfaction was short-lived, though.

Anna was angry. Very angry.

He flinched at the voice issuing from the phone at his ear. "Forget it, Jorge. Go home. Go take a nice coffee. Go back to Argentina! I don't care. You're an idiot! Worse than useless. I'll do it myself. No — I'll find someone else. Franklin, from California — yes, I'll call him."

Jorge's blood froze. Franklin had recently joined the group that met in the back room of Circolo degli Artisti, where Anna led them in planning the world they would create once the Noantri took their rightful places. Franklin was young, Newer than Jorge, and impassioned. He believed in Anna and their mission, and the last thing Jorge wanted was to give up his place at Anna's side to the fresh-faced American.

"No, no, Anna!" Jorge heard himself croaking. He swallowed and went on, "I'm sorry. Let me try again. I'll find the book. I'll find out who that woman is and I'll get it from her. I'll get it for you, Anna. I will."

"You can't, Jorge. You're not the man for the job."

"I am!"

A short pause. "I don't know."

"Anna —"

"All right. One more chance. Do not screw this up, Jorge."

"I won't! I'll find out —"

"I already know who she is."

"What?"

With an exasperated sigh: "I asked around. Livia Pietro. An art historian. Three different people recognized her from your description. Not even Noantri — they were Mortals, art students. She's well known. She lives in Trastevere, in that really old house in Piazza dei Renzi that used to be the watchtower. Do you think that gives you enough to go on, Jorge? Do you think you can do it right this time?"

"Yes! Yes, Anna. Thank you. I'll go there now. I'll get the book."

"You'd better." She clicked off.

Jorge slipped his phone back into his pocket and wiped the sweat from his upper lip. He stood for a moment more, watching the crowds surge this way and that in their eagerness to take in everything they could in their time here. Benighted fools, Anna called them. Far too shortsighted to understand their own best interests from one day to the next. No wonder they'd made such a mess of the world! They fundamentally didn't care about anything that didn't affect them immediately, because in their hearts they knew they'd be gone by the time things got bad.

Was what she said true? Anna was deeply passionate and completely serious about everything she believed, but still, Jorge wasn't sure. He didn't remember feeling that way when he was Mortal. His Change was much more recent than Anna's. She'd been Noantri for four hundred years, so maybe she'd forgotten. Back home in Argentina, where they'd met, Jorge had joined the Communist Party because he and his comrades shared the revolutionary dream of a better future. They knew freedom fighters

187

like themselves were unlikely to live to see it, but they were willing to fight and die for the dream.

Though he couldn't deny that a longer view had its advantages, too. And Anna had done a great deal of thinking about these things. She had been a member of the Party, also, and had urged resistance to the military dictatorship with fiery speeches and acts of breath-taking bravery. Even now, when he understood that, being Noantri, she hadn't been risking, perhaps, quite what he and his friends had, his heart still swelled with pride at her fierce valor.

Bueno. Enough dreaming. The parking lot, that's where he needed to go now, to fetch his *motorino.* As he turned to head in that direction he pulled out the phone again to switch the ringer on. It was required to be off in the Library, and with all that had happened he hadn't thought about it since. He and Anna had just hung up, but she might call back. With new instructions, or to say she'd thought it over and she understood that it wasn't his fault. She had her own ring tone, Anna did: Fuerte Apache's "Vida Clandestina." Hearing it always caused a clash of emotions in Jorge: joy that Anna was calling him and a stab of longing for home. He missed home. Sometimes, before he caught himself, he almost, almost, wished he'd never met Anna, never become Noantri. That the vicious military dictatorship of his beloved Argentina had made him a *desaparecido* like so many of his friends. That he'd died a martyr hero of La Guerra Sucia. It was the fate he was surely headed for until Anna intervened.

But those moments passed. How could he not want what he now had, what everyone would want if they knew it was possible? He had eternal life! He had the power to heal his body, develop his talents, advance his mind! Anna had told him how it would be, in those moments after the Fire, after the Change, when he lay paralyzed and bewildered. He'd been dying, she said; she'd had no choice. He would be grateful, she promised, he'd welcome what she'd done, when he understood. When he learned what she was, and what he now was. The news that he'd been dying had surprised him — the wound was excruciating, but even as he lay writhing he'd known the pain was from a bullet-shattered collarbone — but Anna had risked a great deal, she explained later, to save him. She'd chased off his assailants, but the real risk was what came next. To make someone Noantri without the Conclave's prior assent was forbidden; for Anna,

189

already in exile for previous infractions of the Law, the penalty for such an action could be — Jorge shuddered. He wouldn't think of it. What she had done for him, without his asking or even knowing to ask, proved her love. He owed her this wondrous new life, and he would do whatever Anna needed, whatever Anna desired, for as long as she wanted him to.

For eternity.

And Anna, Anna had a goal! The world would not remain as it was, continuing, day to day, day to day. . . . Anna's ambition held that everyone, Mortal and Noantri, deserved to lead rich and magnificent lives. Lives like hers. It wouldn't be long now until her plans — their plans — succeeded. When they were triumphant and Noantri jurisdiction was established, he could go home then. Once the Church was destroyed, there'd be no reason for Rome to remain the center of Noantri power. He and Anna would go back to Argentina. She would rule from Buenos Aires, and they would be happy.

The ringer was on now, but although Jorge stared at the phone as he walked, it sat inert in his hand. Resigned, he put it away when he reached the parking area and took out his keys. He mounted the *motorino,* revved the engine, and headed for Trastevere, as Anna had told him to do.

19

For the second time that day Thomas Kelly charged blindly out a door. His racing footsteps slapped and echoed through the ornate marble corridors as he ran from the Librarian's suite the way he had from the House of Crazy People. But this time it was much, much worse. Because according to Lorenzo, according to Cardinal Cossa, according to Thomas's friend and rock and spiritual anchor, those people weren't crazy.

It was a nightmare. Wait, yes, that was it! Literally. It was a nightmare, this whole day. He was actually asleep in his bed in the *residenza,* exhausted, disoriented, probably even under the influence of Lorenzo's good red wine from dinner. A nightmare. Thomas slowed his footsteps and waited: in his experience, once you knew you were having a nightmare, you woke up.

He didn't wake up. The crowds still milled in Saint Peter's Square, cameras clicked, groups of tourists swirled this way and that. The vast curve of the Colonnade swept away to encircle the great piazza on two sides, but Thomas saw no grandeur now: only vertigo.

It wasn't a nightmare, then. It was a horror worse than that.

Picking up his pace again, he made his way to Via del Pellegrino. When Lorenzo had informed him he'd be staying in the Jesuit *residenza* inside the Holy See while on this mission, he'd been awed and thrilled. Now all he wanted was to leave as soon as he could, to run as fast as he could, to flee from here to somewhere far, far away.

He heard, *"Buongiorno, Padre,"* as he brushed past another priest, a man heading out into the sunshine, a man who still lived in a normal world. He couldn't answer. At the door to his room he jabbed the key at the lock, could not find the keyhole. **Get a hold of yourself, Thomas!** Who had said that? Lorenzo! Lorenzo dared! Lorenzo Cardinal Cossa, who'd proved, in this last hour, that he'd been lying to Thomas since the day they'd met.

An hour before, in a different lifetime, Thomas had waited in Trastevere as Lorenzo had requested until he'd seen a dark blue Carabinieri Lancia roll to a stop near the café that shielded him. The car parked where it couldn't be seen from the small piazza at Santa Maria della Scala, and when the business-suited young man who got out rounded the corner, he glanced toward the historian's house. All right, the police were here. Thomas jogged to Piazza Trilussa and got in the first cab at the stand. The cab bounced over the cobbles, swung onto Ponte Garibaldi to cross the Tiber, and headed up the broad, busy street on the other side. Thomas tried to think of nothing at all as the *platano* trees slipped rhythmically past the windows. By the time he arrived at the Vatican he'd calmed down. He paid the driver and reported to the Librarian's suite.

He hadn't been kept waiting this time. He was shown in immediately by the young African priest. As Thomas thought back now, did he see a glint in the young man's eye? Did he know, too? Lorenzo had said not, had said no one knew except a very few in the Church's highest ranks. But how could Thomas trust anything Lorenzo said ever again?

When Thomas arrived Lorenzo had dismissed the young priest, pointed Thomas to a chair, and poured cognac into crystal snifters. Thomas, even at this ridiculously early hour, had been grateful for that, but the strong drink made what followed even more surreal.

"Thomas," Lorenzo had said in quiet, measured tones, "tell me what happened. Start in the Library."

So Thomas had recounted the meeting with Livia Pietro, the fight, the flight. Lorenzo said nothing, just sat puffing on a cigar, his eyes searching Thomas's face. Thomas, sure by then the whole thing was an inexplicably elaborate attempt to terrorize him, felt calm, almost amused; but suddenly, when he reached the discussion in Spencer George's study, he had trouble going on. Lorenzo advised him to finish his cognac, and gave him more.

"What happened there, Thomas?" Lorenzo asked. "What did they tell you?"

Feeling the comforting burn of excellent liquor, Thomas continued. "At first, nothing. Just that someone they both seemed to know, someone named Jonah, knew where the Concordat was. And that she — Livia Pietro — was ordered to find it by some group they call the Conclave. Whoever they are, they told her to get me to help her. They know why I'm here."

He looked to Lorenzo but Lorenzo just

nodded.

Thomas said, "She's afraid of them, or of something, but I don't know what. He —" Spencer George's face flashed in front of Thomas and his stomach clenched. "Nasty, sneering man. He — he —"

"He what, Thomas?"

Thomas took another sip. The cognac was warming him. He felt it in his fingertips and along the back of his neck. He was loose, he was safe. "I wouldn't help them. They wouldn't tell me how they knew about the Concordat or what it was or why they wanted it, and finally I told them I'd leave unless they did. I started to go and she said no, sit down, and she told me what they are — what they say they are. Do they believe it themselves?" he suddenly wondered. "Can they be that crazy? How could anyone —"

"Thomas. What did they say?"

Thomas snapped his eyes back to Lorenzo. "Yes. I'm sorry. She said . . ." He drew his brows together and concentrated, peering down at the light reflected in the amber liquid he was holding. As he spoke, the glow shimmered and danced. "She kept using the word 'Noantri.' It's a Romanesco word, a contraction of *noi altri,* it means 'we others,' and residents of Trastevere use it about themselves but she said even though that's what most people mean by it, it didn't just mean that, it meant her people."

"Her people? Thomas, who are her people?"

Thomas lifted his eyes again to meet Lorenzo's. Why was the Cardinal looking so solemn? Thomas burst into a grin. He realized he was tipsy and that this was the most absurd thing he'd ever say to Lorenzo. Dramatically, he lifted his hand toward the ceiling. *"Vampires!"* He started to laugh. Guffaws rocked him and he shook helplessly. The cognac sloshed in his snifter as he cracked up.

Lorenzo reached forward and took the glass from Thomas's hand. He set it down and softly asked, "What else?"

Instantly, the comic mood vanished; instantly, Thomas was sober. "The historian," he heard his own voice in monotone. "I refused to believe them, anything so ludicrous. He said all right then, I should leave, but she said it was important that I stay, important that I help them. So the historian — Spencer George, yes, that's his name — he shrugged and picked up a knife from his desk. He took the flowers from a glass vase — I think they were irises, but I'm not good with flowers —"

"Thomas?"

"He laid them very carefully on the tray. As though he cared about them. He brought the vase and put it on the table right in front of me and then he took the knife and he slit his wrist."

Thomas stopped. Lorenzo repeated, "He slit his wrist."

As though from far away, Thomas noted that Lorenzo phrased that as a statement, not a question. "Over the vase. Blood spurted into the water. Bright red . . . But right away, right *away,* it started to heal. It was a deep wound. He showed it to me, turned his wrist up right in front of me, and I watched it heal. I could see it. The bleeding stopped, the skin moved, crawled together almost. The blood in the water hadn't even mixed, it was still making little trailing threads, and he wasn't bleeding anymore." Thomas looked up at Lorenzo. "How did he do that? What kind of trick . . . ?"

Lorenzo was shaking his head.

"She didn't move," Thomas said. "She just sat there drinking her coffee. As though there weren't . . . weren't blood in the vase. Then he did it again. He did it to his other wrist. The same thing, more blood in the water, and when that one had started to heal he showed me the other one again. It was barely a pink scratch. 'Well,' he said, 'is that dramatic enough? Father?' I didn't answer so he said, 'Livia, I don't think he's convinced.' Then he smiled and handed me the knife. It was bloody. He opened his shirt and tapped himself on the chest. On the heart."

"What did you do?"

"I dropped the knife and ran."

That was it. That was the moment Thomas expected Lorenzo to grin, also, to laugh as hard as Thomas just had, and to explain to him what the Concordat really was, who the other signatory really was, and what the gang of book thieves/terrorists/merry prankster lunatics he'd encountered was really up to.

Lorenzo had not.

Quite, quite the opposite. He'd apologized for withholding this information from Thomas for so long, and said that Thomas's reaction now was proof that he'd been correct in doing so. That of all the Church's secrets, all its hidden truths, the truth of the Concordat was the most difficult for any devout man to learn. That the Noantri, begotten of Satan and birthed in hell, walked the earth. That they had as their purpose the degradation of men's bodies and the destruction of men's souls. That the Noantri promise of eternal life, meaning as it did a never-ending earthly existence and not a rebirth in the presence of the Lord, was a foul and futile pledge.

And that the Church had made a contract with them. And had held to it, to the mutual benefit of both groups, for six hundred years.

20

Thomas Kelly yanked open drawers and grabbed fistfuls of freshly pressed shirts. He pulled jackets and their hangers from the closet, swept the desk clean of pens and notepads, and stuffed everything recklessly into his suitcase. He was normally neat and methodical about his packing, as he was about everything, but nothing right now was normal and the only thing that mattered was to get away from here. To where? He didn't care. The next plane out of Rome, wherever it was going. Beijing, New York, Kuwait City. Somewhere he knew no one, no one knew him, and he could try to understand what had happened to him this day.

The drawers and closets were emptied and the suitcase mashed shut when Thomas, loading his pockets with his passport and wallet, heard his cell phone ring. No! Whoever it was, let them — But conscientious habit had by then forced the phone from the top of the bureau into his hand. An unknown number, a Rome code. Again unconscious routine took over; he'd been at the service of others, trying to be of use, for so long. Before he quite knew what he was doing he'd answered it.

"Thomas Kelly."

"*Buongiorno,* Father." An unrecognized voice, speaking, after that first word, in an English lightly accented. "You don't know me but we have reason to work together. You must bring me the Concordat."

Thomas stopped in the middle of his room, suitcase waiting on the bed. "Who are you? What do you mean?"

"Who I am is not important. You will be more interested, perhaps, in whom I know."

"What are you —"

"Thomas." A new and this time familiar voice. "It's Lorenzo. Whatever this man tells you to do, don't do it!"

"What — What are —"

Through the phone, Thomas heard muffled, unintelligible sounds. Then the other voice was back. "He is a brave man, your friend. Surprising, for a man of the Church. You're usually such cowards. Father Kelly, I don't have much time and neither do you. You'll bring me the Concordat or

202

your friend will die."

Thomas sank into the armchair. He bent forward over the phone. Weakly, he said, "What?"

"My people need that document. It's time the hypocrisy and evil of your Church was revealed for the world to see. Your friend the Cardinal wanted you to find it so he could hide it again and save your Church. Now you'll have to find it to save *him.* He's here with us, and not, believe me, by his own choice. If you don't bring us the Concordat, he will die." A brief pause. "No, better. Yes, much better. He won't die. He'll never die. I'll make him one of us." Thomas heard a horrified intake of breath that could only have come from Lorenzo. "Yes, a marvelous idea," the voice continued. "I'll give your friend eternal life. Isn't that what you men of the Church are always going on about? Eternal life. Won't he love that?"

A foul and futile promise. Lorenzo's words rang in Thomas's head. **The destruction of men's souls.**

"No," Thomas said. "This isn't happening. This isn't real."

"I'm sorry. I'm afraid it is. You'll go back to those of our people you've already met, the two who are searching, and you'll help them. You'll find the Concordat and bring it to me or I'll have the pleasure of welcoming your friend into our Community. We're not unrepresented in your Church, but he'll be our first cardinal. Quite an honor, wouldn't you say?"

"No!" Thomas heard Lorenzo yelling from a distance. "Thomas! Don't help him! They —" His words were cut off.

"Oh, yes, he's very brave." The voice was mocking now. "Willing to die for his Church and his God, I have no doubt. But sadly, I don't think he's going to get that chance. Go join the search for the Concordat, Father Kelly, and wait for my next call."

The connection was cut.

21

Livia Pietro leaned over a map of Trastevere as the area had been in 1840. It had been Spencer's idea to photocopy the map, one of the antique treasures of his collection, and use it to plot the locations of Damiani's subjects. Truth be told, not very much had altered in the district since this map was made, but Spencer thought it would be useful to get as close to Mario Damiani's standpoint as they could.

Livia could see how hard this was for Spencer. She hadn't known Damiani — her own Change had come about during the First World War — and Spencer had never been one to reveal his feelings. But he and Damiani had been together for many decades; as Livia understood it, nearly a century. Noantri unions were the same as those the Unchanged made and also different. Couples came together for the same reasons: an ultimately indefinable compatibility of qualities physical, intellectual, emotional, and spiritual. Among the Unchanged, pairings that started well sometimes came apart nevertheless, as life's events strained them, as the partners grew and became different people from the ones they'd been.

For the Noantri, the challenge was the same, and it was magnified by stretching over greater expanses of time. Through decades and centuries, personalities and behaviors altering as new knowledge, new views, and new experiences were added, a couple could easily find themselves, at last, totally unknown to each other.

But sometimes, the reverse. Sometimes the wealth of years only gave power to a couple's love. Possibly it was the fact that the two had always been opposites that was the strength of Spencer's relationship with Mario Damiani. Livia, despite what she'd led Father Kelly to believe, had known little about Damiani until yesterday, when she'd received the instructions of the Conclave. She'd researched him extensively before heading, just that morning, to the Vatican Library. From what she'd learned, Damiani had been everything Spencer wasn't: enthusiastic, open, optimistic, and spontaneous. Among the Noantri of Rome, she'd discovered, their mutual devotion had been legendary.

"I get the feeling Mario Damiani knew every inch of Trastevere," Livia ventured, glancing at Spencer as she spoke. Working with Damiani's notebook and the map, the two of them were trying to decipher Damiani's passionate, elliptical references and locate the poems' subjects. They'd been at it for nearly two hours, ever since Thomas Kelly had bolted. Spencer, for his part, was delighted to be rid of the priest. Livia, though dismayed, could see that for her to go after Father Kelly would only terrify him more. She had thought, from their short acquaintance, that he might actually be strong enough to accept the difficult truth he was being told. She'd been wrong. She felt bad for him, and worried about the Conclave's reaction when they found out. But perhaps it wouldn't matter, after all, whether he was involved. His knowledge might have been useful, but Damiani's notebook was likely to be the real treasure here. So while Spencer had calmly rinsed out the vase he'd used as a prop in his theatrical display — *Signora* Russo, his cook, was Unchanged, so it wouldn't do for her to come upon it — Livia unrolled the map and began.

"When we met, Mario had been Noantri twenty years, I nearly two hundred." Spencer answered Livia without looking up. "In all the time we were together we never traveled far. Mario didn't care to. Rome, and particularly Trastevere, had his heart. I'd always traveled, even before my Change. I wanted to go back to Asia, but Mario could never be persuaded. He did say he might want to see the New World one day, maybe New York, but such . . . coarseness . . . held no interest for me. So we remained in Rome." Spencer trailed off into a pensive silence. Livia let him be.

"There," Spencer said after a moment, in stronger tones. He laid down his pencil. "I think that's the last of them." He frowned down at the map and then at the notebook. "I have to tell you, though, that whatever was bothering me earlier has not gone away. Something about these poems is so familiar. . . ."

"It's not just that you knew he was working on them?" Livia studied the map, now that they'd completed it, looking for a pattern in the places Damiani had chosen to celebrate.

"I knew it, but I hadn't seen them. He never showed me his work until it was finished. Something here . . . Something about the notebook itself, I think. I —"

The clanking of the brass ring on the front door interrupted him. Livia and Spencer exchanged glances; then Spencer crossed the room to peer through the window overlooking the piazza. "Oh," he said. "My, my. Livia, come see this, and tell me what you want me to do."

22

Carabiniere *Sergente* Raffaele Orsini
scratched his chin (where his stubble was
kept at fashionable two-day length by
Elena's birthday gift of a beard trimmer)
and resettled in his café chair. Even the best
of chairs could get a little uncomfortable
after an hour and a half.

Giulio Aventino, his partner and senior,
was probably back at the station by now,
and livid that the *maresciallo* had given Raffaele permission to do this surveillance. If
Giulio had been there when the request had
come in he'd have fought it, though the
maresciallo would've overruled him and
Raffaele would be here anyway. That was
politics, not piety, Raffaele knew: an uncom-
plicated favor like this for the Vatican was
the sort the Carabinieri were only too happy
to grant, so that when someday the police
needed to, for example, follow a suspect into
San Pietro, the Curia would respond in

kind. Everyone scratched one another's backs, that was the Italian way, and Giulio Aventino was no different except when it came to the Church.

The senior detective wasn't just some kind of blasé unbeliever to whom the Church meant nothing. In Raffaele's view Giulio's soul seemed infused with the bitter cynicism of a heartbroken lover. Giulio Aventino had been devout once, Raffaele was sure of it. Now, his religion was his work. As his sergeant, Raffaele applied himself to learning from a senior officer of long experience, obvious skill, and high reputation. As a man, younger but much stronger in devotion to the Holy Mother Church, he was grateful for his own faith in the face of his partner's gloom.

Here now, what was this? Raffaele, as he'd been trained to do, stayed slouched in his chair, didn't move, as though nothing was on his mind but his mid-afternoon *macchiato.* He reached for his phone, looking for all the world like a *figlio di papà* calling his girlfriend for a romantic chat. What he was, though, was a cop calling his uncle, the Cardinal, for whom the Carabinieri were doing this favor. Raffaele didn't know why he'd been asked to watch this house, and no one had come out; but he thought

Lorenzo Cardinal Cossa might be interested to know that a priest had just arrived, knocked, and was standing on the threshold talking to the black-haired woman whose photo, marking her as Raffaele's surveillance target, the Cardinal had sent.

23

Standing on the cobblestones as the echo of his knock died away, it was all Thomas Kelly could do not to turn and run. He swallowed, bile burning his throat. The idea that he'd soon once again be in the presence of those . . . those *creatures,* made his stomach curdle and his skin crawl.

He still wasn't sure he believed any of it: what he'd seen, what Lorenzo had told him. He'd given up hope that this was a simple nightmare but he was clinging to a new idea, that it was some sort of drug-induced hallucination. There'd been an accident. One of these terrible Rome drivers — some young kid on a *motorino* had almost run him down just moments ago, it was something like that, he was in a hospital all drugged up and his own subconscious had created this insane fantasy out of the depths of who-knows-where. The theory comforted him, but the problem with it was that while he waited for consciousness to return and the world to become right again, he had to take some sort of action. Although in this delusion Lorenzo Cossa had been deceiving and betraying Thomas for fifteen years, the fate threatening the Cardinal now was so horrifying that, though if any of this were true Lorenzo certainly wouldn't deserve his help, Thomas found himself unable to just abandon him. **After all,** Thomas thought, **if you don't act heroically in your own hallucination, what can you hope from yourself in real life?** Somewhere, somehow, Thomas was sure this all had to do with faith. The need to save someone whose treachery cut so deeply must be a test of faith. Thomas didn't know why his subconscious demanded this of him, but he wasn't about to let himself down.

And in a dark, far corner of his mind was a tiny stabbing pain he was trying desperately to ignore. But like a sliver of glass in his shoe, though minute it was agonizing and unremitting: the unspeakable possibility that he was wide awake and it was all true. In which case Lorenzo deserved his help even less, and needed it much more.

The door opened. Thomas stepped back involuntarily at the sight of Livia Pietro. "Don't touch me!"

"No, Father," she said quietly. "Of course not." After a moment she moved back into the foyer, holding the door wide. "Will you come in?"

Thomas found he couldn't cross the threshold, could not enter that house. They stood in silence, regarding each other. Pietro's green eyes seemed kind, even concerned, but Thomas was not going to be taken in again. "You're a monster," he rasped.

She shook her head. "I'm a person. Like you, but different from you."

A person? This creature was claiming to exist in the image of the Lord? He felt the calm that his new theory had brought him begin to slip away. "No!" he barked. "A creature with no soul." Pietro just gazed at him sadly; for some reason that pitying look enraged him more. "You sold your soul for a promise of eternal life. But what you've bought isn't that. It's never-ending corruption. Everlasting decay!" He could feel the heat in his skin, could hear his voice rising, he knew he sounded wild but he couldn't stop himself. "Your bargain is worthless. Worthless! Your false prophet will abandon you. The End of Days will come, even for you, and —"

Pietro held up her hand. Thomas's cheeks

burned; he trembled with rage. But looking at her pale face, her long dark hair — staring into her ocean-green eyes — he felt his flood of accusatory words abate. What was the point? The choice Livia Pietro and the others like her had made couldn't be undone. The sin they'd committed couldn't be confessed, expiated, forgiven. His knotted shoulders fell. Helplessness and sorrow flooded through him where, moments before, righteous anger had blazed.

"Father," Pietro said. "You left here, and I understand. What you're saying is wrong, but many think as you do. But you've come back. Why?"

No, he couldn't do this. Without the heat of his fury he felt cold and clammy, and his breathing caught just standing here in front of her. He couldn't go into that house. **Blood in the vase.**

"Father Kelly? Are you all right?"

"No! How could I be all right? Your . . . your 'people' . . ."

"Father." Now she spoke decisively, commandingly. "Come inside. Or leave."

Lord, Thomas prayed. **Father, help me.** He stood on the threshold another moment, a few more seconds in the cobblestoned, scooter-buzzed, sunny morning, and then he went in.

24

Livia led Thomas Kelly in silence up to Spencer's study. In the doorway, the priest stopped and peered apprehensively into the room.

"Where is he?"

"I asked Spencer to give us some time alone."

Livia sensed his relief, but he straightened and said, "I have no reason to be alone with you."

"Would you rather Spencer were here? Come in and sit down. Please."

She sat first, to appear as unthreatening as she could manage. Thomas Kelly chose a chair in the farthest corner and barely perched on it. He continued to look around uneasily.

"Spencer removed the vase, too," she said. "Why have you come back?"

He snapped his eyes to her like a nervous cat. After a moment: "Cardinal Cossa. The

Vatican Librarian."

"And Archivist. I know who he is. What about him?"

"I got a call. Some of your . . . 'people' have abducted him."

"What?" She sat forward. As she did, he drew back.

"They'll make him one of you." The priest swallowed, then set his jaw and went on. "Unless I bring them the Concordat."

"I don't understand," Livia said. "This is — Who are they?"

"I have no idea. They said to come back here and help you. They'll contact me. Once I have the Concordat I have to give it to them."

Once *you* have it? Livia thought, but only said, "When did this happen?"

"I just got the call. Not fifteen minutes ago, that's how long it took me to get here." Kelly took a handkerchief from his pocket and wiped his sweating face. "The abduction must have happened within the hour. I was with him until then. The Cardinal. He told me — He told me —"

"He told you about the Concordat. And about us. The Noantri."

Kelly nodded, looking sick.

"Father," she said gently, "what you've been told —"

"Your people promised to raise Martin the Fifth to the papacy," he blurted. "If he agreed to stop exterminating you as the Church had always done. If he allowed you to exist and proliferate and defile the world!"

"No, that —"

"And worse: Martin agreed not only to permit you to continue, but to provide you with blood from Catholic hospitals for your filthy rites. Innocent blood!"

"Father," she said firmly. "As far as they go, your facts are correct, but the motivations you ascribe are wrong. As is your characterization of my people. And you're leaving out a great deal. I suppose you haven't been told the whole truth."

"What I was told —"

"What you were told is what most of the Unchanged believe."

" 'Unchanged'?"

"People like you. Please. Wait here a moment. There's something I have to do, urgently. But I want very much to discuss this with you. To tell you —"

"What? Your side? Life from the demon's point of view?"

She stood and saw him recoil. "The news you've brought is troubling. I must discuss it with . . . the people whose instructions

I'm to carry out. I won't be long."

"And what am I supposed to do? Just sit here?"

"I'm asking you to wait for me. But you're not a prisoner here. You can stay or go."

She walked past him out the study door, leaving him pale and staring.

Livia found Spencer where he'd said he'd be, in the drawing room on the next floor. "Well?" Spencer looked up, slipping a bookmark into the volume in his hands. "How is he, your young priest? Has he returned to drive stakes into our hearts? Has he brought his pistol and his silver bullets?"

"He's frightened half to death. You really didn't need to break out the Grand Guignol, Spencer."

"Of course I did. He wasn't believing a word you were calmly saying. He thought you and I were both mad. Two batty people sharing a *folie à deux*."

"I could have convinced him."

"Let me remind you that although you and I have all the time in the world, your priest grows older every minute. By the time your gentle rationality persuaded him, he'd have been too doddering to be of any use. Furthermore, unless I'm wrong, ageless though we may be, we still have a deadline to meet."

Livia dropped into a chair. "You're right. And things just got worse." She told Spencer the news Father Kelly had brought.

Spencer lifted his eyebrows. "An interesting development."

"You're certainly calm about it."

"The abduction of a cardinal is not an event that disquiets me."

"Under these circumstances? This cardinal? It's intensely disquieting, I think." She took out her cell phone. "I have to tell the Conclave. They may not know." She pressed the number and lifted her phone to her ear.

After a moment: *"Salve."* Her call, as she expected, was answered by Filippo Croce, the Pontifex's personal secretary. This man, sober, trustworthy, and devoted, had been the channel for communications to the Conclave since the media for contacting that august body had been quill pen and parchment.

"Salve. Sum Livia Pietro. Quid agis?" Automatically, as her people had for centuries, Livia inquired into the state of the Community before introducing her own affairs.

"Hic nobis omnibus bene est. Quomodo auxilium vobis dare possumus?" **All is well here,** came the response. **How may we be of service?**

The brief ritual completed, Livia switched to Italian and asked to speak to the Pontifex, or, failing that, to Rosa Cartelli. She wasn't asked her mission; clearly she'd been given a priority with the Conclave that, flattering as it was, she'd have preferred not to need. She was assured the Pontifex would speak with her in short order. A brief silence, then the music of Carlo Gesualdo. As with the art hung at the Conclave offices — the paintings of artists such as Ivan Nikitin and Romualdo Locatelli — the music played, even over the phone, was the work of Noantri. Livia had always been uncomfortable with this kind of self-conscious Noantri pride; to her it bordered on separatism. As an art historian, she argued that good art was good and bad art bad, regardless of who produced it. If the paintings of Noantri artists could hang in museums and galleries around the world, as, unbeknownst to Unchanged curators and collectors, they indeed did, then Noantri could have on their walls the work of the best of their own people, and equally, the best of the Unchanged. And better music than Gesualdo's could pour from the Conclave's office phone. She rolled her eyes at Spencer. "I'm on hold."

Spencer sighed, and took the opportunity

to ask, "Whom do you suppose is behind it? This abduction?"

Livia shrugged. "There are other factions, other people besides Jonah who're impatient to Unveil. Any one of them might want to force the issue the same way Jonah does."

Spencer looked skeptical. "To take this action and make this threat — to send the priest back here to us — they'd have to know what you've been told to do and why the priest is in Rome at all."

"Father Thomas Kelly," Livia told Spencer, waiting for the Pontifex to come on the line. "That's his name."

25

It was all Thomas could do to force himself to stay seated. He had to, though. If he stood, he knew he'd run again from this house, and this time he'd keep going. How long should he give her? Half of him hoped she'd never come back. The other half feared the mortal danger — no, the immortal, the eternal danger! — to Lorenzo was becoming more real with every passing second.

This was a terror he'd never encountered before. The late-night seminary arguments and wine-fueled graduate school debates about free will had never covered this territory: the possibility that a man could lose his soul not through his own choices but through the actions of another. Confession, penance, and absolution: these were central to Thomas's faith. Any man, until his dying breath, could repent and be forgiven, could enter into the presence of God though he had denied him all his life. But redemption and God's grace, lost forever because a monster chose to make you a monster, also — neither Thomas nor any of his classmates had for a moment considered this. Their sophistic deliberations of free will had swirled around well-worn issues of the Lord's omnipotence and omniscience, threadbare questions of paradox with the answers always the same: God, in his omnipotence, gives us our own power; in his omniscience he grants us knowledge, in order that we make our own choices. He does this from hope and boundless love, to give each of us the privilege of coming to him freely, of choosing to put our souls into his care.

When this nightmare ended — this drug coma, this hallucination, yes, of course it was that — Thomas hoped he'd remember the foolish naïveté and philosophical bankruptcy of his now-blasted, ever-so-clever theology.

Of course, if this was just a hallucination, and the Noantri didn't exist, then the stealing of one's soul couldn't happen, and all could go back to the way it had been before. Oh, this was marvelous! If he woke, he wouldn't need to remember what he'd just learned, because it would be useless.

225

And if he didn't wake, he wouldn't need to remember it, because he'd never be able to forget it.

He started when the door opened, but this time he was prepared. The silver crucifix that usually hung around his neck was gripped in his hand. He thrust it out as Livia Pietro stepped back into the room. She stopped, stared, and shook her head. "Put that away." Crossing the carpet, she sat again. "The Church has always been our enemy, Father Kelly, but we haven't been yours. To think that the sight of a cross will have any effect on me — I'm sorry, but it's narcissistic."

Thomas slowly lowered his arm as she went crisply on.

"I've relayed your news to the Conclave. It caused a good deal of unease. The situation was already serious. Now it's much worse. That Cardinal Cossa's fate should be dependent on the revelation of the Concordat — this problem is of great concern to our Noantri leaders."

Thomas had to search for his voice, but he found it. "You'll forgive me if I withhold my thanks."

She stared levelly, then continued. "The Conclave is not without resources. They're attempting to find out what they can about what's happened and to intervene if possible."

"No!" Thomas jumped up. "Any interference could jeopardize the Cardinal further!"

"According to your thinking, his position is already dire. We disagree with your characterization of us, but it's one of our First Laws that no Mortal is made Noantri against his will. It's a condition of the Concordat. That document you despise."

She glanced pointedly at his chair. Thomas, not sure he had the strength to stand in any case, sank back down.

"A brief history lesson for you, Father. First: although the Noantri did help Martin the Fifth to achieve the papacy, we weren't the central agents of his rise. He had widespread support in the Church — that is, among *your* people. We aided him because Martin was able to understand the mutual advantages the Concordat would bring to the Noantri and to the Unchanged. His rivals, the Popes of the Avignon line, were blind to these benefits. The Concordat, in essence, obligates the Catholic Church to, as you say, cease trying to annihilate us. And yes, to provide us blood from Catholic hospitals. Blood is our sustenance, Father Kelly. This is not a choice we've made, it's a simple fact. In return, we will make no one

Noantri without his consent — no, more than consent: his request — and the consent of the Conclave." She glanced away as she said that and was silent for a moment. Then she brought her gaze back to him and resumed. "We also, for our part, agree to remain hidden, not revealing our true natures. Not so hidden as we once were, though: we live in Community now, with our own kind, in cities around the world. This is a great comfort to us — just to be together. Because our nourishment is assured, we have no need of stealth, of violence — or of guilt. We're no longer the feral, furtive, degraded people of the past. The Concordat has given us that."

"You still say 'people.' You are not people."

"We are. Each of us started as you are today. As a Mortal man or woman. 'Unchanged' is the word we use. The Change comes about through a micro-organism introduced into the blood. It alters the structure of our DNA." She gave a slight smile. "You look surprised."

"To hear you speak of a devil's bargain in such cold and scientific terms."

"It is science — it's not supernatural. The devil, whether he exists or not, has nothing to do with this. A microbe mutated in the blood of a small number of early humans.

228

Possibly, at first, only one. It causes a need, and a great thirst, for human blood, and grants DNA the ability to rapidly repair cells. Our cells don't deteriorate. So we don't die. That's it."

Thomas drew a breath. "I'll remind you that the very essence of evil is to be subtle. Do you really think that because your unnatural bargain was made with a microbe and not a man with horns and a tail, it's any less the work of Satan?" Who, until today, Thomas might have been willing to argue was only a metaphor, an externalized manifestation of the human capacity for cruelty. Or, alternately, a distilled and focused expression of the evil that did exist in the Universe, brought into being by, and purposefully in contradistinction to, the goodness of God. Right now, though, if Satan walked through the door wearing his horns and tail, Thomas wouldn't blink.

"Couldn't your God have created this microbe?" Pietro asked. "In fact, in your view, how else could it have gotten here?"

"The Lord also created knives and guns. He gives us the privilege of choosing whether to use them." On firmer ground now that he was engaged in theological debate, Thomas added, "People were not meant to live on this earth forever. Only through death can man achieve eternal life."

"Really, Father? Do you say that to the doctors at your hospitals? The ones who stop people from dying every day? Some of whom are Noantri, by the way."

Thomas felt the firm ground slipping. "The doctors?"

"And the lawyers, and the cabdrivers. And" — Pietro pointed to herself — "the university professors. You've lived beside us and known us all your life, Father Kelly."

"No. That can't be true."

"It is. The Noantri came into being long ago. Before your Church, before the religions and belief systems from which your Church sprang. Before written history began. We've been here since the start of humankind."

"So has evil."

"True but irrelevant."

Thomas shook his head. "Even if your explanation is correct, the microbe itself was clearly sent by Satan."

Pietro smiled. "That's not so clear to us. And to your point about eternal life, you may be right. We don't know. What we have may only be longevity. Extreme, but not eternal. Some of our scientists think we may be deteriorating, as you are, just at a rate so slow as to be undetectable."

Thomas found himself asking, in spite of his repugnance, "Can you . . . die?"

"We can. Not of natural causes, because of the rapidity of repair of our cells. And certainly not of silver bullets or stakes to the heart at a crossroads at midnight. Or an overdose of garlic."

"Or," it occurred to Thomas, "sunlight. I was with you, in the sun."

"The Change heightens all the senses and makes us extremely responsive to our environment. We hear and see exceptionally well, for example, so most of us dislike loud noises. By that same token, bright light is painful, and for those of us who're naturally pale, our skin sunburns easily. It's not dangerous but it hurts, and pain is also something we feel more acutely than you do. So we wear sunglasses. And long sleeves, and hats. It was a Noantri chemist who developed sunscreen."

"But stakes to the heart —" A scene from earlier in the day flashed before Thomas. "Surely, if I'd stabbed Spencer George in the heart . . ."

"No. It's complex and still poorly understood, but there seems to be a sort of critical mass of blood and soft tissue that, as long as it's maintained, will eventually repair or, if needed, replicate, the rest of the body.

It can take a long, long time, depending on the damage, but it will happen. In this case, Spencer's heart would have stopped, and the whole thing would've been messy, but after a day or a week of deep coma he'd have been back with us."

"Rising from the coffin. That's why they say you rise from the coffin."

Pietro nodded. "That's exactly right. We don't sleep in coffins, of course not. But once buried, we can 'rise again.' It's not really that, because it's not really death. But we understand why it seems like it, to the Unchanged."

And the dead shall be raised
Incorruptible

Thomas shuddered. The gift promised to all humanity at the Last Trumpet, usurped and perverted. "But you say you can die."

"Yes. In two ways, one more widely understood than the other. First, by fire. Some chemical process involved in the Change makes our flesh more vulnerable to fire than yours. I'm not a scientist so I can't explain it but if you want — yes, all right, never mind. The result is that fire can rapidly destroy us. If our bodies are completely consumed, there's nothing left to initiate the process of regrowth."

"There's always something. A tooth, a bit of bone."

"Bone and tooth don't live in the same way. Or hair, or nails. Soft tissue is what's needed. Living tissue, containing blood, which is what can be destroyed by fire."

"And the other way?"

"Obviously, complete dismemberment would, at some point, eliminate that critical mass. How small you'd have to chop us" — to Thomas's horror, she smiled — "that's something we don't know."

"Why not?"

"Because what Noantri would volunteer for that experiment?"

"Volunteer?" A wild laugh escaped him. Fiends with medical ethics? "Why not just, I don't know what you call it, infect a bunch of people? Then you could chop them into pieces and see if they spring back to life!"

She stared. "You can't really believe we'd do that?"

He didn't answer.

"No," she said, calmly and firmly. "We consider our Changed lives a great gift. A Blessing. What you've suggested would make any Noantri ill even to contemplate."

Thomas felt ill himself. "But you can burn. So when you reach the fires of hell . . .

But how will that happen, if you don't die
. . . ?"

"Well, Father, perhaps you can take comfort in the knowledge that millions of years
from now, the earth will fall into the sun.
Then the Noantri will all be destroyed. We'll
die, and, if there's a Last Judgment, we'll be
judged."

"You can't be judged. You have no souls."

"How can you be sure?"

Thomas looked around him, for help, for
guidance. He was a Jesuit; he wasn't a
scientist, but he was a scholar, trained not
to shy away from the conflicts between fact
and faith. Nor had he, ever. Ultimately, he
saw those contradictions themselves as a
gift from God: they were why faith was
required. If God's goodness, if even his existence, could be proved, then what was man
bringing to the table? What were we offering God? Faith was what God asked of man.
It was our single gift to him. The only thing
man has, and the only thing God wants.

What did that mean, then? Was it possible
these — these creatures, were just another
form of human life? Ultimately, as Pietro
said, to die, and be judged, like all others?

Thomas looked at Livia Pietro again. For
a moment, he saw her eyes as kind and her
face as animated by a lively intelligence.

Then: **Begotten of Satan and birthed in hell!** Inside his head, as clear as if the man himself were sitting here, Thomas heard Lorenzo's roar. **The degradation of men's bodies, the destruction of men's souls. A foul and futile pledge.**

They drink human blood.

It's the essence of evil to be subtle.

Kind eyes, an intelligent face. Better men than he had been deceived by less.

Pietro had been silent, watching him. Now she spoke. "Father, I thought I might be getting through to you but I can see that I haven't. I wish you'd keep an open mind but I know this is hard for you and I can't help what you believe. I think that's enough discussion. We're wasting time. Each of us has a compelling reason to find the stolen copy of the Concordat, and a better chance of succeeding if we act together. Can you put aside your distrust and work with me?"

If only it were merely distrust, Thomas thought helplessly. Revulsion, anger, sadness, and a soul-deep despair opened a chasm within him. This was what Lorenzo had meant when he said, *I'm afraid of what it will do to you, to your faith.*

And Thomas had laughed, because he'd thought that his crisis of faith had come and gone. He saw now that he'd been a man unconcerned about spots on his skin because he'd once survived hives, only to learn, too late, that he has the plague.

"The notebook," Pietro said. "Damiani's notebook. Spencer and I have been studying it. He agrees with me that the pattern of the missing pages may be important."

Thomas stared. Was he really going to do this? As though discussing Damiani's poems, or anything, with her, was reasonable? But, without a sense that he'd decided, he heard his own voice: "How can — How can you tell? You've identified the places the missing pages refer to?"

"No. There are too many possibilities. What we did was to decipher the poems that remain. When we mapped those places out, we found a broad area from here — this house — through Trastevere to the Tiber, with no poems relating to it. It's possible Damiani was heading from here to the river, and hid the Concordat on his way. In some place, some building or statue or fountain, he'd already written about."

Thomas hesitated, then slowly said, "If I do agree to help, what use can I be?"

"You know the significance to the Church of many of these buildings much better than either Spencer or I do," Pietro came back promptly. "And if we do manage to find the right building, we'll still have to locate Damiani's hiding place within it. He was a brilliant and ironic man with a great sense of humor, I'm discovering. Especially if the building he chose was a religious property, as I suspect it was, your knowledge of Church history could be very valuable."

"I'm not sure."

"The Conclave is. And your cardinal."

Yes, the Cardinal. Lorenzo had great faith in Thomas. Not enough to tell him the truth, but enough to ask him to take on this task.

"And if we find the Concordat?" Thomas asked. "What happens then?"

"Our goals are the same: to keep it hidden."

That's your goal, Thomas thought. **And the Cardinal's. Mine, right now, is to save him. If what it takes to do that is giving the Concordat to someone who'd reveal its contents, how bad would that really be? Would it really cause the destruction of the Church?** No: the setting of the Church back on the correct path, a path Thomas could now see had been abandoned six hundred years ago. Would Thomas be able to convince Lorenzo of the rightness of this? Lorenzo had screamed, *Don't help them;* Lorenzo had been willing to sacrifice himself to protect his Church. But Lorenzo, Thomas suddenly realized, could only be anxious to maintain the status quo because all this was theoretical to him. He must never — until they'd seized him — have met one of these Noantri, never been in this insidious, seductive presence. If he had, he'd understand. He'd feel the way Thomas felt now.

Thomas swallowed and asked, "How do we begin?"

"Spencer has the notebook." Pietro's relief was palpable as she stood. "I'll get him. He —"

She stopped as the door opened. Thomas's stomach clenched at the sight of Spencer George, who stood in the doorway holding Damiani's notebook. Thomas had to stop himself from going for his crucifix again. Looking at the historian, Thomas had to admit the man looked none the worse for the great gushing of blood from his wrists a few hours earlier.

None the worse; but he did look odd.

"Livia?" Spencer George spoke in a voice distant and strange. He didn't seem to notice Thomas. "Livia, I have one of these poems."

26

Livia's heart leapt. Spencer had one of Damiani's missing poems; Father Kelly was joining in the search. She was doing as the Conclave had instructed and now had a hope of succeeding. Maybe things would turn out all right.

Maybe Jonah wouldn't have to die.

Spencer crossed the room to a rolltop desk in the corner. Livia watched as he unlocked it and slid the cover open. Laying Damiani's notebook down, he pulled out a drawer and retrieved a small leather case, from which he took a single sheet of paper. He held the sheet, fingering its edges, his eyes moving over it as though searching for something that wasn't to be found — something he'd searched for many times before, something he had never found. Then he laid his paper gently down and opened Mario Damiani's notebook beside it.

The priest started forward but Livia put

out a hand to stop him. They waited; finally, Spencer, still in a soft monotone, said, "Come and look." After a moment, "You, too, Father Kelly, you may look."

They did, and over Spencer's shoulder she could see: the paper, the handwriting, the ink were all the same. Spencer turned pages, comparing torn edges until he located the place the sheet from his desk had originally resided.

"Mario gave it to me," Spencer said. "When he was just starting this book. He was satisfied with this poem — No," Spencer interrupted himself with a sad smile. "It was Mario. He was delighted. He said whether or not the rest of the book ended up any good, this poem did just what he wanted it to and it would always be mine. I thought that's all the note meant."

Livia glanced up at him. "The note?"

From the leather case Spencer drew a second sheet. Though the paper clearly came from another source, and the ink was different, the handwriting was the same. Its single line was Italian, not Romanesco, and scribbled in haste, but no one could mistake that it had been written by Damiani. *Look to your poem,* it said.

"I thought it was a farewell." Now Spencer turned and met her eyes. "When I finally returned to Rome, this was on my desk. I thought he'd left it in case — in case something happened to him. To remind me I had the poem. Had something of him. You see?"

"Yes."

"But maybe that's not what he meant at all. Maybe he wanted me to find the Concordat. Maybe he was telling me where it is."

Heart pounding, Livia peered at the poem; over Spencer's other shoulder, Thomas Kelly did the same.

Quer sbirilluccico che jje strazzia
er gruggno, er ginocchione flesso, è 'n
   passettino
incontro ar Padre nostro: Lui sà ch'è la
   monnezza
tra dde noi che bbatte er cammino,
piede destro, poi er sinistro, che porta
   l'anima a la grazzia.

The Romanesco words lay oddly on the page, their letter groupings not those found in Italian, certainly not in English. But Livia had had a lot of practice at this, as she knew Spencer also had. Nor did Thomas Kelly seem fazed. In Livia's head the poem quickly transformed.

The glow of ecstasy upon the face,
the bended knee, the humblest of steps
toward our Father: He well knows the base
and lowly are the ones who make the trek,
right foot then left, that leads the soul to
    grace.

"If we can understand it," she said, "if we can work it out, you're right, Spencer. Maybe that's what he meant, and this is what we need."

"Work it out?" Spencer seemed bemused.

"What it refers to!" Thomas Kelly snapped. "Where he was sending you!"

Now Spencer smiled. "I'm surprised at you, Father. A Church scholar of your supposed erudition. 'The humblest of steps.' "

Thomas Kelly flushed angrily.

"I'm sorry, Spencer," Livia said. "I don't see it either."

"On the contrary. You do." Spencer pointed out the window, at the shadowed façade of the church of Santa Maria della Scala.

27

Jorge Ocampo lit another cigarette and ordered another coffee. The smoke was his fifth and the coffee his third since he'd sat down in this café in Piazza della Scala. He coughed. Maybe he should cut down. Though Anna said there was no reason. His indestructible Noantri body would repair any damage he was doing. But Jorge found the coughing itself unpleasant.

Anna never coughed.

The *cameriere* brought his coffee. Jorge liked it well enough, this Italian roast, but he'd never been served a coffee here yet that had the depth and strength of an Argentinian brew. He stirred in sugar (they didn't drink it sweet enough here, either), all the while keeping an eye on the door through which the priest had disappeared. Anna would be proud of him. He'd spotted that priest and this time, he wouldn't let him get away.

He admitted it was mostly luck, but a large part of a revolutionary fighter's skill was recognizing the luck that came his way and knowing how to use it. Speeding on his *motorino* to the home of the dark-haired Noantri woman who lived on Piazza dei Renzi, he'd almost collided with the priest who'd been with her in the Vatican Library. He spun his bike around and followed, instinct telling him this man, in such a rush, might lead him where he needed to be.

Besides, this priest had knocked him down, and he owed the man for that, he thought as he sat in the café rubbing his shoulder. Though in truth it didn't hurt anymore. An unfortunate fact about the Noantri body, Jorge had found, was that vastly heightened senses meant pain, like any other physical phenomenon, was amplified far beyond what was experienced by Mortals. But it was also true that quick healing made the pain pass rapidly. Anna had promised, since disability and death were now impossible for him, that eventually the instinctive panic and fear that serious pain occasioned would fade, also.

Jorge hoped so; meanwhile, he was happy to trade occasional bouts of panic and moments of searing pain for the irreplaceable gift his augmented senses had also brought him: the acute, almost unbearable pleasure that surged over him, enveloped him, at Anna's touch. Her velvet lips brushing his lips, his throat; her silken fingertips stroking his face, his chest — and the beautiful blazing agony when she dug her nails into his shoulders, scraped furrows down his back: all this was his, and was worth whatever it cost.

Once or twice, Jorge had caught himself wistfully wondering what it might have been like to make love to Anna if they'd both been Mortal. If all they had were the senses they'd been born with and the desperate, thrilling urgency Jorge remembered as such a vivid part of Mortal embraces. Urgency, of course, underlay all Mortal endeavors, though in daily life it hung almost unnoticed in the background. It came from the simple knowledge that time was finite and one's supply of hours would one day be exhausted. That understanding furnished a piquancy to a Mortal's every moment that, in his unguarded thoughts, Jorge sometimes found that he missed.

But in exchange, look what he had! He had eternal life. And he had Anna.

And right now, he had a chance to make his Anna so very happy. The door he'd been assiduously watching had opened, and from it issued the priest, the black-haired *profes-soressa,* and a third person: a well-dressed man Jorge didn't know but one Jorge could tell by his scent was Noantri. They were walking with purpose across the little piazza, toward the church.

The *professoressa,* in her hand, gripped the stolen notebook.

Jorge stood.

28

Sergente Raffaele Orsini remained seated at his table at the café in Piazza della Scala. The call he'd made half an hour ago to his uncle, Lorenzo Cardinal Cossa, about the priest's arrival at the house Raffaele had been sent to watch had gone to voice mail. He made another call now, and when the Cardinal once again didn't answer, Raffaele called the *maresciallo.*

"The subject has just come out of the house. She's with two people I don't know. One's a priest. I can't reach the Cardinal."

The cell phone in his ear was briefly silent. Raffaele could picture his boss's exasperated frown as he weighed the options. On the one hand, the *maresciallo* was losing the use of one of his men and would eventually have to account to his own superiors for Raffaele's unproductive time. Then again, this was a favor for a cardinal. Sooner or later the *maresciallo* would be able to call it in, thereby impressing his superiors with his Vatican entrée. Good personal connections with the Curia, outside the professionally cordial relationship the Carabinieri were at pains to maintain with the Church, were no small advantage for an ambitious cop on the climb. Raffaele had seen how his own stock had risen in the *maresciallo*'s calculating eyes when his uncle was elevated to cardinal and brought to Rome. He found his boss's transparency amusing, but Raffaele was an ambitious cop, too. That he was a cardinal's nephew was nothing but luck, but he wasn't ashamed to take advantage of what it could bring him. His partner and senior, Giulio Aventino, always said police work was five percent doggedness, five percent luck, and ninety percent the skill to recognize and doggedly use the luck that came your way.

Of course, Giulio Aventino must be the reason the *maresciallo* was hesitating at all over Raffaele's instructions. The work Raffaele should have been doing right now, whether in the office or in the field, would naturally have fallen to his partner. Giulio, with his mustached hangdog face, dislike of paperwork, short temper with technology, and aversion to the Church, had no doubt been grousing nonstop for the past hour and a half about his missing sergeant. This would've been true if the *maresciallo* had given Raffaele the afternoon off to see the dentist; how much truer was it now, when Giulio was left to shoulder their mutual burden because Raffaele was running some nepotistic errand for a cardinal?

Finally the *maresciallo* growled into his ear, "Stay with it. Follow her."

Curia one, Giulio nothing. Raffaele grinned to himself. But his boss's vacillation, though short, had been just long enough to bring up another problem. "They're heading for the church."

"What church, Orsini? Where are you?"

"Sorry, sir. Santa Maria della Scala. In Trastevere."

"They're going in?"

"Yes, sir."

"And one's a priest?" Another moment of thought, much more brief. "Don't go in after them. All we've been asked to do is to keep track of the woman. You sure it's her?"

"I have a photo."

"Well, whatever they're doing in there, they'll have to come out eventually. Wait for them. I don't want you barging into a church. It's always a nightmare even if a crime's been committed, and we don't know that one has. Besides," he added, "I

249

know Santa Maria della Scala. It's small enough that they might notice you."

Showing off, Raffaele thought, but the *maresciallo* couldn't see his smile and he said nothing.

"Just wait for them," his boss said again. "If they go back to that house, keep up your surveillance. If they go somewhere else, follow them, but, Orsini, keep trying your uncle. I want you back here sometime today. Aventino is driving us all mad."

29

Across the cobbled piazza, through the wrought-iron fence, and up the stairs. Not the *scala* for which the church was named; those had belonged to a nearby, long-ago-demolished house. There the miracle of an ill child's recovery had been granted to a mother praying to an icon in a stairway alcove. Thomas hadn't been to Santa Maria della Scala before, but he knew the story. He knew so many of his Church's stories.

The entry doors stood open. Thomas paused minutely and then stepped through as though he were any priest, in the company of any pair of historians, visiting any church in Rome. He felt acutely the presence of Livia Pietro beside him and that of Spencer George a few paces behind. Could they really enter a church? Step onto consecrated ground as easily as he could? A part of him expected — no, admit it, hoped — that they would be struck down at the threshold, reduced to dust and ashes for defiling the sanctified air. Though it was true his crucifix had had no effect. Nor had the mid-morning light in the piazza, any more than the glare of the early sun through which he'd raced with Livia Pietro from the Vatican Library, back in the good old days a few hours ago when he thought she was merely insane.

Livia Pietro followed him and Spencer George followed her and they all crossed the wooden sill and nothing happened. Resigned, Thomas turned through the vestibule to the right-side door. He pushed it open and stopped a few steps in at the marble font to dip his fingers into the holy water and cross himself, perhaps a bit more fervently than usual. He was horrified by the idea that Pietro or Spencer George, as an element of subterfuge, might attempt to do the same. But maybe they couldn't? Maybe contact with holy water would do to them what the sight of a crucifix had not? Maybe they'd melt, and sizzle, and — **Stop it,** he ordered himself, **you sound like a Dominican.** Pietro looked at the font, at him, smiled slightly, and shook her head. Spencer George passed the font without a glance.

Thomas, behind them now, found himself

blinking in the dimness. He squinted to adjust his eyes while Pietro slipped off her sunglasses and seemed quite comfortable. Spencer George had also donned shades and hat as they left his house, even for the brief walk across the piazza. It must be habitual with them. Every time they go outdoors, the way a real person, a human person, puts on clothes. Thomas suddenly flashed on a college friend, an affable physicist who wore photosensitive glasses, their lenses darkening automatically at the first touch of bright light. . . . And a baseball cap, the physicist was rarely seen without his baseball cap . . . No. It couldn't be.

Thomas shuddered that thought off. He couldn't bear, suddenly, the close presence of the two Noantri. He strode along the center aisle toward the altar. Of course they followed. What had he expected? To avoid the sight of them, Thomas looked up, down, around. Santa Maria della Scala was itself a miracle, though a common enough miracle in Rome: its sedate, slightly crumbling façade opened from a small, dark entry into an interior well kept, grand, and imposing. A patterned stone floor — incorporating, as in so many churches, gravestones, identifying the dead who slept beneath your feet — polished wood pews, a soaring vaulted ceiling supported on marble columns; and everywhere, art. None of it, on first glance, exceptional, but its profusion making up for its lack of distinction. Paintings, frescoes, sculpture, gilded candlesticks. Crystal chandeliers over the altar and side chapels, the gift of some pious — or guilt-ridden — nineteenth-century worshipper. They struck an odd note, the chandeliers. But every church had its own oddnesses, its own eccentricities. Its own secrets.

They had come here to find one of those secrets. Father Thomas Kelly, SJ, and two vampires. Thomas felt his composure hanging by a thread.

He stopped at the altar rail, and the other two stopped beside him. "What do we do now?" Thomas spoke not out of hope of an answer, but to keep himself from losing hold.

"I think we were anticipating you'd take the lead from this point, Father Kelly," Spencer George replied. He had, Thomas noted, removed his hat. Anger flared in Thomas at the hypocrisy of the gesture.

"Just how do you expect me to do that? I didn't know Mario Damiani. I've never been in this church before. I first heard of the Concordat just a few days ago and I can't tell you how dearly I wish I never had!"

"Father." Livia Pietro spoke softly, laying a hand on his sleeve. She nodded toward two old women lighting candles in a side chapel.

Thomas pulled back from her touch and dropped his voice to a sarcastic whisper. "Of course, we mustn't disturb the faithful. I know how that upsets you."

Spencer George rolled his eyes. Pietro said, "Actually, it does. I was raised in the same Church you were and I think faith is a precious thing, to be protected wherever it's found. But I know you don't believe that of me and I'm not asking you to. I'm suggesting that you focus on the reason we're here."

Thomas stared at her for a long moment. Then he blew out a breath and looked around helplessly.

Santa Maria della Scala had nave and transept, it had side chapels and high windows. Great bouquets of flowers had greeted them at the church entry with still more standing in the side chapels and others flanking the altar. Because Mass had recently ended, thick incense hung heavy in the air, threading its scent through that of the flowers. What footsteps and soft words were to be heard did not disturb the peaceful hush common to so many churches. It was all comforting and familiar, and

Thomas thought he felt a faint echo of his old sense of home.

But as to a hiding place for a six-hundred-year-old document that detailed a satanic bargain, he could think of none.

"This church," Spencer George said. "What's special about it?"

"You live across the piazza from it! You should know it much better than I do!"

"Really, Father? How much time do you imagine I've spent here? What is it you're thinking I would do if I came? Kneel and pray?"

"No, I can see there'd be no point. Even prayer can't save your mortgaged soul!"

"Then why would I come?"

"Spencer?" Pietro said, speaking to the historian but throwing Thomas a disapproving glance. "Did Mario come here?"

Spencer George unlocked his gaze slowly from Thomas's and looked to Pietro. He nodded. "He loved them all, these little churches. Loved them as art and as history. Once or twice I came inside this one with him. It had always been one of his particular favorites, and he became even more strongly attached to it during the Rebellion because it served as a field hospital for Garibaldi's troops. Mario was an officer in the war against papal power, you know." Spencer

George looked pointedly at Thomas again. Thomas bit his lip and refused to rise to the bait. "Mario's mission," George went on, "the mission he'd given himself, was to take these little jewels back from the stranglehold of the Church and return them to aesthetics and to true spiritual meaning."

"True spiritual meaning?" Thomas hissed, finally unable to contain himself. "As though there were some question? Of the spiritual meaning of a church?"

"As it happens I agree with you. I thought his whole project was absurd. I've spent nearly three centuries in Rome avoiding every church I could."

"You'd have done better —"

"Father? Maybe we can have this conversation later?" As she spoke, Livia Pietro looked back up the center aisle. An elderly monk moved stiffly toward them, his cinctured tan habit whispering. Pietro and George smiled in greeting. Thomas struggled to do the same.

"Buongiorno, Padre," the monk greeted Thomas.

"Buongiorno, Padre," Thomas replied. He continued in Italian, "I'm Thomas Kelly. From Boston. This is Dr. Pietro and — Dr. George. They're historians. As I am," he added.

"Giovanni Battista. Welcome to Santa Maria della Scala." The monk's thin hands were misshapen by arthritis, and his voice rattled with an old-man quaver.

"Thank you," Pietro replied politely. Spencer George murmured some noncommittal courtesy, also, though Thomas could swear his lip was curled. Pietro continued diffidently, "We've come here as part of a project. We're studying the art and history of Trastevere's churches. Each church is unique in some way and we're very interested in seeing the special pieces here."

Father Battista's thin smile told Thomas the monk was well aware of his church's relative lack of artistic riches. Nevertheless, he answered, "Then I'm sure you'll want to see the icon of Our Lady, that holy painting that cured the child. It's in the transept altar, on this side." Without waiting for an answer, he turned to lead the way. Not knowing what else to do, Thomas started after him, peering around, hoping for — what? A ray of heavenly light to strike a painting, an angelic chorus to sing as he passed a piece of sculpture? He walked behind Father Battista, surveying the sanctuary, listening distractedly to the monk's sandals slapping softly on the stone.

Sandals.

Father Battista was a Discalced Carmelite. Discalced. Shoeless.

"Shoeless" meaning in sandals, not bare-foot. They didn't go barefoot.

But they and their order's founder, Saint Teresa of Avila, were often portrayed that way. Even Bernini's celebrated sculpture of Saint Teresa depicted one bare foot peeking from under her robe.

the humblest of steps . . .
right foot then left, that leads the soul . . .

"The relic!" Thomas burst out.

The monk stopped and turned. "Father?"

"The relic," Thomas repeated, stopping also. He brought his voice under control, which could not be said of his racing heart. "Santa Teresa. It's here, isn't it? I'd like very much to see the relic."

Spencer George furrowed his brow. Livia Pietro gave Thomas a quizzical look, but Thomas kept his eyes on Father Battista.

A new interest softened the monk's lined face. "I have to admit that's a pleasant change," he said. "The veneration of relics is out of fashion lately." He gave Thomas a tentatively commiserating smile. Thomas returned it, though "lately" in this case was a relative term: the change dated from 1965,

259

one of the results of the Second Vatican Council. That was before Thomas was born, so he'd come into a religious life that followed the Council's precepts; but the elderly Father Battista had been a young man then, Thomas realized. He wondered if the monk had already taken his vows by the time the Council met. And whether, if young Giovanni Battista had known what changes were coming, he'd have entered holy orders all the same. And if he knew what Thomas knew now? About Thomas's companions, about the Concordat's corrupt bargain? How would he feel about his Holy Mother Church then?

". . . quite a shame," Father Battista was saying. Thomas forced his attention back to the monk. "Communion with the corporeal remains of a departed saint creates an atmosphere for prayer different from any other. It brings the worshipper into an intimate relationship with sanctity. It offers an immediacy that's otherwise much more difficult to reach."

Indeed, Thomas thought. **I've heard that speech before.** Father Battista could spend a pleasant evening over cigars and brandy with Lorenzo, discussing the mistaken direction in which the Church was headed. They could talk about relics and the Latin Mass, the apostolic calling, nuns discarding their habits. Father Battista might not even care that all Lorenzo's piety was a lie.

A lie with which Thomas would never have the opportunity to confront Lorenzo — not in human form, anyway — unless he found the Concordat.

"Yes," he said to Father Battista, nodding as though in earnest agreement. "I'd like very much to see the relic."

30

"What relic is your priest dragging us off to see?" Spencer whispered to Livia as the old monk led them down the side aisle.

"I have no idea. Or why."

She watched Father Battista and Father Kelly walk side by side a few steps ahead, a young man and an old one, sharing the same piety, the same comprehension of the world. Father Kelly's faith had been shaken by what he'd learned today, but Livia expected — she hoped — he'd recover his equilibrium. She'd meant what she told him: she did believe faith was a precious thing. Her own was more complex than his; she wasn't sure at all that that was a good thing, but it was a truth there was no point in denying.

She'd been raised to believe in the same God Thomas Kelly did, though she'd never been as ardent as he. Since her Change, she'd pondered often the question of a deity and also of an afterlife. As she'd told Father Kelly, Noantri could die, though she had not been completely forthcoming with him on that subject: of the three ways death could come to a Noantri, she'd described only two. What she'd said about fire was true, though, and she'd been just half-joking when she'd reassured him that they'd all be devoured when the sun flared out. What then? On that large subject, she'd come to no conclusions. But she was sure of three things.

One was that she could think of no reason why a benevolent God, Thomas Kelly's God, could not be credited with creating the microbe that Blessed the Noantri with their long, rich lives. Thomas Kelly saw the microbe, and the Noantri, as evil. The Unchanged always had, and through the millennia when the Noantri's need for blood nourishment had made them an imminent threat, that view had been understandable. It wasn't true any more than evil accounted for a cat killing a mouse; but you could see the mouse's point. Which led Livia to her second article of faith: that the Concordat was an unqualified good.

The explanation Cardinal Cossa had given Thomas Kelly of how the Concordat came to be was no more the full story than Livia's account of the death of a Noantri had been. It was true as far as it went and so was the history she'd added for him in Spencer's study, but there was more she knew and hadn't told him. And there was a secret at the heart of the Concordat's story that she didn't know. That Martin the Fifth had seen the advantages of ending the Church's virulent and everlasting assault on the Noantri was true enough; but at the time of the Concordat, before Community, before the Law, the Noantri were a fragmented, furtive people. Calling a halt to the hunting, the persecution, was one thing, and would have permitted Martin to concentrate his strength on pressing matters of consolidating papal power. But to sign an agreement with her people, committing the Church to obligations in perpetuity? As a group, in 1431, the Noantri had commanded neither strength nor wealth enough to put in Martin's service in exchange. Why had he done it? And why had the Church continued to abide by it through six centuries?

Possibly the answer to that last question was simple: peace was peace. Even early on, it might have been clear to Church fathers that once the Concordat was signed, the Noantri ceased being a danger. Thus the

Church could turn its attention elsewhere.

As to the larger question, though, Livia had pondered it often, but had come to accept the fact that she did not, probably would never, have an answer. That knowledge was accorded to no Unchanged save the highest ranks of the Church, and to no Noantri outside the Conclave. Ultimately, though, it didn't matter. Whatever had brought the Concordat into being was itself a Blessing.

But though most of the Unchanged didn't know the Concordat existed at all, and the Noantri knew it only insofar as they were required to follow its provisions, the third thing Livia was sure of was that the life she and her people were able to lead because of the Concordat, the life she had come into when she'd Changed, the life so rich and full they had come to think of it as Blessed, was only possible if the agreement was faithfully kept by both parties.

Jonah refused to accept this truth, but he was wrong. And only if she found the lost copy of the Concordat and delivered it to the Conclave did he have any chance of living long enough to understand that.

31

Jorge Ocampo rose quietly from his knees. He waited a few moments and then passed between the pews to the left aisle of the church. The little group he'd slipped into the church to watch had been joined by an old monk and, after a false start in the other direction, was heading beyond the apse. He needed to keep them in view, but not to get too close. Right now the length of the church and the perfume of flowers and incense were keeping the *professoressa* from noticing him. If he were careful, if he were stealthy, that wouldn't change. He hoped the group was planning to view a piece of art or inspect something in one of the side chapels and then leave. When they turned toward the door he'd slip back outside, and as soon as they came out he'd grab the notebook and race around the corner to his *motorino.* He'd bring Anna the notebook and she'd see he was, he truly was, the man for the job.

His only worry was that they were on their way to the church offices, or even worse, to the Carmelite cloister behind Santa Maria itself. How he'd follow them then, he wasn't sure, but he'd find a way. This time, nothing was going to stop him from recovering that notebook for his Anna.

32

Thomas walked beside Father Battista, slowing his own pace to allow for the old man's painfully arthritic steps. What he wanted to do was break into a run, but that would startle the women by the candles, and a young man praying in a rear pew. Not to mention the monk. It wasn't likely that anyone, no matter how devout, had ever raced through Santa Maria della Scala to reach the church's relic.

He'd heard Spencer George's whisper to Livia Pietro. Neither of them had any idea what he was thinking and he didn't enlighten them. Let their preternatural Noantri senses find them an answer. If he was right, he'd be free of them in any case, after this.

An upholstered wooden kneeler stood at a gap in the stone railing, blocking the entrance to a side chapel where a high marble altar rose. "The Reliquary Chapel is through there." Father Battista pointed to the right, at an openwork gate in the chapel's wall. "It's visited rarely now, and we're very few here. We keep it locked."

"I appreciate your willingness to open it for me, Father," Thomas said.

"Certainly." The old monk made to roll the kneeler aside, but Thomas hurried forward to do it. At the gate to the Reliquary Chapel, under a pair of gold angels, Father Battista hoisted a jingling key ring, selected the proper key, and turned the heavy lock.

Thomas followed the monk into a small, high-ceilinged chapel where light glowed through stained glass windows to the left and right of the altar. John of the Cross and Saint Teresa. Paintings adorned the walls, but Thomas barely gave them a glance. Ahead, behind a low stone railing, was the reason he was here. On a marble altar, a flight of solemn gold angels supported a glass-doored case, perhaps eighteen inches high. Inside it, another glass-fronted box stood on golden lion's legs. This was the reliquary itself.

Inside it rested the severed right foot of Saint Teresa.

Thomas's heart beat faster. This must be it, what Damiani meant. Foot, trek, steps — it was all here. The two Noantri exchanged glances but Thomas ignored them. He became aware that the old monk was watching his face.

"Father, would you like to be alone to pray?"

Conscious that his relief and excitement had been mistaken for devotion, and conscious also that he was about to lie to a monk in a consecrated chapel in front of a saint's relic, Thomas answered, "Yes, Father, thank you. I would."

33

Father Giovanni Battista left the Reliquary Chapel, smiling at the sound of the gate behind him clicking shut. It had been a long time — years, he thought, though his clouded memory might be muddling things again, but in any case, a long time — since he'd seen that glow in a visitor's eyes at the sight of the relic of Santa Teresa, that holy object with which he and his brothers were entrusted. He chided himself for his instinctive, mistaken dismissal of this trio. He'd assumed they were interested in Santa Maria della Scala only as art and as history. He'd supposed they'd come to see the icon, as visitors usually did. But three historians, on a project to study churches, what could he be expected to think? The young priests from America were usually the worst, too, taking pride in their own sophistication, their cynicism and worldly-wise ways. And Jesuits! Everything was reason and learning with the Jesuits. In his experience — and his experience was long; though his memory was often too foggy to detail that experience, the existence of the fog itself proved the years were there — Jesuits had no interest in mysticism, cared nothing for those rare, longed-for, and inexplicable ecstatic moments that had made Father Battista's life worth living.

Carmelite monks devoted themselves equally to meditation and service. Giovanni Battista had always considered it one of his own many failings that, though he tried his best to be diligent when performing his pastoral tasks, such as guiding visitors through Santa Maria, he much preferred the solitary, silent hours of contemplation and prayer. Vatican II, which had issued its directives nine years after Giovanni had taken his vows, had greatly disappointed him. The changes, all in the direction of secularization, had been in aid of bringing the Church nearer the flock. In Giovanni's view, this was a great mistake. The Church should be the City of Gold high on Saint Peter's rock: unattainable, but always the glowing goal to strive toward. It was the flock that needed to be helped to come nearer the Church.

But these historians, what a pleasant

surprise. He'd thought only the priest would want to pause in the chapel and pray, but the woman — yes, he knew they'd been introduced, but there was no point in trying to remember her name — had given Father Battista a warm smile and a big thank-you. Such lovely, kind eyes! She'd told him he had no idea how much this meant to all of them, and even the supercilious older gent — older compared with the other two, of course just a pup to Giovanni — had nodded and smiled, also. The priest had seemed a little surprised at his companions himself, but such is the power of the Holy Spirit. Giovanni left them to it.

A warm glow filled him when he thought of the quiet delight with which his brothers would receive this story at the evening collation. Imagine: even Americans, even Jesuits, could still catch one unawares.

With a new spring in his crotchety old bones, Giovanni Battista strode forward to greet the thin young man approaching down the aisle.

34

"Don't look so dismayed, Father," Livia said to Thomas Kelly, turning from the chapel door to face the priest.

"Well, he's disappointed," Spencer said. "He was hoping to have the relic all to himself."

"I'm the one who thought of it," Thomas Kelly snapped.

"Oh, yes, and very clever of you," Spencer acknowledged. "All those feet and steps of Mario's?"

"This is the severed limb of a saint," the priest said coldly. "Teresa of Avila. She founded the Carmelite order."

"Yes, now I remember Mario telling me about it. This chapel was locked when we came, though, so he couldn't show it to me. As it was just now. A lovely bit of subterfuge you used to get us in, by the way. Wanting to pray. My compliments."

The priest stepped forward, fists clenched.

Livia couldn't blame him, and it would almost be worth letting him take a swing at Spencer just to see the look on Spencer's face. But she put up her hand. "Father Battista's not going to leave us alone in here forever. Spencer, do you think it's possible this is the place Mario wanted you to find?"

"Oh, very likely. It's right up his street. The double meanings in the poem, plus the quirky oddness of worshipping desiccated body parts — oh, no offense, Father."

Spencer clearly meant to give offense and Thomas Kelly equally clearly took it, but to the priest's credit, he remained silent. "The chance he took," Spencer continued, "was to imagine I remembered anything at all about what this church contained. That was a mistake. If I had, though, yes, I'd have come straight to this little room."

Livia turned to the priest. "Father Kelly? Now that we're in this chapel" — to make up for Spencer's "little room" — "what are you thinking?"

Thomas Kelly didn't answer her. After a glare at Spencer, he turned and strode through the gap in the altar rail, where he stood looking up at the pair of golden boxes, one inside the other. With a sharp glance Livia pinned Spencer to his spot on the marble floor. Spencer shrugged and re-

275

mained where he was as she followed the priest.

The reliquary's glass front was answered by worked gold panels on the sides and, as far as Livia could see, at the back. The box stood on its raised lion's legs, while inside, its leathery, shrunken, jewel-studded treasure wore a golden sandal and rested on a velvet cloth.

Thomas Kelly hesitated. Stretching his arm, he was just able to reach the bottom of the outer box. He hooked his fingers under the gold frame and tried to pull it open, but it didn't give. He turned to Livia, the set of his shoulder conveying, equally, failure and triumph. "It's locked."

She stepped up. "Let me try."

"I just told you. It's locked."

"And I didn't tell you, but I can open it." She slipped a probe from the zippered pocket of her shoulder bag, plus a nail file to use as a shim. Handing the bag to Spencer, she appraised the high altar and then set herself and jumped. A five-foot vertical leap from a standing start was not an everyday feat even for a Noantri, but Livia was strong and she was motivated. She landed lightly on the marble, to the priest's horrified gasp and Spencer's laughing, "Brava!" She took out her tools and had the flimsy lock open before the priest found words to express his horror.

Spencer was still laughing when she pulled the glass door wide. "Livia! I had no idea."

Livia looked down at Thomas Kelly. "Father?"

His eyes widened. "Me? What do you — Come up there? Onto the reliquary altar? No, no possible way."

"Shall I bring it down, then?"

"No! Don't touch it!" Kelly glanced wildly around. He spied a heavy, brocaded chair near the wall, used by the celebrant while hymns were sung during Mass. He dragged it over and stepped onto it. She extended a hand to help him but he placed his palms flat on the altar and swung himself up with surprising athletic grace.

Standing beside her on the narrow marble shelf, he gave her a resentful glance and then shifted his attention to the reliquary itself. After a moment he said, "See those scrolls inside?" She leaned nearer to look. "They're authentications, blessings, prayers. Maybe Damiani rolled up the Concordat and slipped it in with them. No one ever looks at those scrolls, once they're placed with a relic."

Livia peered skeptically at the beribboned, wax-sealed papers. "I don't think that's likely. They're very small. The Concordat . . . But let's look at them. I imagine you'd prefer to handle them yourself?"

"I certainly would!" She stood aside, letting him be the one to test whether the reliquary was locked, which it wasn't; to ease open the front panel; and to slip out the five scrolls, fastidiously avoiding the saint's foot itself. He stared at the delicate cylinders; then, looking pale, he set his jaw and untied the ribbons and broke the sealing wax scroll by scroll. His face fell as he scanned each and put it aside, until they were all opened and read.

"I'm wrong," he finally said, deflated. "It's not here."

Livia glanced over the scrolls, all in Latin and none anything other than what it purported to be.

From below, Spencer spoke. "No," he said, "this is just too Mario to be wrong." Raising his eyebrows at Livia, he took a step forward. "May I join you up there?"

"No, you may not!" Kelly snapped.

Spencer sighed. "Then you do it. See if there's anything stuck up under the top. Not underfoot, you see. Overhead."

After a moment, with great care, the priest reached inside and felt around the peaked gold cover. He stopped still. Seconds later he drew his hand out again. In it was a single sheet of paper, folded small and yellowed with age.

35

Raffaele Orsini sighed. He hated surveillance. Giulio Aventino didn't seem to mind when they had to sit for hours in a parked car or on a park bench, waiting for someone to appear or something to happen. Raffaele always found it painful, though he was grateful that right now he at least had a chair and a coffee.

To be fair, he had nothing against idling his time away in a café. Before their children were born, he and Elena had spent many pleasant hours over coffee and the morning *La Repubblica.* Even in the past few very busy years they'd made it a point to spend time together doing nothing in languid indolence. The trouble with surveillance was that to do it right you needed to look languid and indolent, while being anything but. Raffaele had found — Giulio had taught him, give the man his due — that often the vital information a surveillance yields comes from some event that takes place before the subject is spotted. It was important to note all comings and goings, to remember faces and clothes, cars and license plates, while lounging lazily and being bored to tears.

Automatically, partly to sharpen his skills of observation and partly to keep his mind from wandering, Raffaele, since he'd arrived, had been cataloging the people crossing the piazza, his fellow café guests, the infrequent cars, and the buzzing *motorini.* Since his subject, the dark-haired woman, had left the house and entered Santa Maria della Scala he'd been particularly focused on visitors coming and going from the church. There had been very few, just four laughing Americans with cameras and one skinny young man who'd been moping in that very café, a few tables over. The signs of lovesickness in him were unmistakable. He'd probably gone to pray to the Virgin to solve his romance problems. The Americans had come out already, consulting guidebooks and wandering away. Raffaele was confident he could describe them all if need be, equally sure he'd never be called upon to do so, and proud of the professionalism with which he committed them to memory just the same. He was wondering idly how many more people besides his surveillance subjects and the skinny young man were actually inside the church when a frantic old woman came out screaming.

36

With fingers he had to order to stop trembling, Thomas unfolded the paper he'd discovered wedged up into the reliquary's roof. It was a small, single sheet, but until he'd flattened it completely, he held on to hope that he'd found the Concordat. Once he opened the last crease, though, that hope was gone.

Still, there could be no question that this paper was what they'd been sent here for.

It was another poem.

"Oh, my God," Spencer George breathed, staring up at the paper in Thomas's hand. Thomas didn't even bother to rebuke him for his blasphemy. "Mario, Mario," George whispered. "What were you up to?"

Livia Pietro leaned over the unfolded poem to examine it. She began to speak, but before she could, she and Spencer George both snapped their heads up.

"What?" said Thomas. "What's happening?"

Pietro shushed him. She stood still, listening, and then even Thomas heard it: a distant shrieking coming from outside the church. Pietro turned to him. "Replace those. We need to close these boxes."

"Those?" For a moment Thomas was lost. Then he realized she meant the prayers, the supplications of devout worshippers to the saint. Of course. What good would prayer do him now, in any case? Thomas slipped the scrolls back into the reliquary and shut the front. He swung the larger door closed, also, and, with the poem still in hand, jumped down. Pietro followed. He replaced the chair he'd climbed up on while Pietro stood still, frowning in concentration. Finally she spoke low. "He's here! The clerk. The incense, the candles — they're confusing me. But I think he's here."

"By 'clerk,' " asked Spencer George, "you mean the Noantri from the Vatican Library?"

Pietro nodded and Thomas demanded, "But what happened? Who's screaming?"

"I don't know. Be quiet." She tilted her head down, seeming to concentrate. "I don't know," she repeated. "But something bad's — Oh, no. Police."

"Gendarmes?"

"No. Carabinieri. Just came inside. Only one, but he's on his radio. He's called an ambulance."

"We have to see what's wrong." Thomas started for the gate.

"Excuse me, Father, but are you insane?" Spencer George stepped in front of him.

"I'm a priest. I might be able to help."

"You're not a doctor, I think? Believe me, if whatever happened needs a priest, they'll have no trouble finding one here."

"We can't just —"

"Father," Pietro said. "We have to. This poem. It must be sending us somewhere else. It's from the notebook, did you see that?"

Thomas looked again at the unfolded sheet in his hand. Paper, ink, and handwriting, all the same. Something else, too, something added in graphite pencil beneath the inked poem: a row of letters. Thomas had no idea what they meant but it was clear Pietro was right. This leaf had been ripped from Damiani's notebook, too.

"It's sending us somewhere else," she repeated.

"Ah." Chuckling, Spencer George snapped his fingers. "Of course. For one thing, there's the matter of the missing leaves. There are seven of them, not just one." Thomas thought about the implications of this as the historian went on. "For another, Mario never did things by halves. Once he'd hidden something as important as the Concordat, he'd make sure it was difficult to find."

The two Noantri froze again and this time Thomas heard what they had: the two-note howl of an approaching siren. No: more than one siren. The ambulance and more police.

"Livia," said Spencer George, "you and the priest must leave." He handed over her shoulder bag. "Whatever happened, if it's important enough for a herd of Carabinieri, you don't want to get tangled up with them. I'll stay and if the subject comes up I'll explain that you two are long gone. And the clerk — he must have followed you. He'll need to be diverted, also."

"You said he'd been arrested." Thomas glared at Livia. "If he'd been arrested he couldn't have —"

"Yes, he could." Pietro dismissed Thomas, turned to George. "Spencer, we need you. Damiani's poems. You might know —"

George was shaking his head. "I told you, I hadn't seen any of them. They'd be as new to me as they will be to you. You know more about the churches of Trastevere than I do. Most importantly, you're the one charged by the Conclave with retrieving the lost Concordat. You, and your priest."

"I'm not her priest!" Thomas snapped. "And short of a little lock-picking and thievery, which they won't be looking for, what do we have to worry about? Why don't we just go out there, tell them we were back in here and don't know anything about whatever it is that went on, and —"

George waved Thomas silent. "If something dire has really happened, this church will be closed down. The authorities will interview everyone here and your search could be delayed for hours. Time, according to both of you for your different reasons, is critical. Your situation, Father, I'm sorry to say, doesn't move me, but I'm quite fond of Livia and I hate to think of the consequences to her if she does not succeed." He looked at them both. "Go now, before they — and that clerk — find you."

"And how are we supposed to get out?" Thomas demanded. "Tip-toe up a side aisle while you distract them with a juggling act in the nave?"

"That does sound like fun. But I'm sure there's a more sensible way." He looked up at the high, thin windows. Thomas followed his gaze. Neither John of the Cross nor Saint Teresa looked as if they'd moved on their hinges in five hundred years.

A bell began to toll in the monastery behind the church. It was a single note, repeated and clanging: not a call to prayer, but a declaration of calamity.

"Yes!" said Pietro suddenly. "Yes, there's another way. Father, come."

Thomas stood rooted to the stone floor. His eyes met Pietro's. A second of stillness, nothing but the tolling: then in a flash Pietro snatched the poem from his hand and stuffed it in her shoulder bag. "Come with me. Or stay here with Spencer and at least buy me some time."

Stay with Spencer George, swear to whatever sneering lies he was going to tell? While Lorenzo's only chance at mortal life — and natural death, and the eternal blessed rest that followed upon that — vanished with this creature? As Livia Pietro slipped out of the Reliquary Chapel and behind the nave screen that separated cloistered monks from parishioners, Thomas sped after her.

37

Giulio Aventino couldn't decide whether to sigh in frustration, snarl in anger, or give in to a satisfied grin. He settled on the grin as he piloted his Fiat through the Trastevere traffic. His dominant emotion at the moment, he had to admit, was smugness. He'd come back to the station to find his sergeant, the well-heeled and pious Raffaele Orsini, out doing the bidding of his cardinal uncle. Not entirely Raffaele's fault, of course: he'd quite properly taken the Cardinal's request to the *maresciallo*. Everything Raffaele did was quite proper. The boss, obviously seeing visions of himself on the Vatican's IOU list, had dispatched Raffaele to sit in a café watching someone the Cardinal, for some secret Vatican reason, wanted watched. Giulio didn't care about the Vatican and its secrets and he wouldn't have given a damn, except that he did.

Two damns.

Damn the *maresciallo* for sending Raffaele out on, basically, an extended coffee break, and thereby sticking Giulio with the mountain of unfiled witness reports on a case he and Raffaele had closed last week.

And damn the Vatican for thinking it could call at any time and the Carabinieri would jump because it said to.

No, three damns.

Damn the Vatican again, for being right.

Still, neither the Vatican's secrets nor the *maresciallo*'s naked ambition nor even the shorts-clad, bottled-water-slugging tourists ambling through the streets as though any car they ignored couldn't hit them quite pierced Giulio's satisfaction. Raffaele's little café break had turned, right under the sergeant's patrician nose, into a homicide. News of which had made the apoplectic *maresciallo* explode from his office and order Giulio Aventino to Santa Maria della Scala immediately, posthaste, and soonest, to go see how much of the situation he could salvage.

The boss, Giulio had noted, and here's where the satisfaction had begun, had showered a few damns of his own on the absent person of Raffaele Orsini.

38

Thomas Kelly was right on her heels as Livia slipped behind the carved wooden screen to the far side of the apse, then through the blue folds of a velvet curtain and around a chapel to an unremarkable door against the far wall. Anyone might think, she reflected, that people made a habit of slinking around Santa Maria della Scala without being seen. Of course, since an order of cloistered friars had lived here for six hundred years, they probably did. The lock on the door was easy and Thomas Kelly, though he tsk'ed in obvious unhappiness when she picked it, had the sense not to speak until it was closed again and they were on the other side.

"What now?" he demanded in a whisper, glancing at a staircase that led up into dimness. "This doesn't look like a way out."

"No. We need to work out what this poem means before we go anywhere. This is a place where we won't be disturbed."

"What happened to 'you and your priest must leave'?"

"I'm not the one who said that. Look, Spencer can be hard to take, I know. But he has a marvelous mind and he's a loyal friend. And his work has been very important to the Noantri." At that the priest scowled. Without knowing why — did she really think Thomas Kelly would ever feel kindly toward her and her people? And did it matter if he did? — Livia went on, "Spencer studies the history of the Noantri, of our people. It's an odd thing, to have lives as long as ours but no sense of continuity *as a people,* no shared history, until a few hundred years ago. I could introduce you to Noantri who rode with Genghis Khan or sailed with Christopher Columbus. Others who helped build the Pyramids, Machu Picchu, the Great Wall of China. Each of them, for centuries, knew only that he was different from those around him. Knew only guilt and fear as he tried to satisfy hungers over which he had no control. Each knew only his own story, do you understand? Since the Concordat it's been possible for us to try to bring our stories together. That's Spencer's work: to help us begin to understand who we are as a people."

She stopped abruptly, feeling her cheeks grow hot. She'd never spoken to any of the Unchanged about her people's history and yearnings, the power of their need for connection, the relief and joy of Community. The few Unchanged outside the inner ranks of the Church who knew about their existence, and the even fewer who were considered friends, were nevertheless rarely presented with any evidence of Noantri misgiving, unhappiness, or doubt.

Livia brushed past Thomas Kelly and started up the curving stone stairs, though she noted as she did that his aversion seemed to have been neutralized, however briefly, by interest, as the scholar in him considered what she'd said.

She led the way up to a landing with a window in the left-side wall and glass-doored cabinets to the right. On the shelves stood ranks of bottles of red, blue, and amber liquids. Most bore labels describing the contents — *Perle della Saggezza, Tonico del Missionario* — in precise and fading script, though on a few of the more recent ones the labels were the work of that at-the-time cutting-edge technology, the manual typewriter. Livia briefly left Thomas Kelly to his surprised inspection of the shelves and worked on the lock on the door between the cabinets. Kelly didn't cluck his tongue this time, though he did catch his breath when she got the door open and they walked into the room beyond.

What had taken him by surprise was not, Livia knew, the trompe l'oeil drapery or the aged wooden counter, not the Murano glass bottles or the ceramic jars with their bright painted lids. This was the eighth or ninth time Livia had been in this room, and the glorious aroma that greeted a visitor as the door creaked back was one of the reasons to keep returning.

Thomas Kelly stood in awe, as most first-time visitors did, though Livia knew he couldn't parse the wave of scent as finely as she could: sweet columbine and spicy goldenrod, the faint rankness of deer's antlers and the astringent bite of arsenic. And so many, many more: the air was a tapestry of olfactory threads, thick and thin, sharp and soft, bile-bitter and honey-sweet. Over two hundred herbs, flowers, leaves and barks, fruit essences and tree saps, ground minerals, cracked bones, and crumbled earths were stored in this room, in drawers, in jars, and in bottles, waiting.

"What is this place?" Kelly breathed.

"The old pharmacy, from the fifteenth century."

"Is it still in use?"

"Not since 1954."

"But it looks so complete. So . . . ready."

She shook her head. "When it closed, the last apothecary monks just locked the door and walked away. Their order had been pharmacists to the Popes for six hundred years. I think they didn't really believe they'd never be called on again."

Now Kelly turned to her. "You think. You knew those monks, didn't you? In 1954. You were here."

Livia faced him, calmly but squarely. "I'd moved away for a time, before the Second World War. We have to, every now and then, no matter how committed we may be to our hometowns. We stay away for years and change our identities before we return. We call it 'Cloaking.' It's our own kind of internal exile, and it's hard on us. But yes, by then I was back."

Once again, she'd told him more than she'd meant to. She braced for his shudder, even a curled lip of disgust; but to her surprise, they didn't come. Nor did a kind smile, or sympathetic eyes, but those would have been too much to ask. Kelly just nodded, as though an academic hypothesis had been confirmed, and returned his gaze to the room.

Above the counter where the apothecary friars had traded herbs and elixirs for customers' coins, a painted angel peered over the trompe l'oeil curtains. He was there, a monk had once told her, to ensure honest dealing.

39

Jorge Ocampo was running like the wind. He shouldn't, he knew. Anna said he must never let the Unchanged see the extent of his Noantri abilities. Their minds were small and they would get frightened; they would shun him, perhaps even attack him, if they felt him to be vastly different from themselves. She assured him they couldn't harm him if they did attack: any pain would be transitory, and in the centuries since the Concordat the Unchanged had lost the understanding of the effects of fire. Still, she said, if Jorge were to arouse suspicion, he would become less valuable to her. That was an alarming thought, but still he sped around the corner at Vicolo del Piede until he reached his goal: the abandoned cinema. The startled gasps as he raced past (*"Madonna! Did you see that guy?"*) would reduce his value to Anna less, he was sure, than being identified as the man responsible for what had happened in Santa Maria della Scala.

The old theater sagged and creaked in the shade of the vines that colonized its flanks. That Vicolo del Piede was never busy was one of the reasons Jorge had chosen this place for his private hideaway. Even Anna didn't know he came here. The street was empty now, as usual, no one to see him leap onto a sill and slip through a half-open window.

Immediately, as it always did, the still darkness of the derelict interior quieted Jorge's heart. His Noantri eyes adjusted immediately to the low light that seeped through the few filthy, cracked windows, but even if they hadn't that would have been all right; he knew every inch of this theater. No films had been shown at Il Pasquino for a decade, but as so often happened in Rome, though the building was now useless it had not been demolished. It had merely been abandoned, as those who'd loved it had moved on to something new.

Anna. He had to call Anna. What would he say? He had to tell her the truth, but he so dreaded her inevitable fury — Anna could detonate with an incendiary heat, just like an Argentinian girl — that though he forced himself to take out his cell phone, he couldn't, for a moment, go further. He gripped the phone tightly and sat where he always did: third row, right side, on the aisle, the seat he'd taken every chance he'd had at any of the movie houses on Avenida Corrientes, back home. Before he'd gotten involved with his brothers of La Guerra Sucia, before he'd met Anna and become part of an even bigger revolutionary movement, Jorge's happiest hours had been spent in the dark theaters of Buenos Aires. Even with the torn upholstery and the spiders and the musty smell, even with no film to watch on the ripped and mildewed screen, Jorge felt more at home in Il Pasquino than anywhere else in Rome.

Oh, how he wanted to go home. He yearned for the day when Anna's plans were accomplished and they could fly off to Argentina, finally together, with only each other to think about. Anna would always be concerned with the welfare of the Noantri, of course, and he would always support her in her efforts on behalf of her people. *Their* people! How many times had she reprimanded him, reminded him that he was Noantri, too, now and forever? But once the last obstacle to Noantri rule had been removed, he and Anna would be free to change their priorities, to trade this necessary work of freedom fighting for the joy of each other's arms.

And though he'd made a bad mistake today, Anna would know how to fix it. She'd give him new instructions, he'd carry them out faithfully, and her plans would not really be disrupted. They'd continue on their path to victory, and home.

Feeling much calmer now, he lifted his phone.

40

Anna Jagiellon threw her phone into her shoulder bag as though to dash it to pieces against the rocks inside. Of course there were no rocks and the phone nestled comfortably next to her makeup kit. She really shouldn't be blaming the phone, anyway, just because that idiot simpering Argentinian was always on the other end. What a mistake he was. It had seemed like a good idea at the time, making Jorge Ocampo Noantri. He already followed her around like a puppy dog, the skinny premed student (premed, because Che had been a doctor: always one for hero worship, Jorge) enraptured by the fiery foreigner. Her Hungarian heritage, which she'd alternately hidden and revealed as she cycled through identities in the years she'd spent in Argentina, had been on full display at the university at the moment Juan Perón returned to power in 1973. They'd all been Communists, all the hottest boys and fiercest girls, out to change the world, and Anna was ever their most articulate organizer, their bravest leader. Oh, the slogans she'd written, the speeches she'd made! On the streets she'd marched and chanted and then, with the others — as though such things could harm her — fled from the tear gas and the bullets down backstreets and twisting alleys. In smoky rooms packed with eager, sweating young bodies, all leaning forward to hear her, to see her, she'd shown them the beauty of the world that could be, the world being kept from them by the rich and the powerful.

They were fools, of course, but that wasn't their fault. The Unchanged, Anna had found, only grew into anything resembling wisdom as they neared their own deaths. Not that it was the approaching obliteration that brought about understanding. Quite the contrary, it was, simply, the years. Wisdom took decades to bloom, and most of the Unchanged were not allotted anything like sufficient time. That might be sad, but it was true. Anna's fellow Party members, her comrade leaders and her wide-eyed followers, were fools because they were young.

Anna had also been young, many years ago, when John Zapolya ascended to the throne of Hungary and Anna was torn from the life that was rightfully hers. Silk and velvet, meat and wine and music, were replaced overnight by sackcloth and filth, coarse bread and foul water. Though she was her father's natural, not legitimate, child, Anna was nevertheless the only remaining heir to the house of Jagiellon, and as such had, of course, to be exterminated. The golden-haired daughter of the soon-to-be extinguished royal line was thrown into a stinking cell where her wishes meant nothing and her degradation was complete.

Until what she thought was to be her final night on earth, with her execution scheduled for dawn. The priest had come to hear her confession in her last hours. Anna had refused to speak to him. They had been a devout family, hearing Mass daily in the palace chapel, taking Holy Communion. Her father was the patron of the monastery on the hill. That the God they'd worshipped with such certainty had allowed this carnage and desolation, and that one of his priests was now offering *Anna* forgiveness — no, no, the man should be on his knees, begging her for hers! She'd turned away stonily, and he'd crept out, and Anna waited in exhausted relief for the dawn and her release from this hell.

Near midnight — as on so many horrific nights before — the jangle of keys heralded a visit by a man intent on having his way with the once-virginal daughter of the dead king. By now long past numb, and intent on the longed-for dawn, Anna just stared at the wall as the man settled in the dirty straw beside her and said he was a friend, a former courtier of her father's, and was here to help. He was lying, she was sure: all her father's intimates had surely been put to death, or had fled. Why he said it, she didn't know. Some of them did, the men who came into her cell. Some of them spoke to her as though to persuade her there was, somewhere, a reason she should not hate them for what they were about to do. She despised those men even more than the ones who silently and roughly threw her on the straw and took her as they wanted.

So she didn't speak to this man, didn't look at him, and when he came close she didn't move. She'd learned to respond as little as she could; in the beginning she'd fought them, but they had always conquered her and her ineffectual struggles only inflamed their lust. Her sole power was in impassiveness and scorn.

The man took her chin gently in his hand, turned her head to face him. He looked into her eyes. She found herself strangely captivated, and was not sure if she could have moved in any case when finally he took her by her shoulders, laid her softly in the straw, and leaned over her. She felt his mouth on her throat, his soft lips, and then a searing, fiery pain engulfed her. It blazed through her as though she were plunging into boiling oil. She lost sight and hearing, could feel nothing but this agonizing Fire. She tried to scream but no sound came. Just when she thought she'd go mad from the pain it started to fade, and when she could see again, she found the man's eyes still on hers. She found also that she could hear the newborn squeak of a baby mouse in its nest inside the walls, and she could smell the aroma of roast meat from the guard's quarters across the courtyard.

He sat her up, this courtier, took her hands, and told her what he was. What she now was. Stunned and unbelieving, she took him for mad. He told her not to fear the dawn. He stroked her hair and, leaning forward again, kissed her. His mouth on hers awoke in her such a clamor of yearning, such vast, unknown pleasure, that it was almost pain again. She still hadn't spoken when he stood and left, locking her cell behind him.

She sat immobile, staring where he'd gone, until they came for her at dawn. Her hands were bound behind her, her eyes blindfolded, and she was hanged, not with a sharp, merciful snap of the neck, but a slow, terrifying strangulation. She fought, kicking, writhing, but darkness flowed gradually in and she was gone. Her last thought was, **At least it's over.**

Until she awoke on silk sheets in a room filled with daylight glowing softly through lace curtains. The courtier sat beside her in a velvet chair. He smiled and she reached her hand to his.

Anna shook herself to bring her thoughts back to this world. Enough memories, enough time-wasting! Each phone call from Jorge brought worse news than the last. She could see no help for it now: she had to involve herself directly, or this golden chance might be lost. If the Church, or the Conclave, recovered the Concordat, another such opportunity could be centuries away. But Jorge was no longer a useful tool. He was a liability, calling attention to himself, and so potentially to her and their movement.

Jorge, the stupid fool, had killed a monk.

41

"Esposito? Come in here a minute."

The *soprintendente*'s command came without urgency, as though it were a request; but the man never raised his voice. Some of Luigi Esposito's fellow Gendarmes had the idea from his manner that their boss was fundamentally unconcerned, with his work, theirs, or anything else, that he was just marking time until he was pensioned off. As so many of them were. But Luigi had learned to read the *soprintendente*'s inflections and the look in his eyes. That's why, though he was just a Naples street kid, he'd become a *vice assistente* when his fellows were still — and would always be — uniformed Gendarmes.

Luigi rose from his desk, where three windows open on his computer linked him to the websites of various law enforcement agencies specializing in art and antiquities theft. Educating himself about the ins and outs of this crime specialty seemed an obvious next step. Especially since he had no suspects to process, no interviews to conduct, and no actual physical evidence to examine.

Well, not entirely no evidence. He'd made a search of the Library passage both the clerk and the black-haired woman had used — and a man claiming to be a priest, one Father Thomas Kelly, a researcher from Boston — and come up with the clerk's Library smock. That he'd thrown it off, obviously the better to blend in, plus the fact that he and the other two had used the same escape route, made it even more glaringly obvious to Luigi that this was a ring of highly professional thieves. Though it was also clear, from the reported fight in the *Manoscritti* Reading Room, that something had gone wrong with this particular attempt at larceny. Maybe the priest really was a priest, and had been trying to prevent the theft? And had chased after the woman to get the stolen book back? But if so, where was he? Why hadn't he come forward? No, to Luigi it seemed more likely that the priest, real or bogus, was a member of the ring, involved up to his clerical collar.

Luigi followed his boss into his office, where the *soprintendente* dropped his round, rumpled body into his desk chair and said, "Close the door. Take a look at this."

Luigi pushed the door shut and took the sheet of paper the *soprintendente* handed him. It was a printout of an incident report, one from a steady stream that flowed through the *soprintendente*'s computer all day. The Rome Polizia, the Italian Carabinieri, and the Vatican Gendarmerie kept one another informed of goings-on in their jurisdictions throughout the day. (And into the endlessly silent Vatican night, when, during Luigi's stints as watch officer, reading the reports of the other police agencies was sometimes the only thing that kept him awake.) It was a professional courtesy, though Luigi couldn't imagine a cop or a Carabiniere scanning the Holy See's crime news with any serious interest.

Glancing over the other agencies' reports was part of the *soprintendente*'s duties, though, and he performed this office faithfully. Luigi knew, from his boss's sharp blue eyes combined with the weary set of his shoulders, that the *soprintendente* had once seen himself sailing the wild seas of true law enforcement, before he'd gotten becalmed in the backwater of the Vatican. It made Luigi wonder how he, Luigi, would survive once he got promoted to a supervisory position and spent all day doing Vatican paperwork, his nose pressed to the glass of actual policing.

Then he read the printout, and his heart skipped a beat.

"That description," the *soprintendente* said. As usual, his manner was casual, but now his eyes were narrowed. "Of their person of interest. Reminiscent of the man you had in here earlier, wouldn't you say?"

Luigi swallowed. "Very much so, sir."

The *soprintendente* stared wordlessly at Luigi for long enough that Luigi found he had to force himself to meet the pale gaze and not squirm. Finally the man spoke. "You don't have the seniority and unless I'm wrong, you haven't worked with the Carabinieri before." He wasn't wrong and he knew he wasn't, so Luigi said nothing. "But if it's the same man, you might be of use. I've spoken to the detective in charge, a man named Giulio Aventino. He's on his way to the church. Santa Maria della Scala." The *soprintendente* gestured to the printout. "His sergeant's already there. He was nearby on some kind of surveillance, I don't know what, when the incident occurred. They'll meet you at the scene."

Trying to appear cool and professional

though he'd already nearly crushed the printout in his grip, Luigi said, "Yes, sir!" and headed for the door.

"Esposito?" The *soprintendente* waited for Luigi to stop and turn. "It's their case. They're willing to have us send someone because it's a homicide of a churchman in a church. You're the obvious choice because of the suspect." **Whom, on the instructions of the Cardinal Librarian, I ordered you to release, and I'm now making it up to you.** Luigi wasn't sure he saw that in the *soprintendente*'s eyes, but he hoped so. "But Santa Maria della Scala's not the Vatican," his boss went on. "It's Italy. You're there to help. To help *them,* Esposito."

Luigi nodded. Anything for a fellow cop. Though, he thought as he loped through the station to the door, if *Vice Assistente* Luigi Esposito of the Gendarmerie were to be any help to a homicide detective of the Carabinieri, it was just possible he might find he was helping himself.

42

Thomas read Mario Damiani's cryptic words with, a tiny corner of his mind was pleased to note, less befuddlement than he'd felt in the Vatican Library when first faced with the poet's works. He was beginning to get inside Damiani's head, he thought. These lines, he was sure, would soon yield to serious and methodical consideration and offer up their meaning.

If he could bring serious and methodical consideration to bear.

The truth was, leaning here on the worn wooden counter beside Livia Pietro, under the scrutiny of a painted angel peeking over a painted curtain, Thomas was having trouble concentrating. Part of it was the distraction created by the aromas swirling through the room. How many weeks, months perhaps, had it been since anyone had opened that door, before he and Pietro had, well, broken in? In all that time the sunlight of summer, now fading to autumn, had continued to fall through the ancient windows. In the quiet warmth, spices, medicinal herbs, flowers, and oils had released their intoxicating scents into the air.

The aromas were part of it; but the other part was that Thomas was noticing them.

Father Thomas Kelly was famous for his scholarly focus, which was another way of saying he was an absentminded professor. Though fond of flowers and sunshine, he generally took as little notice of them while working as he did of howling winter storms and broken water pipes — each of which had landed him in trouble in the past, to the great amusement of his colleagues. ("Until your feet got wet? Seriously?") Faced with a task as monumentally important as the one he was involved in now, it seemed inexplicable to Thomas that he was thinking about scent.

And even more ridiculous, he realized, that he was thinking about thinking about scent. He was distracted by his own distraction. While Lorenzo's life, and death, and afterlife, hung in the balance.

Thomas shifted position, leaning closer to the unfolded paper. Pietro raised her eyebrows as he crowded her, but said nothing.

313

Together they read:

Sarve Reggina, madre de la sorgente
de nasscita e de morte, fragrante ojjo ner
    core
de le lanterne, tutto d'oro, potente
drento. Ave all'anima, ar piede, a la tera
ch'aregge sordati e ssuore, peregrini ner
    gnente.

Ave, Maria, mother of the source
of birth and death, and fragrant, flowing oil
that fuels the lanterns, golden, and the
    force
within. Ave, the soul, the foot, the soil
'neath nuns and soldiers, pilgrims on their
    course.

Just below the last line of the poem: the letters T I V A C, in heavy lead pencil, all uppercase.

At first neither of them spoke. The soft air of the apothecary enfolded them in scent and silence. Finally, Pietro tentatively offered, "Maria. Foot, again. Soil. Pilgrimage. Well, they're pilgrimage poems. And these." She pointed, not touching the paper. "What do you suppose this means?"

"T-I-V-A-C?" With equal uncertainty, Thomas said, "Nothing I can see. Maybe it's initials? Something Spencer George would understand?"

"I suppose. Though we can't very well ask him right now."

"And," Thomas realized, "we can't be sure Damiani wrote them. Uppercase letters, lead, not ink — someone else might have done it."

"In Damiani's notebook? I got the feeling from Spencer that Damiani never showed his notebooks to anyone. But all right, let's let that go for now and focus on the poem."

If only I could focus, Thomas thought. But he redoubled his efforts and stared at the words. And slowly found himself drawn in, absorbed in the old, familiar way, until he all but felt the connections being made in his brain between what he was learning now, and what he already knew. "Something else," he said slowly, as his synapses sizzled and clicked. "Soil, foot, you're right, pilgrimage, but something else . . . Maria, yes, so another church dedicated to Mary. But: Source. Oil. Soldiers, the soldiers are important . . . Lanterns . . . golden lanterns . . . No! Not the lanterns are golden! The oil is golden. The oil. Where the oil bubbled up." He saw the light go on in Pietro's eyes and wondered if it was mirrored in his own.

43

Livia refolded Damiani's poem, slipped it into the pages of her own notebook, and zipped notebook and poem into her bag. The Conclave had been right: having the priest with her was paying off. She was a little surprised at herself for, well, being surprised. The Conclave carried a collective wisdom of thousands of years. Behind them were centuries of debate and study. It was their responsibility to be right. And — with the single, glaring exception of her defying of the Law to make Jonah Noantri — Livia had, since her own Change, always taken it as an article of personal faith that they were. Livia wanted nothing more than a quiet, assimilated life, lived undiscovered among the Unchanged and openly among her own kind; she'd never wanted anything else, except Jonah, and allowing herself to want him was her great error and still her greatest regret.

In silence she led the priest back out of the apothecary — though she caught him casting a look of disappointment on the shelves and bottles, the jars and the drawers he'd had no chance to explore — and across the vestibule to a hallway on the right. She made quick work of the lock on the first door, to, she noticed, no reaction at all from Thomas Kelly. The room held old equipment for crushing and distilling herbs; fascinating devices, and the priest appeared even more pained here, to have to pass them all by. But he made no comment as she crossed to the dusty window, unlatched it, and peered out. Ten feet below lay a courtyard that was even now planted in a formal pattern, though no longer with herbs the monks were cultivating for future use, just with ornamental flowers and shrubs. She pulled the window wide.

"Wait." Thomas Kelly finally spoke, the edginess back in his voice. She'd expected it would return, but still she sighed; his disapproval and objections were wearying. "You can't be planning to go out that way?"

"It's not a far drop. There's a fig tree here." She smiled. "Even a priest in a jacket and collar should be able to make it."

"That's not the point! We can't go through

there. It's the monastery garden. They'll see us."

"The monks? They're all in the church. The bells called them. Look around: there's no one anywhere."

Kelly's face changed. "I should — I should go, too. To see if —"

"No." She turned to look at him full-on. "Father, whatever it was, there's nothing you can do. You and I have a task, as important to you as it is to me. Let's concentrate on it." With that she sat on the windowsill, swung her legs over it, and leapt to the ground. She hadn't needed the help of the fig tree but turned expecting to find Thomas Kelly clambering clumsily down its branches — if he decided to come along at all. She was surprised to see the priest, after hesitating, ignore the tree and grasp the sill, lowering himself on outstretched arms until he let go his handhold and dropped lightly beside her.

As he stood dusting his hands, Livia said, "Nicely done."

"We humans aren't completely without our physical abilities."

She sighed. "Can't we have a truce?" When he didn't answer, she turned away from him. "All right." She surveyed the walled garden. "Now we need to find a way out to the street."

Kelly gave her a pitying look and spun briskly, heading to his left. Livia caught up with him. "Where are you going?"

"Out."

"How do you know it's this way?"

"It's a monastery. I'm a priest."

She couldn't argue with that. She followed, and it turned out he was right. He marched confidently through a small door into a cool, dim corridor, then led her along a smooth-worn stone floor past walls hung with crucifixes and a dark, not very good but clearly deeply felt painting of Santa Teresa. After a brief moment of decision at the intersection with a wider corridor he turned right. A few yards later they reached another door and, through it, a small vestibule. Livia's heart pounded when she saw the sliding scrollwork screen and the desk in the tiny room beyond it, but the vestibule and room were as empty as the corridors. Thomas Kelly crossed to the outer door, eased it open, took a cautious look out, and gestured impatiently as though she were dragging her feet. They issued onto Via del Mattonato, behind the church. No one was about as they hurried away.

"That was impressive," Livia said.

"Tradesman's entrance," was Kelly's short

answer. But after a moment he relented, adding, "The Discalced Carmelites are a semi-cloistered order. Their contact with the outside world is carefully controlled."

"They have a big gate right smack through the rear wall into the monastery."

"That would have been added recently. For trucks. Originally a tradesman would have brought his wares on his back or by handcart as far as the vestibule we just came out of. He'd have been paid by the monk behind the screen and gone off. Then other friars would have been summoned to collect the delivery. Which, you can be sure, is a similar system to the one they use now for the trucks. It's only when the monks are performing their pastoral duties that they have contact with outsiders."

Kelly had assumed the pedantic tones of the university lecturer again, but Livia took care to keep her amusement to herself. To her surprise, though, the corners of the priest's mouth lifted into a small smile.

"What's funny?" she asked.

"You might be the only woman ever to have walked that hallway."

"Don't tell the monks, they'll be scandalized."

Still smiling, Kelly nodded. Then, as if he'd caught himself in an error, his face flushed and he said, "Much more than scandalized if they knew what you really were. What I'd brought to their consecrated halls."

Livia sighed once again. "Give it a rest, Father." She strode past him and then, without looking back, turned down a *vicolo* so narrow it was always in shadow. She kept a few paces ahead of Thomas Kelly as they covered the short distance to the Basilica of Santa Maria in Trastevere.

44

Giulio Aventino had to admit that, notwithstanding the Armani jacket, the elegant two-
day scruff, and the cardinal uncle, Raffaele
Orsini had done an excellent job at the
Santa Maria della Scala crime scene. Once
you got past the fact that he'd sat drinking
coffee in the café across the piazza while it
became a crime scene, of course. Raffaele
had called in the coroner and the forensics
team, used some of the responding officers
to secure the church and some to fan out
and hunt for the alleged perpetrator; and
he'd held on to all the witnesses. That last
must not have been easy in the case of the
sour historian who was sitting in cold
impatience, his arms folded, in a rear pew.
He, according to the sergeant, had to have
it explained to him that the forces of law
and good represented by the Carabinieri
would be most grateful for his continuing
cooperation. As would the substantial

paperwork-generating bureaucratic machine of the civil state, which sadly the Carabinieri could not control once it was unleashed. Giulio nodded. Raffaele was very good at that sort of thing. Giulio himself would just have arrested the man if he'd tried to leave, and sorted it out later.

Not for the first time, Giulio considered the possibility that the *maresciallo* had created their partnership not only because of the things the junior detective could learn from the senior.

The other two witnesses, by contrast, were only too glad to stay. Black-clad *vecchie,* of a type Giulio's twenty-three years on the force had taught him to know well, they had not only been in the church when the homicide had occurred, they'd nearly seen it happen. They'd turned at the yell and the thud, seen the thin young man flee back up the aisle. It was their solemn duty, they assured him, to help the Carabinieri solve this horrible crime, this desecration, this tragedy that offered further proof, if any were needed, that today's young people were lost to God and running completely amok. No, they'd needed no persuasion to stay; in fact, Giulio suspected he'd need a pry bar to get these ladies out of the church in the end.

He'd listened patiently to each as she

objected, disingenuously but huffily, to being made to go through her story again, having already told it to Raffaele. Then, being reassured of her value to the investigation, each launched into a blow-by-blow (". . . lighting candles for my late husband, such a good man, God rest his soul, he was Francesca's brother, we come every day . . .") that eventually wound round to the raised voices, the scuffle, the fall. By the time each of the ladies had told it twice, the story included bellowed blasphemous curses, an unprovoked vicious attack on a man of God by a wild-eyed degenerate, and a morbidly delighted grin lighting up the face of the killer ("I can never forget it, Madonna help me!"); but Giulio thought not. What he heard, between the self-importantly hysterical lines, played out like this: a young man rose from his knees at the rear of the church and sought access to an area in which he was not permitted; the old monk sought to prevent him; in an attempt to shove his way past, the young man had knocked the old monk down. The monk had hit his head on the ancient marble floor — on a gravestone marking a tomb below, but Giulio was long over the ironies that churches could offer — and died, either of the impact or of a heart attack caused by fright or agitation, the specific cause being for the coroner to determine.

Giulio, again from long experience of such matters, suspected the death had been an absurd accident. An overreaction, you might say, on the part of Fate. A satanic disciple, a specimen of today's amok youth with eyes like burning coals, would be unlikely to have been found on his knees at the back of the church to begin with. Had the young man stayed, and assuming he had no record of previous criminal violence, it was likely he'd have gotten a slap on the wrist: at worst, a six-month suspended sentence for assault. As it was, because he'd fled the scene, he was now a suspect in a homicide. The longer and harder the authorities looked for him and the more resources they expended, the angrier the judge they brought him before would be when he was finally caught.

It was that he had, in fact, fled that interested Giulio. That, and the fact that he'd been on his knees in prayer in the first place.

The coroner's men were ready to go, so Giulio dismissed the second *vecchia,* instructing one of the uniformed officers to escort the important lady out. As he'd expected, she balked at leaving, but her sanctimonious respect for authority overcame her desire to be at the center of any tragedy; and finally she went. As was his custom, Giulio went back to the body, lifting the linen over the face for one final look. Raffaele Orsini, standing beside him, crossed himself. That made, since Giulio had arrived, four times. Of course he'd counted; it was one of the little delights of working with Raffaele, the private side bets Giulio made daily about how the sergeant's piety would express itself. Since this case involved the death of a monk in a church, Giulio was looking forward to some inspired devotion.

Giulio nodded to the coroner's team, who started the process of packing the body up for transport. From Giulio's point of view there was nothing of note about the body except the look of peace, even joy, on the old monk's face. Giulio could tell the man had been bent crooked with arthritis, which probably caused him constant pain; and at his age no doubt he had other health problems as well. **As you will soon enough, Aventino,** he told himself, **and at least this one died happy, expecting to meet his Maker.** As Giulio often did, he considered the cheerless irony of how he and his fellow realists (a word he vastly preferred to "nonbelievers," which implied something actually existed in which they refused to believe) had outsmarted themselves. Men like this monk — and Raffaele Orsini — might be deluded about their own purpose, about God existing and having a plan, and most of all, about the afterlife; but they generally died happy.

With a stifled sigh Giulio walked over to the pew where the historian sat. The lemon face turned to look at him.

"Well. The majesty of the law is finally prepared to catechize me, is that it?"

Giulio enjoyed the deliberate misuse of the theological verb, partly because he heard, from the pew behind, Raffaele sucking disapproving air between his teeth. "I'm sorry to have kept you waiting, sir," he said. "Professor Spencer George, is that correct?" Giulio pronounced the English badly but with obvious care, and then returned to Italian with equally obvious relief. "I'm Senior Investigator Giulio Aventino. It's an honor, sir. May I?" Without pausing for an answer Giulio dropped wearily into the pew. "It was those women. They were witnesses to the incident — which I take it you yourself were not, *Professore*?"

He waited, though they both knew he knew the answer. The historian forced out an exasperated "That's correct."

"As I thought. In any case, I needed personally to hear those women's accounts of the situation — as senior investigator on this case I can't rely on secondhand testimony, even from someone as reliable as my sergeant" — his nod to Raffaele, now leaning forward, caused the historian to swivel around to look — "but frankly, sir, it was also that until they were gone I knew I wouldn't be able to think straight. Very pious, of course, and no doubt women of great virtue, but exhausting, don't you find?"

None of this did the *professore* grace with an answer; and all of it was only barely true. Giulio had no special love for the doom-and-gloom sin-sniffing old ladies who came early to Mass and made a point of occupying the pews nearest the confessional, the better to eavesdrop on other people's transgressions. But they didn't make his head spin. Belying his carefully cultivated appearance, very little, in reality, made Giulio Aventino's head spin.

He peered at Spencer George and could tell the historian was seeing right through his rumpled-and-befuddled act. Excellent. George would conclude that Giulio, after having kept him cooling his heels for no good reason, was now making an inept attempt to cozy up to him for the purpose of manipulating him into lowering his guard. Being manipulated tended to irritate people. And, having so easily discovered Giulio's strategy, the *professore* — in any case no doubt accustomed to thinking of himself as smarter than everyone around him; Giulio could see that in the impatient thin lips and the arrogant set of the shoulders — would allow his own condescension free rein.

Irritated, impatient, and condescending. If any constellation of mind-sets was more likely to cause a suspect to make mistakes, Giulio hadn't yet come across it.

Not that Spencer George was a suspect, at least, not in the death of the monk, at least, not directly. But when Giulio had first arrived, after he'd seen the body and gotten the lay of the land, and before he'd questioned any of the witnesses, he'd taken his sergeant outside and had a hushed conversation with him on the church steps. Raffaele had filled him in, with exactly the mixture of apology and pride that Giulio had expected, on his surveillance mission for his cardinal uncle. Giulio, over the half-glasses perennially slipping down his nose as though they wanted to bury themselves in his mustache, had interrupted Raffaele's narrative to ask whether he was absolutely sure he hadn't noticed anything at all amiss about the visitors going in and out of the church. That was by way of reminding the sergeant that all of this had happened while he'd been lounging in the piazza outside on secondment to the Vatican, so perhaps a bit more apology and a touch less pride would have been appropriate. Then, because they were, at the end of the day, partners, and because Raffaele, at bottom, had the makings of a good, solid cop — and because one of Raffaele's better points was that he never made excuses for his mistakes — Giulio had filled the sergeant in on what might turn out to be the intriguing next piece of what might turn out to be a larger puzzle: the anticipated arrival of a member of the Gendarmerie. ("Stop smirking, Raffaele, they're brothers in arms. If anyone should show respect to an officer from the Vatican I'd think it would be a cardinal's nephew.") The Gendarme, so Giulio had heard, had an interesting tale to tell about the homicide suspect who, after causing what Giulio was still sure was an accident, had so rapidly disappeared.

45

Raffaele Orsini was watching his partner work.

He himself had gotten Giulio Aventino's trademark soft-voiced, phrased-as-a-question, piercing-gaze-over-the-eyeglasses reprimand earlier, but he was the first to admit he'd deserved it. Not so much because of what had happened inside Santa Maria della Scala while he sat in the café outside — hadn't the *maresciallo* told him not to enter the church? — but because, though Giulio hadn't mentioned this, the thin young man they now thought of as their suspect must have exploded out of one of the church's main doors just as, through another, Raffaele had been charging in.

Raffaele had been forgiven, though, or at least considered properly chastised, and welcomed back into the fold. In fact, he'd proved his use already. Not only by his rapid, efficient, and book-proper handling of the crime scene. While the historian smoldered in the pew, Giulio Aventino patiently listened to the lamentations of the old ladies. Raffaele would have liked to stay and pick up some pointers on dealing with hysterical witnesses, but he'd been dispatched to run interference with the dyspeptic emissary launched in their direction by the Bishop. This vinegary *Monsignore* had arrived with a flurry and a frown, sent to ensure, in equal measure, that the search for the friar's killer was made a high Carabinieri priority, and that untoward behavior at the monastery of Santa Maria della Scala, should any come to light, not find its way into the official report. Raffaele had done a good job, he was pleased to say, of placating the priest while upholding the honor and independence of the Carabinieri. At the moment the *Monsignore,* in the company of the monastery's prior, was exploring the possibility that some valuable item might have gone missing (a suggestion that made the *Monsignore*'s eyes flash, as though Raffaele, by speaking the words, was in danger of bringing about the fact). After they'd gone off Raffaele had herded the rest of the monks — there were fourteen — into two pews not far from where the body lay. As a detective, he'd have been happier if they'd left the premises altogether, so as not to endanger the evidence; and his partner, as a nonbeliever, would probably be happier if they just vaporized. But Raffaele felt strongly that they had a right to sit in prayer and meditation near the corporeal remains of their brother, to keep vigil and ease his joyous trip into the presence of God.

Until the coroner's men took the body away, of course. Now the monks, on the orders of their prior, had returned to their cloister. The prior and the acidic *Monsignore* were inspecting the side chapels one by one. Uniformed officers, armed with a dialed-back version of the old ladies' descriptions, prowled the streets hunting down the thin young man. And Raffaele was in a rear pew taking lessons in interview technique.

He always enjoyed this process. In some ways observing Giulio with a witness was like watching a soccer game between unmatched teams. Each play unfolded uniquely, and so held individual interest; but the overall organization of the game was familiar and the outcome never in doubt.

"Now, *Professore,* please." Seeming both distracted and ready to be grateful, Giulio addressed the historian. "Tell me what you can about this incident. Where were you when it took place?" The answer, of course,

Giulio already knew, as he could also, no doubt, predict the objection of Spencer George.

"What I told your sergeant —"

"Is what you told my sergeant. I'm sorry, sir, but it's my responsibility to hear all witness statements personally. As I did with those of the *vecchie*," he confided in a tone of shared misery.

"Yes, of course." Spencer George, his eye-roll making it clear he was yielding, unwillingly, to the inevitable, began his tale. It was essentially the same story he'd told Raffaele: he and two friends had entered the Reliquary Chapel at the end of the side aisle "to admire Santa Teresa's chopped-off foot," a phrase near enough to blasphemy that it caused Raffaele to suppress a shudder. George had remained after his friends had gone. He'd heard a scream, come into the main church, and seen the monk lying on the floor with an apparition in black hovering over him. Giulio lifted his eyebrows at this suggestion of the supernatural, until George went on to add, "I believe it was her sister-in-law who'd run howling outside."

"Ah." Giulio nodded and continued. "And the friends you were with, your fellow historians? Livia Pietro and Thomas Kelly? Where are they now?"

From the pause and the widening of the historian's eyes, Raffaele could tell the question had hit home. The *professore* had never been asked, or volunteered, the names or occupations of his companions.

And this was the point and had been all along: the point of keeping Spencer George waiting, of Giulio's pedantic civil servant act, to make him feel superior and therefore get careless.

In their brief conference when Giulio arrived, Raffaele had explained he'd been sent by the Cardinal to keep an eye on Livia Pietro; Giulio in turn told Raffaele about the theft at the Vatican Library and the red-haired American priest easily identified as one Thomas Kelly, who'd been with Pietro then. The third party involved in that fracas, it seemed, was a thin young man of suspiciously similar description to the suspect they were seeking now. The Gendarme detective on that case was on his way; but even without him, Raffaele and his senior partner could see something was going on here that required a more thorough explanation. And that this historian, now that he'd been thrown off-balance, might well be the one to give it.

46

Thomas Kelly realized he'd lost control of the situation once again. He'd boldly led their escape from the monastery, as he'd been the discoverer of the hiding place of the new poem. True, Pietro had chosen for them a serene and splendid retreat in which to decipher the verse, and also true, and more rankling, it had been Spencer George who'd prompted Thomas to check for the folded paper in the reliquary's roof. But as Thomas brought Livia Pietro through the hushed monastery corridors and out onto the street, and then along it, he'd felt less at sea than any time that day.

However, now she was ahead of him in a dark lane he wouldn't have thought to turn down. She knew the way to the Basilica of Santa Maria in Trastevere, and he didn't. He was sure she had no idea what to do when they got there, but neither had he, so they were even on that score.

And she was an unnatural creature with a nimble intellect, a great depth of learning, and an indelible physical presence. A creature who, to hear her tell it, felt a warm, benign joy in the company of others physiologically like herself. Whereas he was a man who'd given his merely human mind, body, and soul to a spiritual community he'd chosen: a Church he'd always understood, even in the days of his darkest doubts, to exist as a place of honest refuge from the evils of the world. About which characterization he was now, at best, unsure.

Where did that put the two of them on the relative-advantage scale?

He pondered that question as he followed Pietro, turning left and then right along narrow streets, then left again onto a busier one, until she suddenly stopped. She thrust out her arm so she could halt Thomas's progress, also. Shades of the Vatican Library. She peered from the mouth of the alley, and then, adjusting her hat and sunglasses, strode confidently into a wide piazza. Thomas followed — what else was he going to do? — as she strolled nonchalantly toward the fountain and then turned to survey the basilica's façade. Wide and imposing, it well suited the first church in Rome, in fact the first in the world, dedicated to Christ's mother. On the pediment the Madonna and Child were flanked by — if he remembered his art history (and he certainly wasn't going to ask Pietro) — a mosaic of ten female saints no one had ever been able to name. He craned up to see them as he trotted by the fountain and through the piazza. Pietro, he noticed, also looked up, with an air of familiarity and happiness, as though seeing old friends. Well, there you go. Maybe they weren't saints. Maybe they were all female Noantri. And maybe that wasn't the Infant Jesus and the Blessed Virgin at their center, it was Baby Damian and the Queen of the Night.

He considered issuing himself a reprimand for his cynical attitude but decided he had a right to it.

Inside the church Thomas's eyes had to adjust once again to the dimness while Pietro headed without pause down the center aisle. Unlike Santa Maria della Scala, he and Pietro didn't have this basilica practically to themselves. A few scattered worshippers were kneeling or sitting quietly in pews, and one or two stood in side chapels lighting candles, while dozens of visitors, some with guidebooks, some without, prowled the splendid aisles.

Now capable of seeing, Thomas hurried

after Pietro, passing between rows of columns of which no two were alike. They'd come from Roman and even Egyptian buildings, he recalled his art history lecturer saying, and he remembered thinking at the time that this reuse of structural elements was a physical manifestation of the supplanting of pagan thoughts and fears by the sheltering truth his faith offered. Resolutely, he turned his gaze away from the columns and from the astounding ceiling with its gold coffers and devotional paintings, there to remind the flock what awaited them in heaven above if only their faith, while they remained below, stayed strong.

Refusing equally to think about the implications of that and to allow himself another cynical interior remark, Thomas stepped to Livia Pietro's side. She stood at a marble railing supported on open stone grillwork; the railing bore a stone plaque. *Fons Olei,* the bronze letters read, marking the spot where, two thousand years before, the miracle responsible for the basilica's existence had occurred. Oil had bubbled up out of the ground here. According to legend, the Jewish residents of Trastevere had recalled an ancient prophecy and hailed the flow as a sign, a herald of the appearance of the Messiah. A few decades later word came

339

from Bethlehem that a Virgin had brought forth a Son; there followed tales of signs and miracles, and later of the Son's sacrifice for love of his Father's flock. The nascent Church declared the prophecy of the oil fulfilled. The building in which it had occurred — by then a social club for retired Roman soldiers — was recognized as sanctified ground, razed, and rebuilt to the glory of the Lord.

That the oil was now understood to have been petroleum, a substance unknown to the locals at the time but not uncommon in the area, and that the ancient Jewish prophecy appeared to be a back-formation of which no trace could be found before the bubbling of the oil, had never bothered Thomas before this.

Pietro turned to Thomas. " *'Fons Olei,'* " she said. "We're here. What now?"

"It's astounding how you people keep expecting me to know what to do next."

She pursed her lips. "You're right. I'm sorry. I was less expecting than hoping, actually."

In Latin it's the same word, he thought, but didn't speak, just squatted and fingered the bronze letters, feeling around their edges. Maybe something had been slipped behind one; but Pietro had apparently had the same thought and already discarded it. "Those letters are too new. They were put there after Damiani's time. You can tell by the typeface."

Thomas could tell no such thing, but she was the expert. Still on his haunches, he examined the marble railing. He ran his gaze along the floor's intricate mosaics, seeking a break in the pattern, a hidden instruction. Nothing presented itself as a hiding place, with one exception: the open stone grillwork on which the railing rested. Behind it, the steps to the altar rose. A piece of paper shoved through the grillwork would have fallen to the floor and could count on resting in that lightless cavern until the entire basilica crumbled to dust. Or until the paper rotted away from mold and damp. Or was devoured by dark-dwelling beetles. From the experience Thomas could claim of Mario Damiani — limited but intense — sliding the next poem, if that's what they were here for, through the grillwork to lie in the dirt was far too slapdash a choice.

Nevertheless, he pressed his face to one of the openings, for a closer look. He felt Pietro kneel beside him, heard her rummage in her bag, and suddenly the area under the steps was illuminated by a bright light. Pietro peered through an opening beside him as he searched the cavern with methodical care.

It was totally, completely empty.

Thomas stuck his hand through the railing anyway. He felt around: perhaps there was a way to fasten something, attach the paper to the back of the grillwork. If so, he'd have to search behind every opening, a tedious process at best. But the masons had been conscientious. The rear side of the stone, though never intended to be seen, was polished to as smooth a finish as the front.

Thomas stood slowly and Pietro straightened up beside him.

"I thought you could see in the dark," he said, unhappily belligerent.

"Better than you. But light always helps."

He saw her drop her cell phone back into her bag.

"That's not a flashlight," he said uselessly.

"On the iPhone. It's an app." She zipped the bag. "You can't really be as disgusted as you look. That a Noantri would have the newest technology?"

With a pang of guilt Thomas realized what he'd been doing. Ruefully grateful she hadn't taken his bait, he said, almost by way of apology, "Some people think it all comes from the devil anyway. There's nothing here.

What are we going to do?"

Pietro looked around, as though hoping for inspiration from the columns, the ceiling, the swirling patterned Cosmatesque floors. Doing that, she reminded Thomas of someone, and then he realized: himself.

"Is it possible Damiani didn't mean this church?" she asked.

"No." Thomas shook his head. " 'Fragrant, flowing oil.' This is the place."

"But the oil . . . If he was leading us to the oil . . ."

Thomas stared at the bronze letters, and then spun to look at her. "There's no oil here. There was. There once was. But if he was leading us to the oil, he didn't mean here."

"But we just agreed, he had to mean here. This church."

"*Basilica.* This basilica. But not here." Rapidly, he turned and started up the aisle, pausing at each side chapel, glancing inside. Pietro didn't ask what he was looking for, just trotted beside him. He reached the narthex and gazed at the front wall, then turned to cross to the left-side aisle. He stopped before he'd taken a step. There it was. Across the narthex, in the side wall, maybe ten feet above the floor, a small golden door in a carved stone frame. Pietro

343

followed his gaze.

"What is it?" she asked.

"An aumbry. A lot of older churches have them but they're not used anymore. This one might not have been opened for years." He barked a humorless laugh. "I'd have said, 'not within living memory,' but —"

"What's in it?"

Right. Serious. This was all serious. "Chalices and other requisites for administering the sacraments. Sacraments like the anointing of the sick." He turned to her. "Requisites like holy oil."

47

Livia stared in wonder at Thomas Kelly. An aumbry. She'd never even heard of an aumbry.

Thomas Kelly turned away from her look to focus, with a frown, on the golden door set high above their heads. He clearly saw the location as an obstacle.

She didn't.

"Father," she said, "it'll take me two minutes if it's locked, one if it's not. Can you give me that?"

"What are you —" The priest's face darkened. He glanced at the offering box at shoulder height directly under the golden door. "You can't be serious."

"If it will hold me."

"No. No, that's —" He stopped himself. "What am I worried about? Such a minor desecration." His sarcastic tone made it clear the words weren't intended for her. After a moment's pause, Thomas Kelly, looking as though his stomach hurt, turned and walked across the narthex and back up the right-side aisle.

He fell. The priest tripped and plowed into a group of tourists, nearly knocking one man over, clumsily recovering, tripping again in his attempt to aid the man and his flummoxed friends. Voices were raised in apology and forgiveness, Thomas Kelly was straightening the man's coat, and then a small exclamation, more apology, and three people in the group fell to their knees. They weren't, Livia realized, praying. They were attempting to recover the contents of a purse knocked away in the confusion.

She looked around. The raised voices and flailing arms had claimed the attention of most people in the church. Good, but it wouldn't last. This leap was higher than the last one she'd made, and the landing area was a nine-inch box. A stretch even for a Noantri, but what choice did she have? She lightly vaulted up, prepared for the box to give, but it didn't. Balancing herself, she reached to test the golden door. She was ready with her pick and shim but the door wasn't locked. Well, really, ten feet above the floor in a basilica, why would it be? She eased it open.

Inside: a pearly marble niche, a shallow

gold shelf, a graceful Murano glass flask of pale yellow oil.

And nothing else.

How could this be? Were they wrong? **No, she heard Spencer's voice in her head. This is just too Mario to be wrong.**

Then what?

The glass flask, the gold shelf, the marble niche. The glass was clear, the oil was pure, the shelf sat firmly on the pearl gray marble.

Except behind the flask the marble wasn't gray.

There, it was black. And it didn't look like marble.

She reached in and removed the stoppered flask with her left hand, taking care not to spill the holy oil. With her other hand she felt the niche's rear wall. No, not stone. Leather. Wedged into the niche, almost the exact dimensions of the rear wall. An unobservant priest replenishing the holy oil would never notice it. She ran a finger around the edge, found a raised corner, peeled it gently toward her. It came away easily.

It was a book cover. Matching exactly the front cover of Damiani's poetry notebook.

Fluttering out from behind it came a single sheet of now-familiar paper.

48

Thomas heard a shout. He whipped around in time to see Livia Pietro, paper and something else in hand, leap down from the offering box, shove a ten-Euro note in it, and dash out the basilica's door. The aumbry was open, the holy oil sitting untroubled within. Three men, clearly more troubled, gave chase, tearing after Pietro while voices echoed around the church in confusion and in umbrage. Thomas's little commotion was suddenly so sixty seconds ago.

Now, if someone steals something from a basilica, shouldn't a priest chase after her? The same as if she steals from, oh, say, the Vatican Library? With a final shamefaced smile to the people he'd been bouncing off of, Thomas ran out the door.

The three chasing men were nowhere to be seen. Neither was Pietro. There was no way they would catch her, Thomas was sure. She could probably fly, or something. No, of course she couldn't. She could run very fast, was all.

What, Thomas? You're starting to buy the nothing-supernatural-about-it line? Careful there.

Well, whether or not she was supernatural, he wasn't. He had complete confidence that her pursuers wouldn't find her. But could he? A cold fear struck him: What if they'd been wrong about how many missing poems they needed to lead them to the Concordat? What if the paper she'd just found was the final one? If she'd realized it would take her to the document and she didn't need him anymore? If so, she'd find it on her own and deliver it to her Conclave. To *her* people. And Lorenzo?

Lorenzo would be condemned.

Thomas stood in the piazza, staring around helplessly. Resolute tourists headed into the basilica while indolent locals strolled toward cafés. Pigeons swooped in to perch on the fountain. A little white dog barked at a big black one, which looked down with amused disdain. Nothing offered a clue to Pietro's course.

Thomas's heart sank.

Against it, in his breast pocket, his phone began to vibrate.

He almost dropped it fumbling it out. A

local number that he didn't recognize. Lorenzo's abductors? He thumbed it on and practically shouted, "Thomas Kelly!"

"I know that, Father. Are you coming?"

For a moment Thomas couldn't speak. "I — *Professoressa*?"

"Try to call me 'Livia.' I'm on Via dei Fienaroli, just past where it intersects with Via della Cisterna. Can you find that?"

"I'm — I will. Stay there. Don't leave!"

"If I were going to leave," he heard her sigh, "why would I have called you?"

49

At the sound of the door latch Lorenzo Cardinal Cossa turned from the open window. Jonah Richter stood on the threshold, golden hair tousled, hands in his trouser pockets, wearing that confident grin Lorenzo despised. Truth be told, there was nothing about the man Lorenzo didn't despise. Starting with the fact that he wasn't a man.

Richter took a few steps into the room, but, as though he were humoring Lorenzo, did not closely approach. "Don't you find it chilly with all the windows open?"

"This room reeks of your kind."

"So strange — before you knew I was Noantri, you didn't complain that I smelled. My stench seems to have arisen simultaneously with your knowledge. What do you make of that?"

"What do you want?"

"I've come to report the hunt is going well."

Lorenzo didn't answer.

"It seems," Richter went on, "that Mario Damiani was a complicated fellow. The trail's longer than it appeared. My historian and your priest have been to two churches and they're on their way to a third."

"What are they finding?" Lorenzo asked in spite of himself.

"I'm not sure. My people can't get that close without being detected by Livia."

Lorenzo turned his back on Richter to gaze out the window again. The room was on the top floor of a building on the Janiculum Hill, and the view was grand. "There. As I said: you stink."

Richter actually laughed. "We can, in fact, detect one another by scent, but we don't feel about it the way you seem to. In any case —" He stopped as his cell phone rang. Lorenzo turned again to face him as Richter answered it and listened. His cheeriness faded into a thoughtful frown. "Thank you," he said, and clicked off. "I have to go," he told Lorenzo.

"Why, is this brilliant scheme malfunctioning?"

"Probably not. But a Noantri who isn't one of my people has been spotted twice in the vicinity of Livia and Kelly. I'd like to know what's going on."

"You can't even trust one another, is that it?"

Richter laughed again. "And you princes and priests of the Church — you can?"

He shut the door behind himself, the latch clicking loudly into place. Lorenzo stood looking where Richter had gone; then he turned once more to the open window and lit a cigar.

50

It took longer than it probably should have for Thomas to arrive at Via dei Fienaroli. That was the fault of the first man he'd asked, who helpfully gave detailed, incorrect directions. Via dei Fienaroli, in fact, was right around the corner from the Basilica of Santa Maria in Trastevere, and it intersected Via della Cisterna another fifty yards along. Via dei Fienaroli was a street so narrow it had no sidewalks. The doors of the shadowed, ancient houses opened directly to the road.

On which, when Thomas got there, no one could be seen.

Of course. She'd sent him on a wild-goose chase. She needed to make sure he couldn't follow her. It wasn't enough that she was an unnatural demon and he just a man, that this city was her home and he had trouble finding his way around it, that she had an entire Community surrounding and supporting her while he was alone with a secret he desperately wished he didn't know, that —

"Father Kelly?"

Not two feet beyond him a battered green door had opened. In the doorway stood a thin young woman with serious eyes and black curly hair. She wore loose white pants and a T-shirt, both of them streaked and splattered with paint, plus a blue stripe on one bare arm and, disarmingly, a smudge on the side of her nose. Smiling, she said, "Father, please come in. Livia's upstairs. I'm Ellen Bird. I'd shake your hand, but I've been told you'd probably rather I didn't."

Her English was American, with a New York tinge. For a moment Thomas felt so relieved, so practically at home, that he began to give her a big answering smile. Then he realized what she must mean about not shaking his hand.

He stepped back. "Are you —" **Seriously, Thomas? What exactly are you going to ask her and how are you going to explain the question if the answer's no?**

The answer, however, was not no. "Am I Noantri? Yes. Please come in."

Thomas stared at Ellen Bird. Her curls, her clear skin, her easy air: she might have been one of his undergraduates. This woman was Noantri? A — **go ahead and say it, Thomas** — a vampire? There was nothing threatening about her. She seemed to be nothing more — or less — than a young American (judging from the paint smudges, an artist) trying her luck in Rome. Not at all like Spencer George, about whom Thomas had gotten an ill feeling from the moment they met. Of course, he reflected, that could have been because the man was arrogant, hostile, and snide. He'd known priests like that whom he hadn't liked any better. Livia Pietro, on the other hand, could be maddeningly manipulative, confusing, and pushy, but even once he knew what she was, she emanated no air of menace. And this Ellen Bird seemed refreshingly straightforward.

But evil was subtle.

"Father Kelly? We can't stand here all day."

No, they couldn't. Livia Pietro, and the new poem, and Lorenzo's fate, were waiting upstairs. Thomas squared his shoulders and, for the second time that day, entered a house whose inhabitants weren't human.

51

From the easy chair by the front window in Ellen's studio Livia heard the conversation on the street, heard the door shut, heard Ellen lead Thomas Kelly up the two flights in silence. He was a brave man, she decided. Brave, because he was obviously so frightened, so repulsed, but still he continued because he wanted to save his friend. That's what courage was about, she'd always believed: not the absence of terror, but the ability to go on in the face of it.

Ellen ushered Thomas Kelly into the room. She said, "I'll leave you two alone for a while," and went out. Kelly stopped and stared around, taking in the bright midday sun streaming through the skylight, the turmoil of pinned-up drawings and sketches, the two easels, each with a painting half-finished; then he turned his gaze to Livia. "Why are we here?"

"Lovely to see you, too, Father." He

frowned. She felt a pang of guilt; she shouldn't tease him. "Please, sit down. Ellen's a friend of mine."

He didn't move from the doorway. "I didn't like what happened the last time we went to see one of your friends."

"I don't blame you. But don't worry. Ellen's not much like Spencer. There won't be any drama."

"Do you have friends everywhere? I suppose you do, a lot of friends. That must be what happens when you have centuries to get acquainted."

"I'm sorry. I know this is hard for you. Please," she said again. "Sit down."

He didn't, but his tone was a shade less belligerent when he said, "I saw you slip money into the collection box."

"Call it penance. That was a nice distraction in the aisle, by the way."

"Thank you," he said automatically, but he remained standing, clearly warring with himself. The scholar, she wondered, against the cleric? If so, the scholar won. Still without moving into the room, he said, "Tell me this. How many of you are there?"

"Of — ?"

"Noantri." He made a face, as though tasting a lemon.

"We borrowed the word 'Noantri' centu-

ries ago, from the native-born Trastever-
ians," she said calmly. "When we use it, we
do mean our kind, but it's not a dirty word."

"Answer my question. How many *Noantri*
are there?"

"Altogether, in the world? Probably ten
thousand, give or take. A third of us here in
Italy, half of that number in Rome, half of
those in Trastevere."

"A third? Three thousand . . . three thousand . . ."

"Three thousand vampires, yes, Father. In
Italy. We were once more scattered, and we
can still be found everywhere, but we
concentrate, for obvious reasons, in coun-
tries and cities with Catholic populations."
Incomprehension clouded his face, so Livia
added, "For the hospitals. For the blood."

Perplexity looked like it was about to give
way to something worse, so she went on
matter-of-factly, "And also, because once
we started to gather, we found we very
much liked living in Community. The comfort we feel in the presence of one another
is something we never knew until the Concordat. In all the years Before, no Noantri
was safe who wasn't furtive and hidden."

"Comfort?"

"We're kin, in a way. We feel it more physi-
cally than the Unchanged do, but everyone

feels heartened in the presence of family."

This was too much for the scholar; the cleric reasserted himself. "Family? Blood relatives, you mean? That's a perverse angle on that concept." Thomas Kelly, his disgust reaffirmed, crossed the room and sat. "Let's get to work. You found another poem."

52

Livia Pietro had just unzipped her bag to draw out the new poem when the door opened. Thomas jumped but settled back again; it was Ellen Bird, bearing a tray. He marveled at himself: **It's okay, nothing to worry about, just a young vampire with some sandwiches.** He realized his coma-hallucination theory had long since faded away and he missed it.

"I know you're hungry, Father Kelly." Ellen Bird smiled, balanced the tray on an art-book pile, and left.

Thomas turned to Pietro. "She knows I'm hungry. How? She sensed my blood sugar falling? Smelled the stomach acid building up?"

"Maybe you have a lean and hungry look. But ask yourself this: If Ellen's Noantri senses did tell her something an Unchanged couldn't have known, is that a reason to reject her food?"

361

Part of Thomas felt it should have been. The other part reached for a napkin, a sandwich, and a bottle of beer.

"You can use that pile of books as a coffee table. Ellen doesn't care much for furniture," Pietro said, replacing the poem in her bag to keep it from damage. "Take a minute to eat. You'll do better when your blood sugar's up."

"You can tell, too?" She just smiled. Thomas examined the sandwich suspiciously. "What's in it?"

"I'm not going to dignify that with an answer."

She was offended. **Well, good. Oh, what, Thomas, now it's all right to offend people on purpose just because you don't like them?** He was startled to hear himself ask that, and reminded himself, **They're not people!** To which the response was even more surprising: **So?** No, really, now he was seriously confused, and Livia Pietro wasn't even doing it. It must be his blood sugar, which was, in fact, low, no matter who knew it. He looked again at the sandwich. It did look like standard Italian fare: salami, cheese, and tomato. But this was a Noantri household. The two parts of his mind were still quarreling when his mouth took a bite. Salty meat, smooth soft

362

cheese, and sharp tomato perfectly set off the crumbly thick bread. A truly great sandwich, or he was starving, or both. He leaned down for a second bite, then stopped as Pietro reached for a sandwich, too.

"I thought you didn't eat. Eat food, I mean."

"We don't need it, no. But we can metabolize it, and the tastes and textures of food are like any other sensations — more powerful and nuanced since we became Noantri. Many of us enjoy eating. It's always been my habit to eat when my Unchanged friends do."

"To keep us company? Or to conceal yourself better?"

She replaced the sandwich on the tray. "I won't if it bothers you."

"No," he said. "No, go ahead. These are amazingly good. You don't want to miss them." He searched his own voice for sarcasm and unexpectedly found none. "Just leave me another two or three."

Pietro smiled. "Don't worry, Father."

"Thomas." That was even more unexpected. "I'd rather you called me Thomas."

"Only if you call me Livia."

"I don't know."

"Then I don't either. Father."

Thomas pulled away from her gaze, uncomfortable. He really needed to raise his blood sugar. He finished what he was holding in three more bites with no conversation in between, drank some beer, and reached for a second sandwich. Pietro was obviously letting him take the lead, set the rhythm, so, as much to break the silence as anything else, he spoke. "These paintings. And the ones in the entrance, and the hallways. I don't know much about art, but they seem quite good. Only, they're in so many different styles. For someone so young —" He stopped, realizing what he was saying.

"It takes some getting used to," Pietro said. Livia. He was going to try to start thinking of her as Livia. "For us, too. When we meet it's one of the first pieces of information we exchange. How long we've been Noantri. It situates us for one another. Ellen's from New York."

"I thought I heard that in her voice."

Pietro — Livia — shook her head. "Her original way of speaking would make her sound like a Brit. She was born in 1745. She's my Elder by about a hundred and fifty years."

"I . . ." Thomas paused, finished his beer. "I don't even know how to think about that."

"Don't try." Livia's voice was gentle. "As I said, it takes some getting used to. Now that your blood sugar's returning to normal, let's look at this poem."

53

Livia leaned forward and placed Mario Damiani's third poem on the art-book coffee table between herself and Thomas, holding it flat on its edges. Before she'd had a chance to work her way through the Romanesco lines, her cell phone rang. She rummaged it out of her bag.

"Livia, it's Spencer."

"Oh, good! Where are you? Are you all right? What happened in the church?"

"I'm home and I'm fine, thank you, apart from some minor psychological brutalization at the hands of the Carabinieri. And more to the point, the Gendarmerie."

"They were there, too?"

"I'm afraid so. The incident was unfortunately serious. That old monk was killed."

Livia drew a sharp breath. Thomas sent her a questioning look. "It's Spencer," she told him. "Spencer, Father Kelly's here with me. Tell me what happened."

"Am I on speaker?" Spencer asked carefully.

"No."

"Good. I'm sure it will be better if you tell him in your way, rather than if he hears it from me."

"That's considerate of you."

"You needn't sound so shocked. I'm not a total beast, Livia. In any case, what seems to have happened is that you were correct about the Vatican Library clerk. He was there, and he tried to follow us into the saint's foot chapel." That sounded more like the Spencer Livia knew.

"He must have come for the book," she said. "Who *is* he?"

"His name is Jorge Ocampo. Does that mean anything to you?"

"No. The police told you that?"

"No, they told each other that. Within my hearing. Careless of them." Except, of course, the Unchanged police officers had no way of knowing how far Spencer's Noantri auditory reach extended. "Ocampo is an Argentinian national." Which, since the clerk was Noantri, did not mean much. "The old monk sought to prevent him from following us. To give us, presumably, our meditative peace. There was an altercation, and the monk fell or was thrown to the

367

ground. He hit his head and gained admission to heaven." Yes, definitely Spencer. "But listen closely, because this is the part that will prove important to you and your priest. Because a churchman died in a church, the Gendarmes sent a representative. A handsome young Neapolitan, who just happens to be the *vice assistente* who arrested this same clerk at the Colosseum Metro station this morning for theft of Vatican property. Though all they found on him of the stolen property was a tracking chip."

"Hmm."

"Don't hmm yet, there's more. The Neapolitan Gendarme has a theory which he's shared with the Carabinieri. It involves a large and well-organized ring of thieves specializing in antiquities, possibly international in scope and clearly effective enough to successfully steal from the Vatican. And to attempt, in the same day with the same personnel, a theft at Santa Maria della Scala."

"The same personnel?"

"The clerk, who was obviously the inside man on the earlier occasion, as he was employed at the Vatican Library. And an art historian, one Livia Pietro. And also — quite appallingly — a priest. An American named

Thomas Kelly."

"Spencer. Are they serious?"

"The Gendarme is entirely serious and he seems to have sold this theory to the Carabinieri. They've become intent on catching the miscreants. It took all my powers of persuasion to convince them I barely know you, I was a touch surprised when you appeared at my door, I'd never met your priest before, and though I had no inkling of your intentions in visiting Santa Maria della Scala, I could assure them that your reputation and character were entirely spotless. You'd have been pleased, I think, to hear the fervor with which I defended your honor."

"Thank you."

"My pleasure. I told them their theory was flatly absurd, and that I was sure you would be able to clear up any misunderstanding as soon as you had the opportunity to speak with them. In order to help you restore your good name, I promised them that, though I had no earthly idea where you'd gone while I was praying over the withered extremity of the sainted Teresa, they could be sure that if I heard from you or of you, they'd be the first to know."

"Did they believe you?"

"I doubt it, but what does it matter? It's

clear they also suspect me, which is why they were willing to share their innermost thoughts: so I'd know how much they know, shiver in my boots, and come clean. However, they had no grounds on which to take me into custody, though keeping me inside a church for over an hour was in my view punitive detention enough. I have no doubt they've set a watch on my home, so you're not to come here. However, if I can be of any assistance to your task by leading them around Robin Hood's barn, do let me know. And talking of your task, how are you progressing?"

"We found another poem, at Santa Maria in Trastevere. In an aumbry."

"In a what?"

"It's — Look it up. We're working on the poem now."

"I'm reaching for my dictionary. I'll leave you to it, but if the poem — or any other you find — doesn't yield to your combined powers, I'd be happy to help. And in any case, do be careful. Your names and faces are all the rage in law enforcement circles."

"Thanks, Spencer. You caught us just in time."

"I endeavor," Spencer drawled, "to give satisfaction."

54

Once again Thomas was having trouble concentrating.

This distraction, so new to him, had first fractured his scholarly focus in the ancient apothecary. There he'd found himself trying to unravel the air, to sort pine bark from rose petal, detach mint from mushroom. Now, leaning with Livia Pietro over Damiani's poem, his mind again popped with unmanageable thoughts and sensations. Partly, he knew, it was the unpleasant news conveyed by Spencer George: that he and Livia were wanted by the Carabinieri and that the old monk was dead. Thomas had said a brief prayer for the soul of Father Battista, though he suspected the friar didn't need the help of a priest as heavily compromised as Thomas Kelly to get into heaven. Guilt was an element of his distraction, too: though Livia had tried to assure him the monk's death wasn't their fault, of course it was. And of course, she knew it was. **What would it be like,** he suddenly wondered, **to live forever, to go through eternity accumulating loss and guilt, with no way to expiate, to make amends, to be forgiven? With no end in sight?** He glanced at Livia, her black hair falling about her face as she leaned forward, her arms wrapped around her in her own posture of concentration that, he realized, was already familiar to him.

Without looking up, she spoke. "The poem, Thomas. I know a lot has happened and it's not easy to deal with. But the poem is what's important now."

He was glad her gaze didn't stray from the torn notebook leaf, because he felt his face grow hot. He straightened his shoulders and stared down at the poem, too.

Dojje de morte? Er piaggnisteo de l'esse nati?
Frammezzo a le crature alate, l'api, l'uscelli,
le sonajjere d'angioli, eccosce volati
a spiarje l'estasi ne l'occhi bbelli,
da dove, simme và, posso scappà coll'ale 'mmacolate.

Death throes? The pure puling of being born?

372

Among the winged creatures, birds and
  bees
and hierarchies of angels, here we swarm,
look down upon her face in ecstasy,
whence, if I chose, could flee, both wings
  untorn.

Again, uppercase blunt lead-pencil letters
along the bottom:

I F I D E.

Nothing. The words gave him nothing at
all. Death or birth? Hierarchies of angels?
Looking down in ecstasy, or looking down
on a face in ecstasy? Who was looking?
Whose face? Whose wings were untorn?
Though that, of all the images here, was the
only one that struck a bell in Thomas's
mind; but it was a bell so faint that, try as
he might, he was unable to call up any
meaning.

The letters, though: they were a different
matter. With growing excitement he stared
at them. The first set had made no sense;
neither did these, but if you added them to
the first ones, and then read them backwards, they almost did.

"Aedificavit," he said tentatively, trying it
out. " 'Built.' "

"Built?" Livia looked up. "Built what?"

"I don't know. But if you read these letters backwards and then the first set backwards, I mean if you read them *together,* they nearly spell *aedificavit.* 'Built.' "

"Nearly?"

"It's missing the initial *a,* but it's a compound letter, *ae,* so maybe he thought he could dispense with it. Or maybe it's in the next line! The *a.* On the next poem."

Livia was silent for a moment. "Are you saying this is a cumulative upside-down acrostic? In Latin?"

"From everything we know, that kind of thing would be right up Damiani's alley."

She nodded. "Yes, that's true. You could be right. It would answer the question of whether the penciled letters are his."

"But the poem itself," Thomas said. "Where to go now. What that means, I have no idea."

"That's all right." Livia smiled. "I do."

55

This time, Jorge Ocampo wasn't going to run. He would do nothing to call attention to himself. He'd covertly, stealthily make his way, an operative whose objective was to remain in deep cover while fulfilling his mission.

What was his mission?

He wasn't exactly sure.

Anna hadn't given him new instructions on the retrieval of the notebook or the surveillance of the *professoressa.* She hadn't told him what to do about the unalterable facts of what had happened in Santa Maria della Scala. She'd drawn in a sharp, angry breath when he'd told her about the accident, but she didn't yell, didn't berate him, didn't let loose that hot stream of vitriol she'd poured on his head on the few other occasions when he'd been unsuccessful at accomplishing a task. She really was unfair to him, Anna. He generally did quite well with the assignments she gave him, and he was — justly, he thought — proud of that. Like anyone, he had his moments of bad luck. Her impatience at those times, her lightning-fast willingness to reproach and blame him, really stung. It wasn't reasonable, it truly wasn't.

Although maybe she was changing. Maybe she was beginning to appreciate how hard he tried, and to understand that misfortune can happen to anyone. He'd expected a storm of anger, he'd braced for it, but instead he'd heard a silence, and then, "All right, Jorge. Are you out of sight?" When he'd assured her he'd taken cover, she asked where, and after he told her, she just said, "Stay there. I'm on my way."

So he'd settled into his velvet seat in the musty theater, waiting for Anna to come and tell him what to do. In the dark he drifted into a reverie, feeling her satin skin and silken hair, hearing the thrilling music of her voice as she whispered to him in his native Spanish. But a horn blared outside and startled him, and the dream vanished and would not come back. As he waited he found himself growing more and more uncomfortable. Il Pasquino was his private place. He didn't know what he should have said. "I'm not going to tell you where I am" hadn't occurred to him, and if it had, Anna wouldn't have put up with it. But he began to feel ill at ease about the idea of seeing Anna. Something in her voice . . . She was angry. She was hiding it, and he thought that sweet of her; clearly she knew the stress he was under and didn't want to upset him further. But she was angry.

And, he realized, disappointed.

That caused Jorge a new kind of pain, the thought that his Anna was disappointed in him. She'd sent him out to be her knight in shining armor, and he'd let her down. He came to a decision. He wasn't going to wait for her. Not right now. Not here, in his theater. He was going to leave Il Pasquino and steal along Vicolo del Piede, keeping to the shadows.

He had no instructions, that was true; but he was capable of formulating his own plans. He would find the *professoressa*. He would retrieve the notebook. He would complete his original assignment before he saw Anna again. Then his mistake in the church wouldn't loom so large. He'd never meant to hurt the old monk. He'd only been trying to move him out of the way. How could he have known he'd lose his balance and fall? After all, Anna was the one who'd drilled into him that he must never use any of his Noantri Blessings in a way that Mortals might notice. So it shouldn't be any surprise that he didn't know his own strength! And people fell all the time, even hit their heads, without dying. What had happened to the monk was definitely not Jorge's fault.

Anna had sounded worried about his safety, making sure he was out of sight, telling him to stay there. She wasn't acting as though what had happened in Santa Maria della Scala was very important.

But even if he couldn't be blamed for the monk's death, he knew it mattered. And he was going to make up for it.

Jorge peeked through the grimy window, waiting for a moment when the street was clear. His mind drifted again, this time not to Anna, but to the accident. It was a strange thing, what had happened to that old monk. The man had died, and Jorge wasn't so far from his own Change that he'd forgotten the terror of a Mortal anticipating that. But among the emotions passing across the old monk's face, Jorge, to his astonishment, hadn't found fear. What he'd seen — what he'd caused — was relief. Then, gratitude. Finally, to Jorge's astonishment, joy.

To his additional astonishment, Jorge

found himself feeling a tiny, transitory twinge of envy.

Back to the window. One of a revolutionary's best weapons was an ability to focus on his mission despite distractions. Ah — now came Jorge's chance. The street was empty. Jorge slipped from the window and sauntered along, in his sunglasses and porkpie hat. He hadn't worn either in the church, and he'd had on a jacket he was leaving in the theater. Sauntering down the street, he blended in beautifully with all the other hipsters. His plan was to head back to the *professoressa*'s house. He'd watch, and surely she'd come home eventually. Then he'd get the notebook Anna wanted and everything would be as it had been before.

That was his plan. But when he hit the intersection with Via della Fonte D'Olio, an amazing thing happened.

The *professoressa*. She'd passed by there. He caught her scent.

She was wearing perfume, this lady, something complicated and tropical. He'd noticed it in the Library and felt a stab of longing; the girls back home wore perfume, but among the Noantri, his new Community, his home now, it was the fashion to shun such things. Anna never wore perfume, petulantly asking, when he'd wondered why, if the fragrance of her own skin was not enough for him. He hadn't mentioned it again.

This *professoressa,* though: the perfume he'd first detected in the Library — maybe gardenias, could that be right? — the scent he'd followed down the winding hidden corridor, and then faintly noted in Santa Maria della Scala (though there the flowers and incense overpowered it) — he could sense it now, trailing from the direction of the piazza.

She'd passed by, and recently.

His heart started to pound. He ordered himself to stay calm. Quickly, but no faster than a Mortal in a hurry would have jogged, he rushed up Via della Fonte D'Olio into the piazza. She was nowhere in sight, but her scent laced the air. The church — she must have gone into the church! Jorge trotted up the steps, and the moment he entered Santa Maria in Trastevere he knew two things: she'd been there, and she was gone.

Something had happened here, though it was over. He could feel the disturbance in the settling air, smell the ozone scent of sudden excitement, the fading but still strongly acrid aroma a jolt of adrenaline adds to sweat. On his left as he entered a priest stood on a ladder locking a small golden door. The Catedral Metropolitana de Buenos Aires — a church he'd been in only once or twice, but oh, how beautiful it was — had a door like that. He'd wondered about it, but never asked anyone, because he liked his own answer. Symbolic sanctuary, he'd decided it meant, a reminder that the church would shelter all who came to it. He'd never seen the one back home open and regretted he hadn't arrived at Santa Maria in Trastevere just a few moments sooner, to see what was in them.

As the priest started down the ladder Jorge ordered himself to stop daydreaming. Revolutionary focus! This Church mumbo jumbo, it was oppressive, it was the enemy. He was only thinking about the Catedral Metropolitana because he missed home. The sooner he accomplished his mission, the sooner Anna and the others could establish Noantri rule, and the sooner he and Anna could return to Argentina. Jorge himself wasn't interested in a position of power in the new order. He didn't need it, because he'd have everything he wanted: to be with Anna, for eternity.

With new resolve, Jorge turned and left the church. He surveyed the streets issuing from the piazza, sniffed the air, and hurried past the fountain to the other side.

56

Rome could be splendid in autumn, clear and bright. The air, even when cool, lacked the sharp edge of Jonah's native Berlin, but he had no argument with a day like today. Rome was a beautiful city. Livia had brought him to it. And Livia was here still.

Shadows and sunlight alternated as his taxi sped — or what passed for speed in Rome traffic — alongside the Tiber. From habit unwilling to risk exposing his Noantri nature — though why it should matter, this near his goal, he wasn't sure — he'd hailed a cab to take him down the Janiculum into Trastevere.

Livia and the priest were apparently inside San Francesco a Ripa, something he'd learned from the man he had watching them. Much as he loved the sight of Livia, Jonah had avoided tailing them himself to keep her from picking up his scent. Or the rhythm of his footsteps, or the sound of his breath. After all the time, and the depth of it, that they'd spent together, she'd know within seconds if he came near.

Now, though, he had to take the chance.

He'd been informed earlier that a Noantri, someone his agent didn't know, had raced by on Vicolo del Piede. It might have been just some newcomer unable to keep his light under the Conclave-required bushel and it was possible the incident had no bearing on Jonah or his plan, beyond underlining the satisfaction he'd feel when it succeeded. After the Concordat had been published and the Noantri all Unveiled, none of his people would ever again be forced into false modesty and painful mediocrity. That was what he'd been thinking; but another of his agents had called just now, as he'd stood with Cardinal Cossa, to say a man who sounded to Jonah very much like the same one had passed by on Via di San Franceso a Ripa in the direction of the church — and to identify him as the clerk from the theft in the Vatican Library. Jonah had been told a third Noantri, besides Livia and the supercilious Spencer George, had been in Santa Maria della Scala, also; it was unclear whether that was again this same man, but Jonah was uneasy enough that he decided to come see for himself.

He understood that not only the Church, but the Conclave, would do everything in their power to thwart him, but he'd thought that at this point he had the upper hand with both.

This unknown Noantri, though, might be working for the Conclave. Jonah wouldn't put that past the Pontifex, to give Livia a task and then set a spy on her. The Noantri leader was a dark and secretive man who'd always made Jonah edgy, whose eyes seemed to see right into him, whom Jonah suspected uneasily of foreseeing Jonah's plan before he, Jonah, had ever had it fully formulated. Foreseeing it, but taking no preemptive action to stop it. As though he were giving Jonah every opportunity to do the right thing himself. This man, who'd emerged from the shadows to lead the Noantri as soon as the Concordat was signed, was an enigma even to his own. His steady voice had long led the opposition to Unveiling. Jonah was well aware that the Pontifex had now ordered his death and also that the only reason that order was stayed was the Conclave's desire to find and re-conceal the lost Concordat. If the Noantri stranger was in fact trailing Livia and the priest at the behest of the Conclave, that was a situation Jonah would have to handle.

Another worrisome possibility existed, also: that he was following Livia and Kelly for someone else. Within the Community, sentiment on the subject of Unveiling ran high on both sides of the line. At this sensitive point, it was imperative that no one, from either camp, interfere with Jonah's plan.

Now, Cardinal Cossa, he thought, as the taxi made the turn onto Viale di Trastevere: the Cardinal was a perfect example of everything that was wrong with the status quo. Because the Noantri were forced to remain hidden, Lorenzo Cossa was unfamiliar with them as people, as individuals; because he had only centuries of lies, tales, and legends by which to judge them, he feared and hated them. He couldn't tell reality from nonsense, claiming, for example, to be revolted by the smell of a Noantri, which Jonah knew no Mortal could detect. As opposed to Cossa's own omnipresent cigars, which could truly stink up a room.

What a sad man he was, too. Sad and bitter. As far as Jonah knew, it had been Cossa's life's goal to become Librarian and Archivist of the Vatican. Now he had. In the short time left to him — if he didn't become Noantri — you'd think he'd revel in the vast, varied collection under his control. The knowledge there, the connections to be made and understood, the possibilities! But he hadn't. He'd focused on the Concordat, set a team searching for it, brought in Thomas Kelly when they didn't find it. Cossa was angry, fearful, and disappointed, and from what Jonah could see, he loved nothing.

No. That was wrong. He did seem to love Thomas Kelly. Although of course Cardinal Cossa would never say anything of the sort to Jonah, still he could sense it in Cossa's voice, in the shift of his shoulders when Kelly was mentioned, in the fear in his eyes for Kelly in the current situation. Thomas Kelly was the son Lorenzo Cossa had never had. The prize pupil, the acolyte. Kelly had done well and Cossa was proud.

Soon, thought Jonah, Kelly would do even better. After which, Jonah would be rid of Lorenzo Cardinal Cossa once and for all.

And his revolting cigars.

57

Jorge Ocampo walked slowly, casually up the shallow steps leading into San Francesco a Ripa. Livia Pietro's perfume trail had brought him straight here, and though Jorge knew following it would have been child's play for any Noantri, still he was pleased with himself. Not just for finding the *professoressa,* but for ensuring he'd be able to get close enough to relieve her of the notebook before *she* detected *him.* He'd stopped at a *farmacia* and bought cologne, not one of the powerful, manly scents he'd worn back home — though he'd been tempted — but a cheap, sharp, unpleasant toilet water no one but a stuffed-nosed Mortal could have enjoyed. He'd have to wash it off before he saw Anna again, of course, but the pungent junk should make an excellent mask as he approached Pietro. What she might be doing here, he didn't know, but it mattered not to Jorge. He was on a mission.

Briefly he considered remaining outside, waiting for his quarry to emerge. His last foray into a church had not gone well. No, he decided. Too many variables, too many chances for her to slip away. Or even just to do whatever she was here for, and keep him waiting. Jorge did not want to wait.

The church's doors stood open, welcoming tourists, pilgrims, and the faithful. The fearful, Anna called them. Jorge's memories of the sweet incense and the echoing cool shadows in La Iglesia de Caacupé, the Buenos Aires church of his childhood, always brought him comfort. He supposed Anna must be right when she said the comfort sprang not from the presence of something ineffable and beyond his understanding, but from yielding to fear and surrendering rational thought, allowing scheming, power-hungry churchmen to deceive him, like millions of other sheep, into believing in that presence. She must be right, but he missed the comfort.

He sidled to the left as he entered, took off his shades, and looked around. At first glance it seemed that San Francesco a Ripa enclosed its visitors in a calm white interior, gilt-trimmed but sedate. Broad streams of sunlight poured from twelve round-topped windows, one over each arch, to crisscross the nave and reflect up off the patterned marble floor. People knelt or sat with bowed heads in some of the pews, and tourists with guidebooks ambled up and down the aisles.

Jorge had been in this church before, though, and he knew the serene nature of the nave and columns only served to emphasize the real pride of San Franceso a Ripa and the real reason to come here. The church was the final resting place of many wealthy and devout parishioners. Their memorials occupied the side chapels, where elaborate commissioned statuary commemorated their exemplary lives and their assured places in the world to come.

Seized with inspiration, Jorge slipped quietly over to, and up, the right-hand aisle, keeping his gaze on the side chapels opposite. Pietro was an art historian. The crowning glory of San Franceso a Ripa's funerary art was the chapel dedicated to Ludovica Albertoni. It depicted the deceased, surrounded by the heads of angels, at the moment of her departure from this life. To Jorge this work had always appeared more erotic than pious, more earthy than ethereal. He wasn't alone in thinking so, but no matter: the work was by Bernini, and in a church full of beautiful things, it stood head and shoulders above the rest.

And — obviously trying to elude him, because she'd changed into loose, cropped white pants, a white T-shirt, and a floppy canvas hat, and was carrying a different shoulder bag — Livia Pietro stood before it, looking up.

58

Five angels gazed out beyond their chapel and over the church, the joy on their faces inviting the congregation to share in the glory of Ludovica Albertoni's ascension to heaven. The sixth angel didn't join them; he was watching Ludovica as the ecstasy of what was happening filled and thrilled her.

"Here?" asked Thomas. "You're sure?"

" 'Death throes? The pure puling of being born?' " Livia quoted. "This is Ludovica Albertoni at the moment of death. There's also always been a theory that it can be read as Saint Ann receiving the Immaculate Conception."

"Simultaneously?"

"He did that sort of thing, Bernini. And see there? 'Among the winged creatures . . . look down upon her face . . .' That one *putto,* he's the only one looking at her." As Thomas followed her pointing finger, she added, "Aren't they beautiful?"

They were, the light from Bernini's hidden window glowing on the angels' heads and on the tomb of the pious woman they were welcoming to paradise. Thomas didn't offer his critical assessment, though, asking instead, "If this is right, where could the poem be?"

Livia paused, then answered, "The only place I can think of is inside that head."

Thomas gazed skeptically at the sculpture. "But this was carved centuries before —"

"They're mounted on steel rods. The heads. They were made separately and installed once the sculpture was in place."

"They come off?"

"So I've read. I've never tried it." Still she didn't move, just stood gazing up at the flowing marble.

"Well?" Thomas said. "If that's where it is, shouldn't we go get it?" By "we" he meant she, and he was sure she knew it. She was clearly the better of the two of them at climbing on things.

Livia glanced around her. "I'm sorry. It's just . . . I'm always so taken with this work. You're right, of course. I'll need something to stand on. I wonder if there's a ladder in the sacristy —"

"What are you talking about? You can reach it from there."

"From where?" she said, so he pointed. Her eyes widened. "You can't be serious. Stand on a Bernini?"

Thomas stared at her. "You climbed onto Santa Teresa's altar. You stood on a collection box!"

Livia blinked. "But this is a Bernini."

They traded looks of mutual incomprehension. With a huffed breath, Thomas turned, approached the sculpture, and said to her, "Then this time you make the distraction." He took a quick look around. No one was near; this was the moment. Without waiting to see what Livia came up with, he slipped off his shoes, turned back to the beatified Ludovica and her angelic escort, grabbed a fold of her marble garment, and hoisted himself up.

59

Livia watched, appalled, as Thomas Kelly
clambered across the supine marble body of
Ludovica Albertoni to reach the angel head.
On their way here, she and he had both
made improvised efforts at disguise. She'd
borrowed pants, a bag, and an *Io ♥ Nuova
York* T-shirt from Ellen; she'd bought tiny
round Yoko Ono sunglasses and braided and
pinned up her hair under a floppy white
canvas hat. Thomas had bought a *Roma*
sweatshirt — black; he was still a priest —
and a baseball cap. They'd both ditched
their cells and bought new, pre-paid phones.
Thomas had fought doing that, in case the
Cardinal called him; when finally persuaded
that their GPS chips were like neon signs
("Even when the phone is off?" "Yes, Father.
Thomas. Yes, Thomas"), the first thing he
did when he got the new phone was to call
Lorenzo Cossa from it. And got no answer.

What all this meant was, Thomas Kelly

wasn't wearing his clerical collar or tabbed shirt anymore. Crawling over the sculpture, he didn't even have that air of authority to separate him from a common vandal. Of course, climbing on a Bernini did just about make him a common vandal, so maybe any separation would've been beside the point. Livia wanted to shout at him to stop, to come down, to be careful, but she clamped her mouth shut: she certainly did not want to alert anyone else in the church to what was going on. A distraction. She needed to cause a distraction. She turned to leave the Albertoni chapel.

The distraction caused itself.

The Noantri clerk from the Library, Jorge Ocampo. The man who, according to Spencer, had killed the old monk. Jorge Ocampo stood right smack in front of her, grinning.

She'd barely registered his presence when he lunged for her. No, not for her. For her bag. He'd wrenched it off her shoulder before she realized what was happening. She reached for it, grabbing nothing but air. Holding the bag high, Ocampo spun away. Livia leapt and tackled him for the second time that day. They both went down, rolling, tangled in each other's clothes. Ocampo's sharp elbow slammed painfully into Livia's cheek. He stank of some disgusting cologne and was slimy with sweat; but though thin, he was strong and determined. She gave him a knee to the gut, tried to yank the bag back. His grip was like glue. He shoved her; her head smacked the chapel railing. She was stunned only for a second, less; but it was enough. Ocampo sprang to his feet and took off with her bag.

He collided, in the aisle, with a broad-shouldered, yellow-haired man.

Jonah.

Dumbfounded, Livia could only stare. Hallucination caused by concussion? Were hallucinations this detailed, carrying scent, glints of gold, the precise web of tiny wrinkles beside laughing eyes? For his part, Jonah, or his phantasm, had no time to acknowledge her presence or answer any of the thousand questions racing around in her head. Livia watched Ocampo try to shove Jonah aside, saw Jonah push back, then sweep his right fist into the clerk's chin and pump his left into his stomach. When Ocampo doubled over, Jonah grabbed the shoulder bag, but Ocampo held tight to the strap and punched Jonah's nose.

With a shout Thomas Kelly jumped from the sculpture to land beside her. He charged forward and grabbed the clerk's arm as Ocampo was pulling back for another blow.

Ocampo spun around snarling and threw Thomas hard to the ground. He raised his leg to stomp Thomas's face. Thomas rolled; in that extra second Jonah slammed his fist into Ocampo's neck. The clerk staggered and loosened his grip on Livia's bag. Jonah yanked it away.

Livia suddenly realized that beyond all this chaos she could hear not only shouts and horrified screams, but sirens. They heralded the law; two officers burst into the church. She rose clumsily to her feet. Jonah, with a grin, tossed her her shoulder bag. He leaned down, helped Thomas up, and then yanked Ocampo to his feet, also. And socked him again. And then, instead of delivering a coup de grâce, he just stood, arms at his sides, and gave Ocampo an opening. The clerk couldn't resist. He threw a punch. Livia stood, openmouthed, until Thomas, shoes in one hand, grabbed her elbow with the other and dragged her down the aisle, saying, "Now that's what I call a distraction. Let's go."

60

The bread was nothing but crumbs, the *salumi* and *formaggio* gone. Giulio Aventino finished his coffee and signaled for another, and for a second for his sergeant, also. Raffaele Orsini drank *caffè macchiato,* into which he stirred sugar, producing a sweet, complicated drink. Giulio preferred the bitter simplicity of espresso. But that was Raffaele. Everything was multilayered and everything was for the best.

They sat at a café in the piazza opposite Santa Maria della Scala, working the phones. Raffaele had been all for dashing out into the streets immediately, but Giulio had suggested mildly that they might do better if they knew which direction to dash in. Carabinieri and *polizia* all over Rome were on the lookout for the suspect, that Vatican Library clerk, and for his associates. Since Giulio and Raffaele both had street sources they cultivated for exactly this type of situation, why not explore whatever assistance the criminal underworld might be able to offer?

Before they'd settled in to run through their contact lists — Giulio wondered if Raffaele had a subfolder labeled "informant" on his cell phone, organized alphabetically or perhaps by specialty — Giulio had called the *maresciallo* to give him a report.

"The Curia's not happy, Aventino," the boss had said darkly.

Giulio stopped himself from asking why a holy friar gaining admission to heaven should displease the Vatican, saying instead, "We're doing what we can."

"Do it faster. Is the Gendarme any use? Or is he in the way? I could get him called off."

"No, don't. I think he's worth having around. But what you could do is tell Central to alert me to any odd goings-on in a church anywhere in the city."

If anyone else had spoken that way the *maresciallo* would probably have reminded him who was boss. Giulio could hear the gritted teeth as he asked, "Why? Is something else about to happen?"

"I have no idea. Just a feeling."

The *maresciallo* allowed himself a snort,

but Giulio didn't care and they both knew that.

"All right, but be judicious in what you respond to. I don't want you to waste your time on wild-goose chases."

"Oh? Well, in that case, we won't." Giulio clicked off.

The Gendarme, Luigi Esposito, had gone off on his own. He wasn't under Giulio's command so Giulio couldn't stop him. Esposito had told them his own sources were better consulted in person. That could be true, but Giulio suspected the young man was just plain excited at the prospect of spending his time on the bustling workaday streets of Rome, instead of the sedate corridors and tourist-choked public rooms of the Holy See.

Giulio himself would have gone out of his mind there.

He'd admonished Raffaele when the sergeant had snickered at the news a Gendarme was coming to join them, but in the pecking order of Roman law enforcement there was no question the Gendarmerie was at the bottom. The Rome *polizia* crowded the middle step, as local lawmen did everywhere in Italy: clumsy, slow-moving bureaucracies at best, or in some places, corrupt and dangerous. The constabulary pinnacle, of course, was occupied by the Carabinieri. A branch of the Italian military, they were well trained and well armed, charged with fighting crime all over the country and occasionally overseas: on any given day you could find Carabinieri on secondment to other nations, and to international agencies; and Carabinieri had been called up for, and had died in, service in the Middle East. Giulio himself had served in Africa, many years ago, and he knew this about his partner: as devoted as Raffaele was to his job and his young family, if called up he'd go proudly. And acquit himself well, Giulio had no doubt. For all Raffaele's religious piety, Giulio had long suspected devotion to duty — to his family, to his job, to his country, and yes, to his Church — was Raffaele's real faith.

Giulio's own faith was simple: that he loved his wife and kids, and they were worth loving; that he was good at his job, and his job was worth doing. Anything else — the next life, or the one after that — would have to take care of itself.

What Luigi Esposito was devoted to, Giulio didn't know. But the young Gendarme had impressed Giulio with his energy, pleased him with his thoroughness, and more or less convinced him with his theory. More or less because hard evidence was the only thing that ever convinced Giulio Aventino of anything. But Esposito's stolen-art-ring idea intrigued him, and tentatively answered some otherwise confounding questions: What had gone on this morning at the Vatican Library? How was it connected to what had happened at Santa Maria della Scala? And why had Raffaele's cardinal uncle requested a surveillance of *Professoressa* Livia Pietro?

That last would have been easier to answer if the cardinal uncle would answer his cell phone, but even his secretary, Father Ateba, when reached at the Vatican, had no idea where Lorenzo Cossa might be.

Giulio nodded his thanks as the new coffees were delivered and dialed the next source on his list, the owner of a fine-art framing shop whom Giulio was sure, but had never tried hard to prove, had a sideline in forged Old Masters. The shop owner was grateful for Giulio's lack of diligence, and Giulio had long since calculated that the man's value as an informant vastly outweighed any potential gain from shutting down his operation, which, after all, only made fools of people drooling after bargains anyone without larceny in his heart would recognize as too good to be true. On this occasion the shop owner had nothing to add, though, beyond promising to contact Giulio immediately should the street start buzzing with tales of audacious, highly professional art thieves.

Giulio thumbed off the phone and grunted. "That makes seven," he said to Raffaele, whose phone was likewise temporarily idle. "And they all claim they haven't heard a thing. You finding anything?"

"*Niente di niente.* I'm beginning to wonder if Esposito's wrong. Or are these people just really good?"

"I've never known Roman crooks to be adept at hiding their traces."

"Well, only one of these three is even Italian."

"Supporting Esposito's international-gang theory. Though you might expect Interpol would've had something on them, then." Which Esposito had said they didn't. The young Gendarme had searched the relevant databases — interesting to find someone so apparently techno-savvy in those hidebound holy halls — and found nothing. Giulio himself, a Luddite, nothing to be proud of but he was too old to change, had done some old-fashioned research: he'd called a friend, Paolo Lucca, who'd been promoted out of general larceny to the elite Nucleo

Tutela Patrimonio Artistico, the Carabinieri's own stolen art bureau. Paolo was
no help: none of the suspects were known
to Il Nucleo. He was interested, but the only
actual theft had occurred at the Vatican,
outside Carabinieri jurisdiction. He'd promised to sniff around, and also, at Giulio's
request, to look into unsolved cases involv-
ing Church-related art anywhere in the
country.

"Around the world, come to that," Giulio
told him. "These people may be new to
Italy. You're buddy-buddy with the hotshots
at Interpol, I assume."

"I thought you said you'd already checked
with them."

"Checked their database. The Gendarme
did. But —"

"But he doesn't know anyone over there
and you're afraid if he calls them they won't
give him the time of day."

"Am I wrong?"

"No. They're worse than we are. Though I
have to admit, the last Gendarme I worked
with was a bona fide idiot."

"This kid's sharp, Paolo. He's wasted over
there."

Giulio sat back now and sipped his coffee.
"I wonder what the point is."

Raffaele looked up. "Point of what?"

"These particular thefts. They've obviously got a specific agenda. And they're in a hurry."

"That could just be because they screwed up this morning and now they're exposed."

"Then why didn't they lay low for a while instead of heading over here? I wish I knew what they were looking for. A notebook from the Vatican Library, some target in the Reliquary Chapel . . ."

"Monsignor Conti said nothing was missing."

"That only means they failed. Possibly because they didn't want that irritating historian to know what they were up to and they couldn't get him to leave."

Raffaele grinned. "If that's it, I sympathize with them."

"What is it they're doing, Raffaele?" Giulio leaned back, staring at the sky. "What's the connection? Come on, you're the church guy. What do you see?"

"Nothing," Raffaele admitted. "But I wonder if they do."

"If they do what?"

"See the connection. Maybe all they have is a list."

Giulio was silent for a moment. "They're working for someone."

Raffaele noddded. "Not just theft, theft to

order. For a client who doesn't want to wait."

"All right. I'll buy it. But that just makes the question: What's the client after?"

"I wonder," Raffaele said, "if the client's impatient enough — or important enough — that they're willing to risk going on now. Accident or not, they did kill someone."

From the table beside his coffee, Giulio's cell phone rang.

"*Ispettore,* this is Dispatch," a woman's voice said. "We've just sent two officers to a fight inside San Francesco a Ripa. There was a bulletin asking that you be alerted to —"

"Yes. Hold on." Giulio looked over at Raffaele. "San Francesco a Ripa. Close, right?" Raffaele nodded. "Thank you," Giulio told Dispatch.

He was about to click off when she said, "*Ispettore*? I have another report here, from an hour ago, before your bulletin came in. I didn't handle the call but when I saw what you wanted I looked back through our files just in case. There was a disturbance in Santa Maria in Trastevere. Nothing seems to be missing but our reports are that a woman stood on the collection box and opened the aumbry. Were you told about that?"

"No. Opened the what?"

"The aumbry, it says. I don't know either."

"But nothing's missing?"

"According to the priests, no."

"Thank you. Good work." By the time he said, "Keep me updated," he'd jumped up and dropped ten Euro on the table. To Raffaele he shouted over his shoulder, "My car's closest. Call Esposito." They took off across the piazza, reached the Fiat, and yanked open the doors at the same moment. Raffaele was poking buttons on his cell phone as they climbed into the car. Giulio fired the engine and peeled out. To Raffaele, holding the phone between ear and shoulder and struggling to buckle his seat belt, Giulio added, "And what's an aumbry?"

61

Livia Pietro tripped. Thomas, his heart pounding, had to grab her to keep her from falling as they ran down San Francesco a Ripa's center aisle. She kept turning to look back; you'd think she'd never seen a fight before. He surveyed the narthex as they neared it. No one there but horrified tourists. The two officers were charging down the left aisle toward the Albertoni chapel, where the clerk and the other man were still brawling. He and Livia could make it out the door. Gripping her arm, he tried to pull her along, but she dug in her heels and said, "No!"

"No, what?"

"We can't leave."

"You made me leave Santa Maria della Scala, and you were right! This is the same. We can't stay here. There's nothing we can —"

"That's not what I mean. There are more

police coming. I can hear them. They'll be pulling into the piazza any second."

As if to prove her words, the wail of a siren and the screech of brakes reached Thomas. Livia, with a look of longing, had turned back toward the fight, which had expanded: now both the clerk — Ocampo, was that his name? — and the blond man were mixing it up with the officers. Thomas tightened his grip on her arm. He stared around desperately, then said, "Come this way!"

The Catholic Church had, over the centuries, evolved many different practices for the administration of its sacraments, and reasons and explanations abounded for each choice. The sacrament of confession, for example: some theologians thought it best that the penitent's side of the confessional be open, with neither door nor drape. Thus the entire congregation could see a fellow believer offer contrition for his sins and seek absolution. They could be a support for him, he an example to them. There was an argument to be made in that direction, to be sure. Right now, however, Thomas was unutterably relieved that the designers of the ecclesiastical furnishings in San Francesco a Ripa had not shared this approach.

He hauled Livia down the center aisle

toward the entrance and then over to the other side of the nave, about as far from the action as they could get. A confessional nestled between two chapels in the side aisle. The booth was of a weighty Baroque style, both priest and penitent hidden behind heavily carved wooden doors. Pulling open the penitent's side, he told Livia, "Get in!" and then, since she seemed frozen, casting yet another look at the scuffling men, he shoved her inside and shut the door on her. **Ah, Thomas, now we're forcing reluctant sinners into the confessional?** He yanked open the other door, jumped in, and pulled it to. Sitting on the narrow bench, he slid the panel, revealing the screen between them.

"What's going on?" he whispered as he pulled his shoes on. When she didn't answer he demanded, "The clerk — that was Ocampo, right?"

"Yes." Livia's own whisper was hoarse. "And Jonah."

"Jonah? Who, the blond man? I thought that was just a good Samaritan, helping you."

"No. Jonah."

"The man — the . . . Noantri — who started all this? The one you're looking for?"

He started to rise but she said, "Don't.

Listen, you can hear it. They're both gone."

Now her voice only sounded sad. He paused, and listened, and found she was right. He heard shouts and clamoring voices, people vying to tell their versions of what they'd seen, what they'd heard. Other voices tried to calm things down, sort them out. Nothing sounded like thrown punches, kicks, flesh striking flesh.

"How do you know they're gone? Not just arrested?"

"Their footsteps when they ran."

"You heard them?"

Wearily, she said, "Of course."

Of course. Thomas sat back down. His skin felt oddly flushed and his heart still beat rapidly as he said, "What *happened*?"

"I don't know. I turned and he was there. Ocampo. He must still be after the notebook because he grabbed my bag."

"How did he find us?"

"I'm not sure. He might have caught my scent."

"Caught your —" Thomas realized that through the confessional screen he was catching her scent, too. Or perhaps not hers — he was human, after all — but the perfume she wore: a deep, gentle fragrance, as of a tropical garden where night flowers bloomed. "All right, fine!" He shook his

411

head to clear it. "And this Jonah? How did *he* find us?"

"I don't know that, either. Or why. He must know what I've been told to do. And that the Conclave is prepared to . . . do it, if I fail. Why doesn't he just stay out of sight?"

"Are they working together?"

"Jonah and Ocampo? You mean, because they're both Noantri? If they are that's some show they just put on." She seemed to rouse herself, her voice beyond the screen taking on a sharper note.

Many questions elbowed one another in Thomas's head, about Jonah, about Livia, about the Noantri; and he felt he didn't want to ask them here, through the confessional screen. He wanted to see her face, look into her eyes. But another question had to be answered first. "Where are the police?"

"What?"

"Use your supersonic hearing! Are they still here?"

For a moment, silence from the other side of the screen. Then, "Yes. More of them. The two officers we saw, and also the man who called for the ambulance in Santa Maria della Scala. He's with someone else. And the Gendarme! From the Colosseum station, I think he's here, too." She drew a

412

sharp breath. "Two of them are heading this way."

"All right," Thomas said. He tried to ignore the odd sensations he was feeling, tried to concentrate on the immediate problem. "Do you remember how this goes?"

"How what goes?"

"Confession. 'Bless me, Father, for I have sinned'? You said you were raised a Catholic. Or is even the memory of that something you've dispensed with?"

"Would you absolve a Noantri if one came to you?" she snapped. "Though in fact you probably have, more than once." Without giving him a chance to answer she intoned, *"Mi benedica, Padre, perché ho peccato."*

She didn't go on, so in soft, droning Italian, which he hoped was quiet enough to barely be heard by, and accentless enough to convince, any passing policeman, Thomas replied with the prompt. "How long has it been, my child, since your last confession?"

A pause; then, "Ninety-six years."

Thomas tried to swallow the choking sound he found himself making. He wasn't sure what to say, but this time, she didn't stop.

"I don't repent of the life I've lived or am living," she said, speaking low. "I'm aware

413

that you think I should — the Unchanged have always thought so — but that belief is born from fear and ignorance."

Thomas started to protest, but was she that wrong? What did he know about her life — their life, these Noantri? And wasn't he, in fact, afraid? He said nothing, only listened as she went on. As, it occurred to him, a priest in a confessional is supposed to do.

"But I committed a great sin, and it's led to others," she said, drawing a slow breath. "I loved a man who wasn't mine to love. Without permission I brought him into my Community. We both could have been expelled, but instead the Community welcomed him. Now he's threatening to destroy it."

At a sound, Thomas glanced through the metal grillwork on the confessional door. The tiny holes that formed a cross showed him two men moving slowly up the aisle in their direction.

"This man you loved." Something inside him resented saying those words; what was wrong with him? They had to keep talking, so he continued, "His actions aren't your fault."

"He's my responsibility. Because I brought him to us. It's one of our Laws. What's worse is, I've been ordered to stop him but I fear that I can't."

"Failure is never a sin."

"Failure to try, though? To do what's right? When it comes to it, I'm afraid I'll let him go. In fact I already did, just now. Instead of . . ." She trailed off.

Thomas paused, as understanding dawned. "Instead of killing him? Is that what you've been ordered to do?"

"It might be necessary."

"To take his life? How could failure to take a life ever be construed as a sin?" He frowned as another question came to him. "Wait. He's — How could that even be done? Throw him on a bonfire? Burn him at the stake?" Would she really do that? Just when he'd begun to think —

"No," she whispered. "There's another way."

"To destroy you? You people, I mean?"

With a faint trace of amusement in her voice she answered, "I'm glad you qualified that. Yes. I —"

She stopped for a moment. He glanced through the door panel. The men walking down the aisle were coming close.

"Don't speak," he said to Livia. "Just let me do this. We'll be fine."

62

". . . in San Francesco a Ripa," Giulio Aventino was telling the *maresciallo.* Raffaele signaled him to keep his voice down — they were standing by an occupied confessional — but all Giulio did was walk a few steps farther down the aisle. They'd come over here for a little peace and quiet. Though the Carabinieri had finished their questioning, tourists and worshippers still milled around by the Albertoni chapel, each offering his own account and disputing the others. If past experience was anything to go on — and in police work, it always was — Raffaele knew the fight was growing in duration and danger with each retelling. By the time the story was told over this afternoon's coffee or tonight's red wine, there would have been knives, brass knuckles, and blood all over the Bernini. Meanwhile, the actual altercation had been over so fast that officers questioning tourists who'd been over here on the right side of the church had found that some hadn't even been aware of the fight and none had seen it.

"Over by the time we got here," Giulio was saying. "It seems to have been a purse-snatching. A tourist. No, some good Samaritan stopped it. That was the fight. But the point is, the witness descriptions of the snatcher fit our suspect. There's a possibility here that he's just some kind of anti-clerical nut job." **Which was funny,** Raffaele thought, **coming from Giulio.** "Yes, you're absolutely right, sir, it would've been easier to know what he's up to if we'd laid our hands on him. You might ask the officers why they let him get away, once they're out of hospital." Giulio rolled his eyes at Raffaele. "The good Samaritan took off after him. Yes, of course we need to keep the search going, but I still think meanwhile — No, I'm not suggesting you provide protection to every church in Rome. Sir. Just to warn them. Yes. All right. Well, it might, but false alarms are better than another death, don't you think? Unless the Vatican doesn't care that we —" He held the phone away from his ear; Raffaele heard the *maresciallo* sputtering, something about Giulio going too far. Giulio brought the phone back and sighed, "Yes. What? Yes,

Esposito's his name, and yes, he's here, too. No, why? As long as they let him stay, I can use him. Yes. We will. No, we haven't, but we're trying. Thank you. Sir."

As Giulio sighed and pocketed the phone, Raffaele said, "He's not happy?"

"Have you ever known him happy? He wanted this wrapped up and it just gets worse. Come on, I need a smoke."

As the priest in the confessional continued to assign penance — judging from the length of the list, this was a prodigal with a wide gulf of time since his or her last confession and an impressive collection of sins — Raffaele and Giulio walked up the aisle and left the church, emerging into the bright autumn afternoon.

"Raffaele," Giulio said, cupping a Marlboro to light it, "you think we're wrong? Esposito's wrong? That this has nothing to do with stolen art, it really is just some lunatic with a grudge against the Church?"

"Lunatic? I've heard you use much more flattering words about people who feel that way."

"Be serious."

"You mean, is this just a wacko trying to create havoc, no worries about killing if someone gets in the way?"

Giulio nodded and blew a stream of

smoke. "Il Nucleo, Interpol, all those bright bulbs, they never heard of this gang. It's the simplest explanation: there is no gang."

"I guess it's possible. But it doesn't explain what Cardinal Cossa wanted with Livia Pietro."

"The boss asked whether we'd reached him. Try him again." While Raffaele took out his phone, Giulio went on, "Maybe this guy's stalking Pietro because she's part of whatever fantasy he's working from. Maybe he has a particular thing about her and Cossa knew it, and wanted you to keep an eye on her to protect her? Or as a way to catch him? That tourist whose purse he went for has her general build, from what the witnesses say."

"Why didn't the Cardinal tell me that, then? I wish that tourist had hung around. She might be able to tell us something."

"Would you stay knowing you'd be wasting your next hour with us? If you weren't hurt and hadn't lost anything?"

"It would've been the right thing to do," Raffaele stoutly maintained. Giulio gave him the over-the-eyeglasses look, and Raffaele admitted, "But if I didn't do it, what I would probably do is head for the nearest café to calm my nerves."

"Hmm. Or wine bar."

While Raffaele dialed his uncle, Giulio dialed Dispatch, asking them to start a search for the intended victim in the cafés and wine bars near San Francesco a Ripa. Raffaele waited until Giulio lowered his phone to say, "Voice mail. So you're thinking that Pietro — and the priest she was with — aren't involved in anything? That there's nothing to be involved in, just some nut?"

Giulio narrowed his eyes at Raffaele through the smoke from his cigarette. "No," he said after a pause. "No. It makes sense and it's simple, but no, I still think something bigger's going on here."

"Good." Raffaele grinned. "So do I. Look, here's Esposito."

63

"You can stop," Livia said, as Thomas droned on about Hail Marys and Our Fathers. "They're gone."

He did stop, and silence filled the confessional. In truth, Livia was grateful. She'd been growing oddly uncomfortable. The need for penance was something she felt acutely, and she was experiencing more than a touch of regret for the days — so long ago — when she believed some prayers and a few good deeds could wipe a slate clean.

"We'll have to wait before we go back," she said. "The Carabinieri are still outside. On the steps."

"Go back where?"

"To look for the poem, of course. Though this time we'll get a ladder. I'm not going to let you climb on the Bernini again."

"Don't worry about it."

"No, I'm serious. Shoes or no shoes, there's no —"

"I mean, don't worry, no one's going to climb on anything. I have it."

"You have — You found it? The poem?"

"That head was heavy, too." She could swear she heard him grinning. "I lifted it off and the sheet of paper was wrapped around the iron bar. It's a little rusty but I think it's readable. I put the head back, by the way."

"I should hope so! Read it to me."

"How about, 'Good work, Father Kelly'?"

"Good work, Father Kelly, now read it to me!"

64

Through the confessional screen, Thomas read to Livia the poem he'd found inside the angel's head.

Ar penitente, quann'è arivato, ce vo' er
  zonno.
J'ammolla la dorce machina lì su la roccia
lisscia com'un guanciale, ppoi casca fonno
frammezzo a 'n zzoggno: du' lupi rampanti,
  'na bboccia
granne ch'aribolle . . . E la nostra
  compaggnia ce stà 'ntorno.

The penitent, at journey's end, needs sleep.
He lays the sweet machine upon the stone
that's smooth enough for pillow, falls to
  deep
dreaming: two gray wolves rampant, a
  cauldron . . .
And dreams lead to the company we keep.

"And there are more penciled letters. A M

A E E. They're spread weirdly far apart, but they're here. And there's the *a.*" Thomas had to force himself to keep his voice down. "The missing *a* from *aedificavit.* There it is."

"If you're right, maybe the next three letters — I mean, the three before, reading right to left — are *eam.* 'It.' 'Built it.' "

"All right, but who built what?"

"That other *e* — it must be part of another word. When we find the next poem, it will tell us."

It was oddly thrilling, he thought. Collaboration. Working with her to solve this puzzle. Building on each other's work, correcting, suggesting, adding. Up until now, all his scholarly work had been done alone. He taught, yes, and so was not lonely; but it was different with students. This joy of teamwork, of equals sparking off each other — he was feeling now an excitement he hadn't felt in years.

Which must be what explained his quickened heartbeat, the tingling in his skin.

"All right," he said. "I think the coast is clear. Let's go."

"Go where?"

"Upstairs, of course."

"Upstairs where?"

He was taken aback. "Really? You don't know? This one's so easy."

65

Luigi Esposito was delighted. He supposed he shouldn't have been, since the case had no breaks yet, but the Carabinieri were treating him like an equal — like a cop! — and he'd been right about that repellent Argentinian clerk. All a mistake, faulty alarm system, hog-wash. It was like breathing fresh mountain air, to be working out here in the real world, where investigating crime was more important than maintaining decorum.

And Luigi had an idea.

He'd arrived at San Francesco a Ripa at almost the same moment as *Ispettore* Aventino and his sergeant, Orsini, which meant none of them had seen the purse-snatching, the fight, or the suspect blasting out of the church with the good Samaritan after him. They found the two damaged officers groaning on the marble floor inside. Both the suspect and his pursuer, apparently, went flying across the piazza and disappeared up Via di San Francesco a Ripa. The suspect, from witness reports, was pulling ahead, which probably meant the good Samaritan eventually gave up, patted himself on the back for the rescue, and went about his business. Carabinieri and *polizia* were out combing the area for the suspect; but they'd done that before, after he escaped from Santa Maria della Scala, and hadn't found a trace. Aventino had requested a bulletin go out to the churches of Rome, ostensibly a warning because the suspect was dangerous. Luigi had caught on, though, and was impressed: the *ispettore,* with that one move, had provided them with many thousands more eyes.

Luigi, though, was interested in a specific set of eyes.

He stood with Aventino and Orsini on the church steps near one of the potted palms, he and Aventino smoking, Orsini scanning the piazza. The sergeant was a man who was in his element in this job, Luigi thought. As he himself would be, if the job were his. They had finished interviewing everyone willing to stay and be interviewed — and everyone who thought they'd slink out the doors; because while the Carabinieri had worked the inside, Luigi, with the help of

an officer he'd been lent (a uniformed officer with a brain! *Miracoloso!*) had ambushed
the slinkers. Afterward, they'd compared
notes. The Carabinieri had told Luigi about
the ruckus with the aumbry in Santa Maria
in Trastevere, and though it wasn't clear
whether it was the same cast of characters
involved in that one, they all agreed: the
Vatican Library and three churches in the
same day meant something big was going
on.

"The historian," Luigi said. "I want to go
back and talk to him."

Aventino squinted through the smoke
from his cigarette. "The Englishman? Spencer George? We grilled him pretty thor-
oughly. You just caught the end."

"So you're satisfied he has nothing to do
with this?"

"I'm never satisfied. We've got people
watching him. I just don't have anything
new to ask him yet."

"I'd like to try."

Orsini grinned. "A hunch?"

Luigi felt his face grow hot. "Not really, I
—"

The *ispettore* shrugged. "Good cops play
their hunches. Let us know what you find
out."

"Yes, sir!" Luigi, thrilled to be just another

cop on a case, playing a hunch, entrusted with the interrogation of a suspect under surveillance, loped to his car. Five minutes later he was back in Piazza della Scala, parking opposite Spencer George's door. He banged the bronze lion knocker and saw the curtain move aside in the upstairs window. For a moment he wondered what he'd do if the historian didn't let him in. He had no authority outside the Holy See, and even if he'd had, a citizen was under no obligation to speak to anyone in law enforcement unless he was under arrest. Or then, either, come to think of it: that's what lawyers were for.

But the door opened and Spencer George stood there, his expression as haughtily bored as it had been when he'd sat on the church pew a few hours ago. **Did his face ever change,** Luigi wondered, **or was this sneer permanent?** He was about to introduce himself when the historian spoke.

"Well. The gentleman from the Gendarmerie. Presumably you're here to ask yet more tiresome questions. I'd hope your position would create in you greater reserves of humility and courtesy than that of your secular peers, but I doubt it does. At least let's be comfortable. Please, come in."

66

Anna's blood started to boil.

Jorge had left the theater. She could tell by sniffing the air when she dropped in the open window: his scent was faded, dissipating in the musty room. She stared around her, picking out, in the dark, all the details Mortal eyes would have needed assistance to see. What was it about this place, Il Pasquino? Why had Jorge chosen to hide here? Dust, mold, and spiderwebs; torn curtains and bubbling plaster. Another object once valuable, now discarded, discounted, by myopic Mortals, who found no worth in what they couldn't use right that instant. This had been a beautiful place once, she could tell, before it was chopped up, then closed and allowed to rot. Sleek, art deco lines, comfortable, wooden-armed seats, even a retractable roof. A place to relax and be transported to someone else's fantasy, where you'd be safe for an hour or two.

Maybe, after she and her followers were successful and Noantri rule was established over a peaceful — a pacified — world, she'd re-open this theater. She'd name it after Jorge, she thought, smiling. L'Ocampo. He'd like that.

Too bad he wouldn't be around to see it.

67

"Ignatius Loyola revered Saint Francis. Ignatius was the son of a noble family whose crest was two gray wolves, rampant, and a cauldron. And of course the wolf is associated with Francis, also." Thomas spoke rapidly, and had fallen back into university lecturer mode, Livia noted, as he led the way up the stone staircase to the left of the altar. To reach these stairs they'd had to cut through the sacristy. Livia had regretted Thomas's lack of ecclesiastical dress at that point, as she had when they left the confessional. She wasn't sure the priests and monks at San Francesco a Ripa would be pleased to see some guy in a sweatshirt climbing out of the box; but speaking through the screen, Thomas had brushed off her worry. "It's not an issue. There's no law about what I wear when. Anyway, my passport photo shows the full regalia. If anyone asks I'll tell them I'm on vacation, we were out sightseeing, and you were overcome with an urge to confess as soon as we walked in here. Believe me, they'll be thrilled." He paused. "I'll be lying, but they'll be thrilled."

"Lying? What about all the things I just told you?"

"We had to keep talking. You had to say something."

"I could have said lots of other things."

He was silent for a moment. "I'm sorry. I don't . . . I didn't . . . even if you were —"

"Oh, never mind. Father. We have work to do. Let's go."

As it happened, they weren't challenged leaving the confessional, or in the sacristy, or on their way up the stone stairway. A number of priests and monks could be seen in the aisles of the church itself, trying to restore tranquillity after the recent excitement. No one noticed Thomas and Livia making their calm way toward the altar. Of course, the two of them did — calmly — stick to as many shadows as they could find.

"Before he founded the Jesuit order — my order — Ignatius made a number of pilgrimages to sites associated with Francis. Including here." Thomas sounded odd to Livia. A peculiar note had found its way into his voice in the confessional, and she could still

433

hear it now. And why was he going on about Ignatius Loyola and Francis? Was he offering what he had to offer — knowledge — as some sort of apology for accusing her of tendering meaningless words just so there would be something for the Carabinieri to hear? Although, to be honest, the raw truth of what she'd said had surprised her, too. Or was Thomas trying to convince her his deciphering of the poem had been correct? Why work so hard? She believed him, or at least, believed him enough to follow where that deciphering led and see if he was right. Still, he kept talking. "This was a Benedictine monastery church when Francis came here, on his visits to Rome to petition the Pope — Innocent the Third — to authorize his new order. He lodged in a tiny cell up these stairs. Nearly three centuries later Ignatius Loyola made a pilgrimage here, asking and receiving permission to sleep in the same room."

He stopped as they reached a small landing at the top. Before them stood a wrought-iron gate, its lines and curlicues allowing a clear view, but no access, to the room beyond. Thomas stepped aside, motioning to the lock. He folded his hands and waited.

He'd certainly gotten used to this process fast, Livia thought, taking out her pick and shim. She didn't call him on it, though, saying instead, "How do you know this is where we're supposed to be? If Ignatius made all those pilgrimages to all those sites?"

"I made this particular one myself, my first time in Rome."

That wasn't actually enlightening, but Livia said nothing, concentrating on the lock. It was at least a century old, which meant her tools were almost too delicate for it, but after thirty seconds of careful work — the faint resistance of tumblers against her fingertips was her guide — she heard it click open. Swinging the gate aside, she stepped into the room. She almost brushed against Thomas on the narrow landing, but he drew back, pressing himself into the stone wall.

"I thought we were past that," she said.

"Past what?"

"You being afraid to touch me."

"I . . . I'm not . . ."

The oddness of his voice made her turn to face him. She saw his flushed cheeks, his wide pupils, and finally she understood.

"It's all right," she said quietly. "It's natural, in a way you don't know."

"What are you talking about? What is?" he croaked.

She stepped back, put more space between them. "Your desire."

"My *what?*"

"Father. You're a priest, but you're a man. I'm Noantri and I'm a woman. What you're feeling right now —" She stopped, looking for the right words. "Our bodies — Noantri bodies — exert a pull on the Unchanged. When I saw Jonah just now, everything I felt for him . . . You couldn't help but sense it, and it made you —" The dismay on his face was so total Livia understood three things: she was right; as funny as he looked, she mustn't laugh; and they'd better get back to work before he ran away again.

68

In stunned disbelief, Thomas watched Livia step into Saint Francis's cell, into the room where that most pious and self-denying of saints had prayed and slept. The horror he felt was not because such an unnatural creature as she was defiling these hallowed stones. Exactly the opposite: it was partly because he realized he'd led her here with no hesitation, no disquiet whatsoever. Worse: with a sense of pride and pleasure. Showing off his cleverness, his erudition. To a Noantri? When had he become so cavalier about who she was, what she was?

And the other cause of his horror was the knowledge that she was right.

The rapid heartbeat, the tingling. The inability to stop talking, to be too near her, to look at her. How many ways, he wondered, could he deceive himself?

He'd felt desire before, of course he had. If ordination meant the end of human frailty there would be no need for vows. He'd felt it, not acted upon it, confessed, and been absolved. Was what was happening now so different?

Yes.

It was stronger, richer, deeper. More immediate, more propulsive. Though he stood two yards from her, his fingertips could feel the silk of her skin, his palms the wildness her hair would offer if, as his hands longed to do, they reached to unfasten her braid. Her scent, that night-blooming jungle, permeated his senses, and every movement she made, every swing of hip or sweep of arm, arrested his gaze. He longed for her. He'd hidden this truth from himself behind a meandering excursus about Saint Ignatius Loyola; but now she'd said it, and he couldn't deny it. And to whom could he confess it? What would he even say? That he, who had vowed to yield to no such wordly hunger, now ached for the touch of a creature not even of this world, a being with no soul and no place in the afterlife?

And how could he confess it, until he really, truly, felt it was wrong?

Ignatius Loyola, who had stood in this very room, had founded an order based on intellectual rigor and natural law. Thomas had joined that order with joy. His life thus far had been spent fearlessly pursuing the truth, confident that the light of reason would chase away the shadows of superstition and ignorance. His Church had agreed, maintaining that belief in the supernatural was error and, even when, in former times of ignorance, indulged in by the Church itself, had ever been so. God's mystical nature and his miracles were one thing, not to be rationally understood; but demons, succubae, and other such creatures were mere metaphors, images useful to reveal the evil in all of us.

But here he was, Father Thomas Kelly, standing in Saint Francis's cell with one of those creatures, yearning for her touch.

Her claim, of course, was that her people were not supernatural, just humans with a virus in the blood. Maybe so, but that didn't change another fundamental point. The Church had always known about the Noantri. For centuries it had hunted them. That path, brutal as it was, made sense in the days of irrational belief. Then — still in those days — Martin the Fifth suddenly signed a document that began six hundred years of simultaneously trafficking with the Noantri, and denying their existence. Six hundred years during which the Church had maintained a position it knew to be false.

What else, then, was false?

The efficacy of confession?

The sanctity of the Host?

The need for priestly celibacy?

An old familiar voice, one he'd thought he'd never hear again, came whispering back to him now.

Thomas — really?

69

Her back to Thomas, Livia stood facing the polished wood and painted saints of the tall altarpiece in Saint Francis's otherwise stark cell. She bit her lip to keep from speaking, planted her feet so she'd stay still, so she wouldn't spin around and demand that Thomas tell her why they were here and how to find the next poem. The priest was teetering on a narrow ledge, she sensed. And so was she.

She'd hidden it from herself behind the immediacy of effort: slipping from the confessional, working their way through the shadows to the sacristy, picking the lock. Listening to Thomas's discourse on saints and holy orders. Worrying about the oddness she sensed in him. Now, in the silence of the stone cell, she could no longer deny it.

Seeing Jonah, his grin and his broad shoulders, smelling his sweat, hearing his laugh, had thrown her into a cyclone of confusion.

She'd thought, for so long, that all that was behind her. Jonah had left her long ago. On a gray autumn afternoon, the entire world outside the windows dispirited, he'd gazed into her eyes across a gulf of disappointment, saying sadly that he could see she wouldn't change. That she'd always be content to follow the rules, to live in the past, to hide her Blessings and mimic the mediocrity of the Unchanged around her. The necessity of that, he said, had ended long ago, and he'd tried every way he could think of to show her he was right; but he realized now that she'd never understand. She was afraid, or she was comfortable, or she was uninterested in a longer, broader view of the world; whatever the chains that were holding her back, he couldn't let them bind him, too. The future was calling him forward, he said, and he kissed her and turned away.

She'd thought then that she'd understood who and what he was. She'd mourned their love, staggered under a weight of loss and guilt, but she'd come back to Italy, to Rome, and started life anew. Through the years since, she hadn't seen him. She hadn't heard from him, or even about him. She'd lived each day still believing she was right and he was wrong. Believing that over the years, as he deepened in understanding of the life he now had, the life of her people, he'd come to realize that.

It would be too late for them then, was too late for them from the moment he strode out the door without looking back, leaving her in the chill of a dusk that came too early. Her victory would be hollow, so personally meaningless that she never thought of it as a victory at all. But she did feel comfort imagining Jonah settling into a rich, fruitful Noantri life. Picturing him somewhere back at his work, studying, exploring, endlessly immersed in beauty: it was their love of art that had brought them together, had given rise to their love of each other. She'd hoped he'd think of her now and then, and that the memory would be a warm one.

But now, suddenly, frighteningly, she wondered.

It was the confessional that had opened the floodgate of her questions, not what she'd said to Thomas as much as the small dark booth itself. Hiding behind a heavy door, concealing herself in fear — this was the Noantri life. This was the life the Concordat had brought about. Yes, and

Community; yes, and assimilation, which brought with it the gift of normal days, of street corner cafés and neighbors who knew her, students to teach and a house to maintain. And friendship, people she loved among both Noantri and Unchanged.

But would all this not still be possible if the Noantri Unveiled?

Maybe Jonah was right. Maybe science was ready to lead the way to Unchanged acceptance of her people, once they were understood to be no threat; and maybe the fear she and every Noantri now felt, not of discovery by the Unchanged as in the days Before, but of the wrath of the Conclave, could be banished forever.

Facing the altarpiece, Livia could not shake off this new idea: that she could find Jonah and tell him she understood now and was ready to join him. That she could disobey the Conclave. Jonah — she knew this from the look she'd just seen in his eyes — would embrace her. He would publish the contents of the Concordat. The Noantri would Unveil, and a new day would begin.

The outlines of that new day, just starting to emerge from the swirl of sensations she was feeling, were shattered by a loud pop.

Before her, the saints on the tall painted panels began to move. She stepped back in instinctive alarm as, with piercing creaks, the panels slowly rotated, vanishing into the altarpiece. The low light in the cell bounced off a moving forest of gold, silver, and glass, which slowed and came to a stop facing her: reliquaries, dozens of them, hidden behind what she hadn't even known were doors.

70

"What . . . ," Livia sputtered. "How did you . . . ?"

"I told you," Thomas said. "I've made this pilgrimage before." He stepped back to the middle of the room, leaving open the small door on the altarpiece where the switch was hidden.

" 'He lays the sweet machine upon the stone.' There." Thomas pointed to a recess in the wall, where an unimposing rock was locked away behind a grate, to be viewed and venerated like the precious object it was. "Francis's pillow. Ignatius used it, too. The sweet machine, *la dorce machina,* that would be his body. But there's another machine here, too. This one. That's what it's called, *Il Macchina.* Thomas of Spoleto built it in 1704 to house relics Lorenzo di Medici donated to this church."

"But — it still works?"

"It's spring-loaded. As long as the friars

replace the springs every few decades, it's fine. I think they need to oil the hinges, though. It shouldn't creak like that."

"And Lorenzo di Medici? He was a fan of Saint Francis? That's a stretch."

"Desperation to get into heaven makes strange bedfellows."

"Desperation of any kind does that, I suppose. Like you and me."

He looked at her. He had to be able, he'd decided, to look at her, if they were to continue. And they had to continue. Lorenzo may have lied to Thomas, the Church may have lied to everyone, but Lorenzo was still a man and even if it were remotely possible that the Noantri were actually people, just a different kind of people, still, becoming one was the sort of choice a man should be able to make for himself. Not have made for him, by someone who considered him an enemy.

"Yes." Steadily, he returned her gaze. "Like you and me." He kept his eyes on hers, found he could, in fact, look at her, and was relieved (though he already regretted the choice of the word "bedfellows"). It might not be wise, though, to stand too near her. He took a step forward, toward the newly revealed shelves of caskets, boxes, stands, and tiny treasure chests in which rested particles of bone and hair that had once been living, breathing saints.

"Well," Livia said, "I'm very impressed." She moved forward, to stand at the altar also, but to his relief she kept a space between them. "But there must be over a hundred reliquaries here." She stepped up on the small stone ledge where the altar-piece sat. Reaching out, she tentatively pushed and pulled at half a dozen of the gold and silver cases. "They're fastened down. Some of them seem to be built in. It would take us hours to remove them all and search them, or search behind them or under them. How —" She stopped. "I'm sorry. I was about to ask you what we should do next."

Thomas nodded and didn't take his eyes off the reliquaries. He'd been trying to get inside the head of Mario Damiani; this might be a good time for the famous Thomas Kelly laser-beam concentration, that blazing focus that allowed for no distractions. "If I were leaving a poem for you" — he felt a flush of heat in his cheeks — "I'd try to think what you'd be likely to look for. Something that meant a lot to the two of us — the two of them, I mean. If I were Mario. That meant a lot to them — to Damiani and Spencer George. What would that be? You knew them."

"Only Spencer." He could tell she was trying to keep amusement out of her voice.

"Yes, I know that. But he — they —" He swallowed. "Or maybe, not something they shared, but something Damiani would expect Spencer George to expect him to think of . . ."

"A place," she said, taking over. "A saint, a name. This was Damiani, so a pun, a joke, an elliptical reference. Maybe —"

Bees, Thomas thought, trying desperately to detour his brain away from the sound of her voice. **Swarm.** It meant something. Those were the words that had led them to Ludovica Albertoni, not to this cell, but still . . . **Wings untorn.** Nothing about the Ludovica tomb particularly called for bee imagery. It was odd, almost forced, in a way nothing of Damiani's had been before this. **Bees . . .**

"Virgil!" he burst out.

"What? Where?"

"Virgil. He thought bees were immortal. That a hive could come back to life after a plague wiped it out. That would've appealed to Damiani, wouldn't it? To one of your people?" The words tumbled out so fast Thomas nearly tripped over them. "He wrote about it. Virgil did. A whole beekeep-

449

ing manual. Part of a larger work called 'Farmers.' In English, it's called that. Virgil wrote it in Latin but he titled it in Greek." He grinned. " 'Farmers,' in Greek. He called it the *Georgics*."

Livia stared at him. "You're amazing. I've spent the last century among academics, but you're amazing. Can all Jesuits do this?"

Thomas turned away to hide the glow of pride suffusing his cheeks. **Honestly, Thomas. A female vampire is impressed by your intellect and that makes you blush?** Add that to the ever-growing list of things to take into the confessional next time he had the chance. He scanned the reliquaries. Each bore a small silver plate inscribed in tiny, flowing script. The low light made them hard for him to read. He knew she could do better, and it wasn't thirty seconds before she pointed and said, "There." Thomas leaned forward to examine one of the larger, more elaborate of the boxes, a gold castle flying a tiny gold flag. The silver script spelled out a name that should have been obvious to them from the start. With his erudition, his love of wordplay — and his love of Spencer — Damiani had chosen images for the poem to the erotic Ludovica sculpture that would have made his lover smile. They were Noantri, the lovers, and they were homosexuals; Thomas supposed he'd have to add to his list of items to take into the confessional the fact that he hoped, when this was over, the historian got a chance to see the poem, and that it did make him smile.

"It's a toe bone," Livia said, gently rocking the golden castle to see if it could be removed. "From the left foot of Saint George."

71

Over his coffee cup, Spencer George considered his visitor. The young Gendarme from Naples was unself-consciously handsome, with his sharp nose, dark eyes, and quick, catlike movements. He was clearly making an effort to appear cool and professional, but Luigi Esposito projected an excitement like a badly banked fire, ready to blaze up at any moment. Spencer found that refreshing. Why the stifling boredom that must attend a year-in, year-out daily presence in those musty Vatican rooms had not smothered in the young man all trace of enthusiasm for anything, Spencer couldn't answer. He didn't seem to be burning with the fervor of faith. It was unlikely he'd chosen the Gendarmerie out of a calling to serve the Holy See, and thereby the Church; but if his vocation was police work, could it really be fulfilling to spend his days chasing pickpockets and confidence men around

Saint Peter's Square?

Probably not, which might be one explanation for the heat in Luigi Esposito's cheeks as he confronted Spencer: the business that had brought him here was real police business, a meaty investigation, a problem that would engage what Spencer gauged as the young man's considerable intelligence — and his even more considerable ambition. Whether a successful resolution to the situation would satisfy Esposito's hopes, Spencer didn't know; he'd still be a Gendarme, after all. Nevertheless, the opportunity this case had handed him couldn't be one he came across very often, and Esposito was pursuing it for all he was worth.

Even if he was headed in the wrong direction.

A smile tugged the corner of Spencer's mouth as he considered the other possible reason for the young man's bright-eyed animation. Spencer had had a number of lovers since he'd lost Mario, men both Noantri and Unchanged. Come to that, he'd had many before Mario, too. Mario was the anomaly, the miracle, the one great love Spencer had thought he'd never find, immortality notwithstanding. After Mario was gone Spencer had spent many years —

decades — alone, a recluse among his papers and books, a Noantri hermit monk whose work was enough for him. But what good is eternal life, if one doesn't live it? Finally the voice of Mario in Spencer's head, berating him, demanding that he re-enter the world and the Community, was too much to bear. Spencer had started to live in the world again. The voice of Mario had of course been right. Spencer had renewed old friendships, found new ones — Livia Pietro, for example — and taken lovers. None of these liaisons were serious and he hadn't pretended they were, to himself or his partners. Nevertheless, he'd enjoyed them.

As he'd enjoy a dalliance with this Neapolitan detective. And if Esposito's heartbeat, temperature, and adrenaline level — all of which Spencer could discern — were any guide, the detective, although Spencer suspected he himself might not know it, would likely enjoy it, too.

However, it was not to be. To hide a sigh, Spencer sipped at his coffee. Too much was at stake — not least, the life Livia had made for herself in the wake of her unfortunate love affair, a life Spencer knew she treasured. Any entanglement between himself and this Vatican detective would create far too many complications in an already precarious situation. The effect of the Noantri body on the Unchanged — especially an Unchanged with his own hungers — was not something Spencer could control, but he could certainly refrain from flirtatious cues, and refuse to respond to any the Gendarme might deliberately or, more likely, involuntarily, offer.

He replaced his cup into the saucer with a small clink, recrossed his legs, and gave the detective an affronted stare. "Let me see if I understand," he said coldly. "The barely credible theory put forward this morning by you and your Carabinieri counterparts — the idea that, one, a ring of art-and-antiquities thieves has been responsible for the recent unpleasantness, and two, that the eminently respectable and highly regarded *Professoressa* Livia Pietro is a member of it — has become firmly entrenched and is the basis for your continuing investigation. Is this correct?"

Luigi Esposito replaced his coffee cup also, leaned back in his chair, and crossed his legs, too. "Please remind me, *Professore*. Where is it you teach?"

Mirroring, Spencer thought. **Put your subject at ease, make him feel you're on the same side underneath it all. A**

good approach. Better than the bogus befuddlement of that mustached Cara- biniere, in any case. "I'm retired," he responded stiffly.

"Yes, of course, I'm sorry." The Gendarme looked around with a lazy gaze. "You have so many unusual and interesting objects here." He swung his sharp eyes back to Spencer. "Antiquities."

Spencer raised an eyebrow. "Are you a connoisseur?"

"No, no." The young man smiled. "I'm just a cop. But I've done a little studying on my own. I try to better myself. Connois- seurship on a Gendarme's pay — it's just not possible. I'm impressed that you've managed to do so well on an academic's salary. This, for example." He tapped the glass top of the small display table where his coffee rested. Under it lay an open bronze hinge, highly polished to show off the delicate vines winding over its surface. "It's beautiful. It must be an important piece?"

Well played. A little self-deprecation, a touch of flattery, the tiniest hint of suspicion, and redirect my attention before I bristle. "You're correct. It's from the door to the Cathedral in Constance. It was in place when the Council of Constance was held." The Gendarme's face was an expectant blank. Spencer continued, "Where the Church's Great Schism was finally ended, and the papal line of succession that's been followed to this day was clarified and established."

Esposito raised his eyebrows. "I got the impression earlier, *Professore,* that you don't highly value the Church."

"How observant of you. However, a historian certainly can't ignore it." Not, at least, a Noantri historian. Particularly the moment in Church history from which sprang the papacy of Martin the Fifth and the beginning of a new era for all Noantri.

"Well. As I said, even a cop can see it's beautiful. How did you come by it?"

"Come by it?" Spencer leaned forward for the silver coffeepot. He refilled Esposito's cup, mostly so he could watch the grace with which the young man added and then stirred his cream and sugar. "*Vice Assistente* Esposito, I'm getting the uncomfortable feeling you're questioning the provenance of my collection."

"Oh, no, sir, not at all. Just, you're clearly a resourceful and dedicated collector."

"And you're clearly a police officer with more urgent issues on which to spend your time than a retired professor's pieces." He couldn't stop himself from adding, "No matter how impressive."

As the Gendarme gave him a rueful smile, Spencer could feel the young man's body temperature rise a fraction. "I'm afraid that's true. But it's occurred to me, *Professore,* that you might be able to tell me where to look."

I certainly could, Spencer thought, but said, "I don't follow." **Well, sometimes I do, and sometimes I lead.**

Esposito leaned confidentially forward. "There's no question in my mind that a reputable academic like yourself would only deal with the most respectable merchants."

"Of course."

"I also have no doubt that you're well known in certain circles."

How true, though they might be different circles from the ones you're thinking about.

"I'm sure, sir," the Gendarme went on, "that, because of your tastes and interests, you've been approached more than once by people much shadier than the ones you usually deal with."

Yes, and if one is careful, they can be rather fun. "I see." Spencer nodded as though he'd just caught on. "And you were wondering whether I might be able to supply you with the names of some of these . . . shadier people. I must say I'm relieved. I was beginning to worry that you thought I myself was caught up in this international theft ring you're postulating. Which, by the way, I still find hard to credit."

"The ring? Or *Professoressa* Pietro's involvement in it? Or maybe the American priest's?"

"The involvement of an American priest in any sort of criminal activity would not come as a shock, I assure you. Livia Pietro's would. I suppose it's possible you could be right, though, no matter how dubious I find the proposition." **There are other propositions I'd accept sooner, but never mind.** "Very well. I believe I can, after all, be of some service to the Gendarmerie. Let me make you a list."

72

Climbing the stairs in the run-down building in the Pigneto district, Giulio heard his cell phone ring. He pulled it out. To Raffaele he said, "It's Esposito." To the Gendarme: "How did it go? Learn anything?"

"He gave me a list of shady dealers who might fence stolen art. I think they ought to be followed up but I don't expect anything to come of it."

"Okay, I can get someone on it. Unless you have people who can do it?" After all, it was Esposito's find.

"They'd be me," Esposito answered shortly.

"Fine. I'll give my boss your number. Someone'll call for the list. That's all?"

"Not exactly." Esposito's grin came through loud and clear. "I insisted that he himself wasn't under suspicion, oh no way. That we overworked cops only wanted the help of an upstanding citizen like himself.

That we felt lucky to have him as a re-
source."

"Did he buy it?"

"Of course not. In fact he tried to distract
me by coming on to me."

"Why, that old dog."

"As you say. I pretended to pretend not to
notice."

"Esposito, you're confusing me," said
Giulio, who wasn't in the least confused.

"I'm sure," Esposito said cheerfully. "Anyway, I'm hoping now he'll tip his hand."

"If he has one to tip."

"He does." The Gendarme sounded completely confident. "I'm not sure how deeply
he's involved but there's no question he's
hiding something. I know you have a man
here, but I'd like to stay on him myself. I
have a feeling things could get interesting."

It didn't escape Giulio's notice that the
idea was phrased as a request, as though
Esposito were under Giulio's authority.
They both knew that wasn't the case, and
that Esposito could stay if he wanted, or go
if he wanted. "You have any experience with
surveillance?"

"Not here. On the force in Naples,
though."

And I bet you're good at it, Giulio
thought. "Okay, go ahead. I'll get my man

461

reassigned." Freeing up a Carabiniere — that should make the *maresciallo* happy. "Let me know right away if anything breaks. Hey, Esposito," Giulio said as a thought struck him. "I don't suppose he gave you anything I could use to get a wiretap warrant?"

"I fished for it, but no such luck. But he's probably using a cell phone anyway."

"True. All right, give me a call when you have something." He was going to add, **Or when you want to be relieved,** but he had a feeling that wouldn't be for a long time.

"I will. If you don't mind my asking, what are you up to?"

Giulio wasn't used to that question from anyone except his partner and his boss. But it had been asked deferentially enough; and the kid had earned an answer. "I had search warrants for Livia Pietro's house and Jorge Ocampo's flat. And through your boss, for the priest's room in the Vatican. Pietro's and Kelly's places haven't given us anything, but we got a call from the team going through Ocampo's place. Orsini and I just got here."

"Anything good?"

"We're about to walk in the door. Don't worry, Esposito, we'll let you know."

At the top of the stairs he handed his cell

phone to an officer, telling him to get the last number that called it to the *maresciallo* and explaining why. The officer was clearly pleased to have a reason to bring himself to the attention of the big boss, and Giulio was equally pleased to avoid him.

Raffaele was waiting for Giulio in the hallway. "Esposito found something?"

"Not yet. He set the guy up. He's pretty good, Raffaele. He's wasted over there." They'd reached the top floor, where the ceilings and the rents were lower than for the other dumps in this exhausted building. The door at the end of the hall was open. An officer standing at it waved Giulio and Raffaele in.

Dingy, rank-smelling, its chipped tile floor sticky under their shoes, Ocampo's one room was more of a mess than even Carabinieri executing a search warrant could have made. Giulio grinned to himself as the dapper Raffaele wrinkled his nose.

"What do you have?" he asked the officer in charge.

"Over here, sir."

Over there, indeed. Giulio would have spotted it himself as soon as he turned around. A wall of photos, a vase of fresh flowers on the shelf below. A silk scarf under the vase. The scarf, the flowers, and the

463

blond girl in the photos were all of them far too high-class for a man who lived in a room like this.

"Who is she?"

"Her name's Anna. That's all we know so far." The officer tapped one of the photos, where the margin was carefully labeled *Anna en la playa.*

"We'd better find her. She might be in danger. This guy just went from thief to serious nutcase."

"Or not," Raffaele said. "Look. The guy — Ocampo — he's in half these pictures with her."

Giulio looked again. It was true. Smiling, sometimes with their arms around each other, Ocampo and this Anna looked out at them from a café, from someone's living room, from a tree-lined street. The girl seemed perfectly happy, even smug, while Ocampo himself had a grateful, puppy-dog air. Giulio's thinking started down an entirely different path. "You know what? Find her anyway."

73

The notebook leaf from the toe-bone reliquary cracked along one of its folds as Livia smoothed it out on the altarpiece. The art historian in her winced and wanted to fold it up again and get it to a conservator as fast as possible. She pushed that thought aside and read along with Thomas.

Er pollarolo co' la frebre se scopre e
   prega. Lei fa miracoli.
S'appiccia 'na cannula, se fanno cappelle
   e cori
de marmo barocco. Li giardinieri, i
   vinajjoli,
li mercanti, ricopreno 'sto paradiso d'ori.
Ma cqui, non tutti l'alati spiccano voli.

The fevered farmer uncloaks, prays. She
   cures.
A lamp is lit and tended, chapels built,
baroque and marble. Vintners, gardeners,

and merchants gild this Eden to the hilt.
But here, not all the winged creatures soar.

Below, the five block letters:

T N A M A

"Amante," Thomas said. "If you add that
other *e.* If it were Italian it would be
'lover.' . . ."

"But the rest makes no sense if it's Italian." Livia concentrated on the page. "In
Latin it's 'loving,' or depending on what
comes next, 'being loved.' The *eam* would
imply there's a feminine object in the
sentence somewhere." She thought for a
moment, then took her cell phone out.

"Livia," came Spencer's dry voice. "A joy
to hear from you. How are you progressing?"

"Damiani's poems are leading us from
church to church," Livia told him. "We're
in San Francesco a Ripa now." That Jonah
had also been here, and that she'd made no
move to try to stop him from leaving, she
didn't add.

"Ah, Mario."

"And there's another thing. Each poem
we've found has five penciled letters on it.
They seem to form some sort of puzzle,

466

maybe an acrostic, reading back to front and bottom to top. In Latin."

Spencer laughed. "I don't mind admitting to you that he was, occasionally, a trial to live with."

"I can believe it. The words we have so far are *amante eam aedificavit.* Do you have any idea what that means?"

'Loving it, built' . . . Feminine form . . . Nothing comes to mind, no."

"Or, stretching, 'being loved, built.' Did you ever build anything together? Or did you build something for him?"

"Livia, I rarely built him a sandwich. And though I'd readily agree I'm no Neanderthal, I'm hardly a woman. I suppose it might refer to an earlier lover, but I don't know who that might have been. If he was ever inclined toward your fair sex, I'm unaware of it."

"All right, it was a long shot. There's at least one more church to go. Maybe we'll figure it out there."

"Call me if you need me. What's the next church?"

"We don't know yet. These poems aren't easy to translate."

"I imagine not. Livia, take care. I've just had a visit from an adorable Gendarme, the same gentleman whose acquaintance you made earlier today. Apparently the narrative of an international art-theft ring has developed a galloping momentum among the forces of the law, and you and your priest have been elevated to leadership positions in this criminal circle. There's some possibility this fascinating theory can be turned to your advantage, but for now I'd recommend looking over your shoulder at all times."

Livia thanked Spencer for his warning and pocketed the phone.

"He's no help?" Thomas asked.

"No. But while we were talking I had a thought." She pointed to the poem. " 'Vintners, gardeners, and merchants.' If you were heading from here to the river, one way to go would take you by Santa Maria dell'Orto. It was a guild church — an *Arciconfraternita* that incorporated guilds of small-holding farmers, livestock breeders, and wine sellers. Could that — ?"

"Yes!" Thomas interrupted with a shout. With a guilty look he dropped his voice. " 'She cures'! That church — it was founded on the site of a miracle. The Blessed Virgin appeared and cured a dying farmer."

"All right." Livia folded the poem back into her bag. "Come on, let's get out of here before someone wants to know what we're up to in Saint Francis's cell."

Pretending she hadn't seen him blush, Livia started down the stone steps. Thomas followed.

"The winged creatures," he whispered as they made their way to the back of the church. "The ones that don't soar. More bees?"

From the shadows just inside the door Livia peered out onto the piazza. No Carabinieri. She gestured to Thomas and trotted down the steps, quick-walking away down the street to the right. "Not more bees," she said as he hurried to catch up with her. "A turkey."

74

Thomas stood beside Livia in a recessed doorway on Via Anicia. Across the street the deepening afternoon had already cast the Baroque façade of Santa Maria dell'Orto into shadow, silhouetting the pyramidal obelisks on its roofline against an intense blue sky. The pace they'd maintained on the way here had been fast, Thomas too intent on breathing to speak; but now that they were staring across at this façade, he said to her, "The turkey's a New World bird. You don't have those in Italy."

"We do. In there. It's enormous. Condor-size. The guilds that made up the *Arciconfraternita* used to compete to make the most impressive donations. The poultry guild trumped everyone when it presented a robing cabinet for the sacristy with a giant turkey on it, to commemorate the arrival in Italy of the first pairs of turkeys for breeding purposes." She added, "They didn't catch on."

"You know," Thomas said, gazing across the street, "you sound just like me."

She grinned. "That's not a good thing, I take it?"

"No. You've seen this turkey?"

"My first area of specialization was representations of the New World in European art."

So, thought Thomas. **I was in Boston studying your world while you were here, studying mine.** But no, not "while": Livia's studies had been decades earlier. And he might have been studying Italy, but in no way had he been studying her world.

He realized she was waiting for him to speak. "The turkey's on the robing cabinet?" he managed.

" 'The fevered farmer uncloaks.' That's bound to be it."

"All right, I'm convinced. So, how will we get in? Can you pick a lock that big?"

"As a matter of fact, no. I'd need heftier tools. I'm impressed you know that."

"I had a cousin," Thomas said.

"I'd like to hear about him."

"Her."

"Even more. But as for getting in, it shouldn't be a problem. It's open until six."

"Open? Santa Maria dell'Orto? It's been

closed to the public for years. I've never been inside, any of the times I've been in Rome."

"It's not only open now, it's in use. It was restored a few years ago. Saved by the Japanese."

"I'm sorry?"

"Japanese Catholic expats. They've made it their home church. They —" She stopped as the church doors swung wide. A portly priest with wavy white hair came to stand in the doorway, dressed in his vestments for Mass, ready to greet and chat with worshippers as they filed out. About two dozen did, all of them Asian.

"Well, thank you, Japan," Thomas said, then froze at the unexpected echo of Lorenzo's voice. **The future of the Church lies in Africa. In Latin America. In Asia! Do you know why? Because they believe.**

"Thomas? Are you all right?"

"I — What? Yes, I'm fine." Thomas shook off the picture in his mind, Lorenzo's sharp, determined face, his ornate office, his hand gesturing with the ever-present cigar.

"I'm fine. But look — we may have a problem."

He pointed across the street, where the priest stood on the pavement chatting with the last of the parishioners.

"What's that?"

"They've just finished Mass. As soon as everyone's gone the priest will be heading back to the sacristy. He'll disrobe. Maybe there's even a sacristan, in which case they'll probably chat. Unless he's in a hurry to get somewhere, it could take a while before the sacristy's empty."

Livia said nothing, but he felt her eyes on him. He looked over at her. "What?"

"Nothing. I was giving you space. You look like a man with a plan."

Slowly, he nodded. "Do you know where the sacristy is?"

"Left of the altar."

"All right," Thomas said. They watched as the priest took the hand of an old woman, the last of the worshippers to leave the church. "I'll distract him. You wander around as though you're looking at the church while you wait for me, then head back there. I'll buy you as much time as I can."

"What are you —" Livia began, but the old woman started down the street and the priest turned to head back into Santa Maria dell'Orto.

"Let's go," Thomas said, and stepped from the doorway into the street. "Father?"

he called in soft Italian as he approached.

The priest turned, his round face open, waiting.

"*Buonasera,* Father. I'm Thomas — O'Brien. Father Thomas O'Brien, SJ. From Boston."

The two men shook hands as the white-haired priest said, "Well, all the way from Boston? A pleasure, Father O'Brien. Marcello Franconi. I was in Boston, oh, ten years ago now. For a conference. A beautiful city."

"It is, but nothing compares to Rome."

Father Franconi smiled almost ruefully, as a kind parent would who can't deny that his child is the most extraordinary in town but doesn't want to embarrass the parents of lesser children.

"This is my friend," Thomas went on. "Ellen Bird. She's a painter."

"*Signora* Bird."

"Father." Livia shook the priest's hand. In Italian more American-accented than Thomas's, she said, "I'm from New York, but I've been living in Rome for many years."

"I came over to see her," Thomas said. "To visit. Father, I — I'm glad I saw you here. I want you to hear my confession."

Father Franconi's face registered mild

surprise. He looked from Thomas to Livia, and in his eyes a new light dawned. "Of course, my son."

"Thank you. A priest's work is never done, is it?"

"Until we've all attained the Kingdom of Heaven, I suppose it never will be. Please, come this way." They entered the church, Thomas and Father Franconi making use of the holy water font. Father Franconi closed the doors behind them. "*Signora* Bird, make yourself comfortable while you wait. You're a painter? You're welcome to view the church. You might find a few things of interest. We have some fine Zuccari frescoes. Father O'Brien, please come this way."

An old Asian man sat waiting near the altar. Father Franconi called across the church to him in Japanese. The old man answered, then, at Father Franconi's response, smiled and bowed. He headed for the door as Father Franconi said to Thomas, "We don't have the budget for a sacristan but Kaoru's retired and he enjoys helping. Actually he's invaluable. I just told him to go home, though. If I can't get out of these by myself by now, I never should have been wearing them in the first place."

He led Thomas to a confessional to the

475

right of the church doors. That was good: as far from the sacristy as they could get. They entered, Thomas kneeling on the penitent's side this time, not sitting on the confessor's.

"Bless me, Father, for I have sinned."

"How long has it been since your last confession?"

Thomas thought. Yesterday; but that was a lifetime ago. That was a different man. This Thomas Kelly, the one who stole books and consorted with vampires, who unsealed reliquaries and climbed Berninis, who knew his friend had been hiding a world-shattering truth from him for decades and his Church had been double-dealing for six hundred years — this Thomas Kelly had never been to confession.

"Father O'Brien?" came Father Franconi's quiet voice through the screen.

Right. Father Kelly wasn't confessing this afternoon. Father O'Brien was, and he could say anything he wanted. He could make stuff up. "Three days."

Father Franconi said nothing, waiting for Thomas to explain what had driven him into the confessional at Santa Maria dell'Orto all the way from Boston.

Thomas had to speak. He opened his mouth, unsure what he was going to say, something to buy Livia time. What he heard, in his own voice, was, "Lust, Father. I've been — experiencing lust." **Wait. This was just a diversion. Father O'Brien was supposed to be making stuff up.**

"Your friend," Father Franconi said. "*Signora* Bird." Not phrased as a question, but not an accusation, either.

"Yes."

"Have you acted upon these feelings?"

"No. No. I haven't touched her. She says it's natural, it's not my fault, but —" **But she's a vampire, so what does she know?**

"She's aware of your feelings for her, then?"

"I didn't tell her, but she knows."

"Well, she's a wise woman. Of course it's natural. The Lord places temptation in our path so we can have the privilege of overcoming it. If you haven't acted on your feelings you're well on your way to defeating them."

"But I . . ." Thomas stopped, unclear on what he'd been about to say.

"But you still feel bad. Especially that you came all the way to Rome."

Bad that I came to Rome isn't the half of it. "Yes, Father."

" 'I should have known better,' you're thinking. 'I should have stayed home. What was I expecting?' Is that it?"

477

I know what I was expecting. I was expecting to be of service to my friend and my Church. "Pretty much."

"But something called you here."

A friendship based on a shocking and enormous lie. "Yes."

"Has it occurred to you that what you're experiencing right now is part of God's purpose for you?"

"I don't see how, Father."

"You're doubting yourself. Your vocation. The need for priestly celibacy. You're thinking, in a different world — perhaps a better world — you might be able to serve your Church and yield to this temptation, also."

Actually, I'm thinking I might as well yield to it, since I don't see any possible way — or reason — to go on serving my Church. Thomas didn't speak. Father Franconi waited, then went on.

"The Lord knows what you're going through, Father O'Brien. Do you think he doesn't see you struggle? Yes, the vows you took were written by men. Poverty, chastity, obedience. They might as easily have been self-improvement, fecundity, and silliness." At the surprise of that, Thomas laughed. "Very good, Father O'Brien. You haven't lost your sense of perspective. Here's my point: they might as easily have been, but

478

they weren't. And when you took your vows, it wasn't to the men who wrote them that you dedicated yourself. It was to God. You promised God you'd live your life in a certain way. He was pleased to receive your vows, and he stands ready to help you live up to them. This is not about what should be or could be. It's about what is."

Again, Thomas didn't answer, this time for a completely different reason. He couldn't. He was thinking: God knew. About the Noantri, about the Church's perfidy. Of course he did. Some would say, *and permitted it?* but Thomas was unconcerned on that score. As Father Franconi had said, we make our own choices; God gives us that privilege. The point was, whatever God's unknowable plan for the Universe, the Noantri were part of it. Part of it because the devil had sent them to test the faithful, or part of it for some other purpose: it didn't matter. What the Church said and did about their existence might be at odds with reality, even at odds with God's intentions, but if there was anything a Jesuit was prepared for it was living with, investigating, even celebrating, that very contradiction.

Another thing Father Franconi had said: Thomas's vows had been made to God. Not to the Church. How simple. How basic. As long as he was a priest he'd keep his vows. His relationship to the Church, and therefore to the priesthood, once all this was over, was a different question. He didn't have to negotiate that path now. That thought filled him with a relief so profound it was like the cessation of pain.

"Of course," he said. "The struggle's the whole point, isn't it, Father?"

"Well, I don't think God's especially pleased that you're struggling. But as long as you have something to struggle against, I'm sure he's proud that you're doing it. Are you ready for the Act of Contrition?"

"What's my penance, Father?"

"None, I think." Thomas could hear the other priest smile. "You paid this account in advance."

"Thank you, Father," Thomas said, and began, "My God, I am heartily sorry . . ."

75

Raffaele couldn't believe it. He'd finally gotten a hit.

Once there was nothing more to be learned at Jorge Ocampo's squalid flat — which was not that long after they'd gotten there — Raffaele and Giulio Aventino had hit the streets. They'd taken copies (Giulio, on paper; Raffaele, in his iPhone) of photos of Ocampo and his ladylove. She turned out to be a comparative literature student at La Sapienza by the name of Anna Jagiellon. She also turned out to be nowhere to be found, including in the Russian poetry seminar where her paper on Akhmatova was supposed to have been presented today. The two detectives went out to show the photos around, to see what they could see.

The Carabinieri had a number of uniformed officers doing the same, of course, and in the general way of things detectives were too valuable to waste on this kind of canvassing. As Giulio had pointed out, however, it was either do the photos, or go back to the station and discuss with the *maresciallo* the current situation: that Ocampo had slipped through their fingers twice already; that Livia Pietro and Thomas Kelly had completely eluded them; and that furthermore they were basing their investigation on the idea that either they had a serial anti-clerical nutcase on their hands, who might or might not be after the aforementioned elusive Pietro (who was in no way, however, a cleric); or they were chasing an international art-theft ring of which the aforementioned Pietro might or might not be a part, in a conspiracy theory promulgated by, horror of horrors, a Gendarme. Raffaele had considered the possible outcomes of such a conversation and agreed the street was preferable. They'd split up, each taking a direction out from San Francesco a Ripa, the last church where Ocampo had been seen.

The calls from churches, monasteries, and convents had been coming thick and fast. Raffaele couldn't tell if the ordained and avowed who were burning up the tip line were worried for their own safety and that of their treasures, or were merely trying to be of service to the authorities. Whichever it was, Carabinieri officers had been criss-crossing Rome all afternoon responding to reports of collection boxes jacked open and tourists' wallets disappearing, which were the kind of thing usually the province of the Rome *polizia;* and also, stories of strange men lurking in church doorways and loud arguments on basilica steps, which on a normal Rome day wouldn't get reported at all.

However, the clerics, to whom Raffaele was used to turning for spiritual but never before professional help, had provided nothing. The only thing these calls had yielded was a sense, disquieting to Raffaele, that church-related disturbances were much more of a quotidian occurrence than he'd thought.

What had borne Raffaele promising fruit was exactly what, in his experience, usually did: two pretty girls drinking wine at a café table, in this case on Via della Luce. Both nodded emphatically when he showed them Ocampo's picture.

"Half an hour, maybe?" The brunette cast a heavily made-up glance at her redheaded companion for confirmation. "He was in a hurry."

"Running?" Raffaele asked.

"No, walking fast, and he kept looking

behind him like someone was following him."

The good Samaritan, Raffaele thought, wishing he had a photo of that man, too. "Was anyone?"

"I don't think so."

"But you're sure it was him?"

"He was gross," the redhead sniffed. "All sweaty. And some kind of awful cologne."

"Sickening," her friend agreed.

"And the way he looked at us when he went by. Like if he weren't in a rush he'd sit right down and buy us a drink."

"I guess I shouldn't try that, huh?" Raffaele grinned.

"Don't flirt, you're on duty," the girl said, but she smiled.

"Did you see where he went?"

"Seriously? I didn't even look at him." A toss of the red hair.

The brunette pointed north. "That way. I think he turned left a couple of blocks up."

"You watched where he was going that far?"

She nodded, then shrugged as the redhead stared. "I don't know, something about him — he was just *interesting,* okay?"

The redhead rolled her eyes.

"How about this woman?" Raffaele intervened, swiping to the photo of Anna Jagiellon. "Was she with him?"

Both girls leaned forward to see. Their eyes met in surprise. "Not with him," the brunette said. "But a few minutes ago. Going the same direction. They know each other?"

"Was she who was following him?" asked the redhead. "That he was afraid of?"

Raffaele didn't answer that, but asked, "The same direction?"

The brunette nodded. The redhead, to prove she could be as helpful to the Carabinieri as her friend — or maybe, to draw Raffaele's attention back to herself — said, "She turned left up there, too. I don't know if it was the same street —"

"It was," the brunette confirmed. The redhead scowled.

"You're sure it was this girl?" Raffaele asked.

"Absolutely. She's, like, completely hot. I mean, not that we're — But she —" The brunette blushed prettily. Raffaele tried not to smile.

"A girl who looks like that," the redhead clarified, "other girls notice."

Raffaele thanked them, walked a few paces away, and called Giulio. "Looks like we're right. Whatever it is, she's involved. Not only wasn't he stalking her, right now it seems like she's looking for him." He boiled the conversation down.

"You're sure they have the right people?"

"They called him gross and brought up the cologne. Her, they were checking out the competition. Girls don't miss much when they're doing that."

"Good work. Keep going. I'll join you as soon as I can get there."

Raffaele pocketed the phone and continued up Via della Luce to the corner the girls had indicated. He stopped a few more times, showing the photos, closing in, once again, on Jorge Ocampo.

76

Livia was examining a side-chapel ceiling in Santa Maria dell'Orto when the two priests stepped from the confessional. She walked to the back of the church, where they stood talking.

"Thanks for waiting," Thomas said to her.

She smiled. "I'd never interfere with the confessional. I just hope your penance doesn't involve giving up coffee — I'm desperate. Father Franconi, your Zuccaris are truly beautiful. And wonderfully restored."

"Thank you. I'm glad you enjoyed them. Please come back to our church. We celebrate Mass every day at four." He added, "There's an excellent café around the corner."

Father Franconi's smile followed them out the church doors. They walked purposefully in the direction he'd pointed them, American tourists in search of caffeine. As soon as she heard the church doors creak shut Livia said to Thomas, "Your blood pressure's about to blow the top of your head off. Relax. I have it."

"The poem? You do?"

"You gave me just about enough time. I guess you found something to talk about."

"Yes. No problem. It was fine. Fine. The turkey's still there?"

"On top of the wardrobe, almost touching the ceiling. Beautifully carved, but huge. I had to tilt the whole thing over. Luckily it's so heavy it just sits up there. They don't fasten it down."

"It's that heavy, but you — Right. Never mind."

She smiled. "The poem was under the base, as far from any of the edges as it could be."

"Did you read it? What does it say?"

"No. I barely made it out of the sacristy when I heard the confessional doors open. It's in my bag. Let's go get coffee."

She saw Thomas pick up on her thought: they needed to get off the street, and two people bending over a page in a café would arouse no suspicions. Besides which, he looked like a man who could use a restorative drink.

At the café they ordered *macchiati.* Once

the waiter had brought them and gone back behind the glass counter, Livia unfolded the sheet of paper on the marble table. Thomas leaned to read it.

Nun se po' vvedé la bbellezza de 'sto vorto
  bbello
come nun se vede pe' gnente l'effimerità
de la musica: e uno, e tre, li diti senz'anello
indicano la grazzia de l'incorrotta santità.
La su' anima lucente rischiara 'sto spazzio
  poverello.

We cannot see the beauty of the face
that turns, music's ephemerality,
and one, and three, the fingers gesture
  grace
and point toward incorrupt sanctity.
Her lucent soul illumes this tiny space.

Below, the expected penciled letters:

R B O R T

Brow furrowed in concentration, Thomas looked from the poem to the letters, back and forth. Livia was about to speak when he blurted, "Bramante! If you add the *b* and the *r*. Going backwards. *Bramante eam aedificavit.* 'Bramante made it.' Not *amante*.

489

Nothing to do with lovers. Bramante. Some-thing Bramante made."

"Well, that doesn't narrow it down much." Donato Bramante, the architect who brought the High Renaissance style to Rome, had held, among other posts, that of papal architect to Julius the Second. Still, it was something; and there were more words to come. "And the *t r o*?"

"I don't know. The next word. I mean, the word before. Whichever of Bramante's buildings Damiani used."

"Good. Now finish up so we can go."

"But the poem —"

"Yes. Let's go."

"Wait. You know where this poem's send-ing us?"

"Of course. You don't?"

"I have no idea."

"Seriously?" She sat back, grinning. "And I had no idea about Saint Francis's cell. Believe me, this one's as easy as you said that one was."

77

This time, Jorge was doing it differently. Slowly, methodically. Scientifically.

For one thing, he had to. After he'd escaped the ambush at San Francesco a Ripa he'd zigzagged through the neighborhood, partly to throw that interfering blond Noantri off his trail. He'd stopped and bought more cologne to aid the purpose, and that and his evasive maneuvers seemed to have worked, because that smirking man was nowhere to be seen.

The other reason for Jorge's serpentine, systematic progress was to pick up the trail of Livia Pietro. There were only so many streets leading away from San Francesco a Ripa. Unless she was still inside, she had to have left by one of them; and if she were still inside, sooner or later she'd come out. And leave by one of them.

He was on Via Anicia, in fact, heading back in the direction of San Francesco a

Ripa to start again, when he got a strong whiff of Pietro's gardenia perfume and the perspiration and skin-scent under it. She'd been here, and fairly recently. He looked back to make sure the blond man wasn't behind him and then picked up his pace. It was an easy trail to follow, for a talented operative like himself. Sticking to the late afternoon shadows, he arrived at, not surprisingly, another church. It was Santa Maria dell'Orto; and it was closed. Why all these churches? Jorge wondered. Was Pietro like him, a Noantri who still missed the comfort of the stained glass and the wooden pews, the wise homily and the glimpse of heaven? Anna said heaven was an outdated and ridiculous concept, a crutch for fearful Mortals. Of course she was right, but Jorge, as he peered down the long, indistinct tunnel of his endless future, sometimes wished he could lean on that crutch just a little bit, even now.

But back to work! Risking leaving the shadows, Jorge worked his way through the intersection in front of the church. Pietro, he decided, had been here, but she wasn't here now. She'd arrived along Via Anicia, but she'd left along Via della Madonna dell'Orto. Her scent was stronger there. Fresher. Madonna dell'Orto, walled on both sides and running east to the river, at this time of day didn't provide much concealing shadow. So be it. Jorge strode into the middle of the street and boldly made his way.

78

Thomas followed Livia through the open gate and into the shadowed garden in front of Santa Cecilia. The streets they'd traveled to get here had been quiet, but when they shut the gate the walled garden surrounded them with a different kind of silence. Thomas stopped for a moment, surprised to feel his heartbeat slow down, his breathing calm. He felt suddenly apart, serenely separated from the tumult his life had turned into on this day.

Almost, he realized with a start, he felt an echo of the old peace.

The basilica's open doors welcomed visitors, but when Thomas and Livia entered they found themselves nearly alone. The air was soft with fading incense; it whispered to Thomas of Asia, of desert caravans and distant cities. Three votive candles flickered in a side chapel. There, a woman knelt before the rail. No one else was about.

Livia didn't hesitate. She trotted up the center aisle. Thomas followed her to the stone rail that stood in front of what he privately considered one of the most beautiful works in Rome. He wasn't an art historian, so maybe he was wrong, but he'd come out of his way on previous trips to Rome just to spend time with this: Stefano Maderno's breathtaking, delicate statue of Saint Cecilia, head so oddly turned away from those who looked on her.

Livia knelt before the statue, and Thomas, though sure she was just inspecting the marble for possible poem locations, knelt with her.

"You're sure it's this one?" he asked.

"There's no question. '. . . the beauty of the face / that turns . . . and one, and three, the fingers gesture grace.' " Livia pointed to Cecilia's hands, their gentle fingers raised to signal the holy trinity. "And," Livia added, "she was one of us."

"What?" He couldn't have heard her correctly. "Cecilia — You're telling me —"

Livia nodded. "They tried three times to chop off her head. They didn't quite succeed, but in any Unchanged the damage and blood loss would surely have caused death. Not only didn't Cecilia die, she remained conscious. It was only after she was allowed to take Communion that she slipped into a coma. The next day they declared her dead and buried her. Stefano Maderno had her disinterred twelve hundred years later, to use her remains as a model for this work. They were intact, undecayed. As you see."

Thomas stared, first at Livia, then at the pure white marble sculpture of the saint. Could this possibly be true? "Is this . . . You said it could take a very long time . . ."

"Yes. In some cases, hundreds of years. Cecilia's Renewal was almost complete when she was disinterred."

"Maderno . . . How did he . . . Why . . . no. I know."

"Yes. Maderno also. They'd known each other two millennia before. In, I believe, Greece. He'd been to her grave. He could tell she was nearly ready. That's why he put himself forward for the commission."

Thomas nodded, a part of him astonished, not by this news, but by his lack of astonishment at it.

"Look." Livia brought him back to the moment, gesturing in the direction of the woman in the side chapel, who rose and turned. "She's leaving. This may be the best chance we'll get."

79

As soon as the woman who'd been praying in the side chapel stepped out the church door Livia was up and over the railing. She'd done this a number of times over the years, waiting her chance to be alone in order to study Maderno's Cecilia. The basilican authorities made it almost impossible to get close to this sculpture. Even to the Unchanged, the evident tenderness, Maderno's skill and joy as he made this piece, was so captivating that the marble cried out to be touched, to be taken in with more senses than just sight. Even the way sound echoed off the stone folds of Cecilia's shroud . . . Livia stopped herself. This was not the time to get lost in the beauty of this work.

Thomas, as usual, was a beat behind her. He'd probably never lose his instinctive horror of trespassing, of breaking the rules. He did seem to have lost a good deal of his horror of her people, though. He'd taken her revelation that Cecilia was both saint and Noantri with a minimum of aversion and no disbelief she could detect.

As he stepped over the railing she knelt and ran her fingertips along the line at Cecilia's throat. That would have been the obvious spot for a Noantri to hide something for a Noantri to find; but the line was as she remembered: a chiseled groove in the solid stone, filled with a thin layer of gold. She moved on, exploring the flowing marble garments, the cavity made by Cecilia's arms resting in front of her torso, the space under her lifted left foot. Livia's fingertips thrilled to every alteration in texture, rough to smooth; her muscles followed Maderno's hammering, his tapping, his polishing. Her delight in experiencing, skin to stone, the cool curves of Maderno's work was so great that it threatened to derail her urgent search.

Or maybe it already had. She was carefully searching the cavity at the statue's feet when Thomas said, "Um, Livia?" She turned to see him prying his key-ring penknife into a small gap at the statue's base. As she watched he dug the blade into a slip of paper and slid it out.

"Oh," she said.

Gingerly, Thomas unfolded the familiar page. He looked up at her. "It's the last." He turned it for her to see. It held no poem. The paper was blank but for five block letters printed in graphite.

EPORP

The last! No new poem, no next church to go to. They had it all, now — the entire puzzle. This final piece would lead them to the Concordat. Heart pounding, Livia knelt beside Thomas. *"Pro,"* she said, reading backwards as they had learned to do. "If that's the first word, and the *p e* goes with what we already had, the word before it is *Petro.*" She looked up to see the dismay she suddenly felt echoed on Thomas's face.

" 'For Peter'?" he said. " 'For Peter Bramante made it'?"

Livia sat back on her heels. "Saint Peter's? He hid the Concordat in Saint Peter's?"

For some moments they sat in silence. Saint Peter's, the Vatican church, was Donato Bramante's grandest work. A huge basilica where the Popes themselves worshipped, it held side chapels, underground rooms and tombs, hundreds of statues, plaques, paintings, gold and silver and precious woods, multiple levels, even tiers to its giant dome. How would you search Saint Peter's? Where would you begin?

"That would be so like Damiani, wouldn't it?" Livia asked rhetorically. "Once he got it out of the Vatican Library he didn't take it anywhere. Just around the corner. To Saint Peter's. But where?"

Thomas made no answer, just shook his head.

"Maybe when we get there," she said. "Maybe something will jump out at us."

Thomas looked as unconvinced as she was, but what else could they do? She stood. He didn't, though. Still crouched beside the sculpture, he said, "He wrote it backwards." Frowning at the floor, which she was sure he wasn't seeing, he asked, "Why did he write it backwards?"

"As extra insurance? If you didn't have the whole thing —"

"You need the whole thing no matter what direction it goes in."

She said nothing, to give him space to follow his thought. He took a pencil from his back pocket, then searched in vain for a piece of paper. Wordlessly, she slipped Damiani's notebook from her shoulder bag and offered it to him.

He didn't reach for it. "Write in that? I can't."

"Damiani would've wanted us to."

"But it's from the Vatican Library."

"The Bernini," she said, "Santa Teresa's relic box. Saint George's."

He met her eyes, sighed, took the notebook, and opened it to a blank page. He tapped the pencil on it a few times, then wrote:

P R O P E T R O B R A M A N T E E A M
A E D I F I C A V I T

He stared at the line of letters, then separated them into the words they made:

PRO PETRO BRAMANTE EAM
AEDIFICAVIT

"Was he telling us to rearrange the words? Once we have it all, to run it backwards? But it's Latin. Word order doesn't matter." He did it anyway.

AEDIFICAVIT EAM BRAMANTE PETRO
PRO

"Or, each word backwards? No. That just gives us Latin gibberish."

Livia realized he was talking as much to himself as to her.

"But he did do it backwards," Thomas went on. "There must be a reason."

Livia withdrew the poems themselves from the zippered pocket of the bag and spread them on the floor in front of the statue. Well, if anyone could help with understanding poems, it would be Santa Cecilia. She read the poems over, taking in the lettered additions. Then she stopped reading, and just looked. Slowly, she said, "If you see it purely as pattern, each line is just below the bottom line of its poem, and the same width."

Thomas turned to her, to the poems, back to her. "As pattern?"

"As graphics. Not meaning."

"All right," he said. "Go on."

"I don't know. But some are stretched out, some are squished up. To me that implies each line's supposed to be kept as a block." She gathered the poems and lapped them over one another, then covered the words of the first poem with her hand. Now only the letters were visible.

TIVAC

IFIDE

AMAEE

502

T N A M A

R B O R T

E P O R P

"Maybe," she said, "some other kind of acrostic? The first letter of each line, or the second, or from one corner to another . . ." She trailed off, seeing nothing at all.

Thomas also stared at the letters, absently tapping his pencil on the marble floor. Beyond its rhythmic sound, Livia's Noantri senses heard a rustle of wind in the courtyard trees, saw the tiny change in the shadows as the votive flames danced. The spices in the faint incense brought her an odd comfort, a connection to distant lands, other times. She realized that, as much time as she'd spent here with Maderno's sculpture, she had never focused on the other works in this church. Maybe, after all this was concluded, once they found the Concordat and her world, so recently upended, was set right again — Upended. Set right. *Thomas!* The pencil-tapping abruptly stopped. "It's not backwards. It's upside down!"

He stared.

She said, " 'For Peter Bramante it made.'

503

Upside down. For Peter, upside down!"
He leapt to his feet and hugged her.

80

Jorge had been right.

He didn't take the time to pat himself on the back, though. As a disciplined guerilla fighter, he shrugged off his satisfaction, not letting it interfere with his strategy. He'd followed Pietro's scent along Via di San Michele to Santa Cecilia and arrived at the perfect moment. He was pondering how to make his incursion — he wasn't afraid of churches, of course not, no matter how many, and how dangerous, the obstacles the opposition had thrown into his course already today — when the *professoressa* and the priest came flying out. It was pitiable to watch the priest try to keep up with her, even more pathetic to watch such a graceful and talented Noantri holding herself back for the convenience of a Mortal. Not that any of that mattered. Jorge's path was clear. Now that they were on the street he'd just trail them to someplace uncrowded, pounce, and wrest the notebook from her. He took off, staying a safe distance behind, ready to drop back if she seemed to be aware of him, or speed up if they turned.

Which they did, left on Via dei Genovesi and left again on Viale di Trastevere. The route they chose, avoiding broad piazzas and skulking in shadows, underlined to Jorge that they were up to no good. That, plus the shamefaced, embarrassed air about them both — the priest more than Pietro, but both — as they exited the church, the way they barely looked at each other and took obvious care not to touch. Jorge didn't know the nature of their wrongdoing and he didn't care: Anna would know, Anna would explain to him what all this was about once, in glowing triumph, he handed her the notebook. He wondered where Anna was, whether she was mad he hadn't waited at the theater, but he decided she must not be because she hadn't called. She probably knew he'd seized the initiative, taken the opportunity to continue his mission. She had faith in him; she was waiting.

Pietro and the priest rushed through the piazza in front of Santa Maria in Trastevere, keeping to the far side of the fountain from the church, she with her hat pulled down, he pretending to shade his eyes but clearly just hiding his face with his hand. Jorge followed as they worked their way to Vicolo della Frusta and then started on the steps up the Janiculum. He gave them a head start and then trotted up the steps himself. They must be going this way to avoid the road, where they'd be more likely to be seen. Probably, since whatever they were doing involved churches, they were making for San Pietro in Montorio, but a good agent would never assume such a thing. Jorge would catch up with them closer to the top; for now, better to hang back. He let some people pass him. Mortals, they were, huffing and puffing on the steps: a French-speaking couple holding hands, three teenage boys in soccer uniforms (How long had it been since Jorge himself had kicked a ball around? he suddenly wondered), and a thin, hatchet-faced older man who'd find himself able to breathe better, Jorge decided, if he threw away his cigar. Focusing on his task, Jorge realized he must really be spooked, because even though they'd left San Francesco a Ripa far behind, he couldn't get over the sense that that blond Noantri was nearby. Well, continuing in the face of fear was the mark of heroism. Not that Jorge was afraid. Far from it. His hanging back on the steps was strategic. He could do that because there wasn't much chance that his quarry would escape him. Actually, there was no chance. Finally, on the Janiculum Hill, Jorge would get what he'd been hoping for.

81

Spencer George, having seen the young Gendarme to the door and pressed his hand in perhaps a more fond farewell than their short acquaintance called for, had been settled in his easy chair deep in thought when Livia's call came. After speaking with her, he'd spent some more time the same way, unmoving, eyes focused on nothing. Now he stood, walked slowly about his house, looking at this and that, contemplating an etching or a bit of silver. Finally he returned to his study. He rang for coffee, and when it had come and he had enjoyed it, he took out his cell phone and made a call.

"*Salve,*" came the voice at the other end of the line.

"*Salve. Sum Spencer George. Quid aegis?*"

"*Hic nobis omnibus bene est. Quomodo auxilium vobis dare possumus?*" **All is well here,** came the response. **How may we be of service?**

82

Trotting up the last of the steep steps to the courtyard above, Livia slowed. Not that she'd been running at any speed, not for her: she'd had to hold herself back to make sure Thomas stayed with her. For an Unchanged — especially a bookish priest — he had impressive stamina and speed; still, a part of her wanted to race ahead and let him catch up when he could. He knew where they were going, after all. But that would be unfair. It might even make him think she was planning to abscond with the Concordat and leave him empty-handed. She didn't want to worry him, and this discovery was as much his as hers.

What she was, in fact, planning to do with the Concordat when they found it, Livia wasn't sure. Thomas was desperate to hand it over to the Noantri who'd abducted his friend the Cardinal. She needed to take it to the Conclave to obey her instructions —

and to save Jonah. Incompatible goals, and though her Noantri strength would give her an easy victory if it came to a wrestling match, the thought of that, after this past day, left her decidedly queasy.

Well, they didn't have it yet. That was a bridge they'd have to cross later. She wondered if Thomas was thinking about that moment, too.

She stopped to wait for him. He jogged up beside her, then leaned over for a moment, hands on knees, catching his breath. He straightened, but didn't speak. Together, wordlessly, they started toward their goal.

Saint Peter's, a mile away at the opposite end of the same long ridge where they were standing, was indisputably Donato Bramante's most magnificent and monumental building. But this one before them now, this tiny chapel, this Tempietto, was arguably his best.

For Peter Bramante made it, Damiani's acrostic had read. Upside down.

Simon Peter, the first Pope, the rock upon whom Jesus built his church, was martyred in Rome. Modern scholarship located the site of his death as, in fact, the ground on which Saint Peter's now stood; but in Bramante's day, and on through Mario Damiani's, Peter was believed to have died on the

Janiculum Hill. Ferdinand and Isabella of Spain commissioned Bramante to create a chapel on what was thought to be the very site. The site where Peter, sentenced to crucifixion and considering himself unworthy to share the fate of his Lord, made a final request, which was granted: that he be crucified upside down.

Livia entered the open gate and stepped into the cloister between San Pietro in Montorio and what had been its monastery, now the Spanish Academy. Crossing the courtyard, she reached the Tempietto and started up the steps, Thomas beside her. They stood for a moment in the faultless colonnade, then entered the single, circular room. Spare, with statuary in wall niches, soft light from high windows glowing off the polished marble floor, the perfect chapel invited contemplation and prayer. It offered proof that though men and women might be incurably flawed, their works occasionally rose to flawlessness; and suggested, therefore, that while sadly not perfectable, people had the power to rise also, to be better than they, until a moment ago, had been.

Perfection, however, Livia thought, gazing around, did not allow for change. For addition or subtraction. It did not, for example, suggest within itself a hiding place.

"Below," Thomas said, as though in response. His voice was completely calm, completely sure. "The place itself."

As soon as he said it she knew he was right. They went back out and around to the Tempietto's far side, where two symmetrical staircases led down to a level below the upper chapel floor. At the bottom where the staircases joined again light slipped through a locked iron gate to glance off a wide glass disk in the floor at the precise center of the chapel above. The glass covered a brick cistern dug, legendarily, on the very spot where Peter's cross had been driven into the earth.

This time when Livia picked the lock Thomas watched her eagerly. She pulled open the creaking gate and started through it, but he placed a gentle hand on her arm. "May I go?"

She stopped at once. "Of course."

83

Hurrying up the steps, Jorge reached the hairpin above Via Garibaldi and started to make the turn. As he came around, his heart, already pounding, surged into another dimension. He whispered, "Anna." Because Anna was here.

She stood just above him, slender and steady, her head cocked, her arms folded. Sunlight blazed in her long pale hair, outlined her slim hips, limned her hat like the dark halos edged in gold on the paintings of saints. Anna! She'd come to be with him in his moment of triumph, to share in the victory his cunning was about to bring them. Desire leapt desperately in him, all the more wild because the sight of her was unexpected. His skin longed for hers. His body ached with the need to enfold her, to surround her and have her enclose him in her heat, her ferocity. More than anything he'd ever wanted, Jorge wanted to touch her at this moment.

He didn't. He forced his arms still, ordered his feet not to move. Discipline was critical for a revolutionary fighter. Their goal was near. The scents in the air told him the *professoressa* and the priest had just passed this way. They would follow, they would have them. He saw the scene, knew with certainty how it would be. He'd leap out in ambush, battle them both, and defeat them. The priest was nothing, the Noantri woman a challenge, but Jorge had no doubt of his success. He'd deliver up the notebook to his Anna. He'd planned to rush to her, bearing it victoriously through the streets. But she was here, standing in the sunlight on the rough stone steps. She was here to watch proudly while her Jorge slew dragons for her.

"*Buonasera,* Jorge." She smiled.

Italian, he thought, puzzled. She'd addressed him in Italian. Usually they spoke Spanish, their private language. Italian was the language she used for the others, sometimes English if she had to, but alone together, she and Jorge shared the melodic, flowing tones of his home. He didn't know why she'd done it — maybe the excitement, she must feel it, too — but he answered in Spanish, as he'd always done.

"Anna. You're so beautiful. Anna, it's almost over."

"Yes," she said. "I know."

A flash of movement on the steps far above caught his eye. The *professoressa* and the priest, arriving at the top. He turned to Anna, to tell her.

She was right there: she'd moved much, much closer. She was still smiling. Her teeth were bared.

"*Buenas tardes,* Jorge," she whispered. "*Adiós.*"

"Anna? They're — Anna, what —"

He stopped as she embraced him. How could he speak? In the warmth of her arms he shivered in an all-consuming ecstasy. It drained away his will. Joyfully, he surrendered his ability to talk, to move, even to want to move. As always when Anna held him, rapture transported him, a bliss so overpowering it was almost pain.

Then it was pain. First, a tiny, tearing twinge, where a moment ago her velvet lips had been kissing his throat. Slowly, from there, a burn began to spread; he felt it reach his side, his stomach, across his hips, replacing with fiery agony the unfathomable joy he'd just known.

"Anna." He wasn't even sure if he'd really said it, if she could hear him.

"Adiós," she murmured again in his ear. "I'll find them myself, Jorge. I can keep looking. Alone. I don't need you."

Find them? They're very near. You don't need to look. They're just above . . . He tried to tell her, but the fire inside him was unbearable and he couldn't speak.

She stepped back. Blood smeared her smile, his blood.

The Lord had re-tasted the Disciple's blood.

Through the excruciating anguish that engulfed him now, Jorge understood. He felt Anna lift him, knew the moment she threw his agonized body over the railing down to Via Garibaldi far below. The pain didn't stop, no, it amplified beyond bearing, but Jorge found himself feeling something else, something that drew his attention away from his agony. As he fell he was suffused with joy, a bliss to match, to far outshine, both the pain, and even the ecstasy, of moments before. Of any of his time with Anna, since their first, transcendent night. His Anna had given him a gift. She'd bestowed on him a final blessing, one that exceeded all the Noantri Blessings he'd ever had. Into his mind flashed the face of the old monk, the man he'd killed in the church, that man's joy and relief, and Jorge understood this gift was one he'd hoped for, yearned for, but never dared admit even to himself. But his Anna knew, and because she loved him, she'd sacrificed her own need for him, given up the dream of a life together on the broad boulevards of Buenos Aires. She'd put her own desires aside to grant Jorge's unspoken, barely imagined, wish.

Anna had re-infected him, and soon, now, now, he was going to die.

84

"If this is wrong," Giulio huffed, "and I'm running up the Janiculum for no reason —"

"I'm running right with you," Raffaele Orsini threw back. "And I smoke more."

"You're fifteen years younger. And," Giulio added, "three steps behind."

Despite burning lungs and aching legs Giulio had to smile as Raffaele shot past him. No one could say his partner wasn't competitive. They'd trailed Jorge Ocampo and Anna Jagiellon through Trastevere, getting enough confirmation on the photos they were showing to determine that, though not together, both were heading up the Janiculum Hill. Giulio had already sent a car to the top, but because there were places to turn off before you got there, Giulio had decided he and Raffaele would follow.

All right, no more talk. Giulio put his head down, got a rhythm, and kept it going, afraid if he slowed he'd stop and never get started again. Step pump step pump step —

"Wait!"

That shout sounded like it came from Raffaele's last breath. Giulio called on a reserve he hadn't known he had and pushed on up, to come even with the sergeant. Raffaele had stopped at a place where the curve of the roadway below became visible. Panting, he pointed over the railing. Jorge Ocampo, eyes open and staring, lay in a lake of blood.

"I guess we can stop running," Raffaele wheezed. "Or one of us can." He grinned, then said, "I'll go check. He may still be alive. He might be able to tell us something."

Giulio, peering down at the broken body, clutched Raffaele's arm as the sergeant turned to head back down the steps. "Raffaele. Don't go near him. Go up above and stop traffic. No one comes down this road."

"What —"

"Go!" Giulio himself turned and jogged down the steps, stopping where they crossed the road below the place where Ocampo lay. He pulled out his cell phone as he ran and called Dispatch. "I need Hazmat," he said. "On Via Garibaldi where it hits Via Mameli, near where the steps go up the Janiculum. Close the road up and down, the staircase, too. Anyone at the top, make them stay. Contact the American Academy, the Spanish Academy, everyone else. No one goes up or down until this is cleared."

"Understood, *Ispettore,*" came the cool voice. "Details on the threat? Do you need the Bomb Squad?"

"No. Hemorrhagic fever."

"I'm sorry?"

"Hazmat will know."

He positioned himself in the roadway below the body, ready to wave off traffic. He hadn't been there thirty seconds when his phone rang.

"Raffaele," he said. "Where are you?"

"Where the hell do you think? Up the damn hill, stopping traffic. What the hell's going on?"

"Did you go near the body?"

"Did you tell me not to?"

"Do you always do what I tell you? He could be highly contagious, Raffaele."

"Contagious? With what?"

Giulio repeated himself. "Hemorrhagic fever. Can you see him from where you are?"

"Yes."

"Then look. He's bleeding. From every orifice. Eyes, ears, mouth. Asshole. He didn't get those injuries in a fall. Look at his skin."

A pause. "Looks like someone beat the

crap out of him."

"No. Subcutaneous bleeding. Every cell in his body's ruptured. We saw this in Zaire. He probably threw himself over the wall. The pain must have driven him mad."

Another pause, longer. "And it's contagious?"

"There are half a dozen types, maybe more. They're all contagious. Some are virulent. You've heard of Ebola?"

"Shit! Are you serious? This guy has Ebola?"

"There are others." Giulio tried to sound reassuring. "Not nearly so bad. But until we know which one this is . . ." He trailed off when he heard sirens in the distance. They grew louder as they neared.

"Giulio," Raffaele said, "could he — You said the pain drove him mad. Could all this, what he's been doing all day . . ."

"I don't know. Whether it affects the brain like that — I don't know how these things progress."

"What about all the people he came into contact with?"

Giulio just shook his head. The potential public health crisis was enormous, but he didn't see any reason to say that. "Hazmat's on the way," he told Raffaele. "They'll wrap him up and get him out of here. You and I will have to go with them, to . . . get checked out." Listening to the sirens down below, there was another thing Giulio didn't see any reason to say: that while most of the hemorrhagic fevers weren't fatal, this one clearly was; and that though some of them would pass on their own after a time, none of them could be cured.

85

Thomas stepped over the threshold and onto the marble floor under the Tempietto, into one of Christendom's most sacred sites. Across the room, at a small altar, an eternal flame steadily burned, fed by a reservoir of oil. The only light beyond that came through the open door behind him where Livia now stood and faintly through the grate in the floor above. This late in the day, no one but he and Livia had been in the upper chapel, and they were alone here in the lower one, too. He paused, breathing the quiet air. Saint Peter had not died here, may never have even set foot here; but relics and churches, paintings and sculptures and holy places, were all just tools, all serving the same purpose: to bring a seeking soul into awareness of the divine. Despite his knowledge, despite the new truths lately learned and old lies newly revealed, Thomas, standing here, couldn't help but feel a deep, cool comfort, a calm and quiet joy.

He understood: faith had created this joy. Not his faith alone; the true belief of pilgrims over centuries that this place was sacred had sanctified it. Faith had brought holiness into being.

Thomas had rarely felt so strongly the desire to fall to his knees in grateful prayer. But this thought came to him also: belief of a different kind could work to equally powerful, and disastrous, ends. Lorenzo, and countless churchmen before him, believed the Noantri to be evil, knew them as Satan's creatures. Had acted upon this belief, had hunted and annihilated them — and in the process, set itself as the enemy of men and women of every kind whom the Church, lost in an overgrowth of fear whose roots were its fear of the Noantri, had also considered *other*. Had done great evil in the name of eradicating evil.

Thomas himself had held to this belief just a few hours earlier. Yet Livia, and Ellen Bird, even Spencer George — and Mario Damiani, and Saint Cecilia herself! — all you had to do was look with open and clear eyes to see the truth.

And the Noantri who had abducted Lorenzo? Without whose demands Thomas would not be here on this holy ground? Yes, they were evil. Proving only that there were malevolent forces at work in the world, in the hearts of Noantri as well as the hearts of churchmen. In the hearts of all people — his, and Livia's. People.

These thoughts were well worth serious reflection, deep contemplation. Not here, though, and not now.

Thomas knelt, but not in prayer. He bent over the thick glass disk, scrabbling for a fingerhold around its edges. He was prepared to work it, to heft it loose. It surprised him by giving without much difficulty, though at two inches thick and three feet wide it made him work to lift it out. Livia could have done it easily, but if anything today had been Thomas's job, it was this. He rolled the glass cover aside, laid it carefully down. The cistern below appeared not as deep as he was tall. Its diameter was the same as the glass cover, perhaps three feet, and its dirt floor was rough in the dim light. With a glance back at Livia, Thomas dropped inside it.

86

Forcing himself calm, Jonah Richter watched from behind a column in the cloister as Livia and Father Kelly entered the Tempietto's lower chapel. Things were unfolding beautifully. When Livia and Kelly exploded out of Santa Cecilia and started doubling back, Jonah knew at once the hunt had entered a new phase. Though he'd been observing them all day, he'd never gotten close enough to learn what their search was based on; still, it was clear the geographical pattern they were following had radically changed. Closer and closer they'd crept to the river, and then suddenly they were running back through Trastevere and up the Janiculum Hill.

Whoever had stolen the Concordat had hidden it well. All of Rome would be demolished and rebuilt, urban-renewed and modernized, before a stone of the Tempietto was ever changed. Silently, Jonah thanked the brave Noantri who'd done it, who'd made possible the coming Unveiling. He had no idea who that had been. That the Concordat was missing at all he'd only learned when like-minded Noantri working in and around the Vatican had begun to whisper to him of odd, esoteric inquiries and recondite trail-following initiated by the new Librarian, Lorenzo Cardinal Cossa. Jonah was the first to grasp the meaning of the Cardinal's research, the only one to arrive at a plan for turning the situation to their use.

This had all taken time, but time was something Jonah had in abundance. He did acknowledge the irony of impatience such as his in someone for whom time unrolled endlessly, world without end, amen. Impetuosity was a trait from his Unchanged days. It had caused him to leave engineering studies for art history, led him to act on his attraction to his dark-haired thesis adviser, though she was clearly at least a decade older. (Such a breathtaking understatement!) It drove him, once he knew, to ask, beg, plead with her to make him Noantri: the world was so huge, so much to be seen, tasted, lived — far more than one meager human lifetime would allow. She'd been reluctant, but once his Change had been accomplished, she'd taken almost as much pleasure in it as he. In their lovemaking, their studies, their play, she was always the more measured, considered, he the more eager and rash. She'd known much better how to choose the routes and byways, metaphorical and real; but once started along them, he could always outrun her.

And he was impatient now: impatient to Unveil, impatient to live freely in the world as the man he was, to stop pretending, stop lying. Impatient to feel Livia's arms around him once again; because she would certainly recognize, once his plans had succeeded — as she always had in all the unorthodox paths he'd taken them down — that the only thing that had been holding her back was an old and burdensome fear.

Impatience, though, could sink him now. He could barely stay still, lurking ridiculously behind this column, but he had to. He'd known that once he made his threat, the Conclave would set Livia on his trail, his and the Concordat's, and that she'd start by searching for it, not him. He knew her that well. He hadn't counted on Father Kelly being of any real use, though he'd admittedly gone to some lengths to keep him around. What he had counted on, and he'd apparently been right, was that if anyone could find the Concordat — the

Cardinal Librarian having failed — his Livia could.

87

Livia watched Thomas sit on the edge of the cistern for a moment, and then slip down. The pit appeared to be about five feet deep; the chapel floor was level with his shoulders. He crouched, disappearing. She waited until impatience got the better of her. She stepped forward and, looking down, said, "What can you see?"

"Nothing. You're in my light."

She rummaged in her bag, stooped, and handed him her new cell phone. It didn't have the flashlight app but the screen was bright. He took his out, too, and trained them together on the cistern floor. No spot stood out from another, but it had been a century and a half since Damiani had hidden the Concordat. Livia was already working out various schemes for digging into the packed earth when Thomas turned the beams to the brick walls. They were five feet high, making a circle three feet in diameter.

Livia searched her geometry training, itself from a century back. If she was right, something over two hundred bricks would need to be painstakingly examined, pulled and prodded to see if any were loose.

But suddenly Thomas stopped the back-and-forth movement of the light, stood for a moment in thought, and then swung the light to a line of bricks in a chosen direction.

"What are you doing?" Livia asked.

"Southeast. Toward Jerusalem. Look!"

How like Damiani. The sacred dimension of Peter's journey might have eluded him, but not its geographical one. There, on a brick exactly halfway down the wall in the row facing Jerusalem, was scratched a small, upside-down cross.

88

Thomas handed Livia both phones. Without a word she sat and held the light steady on the marked brick. He crouched, felt around the mortar joint, found a tiny protruding angle. The brick put up no objection as he wriggled it back and forth. It slid forward until he could get a real grip on it, then eased out into his waiting hand. He slipped his other hand into the crevice its absence created.

A curved wall like this, Thomas knew, would be three or four bricks deep; his hand should have had no more than a three-inch cavity to search before bumping into the next brick. But the two bricks behind the marked one had been removed, leaving a miniature cavern. He felt around and found it immediately: a metal tube. He examined it as he drew it out. Lead, from the dullness of it, six inches long, two inches in diameter, sealed in red wax around its cap.

He looked wordlessly up at Livia. She nodded.

With his thumbnail he pried the wax from the seam. A little wriggling and the cap came loose. Inside the tube was a rolled and folded parchment. Thomas slid it out.

"It may be brittle," Livia warned.

Afraid she was right, he loosened its tight spiral but didn't try to flatten it out. Instead he pulled the outside edge away just enough to see two florid, flowing signatures in ink.

"Martinus V, Pontifex Maximus," he said. "And here — *Pontifex Aliorum?* The Pope of the Others? Who —"

" 'The Pope of the Others,' " Livia repeated calmly. "Our Pontifex. He leads the Noantri, and always has. We —" Without warning, she leapt to her feet and spun around. "Stay down!" she shouted.

Of course Thomas didn't. He stood up just in time to see a man trotting down the steps from the Tempietto's upper level. He knew him: the blond Noantri from San Francesco a Ripa. Jonah Richter, the man who'd started all this.

Richter stepped over the threshold into the small room. The eternal flame flickered shadows across his features. He gazed at Livia with a smile brash but also surprisingly tender. "Hello, Livia."

"Jonah." In that one word Thomas heard anguish: love, fear, longing, loss.

"It'll be all right now," Richter said, with gentle reassurance. "Give it to me."

That voice. Thomas realized he knew it. Before he could stop himself he blurted, "You're the man on the phone! You kidnapped Lorenzo!"

Richter looked down at Thomas, standing in the cistern, and laughed. "Father Kelly, we meet at last. An odd situation, but it's a pleasure."

"It's certainly not! Where's the Cardinal? If you've — If he's —" He wasn't sure how to put it. Before he found the words, Livia spoke.

"Jonah. How did you know we were here? And in the church, before?"

Richter nodded, confirming. "I've been following you."

"The Concordat." Her voice held marvel, not accusation. "You never had it. You never knew where it was."

"No." Richter's smile softened. "But I knew you could find it."

Sparks flew from her words: "I was trying to save *you*!"

"Proving I was right. You've never stopped loving me. Or I you. Give it to me, Livia, and we'll be together again. Together, and free. To live as we please. That's all I ever wanted."

"That's why . . . all this? The threat to reveal it, everything? You suddenly thought, Oh, I know, I'll get the Conclave to scare Livia to death and she'll go out and find the lost Concordat, and I'll steal it from her and make us all Unveil?"

He shook his head. "I wish I could claim that sort of inspiration. No, I learned the new Librarian was hunting it. Before that I didn't even know it was missing. But you can see, it presented a golden opportunity."

"I can't." Her shoulders fell. When she spoke all fire was gone. She sounded small and sad. "All *I* wanted was the life I had. My home, my work." She paused. "You. But you ended that."

"For a while. But now we can have it forever. Give me the Concordat, and we can start a new life. Together. In the sun. Livia, please."

Thomas calmly rerolled the Concordat and replaced it in the tube, making sure the cap was tight. Tube in hand, he muscled himself out of the cistern as though he were leaving a swimming pool. He straightened, stood next to Livia, and, facing Richter, said, "No."

89

"Father," said Jonah. Livia saw him smile at Thomas, saw his smile change. "I understand. You want to negotiate. The Concordat for your friend the Cardinal. Fine. Give it to me and I'll tell you where he is. I promise you, he's" — Jonah's grin broadened — "as you last saw him. So, please."

Talking to Livia, Jonah had been caring, wry, the man she'd never — as he'd known — stopped loving. But as he spoke to Thomas, Livia heard a new note in his voice. His confidence spilled into smug superiority, his resolve into threat. Did he not hear himself?

Momentarily the Tempietto dissolved and Livia was back standing before the Conclave. Rosa Cartelli's shrill fears of terror and of fire if the Noantri Unveiled were balanced by the Pontifex's calm words: *The time will come, but it is not come yet.* The Pontifex, whose understanding of their lives was fathomless and clear: this was what he'd meant. This was the true peril of Unveiling. The greatest danger came not from the Unchanged, was not to the temporal existence of the Noantri. It arose from within, and what was at risk was their very souls. Her people would have much to offer an Unveiled world; but the change she was seeing in Jonah right now was the proof that they were not ready. The Concordat's demand for secrecy, she was suddenly sure, was the very thing that kept the swagger out of the Noantri step.

"No," she said. "What you want is wrong."

"His reasons are wrong," said a new voice. "Twisted as they can be. But his request will be fulfilled."

90

Thomas spun to face the doorway. At the sight of the thin form silhouetted there his heart leapt. "*Lorenzo!* Thank God! You're free!"

The Cardinal, dressed in street clothes and without clerical collar — but carrying a lit cigar — smiled as he stepped into the room. "Thomas. You've done well." He turned to the openmouthed Jonah Richter. "You didn't seriously think I'd stay shut up in that foul-smelling attic waiting for you to come back?"

Richter recovered himself, laughed, and made Lorenzo a mock bow. "Your Eminence. You have to admit I was right, though. It worked."

"It wouldn't have been necessary in the first place if you'd had the least modicum of self-control. How like your kind, though: the arrogance of Satan himself. Thomas, bravo. I'm humbled by your devotion and proud of your erudition. Now please give the Concordat to me."

"Lorenzo." Thomas felt the way he often did translating a fragment of text: he understood the words but couldn't get them to make sense. "How did you get free?"

"He obviously walked out my door." Richter's tone was merry. "The same way he walked in."

"I'm sorry, Thomas," said Lorenzo. "We had to improvise. You'd quit the search and were leaving Rome. Jonah had great faith in *Professoressa* Pietro and was perfectly happy to let you go, but I knew better. You were the key." Lorenzo turned a sour eye on Livia, as though she'd been holding Thomas back. Then: "Thomas. The document. Please." He put out his hand.

"Wait. I don't understand. The phone call . . . Your abduction . . ."

"Catch up, Father!" Richter said. His thumb waggled from Lorenzo to himself.

"Desperation makes strange bedfellows," Lorenzo said matter-of-factly. "Jonah came to me and, after I'd controlled my disgust at his very presence, convinced me the Concordat was more likely to be found if a Noantri was also on the trail. This one, to be precise." He pointed the cigar at Livia. "I was revolted, but it was efficient. Thomas,

540

let's get out of here. It's unbearable to be this close to them for long."

Richter shrugged. "Livia, he thinks we smell funny. This from a man who can't go anywhere without a stinking cigar. To have a flame always nearby, that's it, isn't it, Your Eminence? God, you Mortals are so easy to read. Fine, take it and go. It amounts to the same thing."

Thomas looked from one man to the other. "It does? How can that be? *You* want to make it public. Lorenzo —" He stopped as he met Lorenzo's eyes.

In a voice of infinite patience, Lorenzo spoke. "I told you once: centuries ago, a great mistake was made. It can't be undone, but it can be corrected."

"But the Church — if the world knows about this agreement, that the Church and the Noantri —"

"Yes." Lorenzo stood relaxed and straight, like a man relieved of a burden. "The Church we know, compromised and corrupt, will finally fall."

"And our people" — Jonah Richter smiled at Livia — "will be free."

"Not for long!" Lorenzo spun on Richter in sudden, savage rage. "The new Church that rises will be fearless and mighty! The Church the Savior intended! It will put an

541

end to your filthy kind!" He turned to Thomas; his voice dropped to a plea. "You understand, don't you? All evil flows from them. In God's image, but not human. Among us, not of us, degrading us, destroying us. Mocking the promise of the Resurrection. *They must be stopped!*"

Thomas felt shaky, as though engulfed by a tide that might sweep him away. This was the Lorenzo he knew, the friend he loved, raging against coming disaster as so often before. But this time he was wrong.

Whatever the true colors of Livia's people, whatever the depth of their hearts and the desires inside them — however evil one or another of them might be, as one or another of Thomas's people might also be — the Noantri nature was not as Lorenzo believed.

"No," he said. "Lorenzo —"

"Give it to me!" Lorenzo grasped for the tube in Thomas's hand. Thomas pulled his arm back but no need: Richter seized Lorenzo, flinging him into the altar. The shadows from the eternal flame bounced and danced, though the lamp stayed aright. Richter lunged, clamped a vise grip on Thomas's wrist. He tried to pry the tube loose and would have succeeded but Livia wrapped him from behind in a bear hug. Thomas yanked his hand from Richter's

fingers as Richter, with an earthquake roar, blasted free, throwing Livia to the floor.

Richter leapt on Thomas and the two stumbled back. Thomas felt a sickening thud as his head slammed into the wall. Dizzy, pinned by Richter's weight, he stretched his arm, lifting the tube as high as he could; he was taller than Richter and the man couldn't reach it. Richter laughed. He stopped trying for the tube, instead wrapping both hands around Thomas's throat. He squeezed and shook. Fiery knives sliced through Thomas's skull every time the back of his head hit the stone again. Tiny red lights burst behind his eyes and he knew he'd lost. He couldn't breathe; he couldn't think. The tube began to slip from his fingers. His straining lungs begged for air. **Our Father, who art in heaven . . .**

"NO!" A howl echoed off the stone walls. *"Leave him alone!"* Thomas could barely make out Lorenzo staggering toward them. The Cardinal's face purpled with effort as he tried to pull Richter away. He had no effect at all; then, with wonder, Thomas saw Lorenzo — rail-thin, seventy-three, and never a street fighter — make fists and hammer at Richter's head and face.

The blows were ineffectual but Lorenzo was relentless. *"Let go of him!"* he rasped, and finally Richter turned, snarling. Thomas slipped down the wall as Richter dropped his grip and faced the Cardinal. A second's pause; then one roundhouse punch to the jaw was all it took to lift Lorenzo into the air and hurl him across the room.

91

Livia, winded when Jonah threw her to the floor, pulled in deep breaths. She shook off her daze and looked up just in time to see the Cardinal, flying off Jonah's fist, crash headfirst into a wall. Jonah spared himself a moment to grin in satisfaction. Then he turned back to where Thomas lay gasping on the floor. He reached down for the tube that had dropped from Thomas's grip; but that moment was all Livia needed.

Leaping up, she tackled Jonah as she had the clerk at the Metro station. The tube flew from Jonah's hand and bounced across the room. They rolled and wrestled; in the end he was stronger, though, and leveraged himself on top of her, pinning her down. Looking into her eyes, he grinned. "This was not how I imagined myself back in this position." He leaned down and quickly kissed her. She lost her breath again. Then he jumped up, scanning for the tube. Livia shook off another, much different kind of daze, and followed his eyes. She saw him redden in anger: Thomas had recovered enough to crawl across the floor and grasp the tube, pulling it protectively close.

"Father," Jonah said. "Don't be silly. You'll only get hurt more."

Thomas couldn't do more than shake his head as he lay on the floor, hugging the tube to him. When Jonah leaned down to take it, Thomas held it tight, engaging with all his remaining strength in what Livia knew would be a losing tug-of-war.

She leapt up. "Jonah!" He turned to face her. "Leave it! It isn't time!"

He grinned again. A bead of sweat made a trail down his temple. "No. If I can't make you understand, my darling, I'll continue without you. Once we've Unveiled, you'll know. You'll thank me and come back to me. We have time. I can wait." He reached down again and, with a grunt, yanked the tube from Thomas's weakened grip. "Now move aside," he said, but she filled the doorway and stood. "Livia. If we fight, I'll win."

"Still. I can't let you take it."

"Come with me." His voice was soft. "I became Noantri to be with you. You took on this task to save me, you say. So come with me now."

"And to save our people."

"This will free our people."

"It will destroy them."

He took a step toward her. "There's only one way you could stop me."

She said nothing.

"But you won't do it."

"I will," she said, but she knew he was right.

Another step, and he put a hand on her arm, as if to gently tug her aside. She shook it off and stood firm. "I don't want to hurt you," he said.

Before she could answer Thomas lunged up from the floor, grasping for the tube in Jonah's hand. A second late, Jonah pulled his hand away but he'd lost his grip. The tube flew through the air again, this time landing on the altar shelf. Jonah sprang toward it, stretched for it, but Thomas grabbed at his leg and he tripped. Flailing clumsily, trying simultaneously to kick Thomas away and to reach the tube, Jonah knocked the lamp over. Oil spilled down his arm, and in horror Livia watched flame catch fabric. She rushed forward, threw her arms around him to smother the fire, but he had the Concordat in his hand now and he broke free. The back of his jacket blazed as he leapt for the door.

"No!" she shouted. "If you run the air will feed the flames! Drop! Roll!"

She raced out the door, through the courtyard, and down the steps, wild with fear as she saw the flames engulf him. If she could only catch up to him she could stop him, wrap him in her arms, choke off the fire; but he'd always been able to outrun her.

92

Livia had run after Jonah Richter. Thomas should have followed. She might need his help to wrest the Concordat from Richter's hands. But Thomas could barely stand, certainly couldn't run.

And there was something else.

Staggering to his feet, Thomas crossed the chapel to where Lorenzo lay, his head at an odd angle but otherwise sprawled like a man relaxing in the sun.

"Lorenzo. Father!"

Lorenzo opened his eyes.

"Thank God!" Thomas breathed, fumbling for his phone. "I'm calling for help."

"Thomas." Lorenzo's voice was faint. "Find the Magdalene."

"What? No, don't talk. Help will be here —"

"I can't move," Lorenzo whispered. "I can't feel my arms, my legs. Thomas, let me go. But find the Magdalene."

"What do you mean?"

"This isn't all. The Church you love . . . the Concordat wouldn't have . . . it would have been built anew. Stronger, purer. But it won't . . . you must find . . . find . . ." Slowly, his eyes closed. His lips continued to move, though no sound reached Thomas.

"No. No, Father, please. Lorenzo!" But there was nothing more.

Thomas knelt motionless on the cold marble, trying to will Lorenzo to open his eyes, to speak. Finally, rousing himself, he looked around. Oil from the now-extinguished eternal flame dripped from the altar onto the floor. He stumbled over, dipped his fingers in it, muttered the prayer consecrating it to God's holy purposes. Returning to Lorenzo's side, he traced the sign of the cross on Lorenzo's forehead, and began: "Through this holy unction and his own most tender mercy may God pardon thee . . ."

93

Livia stepped slowly into the chapel under the Tempietto to find Thomas praying over the body of Lorenzo Cossa. In her hand she held the lead tube; in her heart, the indelible sight of Jonah, at the bottom of the steep steps, on his knees as the fire consumed him. His arms were raised high, one hand a triumphal fist; the other, holding the tube, suddenly hurled it out of the flames with what must have been his last strength.

By the time she'd reached him, nothing could be done. He was charred, devoured, destroyed, turning to ash in the still-dancing flames. She'd stood, numb, watching the fire die down. She'd said his name, once; then, carefully, methodically, as though it were someone else doing it, turned away and searched until she found the lead tube. Clutching it to her, she started back up the hill.

In the chapel, she knelt beside Thomas.

After a few moments he turned to look at her.

"I'm so sorry," she said.

His eyes held a question that she answered with a shake of her head.

"I'm sorry, too," he told her.

In the silence, she opened her arms for him. He moved into her embrace. In the dim chapel, they shared their sorrow.

94

Anna had watched Jorge twist and flail as he fell. His descent wasn't long and he'd hit the ground hard. It didn't matter. The fall was camouflage. As a Noantri the impact wouldn't have killed him; but what she'd done would, whether he'd fallen or not. She'd seen it begin. As he lay on the asphalt, tiny drops of blood started to leak from his eyes. There would be more, and then from his mouth, nose, and ears. His skin would turn purple, as though he'd been bruised all over. His internal organs, too, would bleed. Anna had given him a great gift some decades ago. He'd been unworthy of it, and now she had taken it back.

She'd wanted to stay and watch, because although this was a process much discussed among the Noantri, very few had actually seen it. Fascinated as she was, though, she knew she'd better move on. Jorge's body would be discovered soon, and it would be just as well if she weren't around.

Where was she going? She hadn't decided, but it would be far. What she'd said about finding Pietro and the priest was bold talk, and with time she knew she could, but right now she wasn't in a position to look. So far the Conclave didn't seem to know that she'd been trying to thwart their plans; been trying, in fact, to usurp their power. At this point, she judged them likely to win. That idiot Jorge had put her and her faction too far behind. She had no idea where to go to pick up the chase now. To stay in the game she'd have to regroup, and she had a feeling the clock was running out.

She could live with that. She could live with that, she thought with a smile, for a very long time. Her followers were determined that the Noantri should Unveil, and their numbers grew with each passing year. When Anna decided their strength was sufficient, she'd step forward and confront the Conclave directly. She wouldn't need the lost Concordat for that.

Anna had cast one last glance at the dying Jorge, whose blood was by then seeping along the street to flow in little rivulets down the hill. She headed in the same direction, down, saying goodbye to La Sapienza, to comparative lit, and, with a sigh, to the

Serb professor she'd had her eye on. And to Anna Jagiellon, she supposed, for a while. That was all right. It was a big world.

Trotting down the steps, she found herself wondering two things: Why the foul cologne, which had made him so much easier to find? And why, when Jorge's bloody dying eyes met hers, had she read in them, not pain, not anger, but gratitude, and joy?

95

Thomas walked beside Livia in the silence under the trees. The winding way through the Orto Botanico led them down the hill far from the sirens and flashing lights. Leaving the Tempietto they found something had happened, something so big, one wide-eyed tourist told another, that the road down the Janiculum had been closed and they all had to stay up top. The six tourists on the overlook argued among themselves, agreeing the problem was clearly terrorism, debating only what kind: domestic, foreign, bombs, bio-agents. Livia had relayed all this to Thomas as she'd listened in, unnoticed, from the cloister.

"We can't stay here," he said. "How will we get down?"

"Don't worry. Come."

He followed as she turned and headed in the other direction, back around the cloister to the road along the top of the hill.

Thomas, dazed and bruised, moved slowly. Walking at all was an effort, but he found, for the first time today, it didn't take any extra work to keep up with Livia. Her steps were as fatigued as his; she appeared also weary, also dispirited. The Noantri body, he'd learned, could restore itself, come back rapidly from almost any injury. The Noantri heart, it seemed, not so.

She'd led him to the gates of the Orto Botanico, Rome's Botanical Garden. They'd been prepared to climb the fence in case the Orto had been shut down, but in typical Roman style, either the word that no one was to go up or down the Janiculum hadn't reached the Orto, or more likely, it had been received with a shrug and was being ignored. They paid their entrance fee, hoping the young man in the booth wasn't on the lookout for fugitives. As it turned out, he was not, being barely sentient enough to notice customers. They headed down the curving pathway where fallen leaves whispered underfoot. The tracery of branches revealed the fading autumn afternoon, as though the tree canopy had given up trying to hide the sky. The few blooms still to be seen had withered; even the bamboo grove was fading from green to yellow.

Whatever had happened on the road

they'd have to learn later. They couldn't afford to be seen by the *polizia* or Carabinieri; and they couldn't afford to wait. Richter was gone beyond recognition, an unexplained blaze exhausted to a smoking mound of ashes on a flight of stone steps; but Lorenzo's body would not lie in the chapel long without someone, sightseer or caretaker, stumbling upon it.

Lorenzo's body. Lorenzo had lied to Thomas and used him, had betrayed his trust and had intended to betray the Church. But anger, indignation, resentment, even relief that Lorenzo's plans had been thwarted — Thomas felt none of these. Instead, walking under empty branches, he searched himself, searched their fifteen years of friendship, for the failing. What in Thomas had made Lorenzo unwilling to trust him with this secret, unable to share his knowledge and his fears? They could have debated, talked, studied over it. They could have found another path. Why had it come to this?

96

Seated at the café in Piazza della Scala, Luigi Esposito had to admit to himself that he might be wrong. Wrong about Spencer George's involvement in whatever was going on? No. The man was so clearly hiding something that Luigi suspected the uniformed *scemi* he'd been stuck with this morning could've seen it. But it was possible he was wrong about the value of a surveillance. It had been an hour since he left the interview with the historian and the man had not emerged. If nothing happened in the next hour or so, no one in or out, maybe the most useful thing Luigi could do would be to go back to the office and dig into George's life. People peddling stolen art didn't exist in vacuums. He'd find another path.

These were the thoughts running through his head when his cell phone rang. He didn't need to check the screen; he'd thought it prudent to give the *soprintendente* his own ring tone.

"Esposito, where are you?"

"Piazza della Scala, sir. Still on the surveillance."

"Leave. Your car's close?"

"Yes, sir, but —"

"Take it, not a cab. Go to the Ambulatorio di Medicina Tropicale. On Via Portuense. The emergency room. Tell them who you are."

"The emergency room? Who's there?"

"You. They're waiting for you."

"I — Sir, what are you talking about? I'm fine."

"Maybe not. That Argentinian, your suspect? He's dead. Of a hemorrhagic fever."

"A what?"

"Deadly and contagious. The officers you had with you this morning are already there. So are the Carabinieri you're working with, and from what you say they had no physical contact with him."

"No, they didn't. But, sir, he —"

"Esposito. It's an order. They'll keep you until they finish the autopsy and isolate the virus. It's not just for you. It's to keep you from infecting anyone else. I'm sure you're fine," he said, in tones that made it clear he wasn't. "But go."

This wasn't happening, Luigi thought. He had a case! A real crime to solve. A theory that was right, he knew it was. Two Carabinieri detectives who respected him. This was his chance — this was his blue uniform —

"Esposito! Do I have to send an ambulance to find you?"

"No." Luigi cast a last, longing glance at Spencer George's door. "Sir. Not necessary. I'm on my way."

97

Neither Livia nor Thomas had spoken since they entered the Orto Botanico; their silence continued as they emerged at the bottom of the hill and made their way through Trastevere. Livia kept them to the less-traveled, more-shadowed streets, though they saw few Carabinieri or *polizia;* whatever had happened on the Janiculum seemed to have drawn all the law officers in Rome. Livia's thoughts, unbidden but uncontrollable, kept returning to that long-ago violet evening, to the cobalt cloth in the candlelit room, to the moment she'd given in to her own desires, and his, and made Jonah Noantri.

The fault was hers. He wasn't strong enough, and if she'd brought the request to the Conclave, as the Law required, they would have told her that. She had ignored the Law, because she already knew.

She'd done it, as she'd revealed herself to him at all, because she was afraid of losing him. Now he was lost: to her, to the world. To himself.

Thomas hadn't asked where they were going, but as they reached the middle of the Ponte Sisto, Livia stopped and faced him. "The place where the Conclave meets is just over the bridge."

Thomas leaned on the stone balustrade and watched the Tiber flow. "You intend to give the Concordat to them?"

"They'll keep it hidden. I wasn't sure that was still necessary, even as late as this morning. But now . . ." She leaned beside him, trying to marshal an argument. This was his Church's copy; by rights it should be returned. Still staring out over the water, he held up a hand to stop her.

"I agree. I don't know how many in the Church know it exists, but Lorenzo can't be the only one who feels — who felt as he did. About your people. I don't think we can return it to the Church."

"Jonah wasn't alone, either," she said quietly. "The Conclave will protect both copies. Until it's time."

He nodded and straightened, and they walked on.

98

Father Thierry Ateba unlocked the Librarian's office suite, entered, and closed the ornate door behind. He crossed himself as though in the presence of death, although the death of Cardinal Cossa, of which Father Ateba had just learned, had occurred within the hour on the Janiculum Hill, not here. The room, of course, did not know its occupant was gone forever, and the Cardinal's open books, his papers, and his humidor all sat as he had left them, awaiting his return.

It would fall to Father Ateba, as Lorenzo Cossa's personal secretary, to sort and organize these items, to separate Cardinal Cossa's possessions from those of the Church and ensure that each item was ultimately disposed of as it must be. It would take time, but meticulousness and patience were two of Father Ateba's virtues. He glanced about the room, unconsciously planning his strategy for where to begin, how to conscientiously, efficiently fulfill this final responsibility. After his work was complete, he himself would no longer be needed here. The new Librarian and Archivist would bring with him his own assistant.

Father Ateba moved to the window and threw it open to rid the air of the lingering smell of cigar smoke; not offensive, but an odor he had never liked. Turning back to the room, he regarded the books and papers on the late Cardinal's desk. Father Ateba had been made privy to the work the Cardinal was doing, and he wondered if the new Librarian would want to continue it.

He walked to the desk, the obvious place to begin. First, though, now that he was alone here where he wouldn't be disturbed, one other task demanded his attention. As he'd been requested to do when he'd received the sad news, he took his cell phone from his jacket pocket and pressed in a number. He was greeted by a voice familiar to him for many, many years.

"Salve."

"Salve. Sum Thierry Ateba. Quid aegis?"

"Hic nobis omnibus bene est. Quomodo auxilium vobis dare possumus?"

99

"You've done well, Livia," said a deep, slow voice. "And you, Father Kelly. The Noantri thank you."

Thomas nodded, unable to speak. As he'd walked with Livia through the twilight from the Ponte Sisto to Santa Maria dell'Orazione e Morte, she'd told him where they were going and what to expect. She'd tried to prepare him, but how could he have been prepared for this? This morning he'd have laughed at the idea that vampires existed. Twelve hours later he was standing beside one, in front of thirteen more, in the light of two great candelabra in the basement of a bone church.

Arrayed before him, robed in black, were what had been described as the most powerful figures in the Noantri world. Their College of Cardinals, in a way. He suddenly realized: their ruling body! Body, now *that* was funny. A laugh threatened to explode out of him; understanding himself to be on the edge of a cliff of exhaustion, shock, and grief-fueled wildness, he clamped his jaw shut and forced himself still.

"We will keep this copy of the Concordat safe," the voice went on. "As we have the other, all these years." The speaker was the Noantri leader, the Pontifex Aliorum. It was he himself who had signed the Concordat. He spoke in English; Livia had said that would be the case, out of courtesy to Thomas. His was the first voice heard in the room since Livia had presented the lead tube, along with Mario Damiani's notebook and its missing pages. The Pontifex had passed the notebook to the woman on his right and opened the tube in silence and with great care. Once he'd unfolded the document Thomas could have sworn he saw the man's face lose some of its somber tension, though you couldn't say he relaxed. Probably — like Lorenzo — this man never relaxed. He'd passed the document, also, to the woman on his right; each Counsellor had taken it in turn and looked it over while Livia and Thomas stood before them.

"The time will come when our peoples — yours, Father, and ours — will be released from the requirements of this agreement. On that day, your names will be spoken in praise. Until then, what's happened must remain our secret." He regarded Thomas. "Father Kelly, you've lost a friend today. Please accept our deepest sympathy, and understand none among us sought this outcome."

Again, Thomas could only nod. The Pontifex turned his attention to Livia.

"Livia, you've also suffered a loss. That it was inevitable makes it no less tragic. We offer our sympathy to you, also."

"Thank you, Lord," Livia said, her voice quiet but steady.

A long moment of silence followed. All eyes rested on Livia as the Pontifex said, *"Mandatum exsecuta es et opus perfectum est."* **You have followed your instructions and your task is complete.** It was a formal acknowledgment, no doubt part of a ritual centuries old. What other rituals, Thomas wondered, were observed here?

"Officio perfungi mihi gratum est." Livia responded formally. **I am grateful to be of service.** She took a breath and, switching back to English, she said, "Lord, might I make a request?"

The Pontifex traded glances with the woman beside him. He nodded. "Speak."

"Thank you, Lord. The circumstances of the day have left many questions in the

Unchanged world. The Carabinieri are searching for Father Kelly and myself. Jonah's —" Thomas saw her swallow and blink back tears. She recovered and continued, "His death will go unnoticed by the Unchanged, but two men, churchmen, are also dead."

"And a Noantri who certainly has not gone unnoticed," said the woman beside the Pontifex. "The clerk from the Library. On the Janiculum Hill. You didn't know?"

Livia gasped. "Not unnoticed? Was he —"

She stopped as the woman nodded. "Yes. His Lord destroyed him."

Thomas wasn't sure of the significance of that, but Livia clearly was. She paled. "Who is that?"

"A woman named Anna Jagiellon. She made him without our consent, and has done this without it, also. She will be dealt with."

"On the Janiculum." Thomas was surprised to hear his own voice. The Counsellors turned to him. "Is that why the emergency vehicles were there?"

A rotund man answered, someone who hadn't previously spoken. "Yes. The death of a Noantri, when brought about this way, resembles some of the more frightening human illnesses." Unlike the other two, this man spoke English — American English — without a trace of an accent. No, Thomas realized: with an accent like his own. A Boston Noantri, from Southie. Thomas set that aside, to think about later. "The body was removed and will be autopsied," the man said. "Nothing, of course, will be found."

"The microbe?" Thomas asked.

The man smiled. "Ever the scholar, eh, Father Kelly? The autoimmune reaction triggered by re-exposure — the cause of death — destroys the microbe. Nothing," he repeated, "will be found."

Thomas felt questions arising in his mind in infinite number, but their sheer quantity prevented his articulating any single one.

"Father Kelly," the Pontifex said, "your curiosity regarding our natures is obvious. So is your weariness. Perhaps you'd prefer to renew our dialogue at some future time? Because of your services to the Noantri this day, I speak for each member of this Conclave, including myself, when I say we will be pleased to make ourselves available to you for further discussion, whenever you choose. We have held these dialogues from time to time, through the years, with friends of the Noantri. You are one."

As exhausted and grief-stricken as he was,

Thomas still understood the value of the gift he'd just been given. "Yes," he said. "I'd welcome that. Thank you."

The Pontifex turned back to Livia.

"You, too, are weary. But you have a request to make of us?"

"Yes, Lord," Livia said. "I, of course, will leave Rome, but I'm concerned about Ellen Bird and Spencer George. Most of all, about Father Kelly. The authorities will continue their investigations, and I don't want Spencer's or Ellen's lives interrupted. And Thomas — Father Kelly — can't just change identities and vanish, as we can. Nor, I think, would he want to." Her gaze briefly met Thomas's, then returned to the Counsellors. "If there's any way the Conclave can . . . affect the course of the authorities' processes? I'm not sure what I'm asking you to do, but . . ." She trailed off.

"There is no reason for you to leave Rome," the Pontifex said. "Or to Cloak."

"The Carabinieri have been looking for us since Father Battista died in Santa Maria della Scala. Spencer told me that. And surely someone will have seen us near the Tempietto. We're suspects and, at this point, fugitives."

"At the moment, yes. But you have a very good friend in Spencer George. He contacted us a few hours ago, with a clever proposal. Arrangements have already been made."

"Arrangements, Lord?"

The Pontifex looked to the woman on his right.

"The Carabinieri and the Gendarmerie are in fact looking for you," she said, "though their theories about the basis of your involvement keep changing." In her dry voice Thomas heard her disdain for the quotidian forces of the law. "What they are sure of is the existence of an international ring of art thieves. Spencer George has elected himself head of this cabal. When his home is searched, as it will soon be, many valuable items belonging to the Vatican will be found. They're being selected as we speak, from the office of the Cardinal Librarian, and will be scattered about. They will include this notebook. Certain other treasures will also be found, which will be traced back to other collections. On those items the provenance marks are recent and false, provided by Spencer George himself. Evidence planted in certain places will make it clear that you, Livia, were aiding Father Kelly in a search, instigated by Cardinal Cossa, to find the leader of this criminal organization, and to do it with utmost discretion, in order that the Vatican not be embarrassed by the ease with which its collections have apparently been raided. The Holy See, realizing you were both in service to the Cardinal, will intervene with the Carabinieri on your behalf."

"I . . ."

Livia seemed no more able to take all this in than Thomas was himself. The woman continued.

"Ellen Bird, if she's noticed at all, will be considered an ally of yours and therefore of the Vatican's. The unfortunate death of Father Battista will be ascribed — correctly, I think? — to Jorge Ocampo, now dead himself, and a member of this ring of thieves, though his murderous behavior will most likely be attributed not to the requirements of larceny but to a mental instability brought about by the infectious fever that killed him. Cardinal Cossa" — she gave Thomas a brief, piercing look — "will be thought to have been slain in a confrontation with these thieves. Whose leader, by the time this has all been worked out — the Carabinieri and Gendarmerie detectives involved in the case being temporarily indisposed — will be found to have fled the country."

"Leader?" Livia asked. "Spencer? Fled the

country?"

"He'll be traceable for a time, to give the authorities something to do. His ultimate plan, once he's finally disappeared, is to spend some years in America."

"Spencer?" Livia repeated. "America?"

"He expressed a desire to see the New World."

"The New . . ." A pause. "Yes, I see. And his collection?"

"The most valuable pieces — valuable to the Noantri, I mean — will be found to have unassailable provenance. They, and his home, will turn out to be not strictly Dr. George's possessions, but actually those of a distant cousin in Wales. This cousin will continue to pay the taxes and costs of upkeep on the home and will visit occasionally. A number of years hence he will, I believe, retire to Italy."

She settled back in her chair with a satisfied huff. The Pontifex spoke. "You have, as I said, a very good friend in Spencer George." With a small smile, he added, "As does the Gendarme detective. Apparently the entire idea of an art-theft ring was his. Dr. George feels he's wasted on the Gendarmerie and has requested that, in return for Dr. George's participation in this scheme, we arrange for the young man to be reassigned — transferred to the Carabinieri. If, of course, he's willing to go."

"I see," said Livia again. "So, I may just . . . go home?"

"You may, but I wouldn't suggest that you do, just yet. You and Father Kelly will be cleared of all suspicion shortly, but not until the various detectives become available, sometime tomorrow. Until then your house is being watched by officers who have instructions to bring you in for questioning. I assume you'd rather avoid that eventuality?"

"Very much so, Lord."

"Well, then. As I'm sure you know, we maintain a number of residences throughout Rome for the convenience of visitors. May we offer you both our hospitality this evening?"

100

In fitful sleep that night, Livia was haunted by shadowy, oppressive dreams; between them, lying awake, by the image of Jonah engulfed in fire. Arising with the sun, she showered, then chose gray slacks and a soft blue sweater from among the items they'd been told would be waiting at the spacious apartment on Via Giulia for their use. "You both look rather the worse for wear," had been Rosa Cartelli's assessment.

Livia made her way into the kitchen. She and Thomas had been met the night before by a friendly young Noantri — though, from his manner of speech, Elder to her, Livia thought — who had shown them their rooms and served a light supper of *pasta al limone* before retiring discreetly to his own apartment across the hall. Now, at this early hour, she expected to be alone; but she found Thomas already at the table in the bright room. He was drinking a cappuccino, and grounds in the sink indicated it wasn't his first.

"Good morning," Livia said, smiling softly. "How are you doing?"

She could see he'd also had a shower; his wet hair was neatly combed and parted. The purple bruises from Jonah's hands were visible above the collar of a new sweatshirt, plain and black. He considered her question as though it were complex and arcane. At last he said, "I'm not the same man I was yesterday, that's for sure."

"I hope," she said, "that I like this man as well as I liked that one. Do you want more coffee?"

At his nod, she opened a ceramic canister and spooned coffee into the *moka* pot. She put it on the stove and unwrapped the blue and white paper around the *cornetti* that sat in a bowl in the center of the table. In a small pitcher she steamed milk and drizzled it into their coffee cups. Bringing the coffee to the table, she sat down across from him. "Were you able to sleep?"

"Not really."

"I'm not surprised. It will be a long time, for both of us, I think."

He nodded, reached for a *cornetto*. He ate; she leaned back in her chair and sipped her coffee, looking beyond him to the window and the glorious blue sky. In this quiet moment, in this bright, airy place her people maintained to shelter their own, she began to feel, not the end of her shock and sadness over what had happened yesterday, but the possibility of that end. The Noantri sense of time and thus of potential was different from that of the Unchanged. To Livia's people, even to the Eldest, the future was always longer than the past. Thomas's relationship to his own history was quite different, but she hoped he could feel some echo of optimism, too.

"There's something else," he said.

She turned from the window. "Something else?"

"That kept me awake. Not just what happened. What Lorenzo said."

Livia thought back, found nothing to fasten on. "What did he say?"

"As he was . . . The last thing he said to me was that the Church would have been built anew after the revelation of the Concordat. But he seemed to be trying to tell me there was another secret, something even more dangerous. He died . . . before he could tell me more. But he said, 'Find the Magdalene.'"

"The Magdalene? Do you have any idea what he meant?"

Thomas shook his head.

Tentatively, Livia said, "There are art-works all over Rome, paintings and sculptures, depicting Mary Magdalene. Hundreds, I'd guess. But there's only one church dedicated to her. Santa Maria Maddalena, near the Pantheon. Could he have wanted us to go there? You, wanted you to go. He wouldn't have wanted anything from me."

Thomas met her eyes. "I'm sorry," he said. "Hate like his . . . I always thought he was such a good man. Tough, and often angry, but at heart so good."

"The tragedy," she said softly, "is that he thought so, too. He meant to do good. He thought he was. So few people are wicked by their own lights. Thomas, you loved him. And he loved you. Remember that."

"He used me," Thomas said bitterly. "My studies — my focus on the period around the Risorgimento — it was his idea. Our friendship, keeping me close — it was all so I'd be ready for this. For when he had the chance to find the Concordat."

"Because he thought it was important. He thought the Church you both loved needed him, needed you, to do this." She put her hand over his. "And I doubt if your friendship was any less real, or less deep, for all that."

"How real? He didn't trust me enough to tell me about the Concordat. About your people."

She was quiet a moment. "I trusted Jonah enough to tell him. It was wrong."

Thomas entwined his fingers with hers. They sat in silence for a long time.

"I want to go there," Thomas said. "To Santa Maria Maddalena."

Livia met his eyes. "What I was instructed to do, I've done," she said. "Whatever the Cardinal's words meant, he intended them for you. If you want to go without me, I'll understand."

"No," Thomas said, without pause. "I'd like you to come."

101

They walked through the fresh Rome morning along streets just waking for the day. Their footsteps, in rhythm with one another, were purposeful but no longer racing, no longer furtive. Thomas tried to soothe the heaviness in his heart and the confusion in his mind by not thinking at all, not about where they were going or about what had happened yesterday. He watched shopkeepers put out their signs and sidewalk racks, café owners wipe off tables and bustle out with coffee for early customers; but the extraordinary choreography of everyday activity, usually a source of delight to him, today didn't provide enough distraction. He turned to something else, something that had always worked: the search for knowledge.

"May I ask you something? Some things?" he said to Livia.

"Of course."

"About your people?"

"I just hope I know the answers. It might really be Spencer you want."

"No, it's not your history. It's your . . . your nature, I suppose you'd say." They walked on, Thomas organizing his thoughts, welcoming the calm that came with focus. "Stop me if I get too personal. Can you . . . have children?"

"No." A few steps later, she added, "Some Noantri, who either didn't know that when they were made, or thought they didn't care, find it a source of great sadness later on." She paused again. "There are children among us. Or rather, Noantri who were made when they were children. Since the Concordat it's been an unforgivable infraction of the Law to do that, and even before, it's something most Noantri would have balked at. But these people — no more than a dozen or so — were made long ago. They occupy a special place in our Community — one or two of them are among the Eldest."

Thomas reflected upon that. Everything he'd learned this past day would take so much reflection. "Is anyone ever sorry?"

"About becoming Noantri?"

"Because it's irreversible. And . . . endless."

He thought he knew her answer: that she'd say absolutely not, that with senses enhanced and all the time in the world to study, to hone, to learn, to love, what could anyone regret?

"Yes," she said quietly. "This life becomes a burden for some. Many people find they never actually wanted to live forever. What they wanted was not to die."

They turned a corner, had to part for a large group of small children in two ragged, giggling lines. When the little ones had been herded past by their frazzled guardians, Thomas and Livia came together again.

"This time yesterday," he said, "I didn't know you existed. Tell me, are there — others?"

"Other Noantri?" Livia looked confused. "Besides those of us you've met? Of course."

"No, no. Other . . . I'd have said, 'supernatural beings,' but . . ."

Livia laughed. "I see. You want to know if I party with werewolves and zombies? Dance with skeletons, go hiking with Bigfoot?"

"I . . ." Thomas felt himself reddening. "When you put it that way, it does sound idiotic."

"It's not idiotic." Her voice softened. "I just don't know. There have always been legends — we hear them just as you do. But there've been legends about us, too: that we turn into bats, that we can't be seen in mirrors. On book covers we're shown with eyes like red-hot coals, in films with skin like dirty snow. Some of those ideas, we're guilty of fostering, once they start making the rounds. Bram Stoker, who was one of us, did us a great service. Stories about us had started to circulate, interest had been renewed. It was a daring move to write *Dracula.* Some Noantri were horrified, but it turned out to be brilliant. He made us seem at once completely outlandish, and identifiable. Anyone who could go out in daylight, who didn't have pointy teeth and didn't smell like rank earth, couldn't possibly be a vampire. Those kinds of myths allow us to live among the Unchanged more easily. I'd imagine if other" — she paused — "other varieties of people, people with different natures, do exist, they're not much like the stories about them, either."

Pondering that, the meaning and possibilities, how wide the world was and how narrow human knowledge, Thomas found himself beside Livia rounding the corner into Piazza della Rotonda without being quite sure how they'd gotten there. To their right, the Pantheon itself, one of the world's truest gems of architectural creation. To their left, a café, people relaxing with a morning coffee or using the coffee to rev up for the day: contradictory uses, the same pleasure. Livia led the way past tourists getting an early start and up a little street called Via della Rosetta. A few short, shadowy blocks, and then straight ahead rose the elaborate Baroque façade of Santa Maria Maddalena, golden limestone glowing.

Thomas and Livia entered the open church doors, stepped through the small entry on the right into the sanctuary. Thomas dipped his fingers in the font of holy water and crossed himself, Livia waiting for this brief ritual to be complete before, together, they walked forward. Reaching the last row of pews, they stopped. Soaring marble, polished wood, gilt and silver and a blood-red cross in the stained glass of the rose window; but nothing offered a direction, a hint of what Lorenzo might have meant.

"Damiani's notebook," Thomas said. "Maybe there was a poem . . . ?"

But Livia shook her head. "They were all in Trastevere, the places he wrote about."

Thomas hadn't really expected that to work. "Well," he said, scanning the ornate ceiling, the patterned floor, the side chapels with their marble tombs, none of which sparked any flashes of inspiration, "I guess it's time to ask someone."

"Ask what?" Livia said, but Thomas was already striding down the center aisle.

102

Livia followed Thomas to the front of the church, where a black-robed monk whose habit bore a large crimson cross laid an altar cloth in one of the side chapels.

"*Buongiorno,* Father," Thomas said, and continued in Italian. "Thomas Kelly, SJ, and *Professoressa* Livia Pietro. Do you have a moment? We have some questions about this church."

The monk turned his lean, unsmiling face to them. "Emilio Creci. I'll be glad to help." Meeting his eyes, "glad" was not the first word that sprang to Livia's mind.

"Thank you." Thomas smiled, not reacting to the monk's frostiness. "We're both historians, Livia and I. We were advised to come here by . . . another historian, who has since died. We're hoping to honor his guidance, but we don't know what it was he particularly wanted us to study. I'm sure your church has many treasures, but does anything stand out to you, something a pair of bookish academics might have been sent to see?" He spoke with a self-deprecating diffidence, clearly calculated to make the other man feel both superior and impatient. This wasn't exactly flimflam, Livia thought, but it could without fear of contradiction be called misdirection. What he'd said over breakfast was true: Thomas Kelly wasn't the same man he'd been yesterday.

And, Livia was delighted to find, she liked this one even better.

Father Creci shrugged. "We're a poor order, dedicated to the sick. This church is grand, but in Rome" — he smiled thinly — "undistinguished. Like many of the smaller orders, we're . . . honoured with the responsibility of maintaining a property whose demands threaten to outstrip our resources. Not a problem I believe Jesuits encounter often?"

Oho, thought Livia. **Sibling rivalry: so that's his problem.**

Thomas smiled beneficently. "If that's the case, you're due even more praise, Father." He spread his hands to indicate the gleaming marble and glowing stained glass, the elaborate side chapels and polished wood pews. The church's rococo interior was wild with gilt and Technicolor frescoes: in Livia's

opinion, over the top, but admirable none-
theless. "The beauty of Santa Maria Maddalena — and of the obvious treasures here —
is a testament to you and your brothers,"
Thomas said. "You must spend a great deal
of time working here. Each of you must
come to know this church intimately."

Thomas was obviously trying to steer the
conversation back to the church building
and its contents, but Father Creci still had
a point to make.

"As much as needed. As I said, our mission is to the indigent sick. The resources I
spoke of include our time. We resist as well
as we can being caught up in the needs of
the material world."

"And yet you serve your immediate material world — your obligation to this church
— so well."

"Thank you," said the monk. He was
forced to acknowledge the compliment, but
rose to the defense of his fellows and how
they spent their time. "The endowment
helps a great deal, of course."

Thomas and Livia glanced at each other.
"Endowment?" Thomas asked.

"Strictly for the upkeep of the church and
its possessions. Not for our ministry, which
is always in need."

"Really?" Thomas murmured. "How narrow. Who is your benefactor?"

"We've never known," the monk answered with a combination of resentment and pride. "The endowment dates to 1601. It enabled us to maintain our first church, and later build this one. We're charged with the particular responsibility of the Maddalena statue, but in return for constant vigilance with regard to that, the endowment enables us to provide for, as you say, this immediate material world, while allowing my brothers and myself to focus on our true calling."

Livia felt her pulse quickening, but she didn't speak, letting Thomas continue. Betraying no excitement, he said, "The Maddalena statue? An endowment — that must be an important piece."

"To us it is, for the freedom its upkeep allows us. It dates from the late fifteenth century. Personally — though of course I haven't a Jesuit's erudition, so I can only think what I think — I find it neither good nor particularly beautiful. It was of obvious value to someone in 1601, however."

Smiling, Thomas asked, "May we see it?"

103

The grudging Father Creci led them across the front of the church to a chapel on the right. Tucked in a corner on a two-foot marble plinth stood a large wooden statue of Mary Magdalene. Life-size, Livia thought, if you took into account people's smaller stature then. Of course, it wasn't made in Mary's time, it was made in the fifteenth century. Still, people were smaller during the Renaissance, also. It was an ongoing source of needling from the Elder Noantri to the Newer, if one of the relatively few made in the nineteenth and twentieth centuries should show himself to be no physical match for a smaller, slighter — but no less everlasting — senior.

Examining the statue with a practiced eye, Livia found herself agreeing with the belligerently untutored monk. As a work of art, it wasn't very good. Its proportions were off, its carving in some places clumsy. The iconography was here: the long loose hair, the left hand holding the unguent jar, that marvelous contradiction signaling Mary Magdalene's dual nature: her debased early life as a prostitute, and her later devotion, because it was that same costly unguent with which she washed Christ's feet. This Magdalene wore no jewels or gold chains, and neither her clothing nor the body beneath it could be called voluptuous. Those facts and the half-closed eyes and pensive face told Livia the sculptor was depicting Mary after her repentance and conversion.

"Livia," Thomas said, in casual tones that belied the rise in his pulse rate and adrenaline level, which Livia could feel, and which echoed her own. "I think this might be it, don't you? What we were sent to see."

"It could be," Livia answered, putting doubt into her voice although she felt none. She turned and smiled at the monk. "Father Creci, you're obviously dedicated to your mission and we've already taken you from it for too long. Might we be allowed to spend some time with your sculpture? I understand you have a great deal to do. I think I speak for Father Kelly, also, when I say your devotion to your ministry is inspiring. If I may be allowed to make an offering?" She

slipped three one-hundred-Euro notes from
her wallet. "Or shall I place this in the offering box on our way out?"

The monk all but snatched the bills from
her hand. "No, no need to trouble yourself,
I'll take care of it. Thank you. Yes, please,
take as much time as you like. If you have
any further questions, don't hesitate to ask."

They watched him walk quickly away, a
bit more bounce in his step now than before.

"Do you think he thought I wasn't actually going to stuff the bills in the box?" Livia
asked Thomas.

"I'm sure of it." Thomas grinned. He
turned his attention to the statue and his
face grew serious. "If this is it, what Lorenzo
meant, what about it did he mean?"

"I don't know," Livia said slowly, considering the piece. "Either its iconography
conceals something . . ."

"Or it conceals something."

"Another Damiani poem?"

"Possible," said Thomas. "Personally, I
hope not. I'd like to think we're done with
that."

Livia walked slowly around, leaned to peer
behind the statue. She put out a tentative
hand, felt it, pushed gently. Firmly positioned on its base, solid and tremendously
heavy, it didn't move. Returning to the

front, she stood and looked, letting her eyes move slowly over the piece, as the art historian in her would with any new work.

The statue's face wasn't beautiful: elongated and flat, with a high forehead, a crooked nose, a cleft chin. The folds of cloth, so often a breathtaking element of Renaissance art, were uninteresting, and the unguent jar was held at a strange angle. The face had an undeniable power, its emotions growing deeper and more complex the longer Livia regarded it. The force exerted by it, though, required time spent before it. In a church — and a city — so full of glories, this statue would almost assuredly have passed unnoticed through the centuries; Livia herself, whose vocation gave her reason to be familiar with many more pieces than most people could claim, couldn't recall having seen it before. A strange piece to carry its own endowment.

Unless that were the point.

"The face is beautiful," Thomas said. "No, I don't mean beautiful. But I can't stop looking at it."

"I think the sculptor felt the same way about his model." The tiny contractions in Livia's muscles were showing her the artist's path through the work. "Thomas, look at this. The jar is tipping — if you really carried oil like that, you'd spill it. And the right hand — it looks like it's pointing straight to it."

"Does that mean something?"

"Maybe not. Or maybe it's saying what the jar holds is important. And isn't liquid." She looked around. The few resolute early tourists they'd passed on their way up the aisle might make their eventual way to this chapel, but right now, none were near. Livia handed Thomas her shoulder bag and stepped up lightly onto the plinth. Balancing easily, she ran her hands over the unguent jar. She rapped with her knuckles, listening for a change of tone. "Thomas?" she said quietly. "It's hollow."

104

Thomas watched Livia explore the unguent jar on the wooden statue of Mary Magdalene. He found himself oddly calm, his heart no longer pounding with the urgency and fright of the day before. Whatever they found — if there was anything to find — might reveal to him the meaning of Lorenzo's final words. Or those words might remain forever a mystery. Of more importance to Thomas was his own mystery: Would he be able to forgive Lorenzo for his betrayal? For his hate?

Livia's searching hands suddenly stopped still. After a moment she repositioned herself, gripped the jar with her left hand, and placed her right on its carved lid. Thomas could see the slow, steady force she was using in the set of her shoulders. The lid didn't move. Livia dropped her arms and stared at it. "Thomas? In my bag there's a vial. Can you hand it to me?"

Thomas, not used to rummaging through a woman's handbag, spent a minute finding it. "This?"

"Yes. It's the scent I use. Not really a perfume. An essential oil." She took the vial he handed her, unscrewed the top, and poured the oil carefully on the seam between the jar and its lid. The heady scent of gardenias wafted down to Thomas as the oil perched on the surface of the wood and then gradually began to seep in. Livia re-stoppered the vial and handed it back down. Slowly, she started to work at the lid again. Nothing, nothing, nothing — then, finally, Thomas could see it begin to give. With calm patience Livia pressured it, pushing down, turning, until at last, millimeter by millimeter, she was able to unscrew it. Slowly and deliberately, she took the lid off, reached into the hollow jar, and removed a rolled, beribboned, wax-sealed scroll.

105

Standing at the back of the church, he could see only that Livia Pietro and Thomas Kelly had been escorted by a monk to the Magdalene chapel. But he didn't need to be near to see — to know — what they were doing. When he'd gotten the call telling him they'd left the apartment, he'd gone out, too, into the fresh Rome morning. He didn't try to follow them. Anywhere they had it in mind to go was their own business and they had his blessing. Anywhere but here. He came straight to Santa Maria Maddalena, hoping that they wouldn't appear, but knowing they would.

He'd never been sure how much of the truth Lorenzo Cossa knew. It was possible, he'd thought, that though the contents of the document Livia Pietro and Thomas Kelly had just found were known to the Cardinal, its hiding place might not be. It had also seemed possible that, even if he knew, he hadn't had a chance to pass his knowledge on. When Livia and Kelly walked into the church, though, that possibility was lost. He took heart when it became clear that they didn't know what next step to take, but the resourcefulness they'd proved yesterday came into play here, too. He wasn't sure how they'd done it and it didn't matter: once they'd found the statue, it was all but assured they'd find the treasure it held.

This day was a long time coming, but it was always bound to come. He'd been given, not instructions to follow, but the immeasurable honor and immense responsibility of deciding what to do when it came. He'd pondered the question long and hard, never coming to a conclusion. Now he'd reached one. Now he had to.

Stepping from the shadows, the Pontifex strode forward.

106

Thomas sank slowly onto the marble plinth. Livia stood beside him, the unrolled vellum scroll from the unguent jar in her hand. Around him Santa Maria Maddalena faded, became a still photograph, a frozen stage set. Nothing lived, moved, breathed. He was ice-cold. The words he'd just read — he wanted to never have seen them; if that wasn't possible, to instantly forget them. But they swam before his eyes and, though he'd never heard them spoken, they sounded in his head.

Roma profecturi hoc testamentum relinquimus. Nobis praesentibus non erat opus talibus litteris; nos ipsi vitaque nostra pro testibus veritatis erant. Quamquam ex hac urbe discedimus, testimonium illud manet. Sumus etiamnunc inter vos. Estote certi: si necessarium fiet, nos revelabimus naturamque nostrum duplicem manifesta-

bimus, id quod non prius necessarium erit quam aut Ecclesia aut Noantri pacto inter duas nostras gentes valenti deficiant. Ad quod tempus — utinam ne veniat — fidem servabimus atque occultum tenebimus et pactum et nostrum ipsorum naturam.

Preparing to depart from Rome, we leave behind this Testament. While we remained, no such document was required. The proof of its truth was ourselves and our lived lives. Though we leave this city, that proof remains. We are still among you. If necessary, be sure we will reveal ourselves, and make our dual natures known. That necessity will not arise until the day either the Church or the Noantri fail to conform to the Concordat between our peoples. Until such time — may it never come! — we will honor our vows, revealing neither the secret of the Concordat nor the secret of our own natures.

Below this brief, world-changing text, a date:

DIE DOMINICA X XII APRILIS ANNO DOMINI MDCI

Sunday, 22 April, the Year of Our Lord 1601.

and the signatures.

On the left, *Maria Magdalena*.

On the right, *Jesus Nazarenus*.

Mary Magdalene.

Jesus of Nazareth.

This was what it was, then: the secret Lorenzo had thought the Church could not survive. Thomas wasn't sure he'd survive it himself. *Dual natures.* Could this document be real? Could it be authenticated? But even as the scholar in him, desperate for a hand-hold, asked the question, the priest knew it was beside the point. The Concordat existed; the Noantri existed. Even if this Testament couldn't be proved real by any science known to man, its revelation, with its signatures and its date, would force the Concordat and the Noantri into the light. The ensuing whirlwind would bring down the Church, and who knew what would fall with it? If the . . . if the signatories . . . Thomas couldn't bring himself to say their names, even in his own head. **Come on,**

Father Kelly, you're a Jesuit, he told himself. **You don't fear knowledge.** If he hadn't been frozen, he'd have laughed. Had he been just a tiny bit proud of how he'd accepted the Noantri, even come to respect and feel fondness for them, in so short a time? **Then accept this, Father Kelly: your Savior is also . . . is also . . .**

"So that's it." Someone spoke, a warm voice penetrating the ice in which Thomas was locked. Slowly, he looked up. Livia, appearing as shaken as he was, stared at the scroll in her hand. "That's the reason," she breathed. "Why Martin the Fifth signed the Concordat at all. What forced him into it. They did. It was this."

Yes, Thomas thought. **Fine.** That question now was answered. What of it? What did such a thing matter now, when . . .

"Yes." Another voice, dark and quiet. Thomas turned; Livia gasped. Before them stood the man — the Noantri — who'd sat at the center of the Conclave yesterday. The Pontifex Aliorum. The Pope of the Others. The Noantri ruler.

"Yes," he said again. The Pontifex stepped closer, pointing to the document Livia held. "You now know the final secret."

A long silence; then Thomas, to his surprise, heard a ghost of his own voice. "Who

603

else . . ."

"Only the Conclave," the Pontifex replied. "No other Noantri, and no one in the Church, have this knowledge. The Church has swirled with dark rumors for centuries, stories of another document even more dangerous than the Concordat. But that the Concordat — and we — exist is perilous enough for the Church."

"But Lorenzo knew. How?"

The Pontifex turned his dark gaze on Thomas. He waited; then he spoke. "Ending the persecution of the Noantri, and accepting the help we could give him, brought Martin the Fifth to power over the rival line of Popes then at Avignon. If he had lost that struggle, the Antipope John would have reigned. John was his papal name. He was born Baldassare Cossa."

"Cossa," Thomas repeated. He felt simultaneously that vast knowledge was being revealed to him, and that he was unbearably stupid.

"Lorenzo Cardinal Cossa was descended from Baldassare's brother's line. The Cossas, believing the Church illegitimate from the moment the Concordat was signed, have been determined to regain the papacy since."

"Regain? Lorenzo? He'd have . . . made

himself Pope?"

"A spy in the retinue of Martin the Fifth brought the knowledge of this" — again, a gesture at the document — "to Baldassare Cossa. Once the Avignon Popes lost the struggle for power, the Cossa family understood what they'd need to regain it: both the Concordat and this Testament. It's an odd irony that, though it is the Noantri to whom time is no enemy, the Cossas have been willing to wait as long as necessary, passing this knowledge from father to son."

"And Lorenzo also passed it on?"

"We think not — except to you."

Thomas felt the meaning of the Pontifex's words as a physical blow.

"It took more than one hundred and fifty years after the signing of the Concordat to bring the entire Church into line. The last man executed by fire died in 1600. The resulting outcry ended the practice and convinced Jesus and Mary that they could vanish again — could return the Church, and the choice to believe and follow, to men.

"They wrote this Testament. The Noantri were told of its existence, and that it had been placed in the care of the Order of Saint Camillus, chosen because of their humble devotion to the infirm and the dying. We were not told what form the Testament took nor where it was placed. The friars were given to understand their work would be supported as long as they took especial care of this statue, without a reason given."

"But surely," Thomas said, "you must have deduced its location. Why not take it into your care? Why leave it here for . . . for someone to find?" By which he meant, **For me to find, and read, and learn.** He meant, **Why force this unwanted knowledge upon me?**

The Pontifex nodded. "We had. But it wasn't ours to move. It was done thus to assure that its keeping would be in the hands of both parties. The Noantri have kept watch over this church since that time, and the friars, over the statue. All was well until the ascendancy of Lorenzo Cossa. He felt himself uniquely positioned for the search for the Concordat."

"He positioned himself. He positioned me."

"Thomas?" Livia said. "What I said before, I still think it's true. The Cardinal believed himself to be doing good."

Thomas didn't answer.

In the silence, Livia turned to the Pontifex. "Lord. This knowledge — you understand what a tremendous shock it is. To us both."

"Of course. It will take time to fully understand it."

"May I ask —"

"When the Savior," Thomas interrupted, needing to know the answer to the question Livia was having trouble framing — or maybe her question was different, but he didn't care, it was this he needed to know — "when he promised eternal life, was it this he meant? Endless human existence? Not transcendent heavenly life, eternally with the Father?" Did he also, then, lie?

"No," the Pontifex said calmly. "The opposite. He was ready to die for his flock, Father Kelly, to prove his faith and sustain yours. He nearly did. When he was cut down from the cross he was thought to be dead. But Mary Magdalene was Noantri. She knew he still lived — barely, but lived." He gazed at the wooden statue. "Art and legend have always depicted Mary as miserable and debased until she met Jesus of Nazareth. That was indeed her condition, but not because she was a prostitute — she was not. At that time, the Noantri, with no understanding of what we were, no knowledge of others like ourselves, lived constrained, degraded, furtive lives. The preaching of Jesus, the promise that the least among us could be redeemed, was a revelation to

607

Mary. When he was on the edge of death she struggled with her newfound faith, and realized she could in her way give him what he'd given her: the promise of eternal life."

"And if he chose not to accept her gift . . ."

The Pontifex nodded again. "She could restore him to his mortality."

"But he chose to remain," Thomas whispered.

"As always, he assented to what he saw as the will of his Father."

The grand church dedicated to the lowliest of Jesus' followers fell completely silent. Not a footfall or a whisper interposed itself, waiting for Thomas to say, "So he is still here."

"Yes."

"Where?" Thomas had never wanted the answer to a question as much as he wanted this one.

The Pontifex smiled and spoke softly. "I don't know."

Thomas, stricken, could not reply.

"Understand," the Pontifex said, "that he could have revealed himself at any moment before the writing of this Testament — or any moment since. But from the start of time, good has rarely come from religion. When it comes, it comes from faith. The Concordat was an attempt to set the Church founded in his name — a Church founded on faith — back onto a righteous path. Ultimately, though, each of us, Unchanged and Noantri, must choose our own way. If any good is to come of religion, faith must guide that choice, and faith does not merely allow, it absolutely *requires,* a lack of proof."

In his head, Thomas heard his own earlier thoughts: **If God's existence could be "proved," what was man offering God? Faith was what God asked of man. The only thing man has, and the only thing God wants.**

Faith was our single gift to him.

107

What Livia felt now, she'd felt only once before, at the moment of her own Change: that the world had been revealed to her as overflowing, churning, mad with color and sound and scent, with promises she'd never thought to ask for and answers to questions she'd never thought to ask. This kaleido-scopic symphony, this vast, endless tapestry was before her now, again, in this silent church. What a gift! What a marvel, to live in such a world!

But a question grew in her, and with it a fear. One question, that did have to be asked.

"Lord," she addressed the Pontifex, "what do you intend to do?"

"I?"

"Now that Father Kelly and I have come upon this knowledge."

He regarded them without words for quite some time. "From the moment I was asked to lead our people," he said quietly, "it was clear this day would sometime come. I have given much thought to this question and never found an answer. Even as I stepped forward to speak with you here, I was not sure what my duty required. Now, I am." He paused. "Father Kelly. Livia. The choice is yours."

Livia had to swallow before she could speak. "Ours, Lord?"

"As faith was put in me, I put mine in you, to make the correct choice. If you choose a path that I would not have, my faith will continue to guide me as we travel that path. Reveal what you know, or hide this secret again. I await your decision."

Livia was struck dumb, unable even to think. She stood motionless, staring at the Pontifex, the dark eyes that seemed to see into her. For a few long moments, that was all. Then Thomas spoke.

"We will replace it."

Slowly, he rose from the plinth and faced them. "I can't claim to understand the meaning of what we've learned today. That will take a long time, perhaps a lifetime, of contemplation and prayer." Unexpectedly, he smiled. "My lifetime. Not yours."

"I think," Livia said, "mine, also."

Thomas met her eyes and went on. "That

this document was written at all tells me there will come a time when these facts will be revealed. That it was hidden tells me that that time will come at the choosing of someone much greater than myself. Sir, your faith in us is an honor that will forever humble me. But the choice is not, in fact, ours. Jesus of Nazareth chose to keep this secret. Until he chooses otherwise, it will remain a secret."

The Pontifex nodded slowly, but said, "Others — Unchanged, or Noantri — might one day discover what you have."

"Then they will make their choices. I've made mine."

Wordlessly, Livia handed the scroll to the Pontifex. He took it and glanced over it, a ghost of a smile playing on his lips. Then he rerolled it and, as lightly as she had, he stepped onto the marble plinth, removed the jar's cap, and slipped the scroll inside. No one said anything until he was standing beside them again. Then it was the Pontifex who spoke.

"Thank you."

Nothing else needed to be said. He turned to leave them. Before he could take a step, though, Thomas said, "Sir?"

The Pontifex turned back.

"May I ask something?"

"You may."

"Thank you. You speak as one who . . . knew them. Knew him."

"I did. And loved them both. My own Change dates from not long before his. Father Kelly, you know my story, though it's not as you've long thought."

To Thomas's puzzled look, the Pontifex continued.

"I also was thought to be in the arms of death, I also was brought back to this world. Jesus of Nazareth, however, did not accomplish that 'miracle.' It has been attributed to him, but in truth it was brought about by the same Noantri who later performed his. Mary Magdalene. She who was also" — he smiled again — "despite what biblical scholars say, Mary of Bethany. My sister."

The Pontifex's smile broadened as understanding dawned in Thomas's eyes, though Livia herself didn't quite believe it until she heard him say it.

"I am Lazarus."

Then he turned in the aisle, and was gone.

POSTSCRIPT

Notable Noantri — A Brief List

Most Noantri, of course, take some pains not to become famous. The spotlight makes disappearing, and reappearing in another place as another person — a necessity of eternal life — more difficult. Some, however, especially those in the arts, are unable to avoid public notice; and some frankly enjoy both the acclaim, and the thrill of danger that comes with it. Listed on the following pages are some men and women claimed by the Noantri as their own. It must be said that the siren song of fame is heard, perhaps, more clearly in some nations than in others; thus it will be noted that this list is heavy with Americans. The birth dates given for some here are the actual date of birth of the person before his or her Change; for others, they are the birth date associated with the identity we have come to know — a false date, in other words. Which are which are facts deeper in the Noantri Archive than your scribe was permitted to go.

Sam Cabot
January 1, 2013

Khachatur Abovian, b. 1809, Armenian writer.

Al-Hakim bi-Amr Allah, b. 996, sixth Fatimid caliph.

Theodosia Burr Alston, b. June 21, 1783, daughter of U.S. vice president Aaron Burr.

Dorothy Arnold, b. 1884, American socialite.

Benjamin Bathurst, b. March 18, 1784, British diplomat.

Ambrose Bierce, b. June 24, 1842, American writer.

Captain James William Boyd, b. 1822, Confederate States of America military officer.

Matthew Brady, b. 1822, American photographer.

Giordano Bruno, b. 1548, Dominican friar, mathematician, astronomer, philosopher.

John Cabot, b. 1450, Italian explorer.

Saint Cecilia, b. second century AD, Roman, Catholic martyr and saint, patroness of poets and musicians.

Thomas P. "Boston" Corbett, b. 1832, Union Army soldier.

Hart Crane, b. July 21, 1899, American poet.

Joseph Force Crater, b. January 5, 1889, New York judge.

Arthur Cravan (Favian Avenarius Lloyd), b. May 22, 1887, Swiss boxer, poet, surrealist figure.

Emilio de' Cavalieri, b. 1550, Italian composer.

Amelia Earhart, b. July 24, 1897, American aviatrix.

The Eight Taoist Immortals, b. during Tang or Song Dynasty, Chinese "mythological" characters.

Carlo Gesualdo, b. March 8, 1566, Italian composer.

Franz Greiter, b. 1918, Austrian scientist, inventor of sunscreen.

Jesus of Nazareth, b. 1 AD, central figure of Christianity.

Louis Aimé Augustin Le Prince, b. August 28, 1841, French inventor.

Romualdo Locatelli, b. 1905, Italian painter.

Thomas Lynch, Jr., b. August 5, 1749, American patriot, signer of the U.S. Declaration of Independence.

Stefano Maderno, b. 1576, Italian sculptor.

Mary Magdalene, b. first century AD, early disciple of Jesus of Nazareth.

Philip Mazzei, b. December 25, 1730, Italian physician, confidant of Thomas Jefferson, originator of the phrase "All men are created equal."

Methuselah, b. 1,656 years after creation, figure mentioned in Hebrew Bible.

Nefertiti, b. 1370 BC, "Great Royal Wife" of Pharaoh Akhenaten.

Ivan Nikitin, b. 1690, Russian painter.

Qin Shi Huang, b. 259 BC, Chinese emperor.

The Seven Sleepers of Ephesus, b. 250, Christian martyrs.

Spartacus, b. 109 BC, Thracian rebel slave.

Bram Stoker, b. November 8, 1847, Irish novelist.

Horace Sumner, b. 1826, American passenger on ill-fated ship on which Margaret Fuller (American writer) was lost.

Jan van Eyck, b. 1390, Flemish painter.

Yellow Emperor or Huangdi, b. 2724 BC, Chinese emperor, reigned 2696–2598 BC.

ACKNOWLEDGMENTS

Without the hard work of many people, this book would not exist. For that, Sam Cabot would like to thank Damiano Abeni, Dana Cameron, Moira Egan, Conor Fitzgerald, Massimo Gatto, Tom Govero, Betsy Harding, the late Royal Huber, Tyler Lansford, Dermot O'Connell, Franco Onorati, Ingrid Rowland, Tom Savage, Barbara Shoup, the secret map-maker, and all the believers and nonbelievers at Rancho Obsesso. Sam would also like to offer a particular tip of the biretta to Steve Axelrod of The Axelrod Agency, and to David Rosenthal, Vanessa Kehren, and the fine folks at Blue Rider. *Grazie.*

Without the electricity of Art Workshop International in Assisi, Sam Cabot would not exist. For that, Carlos Dews and S. J. Rozan would like to thank Edith Isaac-Rose, Bea Kreloff, Charles Kreloff, Chris

Spencer, and the Hotel Giotto. *Pax et bonum.*

ABOUT THE AUTHOR

Sam Cabot is the pseudonym of Carlos Dews and S. J. Rozan.

Carlos Dews is an associate professor and chair of the Department of English Language and Literature at John Cabot University, where he directs the Institute for Creative Writing and Literary Translation. He lives in Rome, Italy.

S. J. Rozan is the author of many critically acclaimed novels and short stories that have won crime fiction's greatest honors, including the Edgar, Shamus, Anthony, Macavity, and Nero awards. Born and raised in the Bronx, Rozan now lives in Lower Manhattan.

The employees of Thorndike Press hope you have enjoyed this Large Print book. All our Thorndike, Wheeler, and Kennebec Large Print titles are designed for easy reading, and all our books are made to last. Other Thorndike Press Large Print books are available at your library, through selected bookstores, or directly from us.

For information about titles, please call:
(800) 223-1244

or visit our Web site at:
http://gale.cengage.com/thorndike

To share your comments, please write:
Publisher
Thorndike Press
10 Water St., Suite 310
Waterville, ME 04901